Number-one *New York Times* bestselling author Nora Roberts presents the electrifying conclusion to her powerful new trilogy. Worlds have collided and centuries have elapsed as six people have brought their unique powers, their courage and their hearts to a battle that could drown humanity in darkness . . .

Her face, so pale when she'd removed her cloak, had bloomed when her hand had taken the sword. Her eyes, so heavy, so somber, had gone as brilliant as the blade. And had simply sliced through him, keen as a sword, when they'd met his . . .

In the kingdom of Geall, the scholarly Moira has taken up the sword of her people. Now, as queen, she must prepare her subjects for the greatest battle they will ever fight—against an enemy more vicious than any they have seen. For Lilith, the most powerful vampire in the world, has followed the circle of six through time to Geall.

Moira also has a personal score to settle. Vampires killed her mother—and now, she is ready to exact her revenge. But there is one vampire to whom she would trust her soul . . .

Cian was changed by Lilith centuries ago. But now, he stands with the circle. Without hesitation, he will kill others of his kind—and has earned the respect of sorcerer, witch, warrior and shape-shifter. But he wants more than respect from Moira—even though his desire for her makes him vulnerable. For how can a man with an eternity to live love a woman whose life is sure to end—if not by Lilith's hand, then by the curse of time?

"[Roberts] is one of the best writers in the romance world."
—***The Best Reviews***

Turn the page for a complete list of titles by
Nora Roberts and J. D. Robb
from the Berkley Publishing Group . . .

Nora Roberts & J. D. Robb

REMEMBER WHEN

Nora Roberts

HOT ICE
SACRED SINS
BRAZEN VIRTUE
SWEET REVENGE
PUBLIC SECRETS
GENUINE LIES
CARNAL INNOCENCE
DIVINE EVIL
HONEST ILLUSIONS
PRIVATE SCANDALS
HIDDEN RICHES
TRUE BETRAYALS
MONTANA SKY
SANCTUARY
HOMEPORT
THE REEF
RIVER'S END
CAROLINA MOON
THE VILLA
MIDNIGHT BAYOU
THREE FATES
BIRTHRIGHT
NORTHERN LIGHTS
BLUE SMOKE
ANGELS FALL

Series

Circle Trilogy

MORRIGAN'S CROSS
DANCE OF THE GODS
VALLEY OF SILENCE

In the Garden Trilogy

BLUE DAHLIA
BLACK ROSE
RED LILY

Key Trilogy

KEY OF LIGHT
KEY OF KNOWLEDGE
KEY OF VALOR

Three Sisters Island Trilogy

DANCE UPON THE AIR
HEAVEN AND EARTH
FACE THE FIRE

Gallaghers of Ardmore Trilogy

JEWELS OF THE SUN
TEARS OF THE MOON
HEART OF THE SEA

Born In Trilogy

BORN IN FIRE
BORN IN ICE
BORN IN SHAME

Chesapeake Bay Saga

SEA SWEPT
RISING TIDES
INNER HARBOR
CHESAPEAKE BLUE

Dream Trilogy

DARING TO DREAM
HOLDING THE DREAM
FINDING THE DREAM

Anthologies

FROM THE HEART
A LITTLE MAGIC
A LITTLE FATE

MOON SHADOWS
(with Jill Gregory, Ruth Ryan Langan, and Marianne Willman)

The Once Upon Series
(with Jill Gregory, Ruth Ryan Langan, and Marianne Willman)

ONCE UPON A CASTLE
ONCE UPON A STAR
ONCE UPON A DREAM
ONCE UPON A ROSE
ONCE UPON A KISS
ONCE UPON A MIDNIGHT

J. D. Robb

NAKED IN DEATH
GLORY IN DEATH
IMMORTAL IN DEATH
RAPTURE IN DEATH
CEREMONY IN DEATH
VENGEANCE IN DEATH
HOLIDAY IN DEATH
CONSPIRACY IN DEATH
LOYALTY IN DEATH
WITNESS IN DEATH
JUDGMENT IN DEATH
BETRAYAL IN DEATH
SEDUCTION IN DEATH
REUNION IN DEATH
PURITY IN DEATH
PORTRAIT IN DEATH
IMITATION IN DEATH
DIVIDED IN DEATH
VISIONS IN DEATH
SURVIVOR IN DEATH
ORIGIN IN DEATH
MEMORY IN DEATH

Anthologies

SILENT NIGHT
(with Susan Plunkett, Dee Holmes, and Claire Cross)

OUT OF THIS WORLD
(with Laurell K. Hamilton, Susan Krinard, and Maggie Shayne)

BUMP IN THE NIGHT
(with Mary Blayney, Ruth Ryan Langan, and Mary Kay McComas)

Also available . . .

THE OFFICIAL NORA ROBERTS COMPANION
(edited by Denise Little and Laura Hayden)

Valley of Silence

NORA ROBERTS

JOVE BOOKS, NEW YORK

THE BERKLEY PUBLISHING GROUP
Published by the Penguin Group
Penguin Group (USA) Inc.
375 Hudson Street, New York, New York 10014, USA
Penguin Group (Canada), 90 Eglinton Avenue East, Suite 700, Toronto, Ontario M4P 2Y3, Canada
(a division of Pearson Penguin Canada Inc.)
Penguin Books Ltd., 80 Strand, London WC2R 0RL, England
Penguin Group Ireland, 25 St. Stephen's Green, Dublin 2, Ireland (a division of Penguin Books Ltd.)
Penguin Group (Australia), 250 Camberwell Road, Camberwell, Victoria 3124, Australia
(a division of Pearson Australia Group Pty. Ltd.)
Penguin Books India Pvt. Ltd., 11 Community Centre, Panchsheel Park, New Delhi—110 017, India
Penguin Group (NZ), Cnr. Airborne and Rosedale Roads, Albany, Auckland 1310, New Zealand
(a division of Pearson New Zealand Ltd.)
Penguin Books (South Africa) (Pty.) Ltd., 24 Sturdee Avenue, Rosebank, Johannesburg 2196,
South Africa

Penguin Books Ltd., Registered Offices: 80 Strand, London WC2R 0RL, England

VALLEY OF SILENCE

A Jove Book / published by arrangement with the author

Cover design by Richard Hasselberger.
Cover illustration by Pyrographx/David S. Reinhardt.
Stepback art: Mountain Range by Carl Lyttle/Getty Images; Lightning by Daniel Furon/Getty Images.
Text design by Kristin del Rosario.

For information, address: The Berkley Publishing Group,
a division of Penguin Group (USA) Inc.,
375 Hudson Street, New York, New York 10014.

ISBN: 978-0-7394-7629-1

JOVE®
Jove Books are published by The Berkley Publishing Group,
a division of Penguin Group (USA) Inc.,
375 Hudson Street, New York, New York 10014.
JOVE is a registered trademark of Penguin Group (USA) Inc.
The "J" design is a trademark belonging to Penguin Group (USA) Inc.

PRINTED IN THE UNITED STATES OF AMERICA

To my own circle,
friends and family.

Good and evil, we know, in the field of this world
grow up together almost inseparably.
—JOHN MILTON

Presume not that I am the thing I was.
—SHAKESPEARE

Prologue

There were pictures in the fire. Dragons and demons and warriors. The children would see them, as he did. The old man knew the very young and the very old often saw what others could not. Or would not.

He had told them much already. His tale had begun with the sorcerer who was called by the goddess Morrigan. Hoyt of the Mac Cionaoith was charged by the gods to travel to other worlds, to other times, and gather an army to stand strong against the vampire queen. The great battle between human and demon would take place on the sabbot of Samhain, in the Valley of Silence, in the land of Geall.

He had told them of Hoyt the sorcerer's brother, killed and changed by the wily Lilith, who had existed near a thousand years as a vampire before making Cian one of her kind. Nearly another thousand years would pass for Cian before he would join Hoyt and the witch Glenna to make those first links in the circle of six. The next links were forged by two Geallians—the shifter of shapes and the scholar who traveled between worlds to gather in those first days. And the last of the circle was joined by the warrior, a demon hunter of the Mac Cionaoith blood.

The tales he had told them were of battles and courage, of death and friendship. And of love. The love that had bloomed between sorcerer and witch, and between the shifter and the warrior, had strengthened the circle as true magic must.

But there was more to tell. Triumphs and loss, fear and valor, love and sacrifice—and all that came with the dark and the light.

As the children waited for more, he wondered how best to begin the end of the tale.

"There were six," he said, still watching the fire while the children's whispers silenced and their squirming stilled in anticipation. "And each had the choice to accept or refuse. For even when worlds are held in your hands, you must choose to face what would destroy them, or to turn away. And with this choice," he continued, "there are many other choices to be made."

"They were brave and true," one of the children called out. "They chose to fight!"

The old man smiled a little. "And so they did. But still, every day, every night of the time they were given, that choice remained, and had to be made anew. One among them, you remember, was no longer human, but vampire. Every day, every night of the time they were given, he was reminded he was no longer human. He was but a shadow in the worlds he had chosen to protect.

"And so," the old man said, "the vampire dreamed."

Chapter 1

He dreamed. And dreaming, he was still a man. Young, perhaps foolish, undoubtedly rash. But then, what he believed was a woman had such beauty, such allure.

She wore a fine gown in a deep shade of red, more elegant than the country pub deserved, with its long, sweeping sleeves. Like a good claret it poured over her form to set her pure white skin glowing. Her hair was gold, the curls of it glinting against her headdress.

The gown, her bearing, the jewels that were sparkling at her throat, on her fingers, told him she was a lady of some means and fashion.

He thought, in the dim light of the public house, she was like a flame that burned at shadows.

Two servants had arranged for a private room for her to sup before she swept in, and simply by being had silenced the talk and the music. But her eyes, blue as a summer sky, had met his. Only his.

When one of the servants had come out again, walked to him and announced that the lady requested he dine with her, he hadn't hesitated.

Why would he?

He might have grinned at the good-natured comments of the men he was drinking with, but he left them without a thought.

She stood in firelight and candlelight, already pouring wine into cups.

"I'm so glad," she said, "you would agree to join me. I hate to dine alone, don't you?" She came toward him, her movements so graceful she almost seemed to float. "I'm called Lilith." And she handed him wine.

In her speech there was something exotic, some cadence of speech that hinted of hot sand and riotous blooming vines. So he was already half seduced, and completely enchanted.

They shared the simple meal, though he had no appetite for food. It was her words he devoured. She spoke of the lands to which she had traveled, those which he'd only read of. She had walked among the pyramids, she told him, in the moonlight, had ridden the hills of Rome and stood in the ruined temples of Greece.

He had never traveled beyond Ireland, and her words, the images they invoked, were nearly as exciting as she herself.

He thought she was young to have done so much, but when he said as much she only smiled over the rim of her cup.

"What good are worlds," she asked, "if you don't make use of them? I'll make use of much more. Wine to be drunk, food to be tasted, lands to be explored. You're young," she said with a slow and knowing smile, "to settle for so little. Have you no wish to see beyond what you've seen?"

"I thought perhaps to take a year when I'm able, to see more of the world."

"A year?" With a light laugh, she snapped her fingers. "That is a year. Nothing, a blink of time. What would you do if you had an eternity of time?" Her eyes seemed like depthless blue seas as she leaned toward him. "What would you do with it?"

Without waiting for his answer, she rose, leaving the trail of her scent behind as she walked to the small window. "Ah, the night, it's so soft. Like silk against the skin." She turned back with a gleam in those bold blue eyes. "I am a night creature. And so, I think, are you. We, such as we, are at our best in the dark."

He had risen when she did, and now as she came back to him, her scent and the wine swam through his senses. And something more, something thick and smoky that hazed over his mind like a drug.

She tipped her head up, and back, then laid her mouth over his. "And why, when we're best in the dark, would we spend the dark hours alone?"

And in the dream, it was like a dream, misty and muddled. He was in her carriage, with her full white breasts in his hands, her mouth hot and avid on his. She laughed when he fumbled with her kirtle, and spread her legs in seductive invitation.

"Strong hands," she murmured. "A pleasing face. It's what I need, and need, and take. Will you do my bidding?" With another light laugh, she nipped at his ear. "Will you? Will you, young, handsome Cian with the strong hands?"

"Aye, of course. Aye." He could think of nothing but burying himself in her. When he did, with the carriage swaying madly, her head fell back in abandon.

"Yes, yes, yes! So hard, so hot. Give me more, and more! And I'll take you beyond all that you know."

As he plunged, his breath coming short as he neared climax, her head reared up again.

Her eyes were no longer blue and bold but red and feral. The shock that rushed into him had him trying to pull back, but her arms suddenly wrapped around him, implacable as iron chains. Her legs hooked around his waist, keeping him inside her, trapped. While he struggled against her impossible strength, she smiled with fangs gleaming in the dark.

"What are you?" There were no prayers in his head; fear left no room for them. "What are you?"

Her hips continued to rise and fall, riding him, so he

was helplessly driven closer to peak. She fisted a hand in his hair, yanking back his head to expose his throat. "Magnificent," she said. "I am magnificent, and so will you be."

She struck, the fangs piercing his flesh. He heard his own scream, somewhere in the madness and pain he heard it. The burn was unspeakable, searing through skin, into blood, beyond the bone. And mixed with it, sliding through it was a terrible, terrible pleasure.

He came, in the whirling, singing dark, betrayed by his body even as it dipped toward death. He struggled still, some part of him clawing for the light, for survival. But the pain, the pleasure dragged him deeper into the abyss.

"You and I, my handsome boy. You and I." She dipped back, cradling him in her arms now. With her own fingernail, she sliced a shallow slice across her breast so that blood dripped from it as it did, horribly, from her lips. "Now drink. Drink me, and you are forever."

No. His lips wouldn't form the word, but it screamed through his mind. Feeling his life slipping away, he struggled weakly for that last hold on it. Even when she pulled his head to her breast he fought her with what was left of him.

Then he tasted it, the rich and heady flavor that flowed from her. The bulging life of it. And like a babe at its mother's breast, he drank his own death.

The vampire woke in absolute dark, in absolute silence. Such was the way for him since the change so long ago, that he roused each sunset with not even the sound of his own heartbeat to stir the air.

Though he had dreamed the dream countless times over countless years, it disturbed him to fall from that edge yet again. To see himself as he'd been, to see his own face—one he'd not seen while awake since that night—made him edgy and annoyed.

He didn't brood over his fate. That was a useless occupation. He accepted and used what he was, and had through his personal eternity accumulated wealth, women, comfort, freedom. What else could a man want?

Having no heartbeat was a small price to pay, in the larger scheme of things. A heart that beat aged and weakened, and eventually stopped like a broken clock in any case.

How many bodies had he seen decay and die over his nine hundred years? He couldn't count them. And while he couldn't see the reflection of his own face, he knew it was the same as the night Lilith had taken him. The bones were still strong, the skin over them firm, supple and unlined. His eyes were sharp of sight and unfaded. There was not, and would never be, any gray in his hair, any sagging in his jowls.

Perhaps there were times, in the dark, in private, when he used his fingers to see his own face. There the high, prominent cheekbones, the shallow cleft in the chin, the deep-set eyes he knew were a strong blue. The blade of his nose, the firm curve of his lips.

The same. Always the same. But still, a small indulgence to spend a moment reminding himself.

He rose in the dark, his leanly muscled body naked, shook back the black hair that framed his face. He'd been born Cian Mac Cionaoith, and had gone by many names since. He was back to Cian—his brother's doing. Hoyt would call him nothing else, and since this war he'd agreed to fight might end him, Cian decided it was only right he should wear the name of his birth.

He'd prefer not to be ended. In his opinion, only the mad or the very young considered dying an adventure. But if that was his fate, at this time and place, at least he'd go out with style. And if there were any justice in any world, he would take Lilith with him to dust.

His eyes were as keen as his other senses, so he moved easily in the dark, going to a chest for one of the packets of blood that had been transported from Ireland. Apparently, the gods had deemed to allow the blood, as well as the vampire who required it, to travel through worlds from their circle of stones.

Then again, it was pigs' blood. Cian hadn't fed on humans in centuries. A personal choice, he mused as he broke open the packet, poured its contents into a cup. A matter of will, he thought, and well, manners, come to that. He lived among them, did business with them, slept with them when he was in the mood. It seemed rude to feed off them.

In any case, he'd found it simpler to live as he liked, to stay off the radar, if he didn't kill some hapless soul on a nightly basis. Live feeding added both thrill and flavor nothing else matched, but it was, by nature, a messy business.

He'd grown accustomed to the more banal flavor of pigs' blood, and the simple convenience of having it at his fingertips rather than having to go out and hunt something up every time hunger stirred in him.

He drank the blood as a man might his morning coffee—out of habit and the need for a kick on waking. It cleared his mind, jump-started his system.

He troubled neither with candles nor fire as he washed. He couldn't say he was overly pleased with the accommodations of Geall. Castle or not, he imagined he was as out of place in this medieval atmosphere as both Glenna and Blair.

He'd lived through this sort of era once, and once was enough for anyone. He preferred—much preferred—the daily conveniences of indoor plumbing, electricity, Chinese bloody take-out, come to that.

He missed his car, his bed, the damn microwave. He missed the life and sounds of city life and all it offered. Fate would have given him a solid kick in the ass if it ended him here, in the era, if not the world, of his beginnings.

Dressed, he left his room to make his way to the stables, and his horse.

There were people about—servants, guards, courtiers—those who lived and worked within the Castle Geall. Most avoided him, averting their eyes, quickening their pace.

Some made the sign against evil behind their backs. It didn't trouble him.

They knew what he was—and had seen what creatures like him were capable of since Moira, the scholarly gladiator, had battled one in the playing field.

It had been good strategy, he thought now, for Moira to ask him along with Blair and Larkin to hunt down the two vampires who'd killed her mother, the queen. Moira had understood the importance, the value of having vampires brought back alive so the people could see them for what they were. And see Moira herself fight and end one, proving herself a warrior.

She would, in a matter of weeks, lead her people to war. When a land had been at peace as long as Geall was reputed to have been, it would take a strong leader, a forceful one, to whip farmers and merchants, ladies-in-waiting and creaky advisors into soldiers.

He wasn't sure she was up to the task. Brave enough, he mused as he slipped out of the castle, crossed a courtyard toward the stables. More than bright enough. And it was true she'd honed considerable fighting skills over the past two months. No doubt she'd been trained since birth in matters of state and protocol, and her mind was clever and open.

In peace, he imagined she'd rule her pretty little world quite well. But in wartime, a ruler was general as well as figurehead.

If it had been up to him, he would have left Riddock, her uncle, in charge. But little of this business was up to him.

He heard her before he saw her, and scented her before that. Cian very nearly turned around to go back the way he'd come. It was just another annoyance to come across the woman when he'd been thinking of her.

The problem was, he thought of her entirely too often.

Avoiding her wasn't an option as they were inexorably bound together in this war. Slipping away now unseen was easily done. And cowardly. Pride, as always, refused to let him take the easy way.

They'd housed his stallion at the far end of the stables, two stalls away from any of the other horses. He understood and tolerated the fact that the grooms and farriers were wary of tending to the horse of a demon. Just as he was aware either Larkin or Hoyt groomed and fed his temperamental Vlad in the mornings.

Now it seemed Moira had taken it upon herself to spoil the animal. She had carrots, Cian saw, and was balancing one on her shoulder, cajoling Vlad to nip it off.

"You know you want it," she murmured. "It's so tasty. All you have to do is take it."

He'd thought the same about the woman, Cian mused.

She was gowned, her dress draped over a plain linen kirtle, so he assumed whatever training she'd done that day was complete. Still, she dressed simply for a princess, in quiet blue with only a hint of lace at the bodice. She wore the silver cross, one of nine Hoyt and Glenna had conjured. Her hair was loose, all that glossy brown falling down her back to her waist, and crowned with the thin circlet of her office.

She wasn't beautiful. He reminded himself of that often, nearly as often as he thought of her. She was, at best, a pretty thing. Slender and small-framed, small of feature as well. But for the eyes. They were long and dominant in that face of hers. Dove gray when she was quiet, pensive, listening. Hell smoke when she was roused.

He'd had his choice of great beauties in his time—as a man with any sense and skill would given a few centuries. She wasn't beautiful, but he couldn't, for all the effort, lock her out of his mind.

He knew he could have her if he put any of that effort into a seduction. She was young and innocent and curious, and therefore, very susceptible. Which was why, above all else, he knew he'd be better off seducing one of her ladies if he wanted the entertainment, the companionship, the release.

He'd had his fill of innocence long ago, just as he'd had his fill of human blood.

His horse, however, appeared to have less willpower. It took only moments before Vlad dipped his head and nipped the carrot from Moira's shoulder.

She laughed, stroked the stallion's ears as he chomped. "There now, that wasn't so hard, was it? We're friends, you and I. And I know you get lonely from time to time. Don't we all?"

She was lifting another carrot when Cian stepped out of the shadows. "You'll make a puppy out of him, then what sort of war horse will he be come Samhain?"

Her body jerked, then stiffened. But when she turned toward Cian, her face was composed. "Sure you don't really mind, do you? He so enjoys a bit of a treat now and then."

"Don't we all," he murmured.

Only the faintest flush of heat along her cheekbones betrayed any embarrassment at being overheard. "The training went well today. People are coming in from all over Geall. So many willing to fight we've decided we'll be setting up a second training area on my uncle's land. We'll have Tynan and Niall working there."

"Lodging?"

"Aye, that's becoming a bit of a thing. We'll house as many here as we can manage, and at my uncle's as well. There's the inn, and many of the farmers and crofters nearby are sheltering family and friends already. No one will be turned off. We'll find a way."

She fiddled with her cross as she spoke. Not, Cian thought, out of fear of him, but out of nervous habit. "There's food as well to think of. So many had to leave their crops and cattle behind to come here. But we'll manage. Have you eaten?"

She flushed a little deeper as soon as the words were out. "What I meant is there'd be supper in the parlor if—"

"I know what you meant. No. I thought to see to the horse first, but he appears well groomed and fed." On the heels of the words, Vlad bumped his head against Moira's shoulder. "And spoiled," Cian added.

Her brows drew together as they did, he knew, when she

was annoyed or thoughtful. "It's only carrots, and they're good for him."

"Speaking of food, I'll need blood in another week. You might make certain the next pigs that are slaughtered, their blood isn't wasted."

"Of course."

"Aren't you the cool one."

Now the faintest sign of irritation crossed her face. "You take what you need from the pig. I'm not after turning my nose up at a slab of bacon, am I?" She shoved the last carrot into Cian's hand and started to sweep out.

She stopped herself, "I don't know why you fire me up so easily. If you mean to or not. And no." She held up a hand. "I don't think I want to know the answer to that. But I would like to speak to you for a moment or two about another matter."

No, avoiding her wasn't possible, he reminded himself. "I have a moment or two."

She glanced around the stables. It wasn't only horses that had ears in such places. "I wonder if you could take that moment or two to walk with me. I'd be private on this."

He shrugged, and giving Vlad the last carrot joined Moira to walk out of the stables. "State secrets, Your Highness?"

"Why must you mock me?"

"Actually, I wasn't. Irritable tonight, are you?"

"It might be I am." She shoved back the hair that spilled over her shoulder. "What with war and end of days, and the practical matters of washing linens and providing food for an army meanwhile, it might be I am a bit irritable."

"Delegate."

"I am. I do. But it still takes time and thought to push chores into other hands—finding the right ones, explaining how it must be done. And this isn't what I wanted to speak to you about."

"Sit."

"What?"

"Sit." He took her arm, ignoring the way the muscles tensed against his hand, and pulled her down onto a bench.

"Sit, give your feet a rest if you won't turn off that busy brain of yours for five minutes."

"I can't remember the last time I had an hour, all to myself and a book. Well, I can, actually. Back in Ireland, in your house. I miss it—the books, the quiet of them."

"You need to take it, that hour now and again. You'll burn out otherwise, and won't be any good to yourself or anyone else."

"My hands feel so full, they make my arms ache." She looked down at them where they lay in her lap, and sighed. "And there, I'm off again. What is it Blair says? Bitch, bitch, bitch."

She surprised a laugh out of him, and turned her head to smile into his face.

"I suspect Geall has never had a queen such as you."

And her smile faded away. "No, you've the right of that. And we'll soon see. We go tomorrow, at first light, to the stone."

"I see."

"If I lift the sword from it, as my mother did in her time, and her father in his, and back to the first, Geall will have a queen such as me." She looked off, over the shrubberies toward the gates. "Geall will have no choice in it. Nor will I."

"Do you wish it otherwise?"

"I don't know what I wish, so I don't wish at all—except that it was done and over. Then I could do, well, whatever needs to be done next. I wanted to tell you." She shifted her gaze from whatever she saw in her mind, and met his eyes again. "I'd hoped we'd find a way to do this thing at night."

Soft eyes, he thought, and so serious. "It's too dangerous to have any sort of ceremony outside after sunset beyond the castle walls."

"I know it. All who wish to witness this rite may attend. You can't, I know. I'm sorry for it. It feels wrong. I feel the six of us, our circle, should be together at such a time."

Her hand reached up for her cross again. "Geall isn't yours, I know that as well, but the moment of this, it's important for what comes after. More than I knew before. More than I could have known."

She took a shaky breath. "They killed my father."

"What are you saying?"

"I have to walk again. I can't sit." She got up quickly, rubbing her arms to warm them from the sudden chill in the air, and in her blood. She moved through the courtyard into one of the gardens.

"I haven't told anyone—I didn't mean to tell you. What purpose does it serve? And I've no proof, just a knowing."

"What do you know?"

Easier than she'd believed it would be to talk to him, to tell him, she realized, because he was also so to the point. "One of the two that killed my mother, that you brought here. The one I fought." She held a hand up, and he watched her draw in her composure again. "Before I killed it, he said something of my father, and how he died."

"Likely trying to get a rise out of you, break your concentration."

"It did that well enough, but was more, you see. I know it, inside me." Looking at him, she pressed a hand to her heart. "I knew it when I looked at the one I killed. Not just my mother, but my father as well. I think Lilith sent them here this time because she'd had success with it before. When I was a child."

She continued to walk, her head bowed with the weight of her thoughts, her circlet glinting in the light of the torches. "They thought it was a bear gone mad. He was in the mountains, hunting. He was killed, he and my mother's young brother. My uncle Riddock didn't go as my aunt was close to her time with child. I . . ."

She broke off again as footsteps echoed, keeping her silence until the sound of them drifted away. "They thought, those who found them and brought them home, they thought it was animals. And so it was," she continued with steel in her tone now. "But these walk like a man. She sent them to kill him, so there would be no child but me."

She turned to him then, the torchlight washing red over

her pale face. "Perhaps, at that time, she knew only the ruler of Geall would be one of the circle. Or perhaps it was easier to kill him than me at that time, as I was hardly more than a baby and kept close watch on. Plenty of time for her to send assassins back for me. But instead they killed my mother."

"Those that did are dead."

"Is that comfort?" she wondered, and thought—from him—it likely was an offer of it. "I don't know what to feel. But I know she took my parents from me. She took them to stop what can't be stopped. We'll meet her on the battlefield come Samhain, because it's meant. Whether I fight as queen or not, I fight. She killed them for nothing."

"And nothing you could have done would have stopped it."

Yes, comfort, she thought again. Oddly, his pithy statement gave her just that. "I pray that's true. But I know because of what was done, what was not done, what had to be, what comes tomorrow is more important than rite and ritual. Whoever holds that sword tomorrow leads this war, and wields it with the blood of my murdered parents. She couldn't stop it. She cannot stop it."

She stepped back, gestured up. "Do you see the flags? The dragon and the claddaugh. The symbols of Geall since its beginning. Before this is done, I will ask that one more be hoisted."

He thought of all she might choose—a sword, a stake, an arrow. Then he knew. Not a weapon, not an instrument of war and death, but a symbol of hope and endurance. "A sun. To shed its light on the world."

Surprise, with pleasure running just behind it, lit her face. "Aye. You understand my thinking, and the need. A gold sun on the white flag to stand for the light, the tomorrows we fight for. This sun, gold as glory, will be the third symbol of Geall, one I bring to it. And damned to her. Damned to her and what she brought here."

Flushed now, Moira drew a deep breath. "You listen well—and I talk too much. You must come inside. The others will be gathering for supper."

He touched a hand to her arm to stop her. "Earlier I thought you'd make a poor wartime queen. I believe it might have been one of the rare times I was wrong."

"If the sword is mine," she said, "you will be wrong."

It occurred to him as they started inside, that they'd just shared their longest conversation in the two months they had known each other.

"You need to tell the others. You need to tell them what you believe about your father. If this is a circle, there should be no secrets to weaken in."

"You're right. Aye, you've the right of it."

Her head was lifted now, her eyes clear as she led the way.

Chapter 2

She didn't sleep. How could a woman sleep on what was, in Moira's mind, essentially the last night of her life? If in the morning it was her destiny to free the sword from its stone scabbard, she would be queen of Geall. As queen she would rule and govern and reign, and those were duties she'd been trained for since birth. But as queen on this coming dawn and the ones to follow, she would lead her people to war. If it wasn't her destiny to raise the sword, she would follow another, willingly, into battle.

Could weeks of training prepare anyone for such an action, such a weight of responsibility? So this night was the last she could be the woman she'd believed she would be, even the queen she'd hoped she might be.

Whatever dawn brought her, she knew nothing would ever be quite the same again.

Before her mother's death, she'd believed this coming dawn was years away. She'd assumed she would have years of her mother's company and comfort and counsel, years of peace and study so that when her time came she'd be not only ready for the crown, but worthy of it.

A part of her had assumed her mother would reign for decades longer, and she herself would marry. In the dim and distant future, one of the children she bore would take the crown in her stead.

All of that had changed on the night of her mother's death. No, Moira corrected, it had changed before, years before when her father had been murdered.

Perhaps it had not changed at all, but was simply unfolding as the pages of the book of fate were written.

Now she could only wish for her mother's wisdom, and look inside herself for the courage to bear both crown and sword.

She stood now on the high reaches of the castle under a thumbnail moon. When it waxed full again, she would be far from here, on the cold ground of a battlefield.

She'd come to the battlement because she could see the torches lighting the playing field. Here the sights and sounds of night training could reach her. Cian, she thought, used hours of his night to teach men and women how to fight something stronger and faster than humans. He would push them, she knew, until they were ready to drop. As he had pushed her, and the others of the circle, night after night during their weeks in Ireland.

Not all of them trusted him, she knew that as well. Some actively feared him, but that might be to the good. She understood he wasn't after making friends here, but warriors.

In truth, he'd had a strong part of making one of her.

She thought she understood why he fought with them—or at least had a glimmer of understanding why he would risk so much for humankind. Part of it was pride of which she knew he had abundance. He would not bow to Lilith. Part, whether he admitted it or not, was loyalty to his brother. And the rest, well, it dealt with courage and his own conflicted emotions.

For he had emotions, she knew. She couldn't imagine how they struggled and whirled inside him after a thousand years of existence. Her own were so conflicted and torn after only two months of blood and death she hardly recognized herself.

What must it be like for him, after all he'd seen and done, all he'd gained and lost? He knew more than any of them of the world, of its pleasures, its pains, its potentials. No, she couldn't imagine what it was like to know all he knew and still risk his own survival.

That he did risk it, that he was even now lending his time and skill to train troops, earned her respect. While the mystery of him, the hows and whys of him, continued to fascinate.

She couldn't be sure what he thought of her. Even when he'd kissed her—that single hot and desperate moment—she couldn't be sure. And getting to the inside of matters had always been irresistible to her.

She heard footsteps, and turning, saw Larkin coming toward her.

"You should be in your bed," he said.

"I'd only stare at the ceiling. The view's better here." She reached for his hand—her cousin, her friend—and was instantly comforted. "And why aren't you in yours?"

"I saw you. Blair and I went out to help Cian for a bit." Like hers, his gaze scanned the field below. "I saw you standing up here alone."

"I'm poor company, even for myself tonight. I only wish it were done, then there would be what happens next. So I came up here to brood over it." She tipped her head toward his shoulder. "It passes the time."

"We could go down to the family parlor. I'll let you beat me at chess."

"Let me? Oh, will you listen to him." She looked up at him. His eyes were golden brown, long-lidded like her own. The smile in them didn't quite mask his concern. "And I suppose you've *let* me win the hundreds of matches we've had over the years."

"I thought it good for your sense of confidence."

She laughed even as she poked him. "It's confident I am I can beat you at chess nine times out of every ten."

"We'll just put that to the test then."

"We will not." Now she kissed him, brushing his tawny hair away from his face. "You'll go to your bed and to your lady, and not spend these hours distracting me from my sorry mood. Come, we'll go in. It may be the limited view of my ceiling will bore me to sleep after all."

"You've only to tap on the door if you're wanting company."

"I know it."

Just as she knew she would keep her own counsel until the first light of dawn.

But she did not sleep.

In the way of tradition she would be dressed and tended to by her ladies in the last hour before dawn. Though it was urged on her, she refused the red gown. Moira knew well enough it wasn't a color that flattered her, however royal it might be. In its stead she wore the hues of the forest, a deep green over a paler green kirtle.

She agreed to jewels—they had been her mother's after all. So she allowed the heavy stones of citrine to be fastened around her neck. But she would not remove the silver cross.

She would wear her hair down and uncovered, and sat letting the female chatter chirp around her as Dervil brushed it tirelessly.

"Will you not eat just a little, Highness?"

Ceara, one of her women, once again urged a plate of honey cakes on her. "After," Moira told her. "I'll feel more settled after."

Moira got to her feet, her relief profound when Glenna stepped into the room. "How wonderful you look!" Moira held out her hands. She'd chosen the gowns herself for both Glenna and Blair, and saw now she'd chosen well. Then again, she thought, Glenna was so striking there was nothing that wouldn't flatter her.

Still, the choice of deep blue velvet highlighted her creamy skin and the fire of her hair.

"I feel a bit like a princess myself," Glenna told her. "Thank you so much. And you, Moira, look every inch the queen."

"Do I?" She turned to her glass, but saw only herself. But she smiled when she saw Blair come in. She'd chosen russet for Blair, with a kirtle of dull gold. "I've never seen you in a dress."

"Hell of a dress." Blair studied her friends, then herself. "We've got that whole fairy tale thing going." She threaded her fingers through her short, dark hair to settle it into place.

"You don't mind then? Tradition requires the more formal attire."

"I like being a girl. I don't mind dressing like one, even one who's not in my own fashion era." Blair spotted the honey cakes, and helped herself to one. "Nervous?"

"Well beyond it. I'd like a moment with the ladies Glenna and Blair," Moira told her women. When they scurried out, Moira dropped into the chair in front of the fire. "They've been fussing around me for an hour. It's tiring."

"You look beat." Blair sat on the arm of the chair. "You didn't sleep."

"My mind wouldn't rest."

"You didn't take the potion I gave you." Glenna let out a sigh. "You should be rested for this, Moira."

"I needed to think. It's not the usual way of it, but I want both of you, and Hoyt and Larkin to walk with me to the stone."

"Wasn't that the plan?" Blair asked with her mouth full.

"You would be part of the procession, yes. But in the usual way, I would walk ahead, alone. This must be, as it always has been. But behind me, would be only my family. My uncle, and my aunt, Larkin, my other cousins. After them, according to rank and position would walk others. I want you to walk with my family, as you are my family. I do this for myself, but also for the people of Geall. I want them to see what you are. Cian isn't able to be part of this, as I wish he could."

"It can't be done at night, Moira." Blair touched a hand to Moira's shoulder. "It's too much of a risk."

"I know. But while the circle won't be complete at the place of the stone, he'll be in my thoughts." She rose now to go to the window. "Dawn's coming," she murmured. "And the day follows."

She turned back as the last stars died. "I'm ready for what comes with it."

Her family and her women were already gathered below. She accepted the cloak from Dervil, and fastened the dragon brooch herself.

When she looked up from the task, she saw Cian. She assumed he might have stopped for a moment on his way to retire, until she saw he carried the cloak Glenna and Hoyt had charmed to block the killing rays of the sun.

She stepped away from her uncle's side, and up to Cian. "You would do this?" she said quietly.

"I rarely have the opportunity for a morning walk."

However light his words, she heard what was under them. "I'm grateful you've chosen this morning to take one."

"Dawn's broke," Riddock said. "The people wait."

She only nodded, then drew up her hood as was the custom before stepping out into the early light.

The air was cool and misty with barely a breeze to stir the fingers of vapor. Through the rising curtain of it, Moira crossed the courtyard to the gates alone, while her party fell in behind her. In the muffled quiet, she heard the morning birds singing, and the faint whisper of the damp air.

She thought of her mother, who had once walked this way on a cool, misty morning. And all the others who'd walked before her out of the castle gates, across the brown road, over the green grass so thick with dew it was like wading through a river. She knew others trailed behind her, merchants and craftsmen, harpers and bards. Mothers and daughters, soldiers and sons.

The sky was streaked with pink in the east, and the ground fog sparkled silver.

She smelled the river and the earth, and continued up, over the gentle rise with the dew dampening the hem of her gown.

The place of the stone stood on a faerie hill where a little glade of trees offered shelter. Gorse and moss grew, pale yellow, quiet green, over the rocks near the holy well.

In the spring there would be the cheery orange of lilies, dancing heads of columbine, and later the sweet spires of foxglove, all growing where they would.

But for now, the flowers slept and the leaves of the trees had taken on that first blush of color that portended their death.

The sword stone itself was wide and white, altarlike on an ancient dolmen of flat gray.

Through the leaves and the mists, beams of sun lanced, crossing that white stone and glinting on the silver hilt of the sword buried in it.

Her hands felt cold, so very cold.

All of her life she had known the story. How the gods had forged the sword from lightning, from the sea, and the earth and the wind. How Morrigan had brought it and the altar stone herself to this place. And there she had buried it to the hilt, carved the words on the stone with her fiery finger.

SHEATHED BY THE HAND OF GODS
FREED BY THE HAND OF A MORTAL
AND SO WITH THIS SWORD
SHALL THAT HAND RULE GEALL

Moira paused at the base of the stones to read the words again. If the gods deemed it, that hand would be hers.

With her cloak sweeping over the dew-drenched grass, she walked through sun and mist to the top of the faerie hill. And took her place behind the stone.

For the first time she looked, and she saw. Hundreds of people, her people, with their eyes on hers spread over the field, down toward that brown ribbon of road. Every one of them, if the sword came to her, would be her responsibility. Her cold hands wanted to shake.

She calmed herself as she scanned the faces and waited for the trio of holy men to take their places behind her.

Some were still coming over that last rise, hurrying lest they miss the moment. She wanted her breath steady when she spoke, so waited a little longer and let herself meet the eyes of those she loved best.

"My lady," one of the holy men murmured.

"Yes. A moment."

Slowly, she unpinned the brooch, passed her cloak behind her. The wide sweep of her sleeves flowed back as she lifted her arms, but she didn't feel the chill against her skin. She felt heat.

"I am a servant of Geall," she called out. "I am a child of the gods. I come here to this place to bow to the will of both. By my blood, by my heart, by my spirit."

She took the last step toward the stone.

There was no sound now. It seemed even the air held its breath. Moira reached out, curled her fingers around the silver hilt.

And oh, she thought as she felt the heat of it, as she heard somewhere in her mind the murmur of its music. Of course, aye, of course. It's mine, and always was.

With a whisper of steel against rock, she drew it free and raised its point to the sky.

She knew they cheered, and some of them wept. She knew that to a man they lowered to one knee. But her eyes were on that point and the flash of light that streaked from the sky to strike it.

She felt it inside her, that light, a burst of heat and color and strength. There was a sudden burn on her arm, and as if the gods etched it, the symbol of the claddaugh formed there to brand her queen of Geall. Rocked by it, thrilled and humbled, she looked down at her people. And her eyes met Cian's.

All else seemed to melt away in that moment, for a

moment. There was only him, his face shadowed by the hood of his cloak, and his eyes so brilliant and blue.

How could it be, she wondered, that she should hold her destiny in her hand, and see only him? How, meeting his eyes like this, could it be like looking deeper, deeper yet, into her own destiny?

"I am a servant of Geall," she said, unable to look away from him. "I am a child of the gods. This sword, and all it protects is mine. I am Moira, warrior queen of Geall. Rise, and know I love you."

She stood as she was, the sword still pointing skyward as the hands of the holy man placed the crown on her head.

He was no stranger to magic, the black or the white, but Cian thought he'd never seen anything more powerful. Her face, so pale when she'd removed her cloak, had bloomed when her hand had taken the sword. Her eyes, so heavy, so somber, had gone as brilliant as the blade.

And had simply sliced through him, keen as a sword, when they'd met his.

There she stood, he thought, slender and slight, and as magnificent as any Amazon. Suddenly regal, suddenly fierce, suddenly beautiful.

What moved inside him had no place there.

He stepped back, turned to go. Hoyt laid a hand on his arm.

"You must wait for her, for the queen."

Cian lifted a brow. "You forget, I have no queen. And I've been under this bloody cloak long enough."

He moved quickly. He wanted to get away from the light, from the smell of humanity. Away from the power of those gray eyes. He needed the cool and the dark, and the silence.

He was barely a league away when Larkin trotted up to him. "Moira asked me to see if you wanted a ride back."

"I'm fine, but thanks."

"It was amazing, wasn't it? And she was . . . well, brilliant as the sun. I always knew she'd be the one, but seeing it happen is a different matter. She was queen the moment she touched the sword. You could see it."

"If she wants to stay queen, have anyone to rule, she better make use of that sword."

"So she will. Come now, Cian, this isn't the day for gloom and doom. We're entitled to a few hours of joy and celebration. And feasting." With another grin, Larkin gave Cian an elbow poke. "She might be queen, but I can promise the rest of us will eat like kings this day."

"Well, an army travels on its belly."

"Do they?"

"So it was said by . . . someone or another. Have your feasting and celebration. Tomorrow queens, kings and peasants alike best be preparing for war."

"Feels like we've been doing nothing else. Not complaining, mind," he continued before Cian could speak. "I guess the matter is I'm tired of preparing for it, and want to get to it."

"Haven't had enough fighting the last little while?"

"I've payment to make for what was nearly done to Blair. She's still tender along the ribs, and wears down quicker than she'd admit." His face was hard and grim as he remembered it. "Healing fast, as she does, but I won't forget how they hurt her."

"It's dangerous to go into battle with a personal agenda."

"Ah, bollocks. We've all of us something personal to settle, or what's the point? And you won't tell me that a part of you won't be going into it with what that bitch did to King in your mind and in your heart."

Because Cian couldn't deny it, he left it alone. "Are you . . . escorting me back, Larkin?"

"As it happens. There was some mention of me throwing myself bodily over you to shield you from the sunlight should the magic in that cloak fade out."

"That would be fine. We'd both go up like torches." Cian said it casually, but he had to admit he felt easier when he stepped into the shadow cast by Castle Geall.

"I'm also asked to request you come to the family parlor if you're not too weary. We're to have a private breakfast there. Moira would be grateful if you could spare a few minutes at least."

She would have liked a few minutes herself, alone. But Moira was surrounded. The walk back to the castle was a blur of movement and voices wrapped in mists. She felt the weight of the sword in her hand, the crown on her head even as she was swept along by her family and friends. Cheers echoed over the hills and fields, a celebration of Geall's new queen.

"You'll need to show yourself," Riddock told her. "From the royal terrace. It's expected."

"Aye. But not alone. I know it's the way it's been done," she continued before her uncle could object. "But these are different times. My circle will stand with me." She looked at Glenna now, then Hoyt and Blair. "The people won't just see their queen, but those who have been chosen to lead this war."

"It's for you to say, you to do," Riddick said with a slight bow. "But on such a day, Geall should be free of the shadow of war."

"Until Samhain has passed, Geall remains always in the shadow of war. Every Geallian must know that until that day, I rule with a sword. And that I'm part of six the gods have chosen."

She laid a hand on his as they passed through the gates. "We will have feasting and celebration. I value your advice, as always, and I will show myself, and I will speak. But on this day, the gods have chosen both queen and warrior in me. And this is what I will be. This is what I'll give to Geall, to my last breath. I won't shame you."

He took her hand from his arm, brought it to his lips. "My sweet girl. You have and always will bring me nothing but pride. And from this day, to my last breath, I am the queen's man."

The servants were gathered, and knelt when the royal party entered the castle. She knew their names, their faces. Some of them had served her mother before Moira herself was born.

But it was no longer the same. She wasn't the daughter of the house now, but its mistress. And theirs.

"Rise," she said, "and know I am grateful for your loyalty and service. Know, too, that you and all of Geall have my loyalty and service as long as I am queen."

Later, she told herself as she started up the stairs, she would speak with each of them individually. It was important to do so. But for now, there were other duties.

In the family parlor the fire roared. Flowers cut fresh from garden and hothouse spilled from vases and bowls. The table was set with the finest silver and crystal, with wine waiting for Moira's inner circle to toast the new queen.

She took a breath, then two, trying to find the words she would say, her first, to those she loved best.

Then Glenna simply wrapped arms around her. "You were magnificent." She kissed both Moira's cheeks. "Luminous."

The tension she'd held tight in her shoulders eased. "I feel the same, but not. Do you know?"

"I can only imagine."

"Nice job." Blair stepped up, gave her a quick hug. "Can I see it?"

Warrior to warrior, Moira thought and offered Blair the sword.

"Excellent," Blair said softly. "Good weight for you. You expect it to be crusted with jewels or whatever. It's good that it's not. It's good and right that it's a fighting sword, not just a symbol."

"It felt as though the hilt was made for my hand. As soon as I touched it, it felt . . . mine."

"It is." Blair handed it back. "It's yours."

For the moment, Moira set the sword on the table to accept Hoyt's embrace. "The power in you is warm and steady," he said close to her ear. "Geall is fortunate in its queen."

"Thank you." Then she let out a laugh as Larkin swept her off her feet and in three dizzying circles.

"Look at you. Majesty."

"You mock my dignity."

"Always. But never you, *a stór.*"

When Larkin set her back on her feet, she turned to Cian. "Thank you for coming. It meant a great deal to me."

He neither embraced nor touched her, but only inclined his head. "It was a moment not to be missed."

"A moment more important to me that you would come. All of you," she continued and started to turn when her young cousin tugged on her skirts. "Aideen." She lifted the child, accepted the damp kiss. "And don't you look pretty today."

"Pretty," Aideen repeated, reaching up to touch Moira's jeweled crown. Then she turned her head with a smile both shy and sly for Cian. "Pretty," she said again.

"An astute female," Cian observed. He saw the little girl's gaze drop to the pendant he wore, and in an absent gesture lifted it so that she could touch.

Even as Aideen reached out, her mother all but flew across the room. "Aideen, don't!"

Sinann pulled the girl from Moira, gripped her tight against her belly, burgeoning with her third child.

In the shocked silence, Moira could do no more than breathe her cousin's name.

"I never had a taste for children," Cian said coolly. "You'll excuse me."

"Cian." With one damning look toward Sinann, Moira hurried after him. "Please, a moment."

"I've had enough moments for the morning. I want my bed."

"I would apologize." She took his arm, holding firm until he stopped and turned. His eyes were hard; blue stone. "My cousin Sinann, she's a simple woman. I'll speak with her."

"Don't trouble on my account."

"Sir." Pale as wax, Sinann walked toward them. "I beg your pardon, most sincerely. I have insulted you, and my queen, her honored guests. I ask your forgiveness for a mother's foolishness."

She regretted the insult, Cian thought, but not the act. The child was on the far side of the room now, in her father's arms. "Accepted." He dismissed her with barely a glance. "Now if you'll release my arm. Majesty."

"A favor," Moira began.

"You're racking them up."

"And I'm in your debt," she said evenly. "I need to go out, onto the terrace. The people need to see their queen, and, I feel, those who are her circle. If you'd give me a few minutes more of your time I'd be grateful."

"In the buggering sun."

She managed a smile, and relaxed as she recognized the frustration in his tone meant he'd do as she asked. "A few moments. Then you can go find some solitude with the satisfaction of knowing I'll be envying you for it."

"Then make it quick. I'd enjoy some solitude and satisfaction."

Moira arranged it deliberately, with Larkin on one side of her—a figure Geall loved and respected—and Cian on the other. The stranger some of them feared. Having them flank her would, she hoped, show her people she considered them equals, and that both had her trust.

The crowd cheered and called her name, with the cheers rising to a roar when she lifted the sword. It was also a deliberate gesture for her to pass that sword to Blair to hold for her while she spoke. The people should see that the woman Larkin was betrothed to was worthy to hold it.

"People of Geall!" She shouted it, but the cheering continued. It came in waves that didn't ebb until she stepped closer to the stone rail and raised her hands.

"People of Geall, I come to you as queen, as citizen, as protector. I stand before you as did my mother, as did her sire, and as did all those back to the first days. And I stand as part of a circle chosen by the gods. Not just a circle of Geallian rulers, but a circle of warriors."

Now she spread her arms to encompass the five who stood with her. "With these who stand with me, that circle is formed. These are my most trusted and beloved. As a citizen, I ask you give them your loyalty, your trust, your respect as you do me. As your queen, I command it."

She had to pause every few moments until the shouts and cheers abated again. "Today, the sun shines on Geall. But it will not always be so. What is coming seeks the dark, and we will meet it. We will defeat it. Today, we celebrate, we feast, we give thanks. Come the morrow, we continue our preparations for war. Every Geallian who can bear arms will do so. And we will march to *Ciunas.* We will march to the Valley of Silence. We will flood that ground with our strength and our will, and we will drown those who would destroy us in the light."

She held her hand out for the sword, then held it high again. "This sword will not, as it has since the first days, hang cool and quiet during my reign. It will flame and sing in my hand as I fight for you, for Geall, and for all humankind."

The roars of approval rose like a torrent.

Then there were screams as an arrow streaked the air.

Before she could react, Cian shoved her down. Under the shouting and chaos, she heard his low, steady cursing. And felt his blood warm on her hand.

"Oh God, my God, you're shot."

"Missed the heart." He spoke through gritted teeth. She saw the pain on his face as he pushed away from her to sit.

When he reached up to grip the arrow out of his side, Glenna dropped to a crouch, pushed his hand aside. "Let me see."

"Missed the heart," he repeated, and once again gripped the arrow. He yanked it out. "Bugger it. Bloody fucking hell."

"Inside," Glenna began briskly. "Get him inside."

"Wait." Though her hand trembled a little, Moira gripped Cian's shoulder. "Can you stand?"

"Of course I can bloody stand. What do you take me for?"

"Please, let them see you." Her free hand fluttered over his cheek for just an instant, like a brush of wings. "Let them see us. Please."

When she linked her fingers with his she thought she saw something stir in his eyes, and felt its twin shift inside her heart.

Then it was gone, and his voice was rough with impatience. "Give me some damn room then."

She got to her feet again. Below was chaos. The man she assumed was the assassin was being kicked and pummeled by every hand or foot that could reach him.

"Hold!" She shouted it with all her strength. "I command you, hold! Guards, bring that man to the great hall. People of Geall! You see that even on this day, even when the sun shines on us, this darkness seeks to destroy us. And it fails." She gripped Cian's hand, lifted it high with her own. "It fails because there are champions in this world who would risk their lives for another."

She laid a hand on Cian's side, felt his wince. Then held up her bloody hand. "He bleeds for us. And by this blood he shed for me, for all of you, I raise him to be Sir Cian, Lord of Oiche."

"Oh, for Christ's sake," Cian muttered.

"Be quiet." Moira said it softly, with steel, and her eyes on the crowd.

Chapter 3

"Half-vamp," Blair announced as she strode back into the parlor. "Multiple bite scars. Crowd did a number on him," she added. "A regular human would be toast after the beating he took. And he's not feeling so well himself."

"He can be treated after I've spoken to him. Cian requires care first."

Blair looked over Moira's shoulder to where Glenna was bandaging Cian's side. "How's he doing?"

"He's angry and uncooperative, so I would say he's doing well enough."

"We can all be grateful for his reflexes. You handled it," Blair added, looking back at Moira. "Kept your cool, kept control. Tough first day on the job, nearly getting assassinated and all that, but you did good."

"Not good enough to have anticipated a daylight attack. To remember that not all Lilith's dogs require an invitation to come within these walls." She thought of how Cian's blood had run against her hand—warm and red. "I won't make that mistake again."

"None of us will. What we need is to get information out of this asshole Lilith sent. But there's a problem. He either can't or won't speak English. Or Gaelic."

"He's mute?"

"No, no. He talks, it's just none of us can understand him. Sounds Eastern European. Maybe Czech."

"I see." Moira glanced back at Cian. He was stripped to the waist, with only the bandage against his skin. Annoyance more than pain darkened his face as he sipped from a goblet she assumed held blood. Though he didn't look to be in the best of moods, she knew she was about to ask another favor.

"Give me a moment," she murmured to Blair. She approached Cian, ordering herself not to shrink under his hot blue stare. "Is there something more that can be done for you, to make you more comfortable?"

"Peace, quiet, privacy."

Though each of his words had the lash of a whip, she kept her own calm and pleasant. "I'm sorry, but those items are in short supply right at the moment. I'll order them up for you as soon as I can."

"Smart-ass," he mumbled.

"Indeed. The man whose arrow you intercepted speaks in a foreign tongue. Your brother told me once that you knew many languages."

He took a long, deep drink, with his eyes deliberately on hers. "It's not enough that I *intercepted* the arrow? Now you want me to interrogate your assassin?"

"I would be grateful if you would try, or at least interpret. If indeed, his tongue is one you know. There are likely a few things in the world you don't know, so you may be of no use to me at all."

Amusement flickered briefly in his eyes. "Now you're being nasty."

"Tit for tat."

"All right, all right. Glenna, my beauty, stop hovering."

"You lost considerable blood," she began, but he only lifted the goblet.

"Replacing, even as we speak." With a slight grimace, he got to his feet. "I need a goddamn shirt."

"Blair," Moira said in even tones, "would you fetch Cian a goddamn shirt?"

"On that."

"You've made a habit of saving my life," Moira said to Cian.

"Apparently. I'm thinking of giving that up."

"I could hardly blame you."

"Here you go, champ." Blair offered Cian a fresh white shirt. "I think the guy's Czech, or possibly Bulgarian. Can you handle either of those?"

"As it happens."

They went into the great hall where the assassin sat, bruised, bleeding and chained, under heavy guard. That guard included both Larkin and Hoyt. When Cian entered, Hoyt stepped away from his post.

"Well enough?" he asked Cian.

"I'll do. And it cheers me considerably that he looks a hell of a lot worse than I do. Pull your guards back," he said to Moira. "He won't be going anywhere."

"Stand down. Sir Cian will be in charge here."

"Sir Cian, my ass." But he only muttered it as he approached the prisoner.

Cian circled him, gauging ground. The man was slight of build and dressed in what would be the rough clothes of a farmer or shepherd. One eye was swollen shut, the other going black and blue. He'd lost a couple of teeth.

Cian snapped out a command in Czech. The man jolted, his single working eye rolling up in surprise.

But he didn't speak.

"You understood that," Cian continued in the same language. "I asked if there are others with you. I won't ask again."

When he was met with silence, Cian struck out with enough force to have the prisoner slamming back against the wall, along with the chair he was chained to.

"For every thirty seconds of silence, I'll give you pain."

"I'm not afraid of pain."

"Oh, you will be." Cian jerked the chair and the man upright, kept his face close. "Do you know what I am?"

"I know what you are." The man used his bloodied mouth to sneer. "Traitor."

"That's one viewpoint. But the important thing to remember is that I can give you pain beyond what even such as you can stand. I can keep you alive for days, weeks, come to that. And in constant agony." He lowered his voice to a hiss. "I'd enjoy it. So let's begin again."

He didn't bother to ask the question, as he'd warned he wouldn't repeat it.

"Could use a spoon," he said conversationally. "That left eye looks painful. If I had a spoon handy, I could scoop it right out of its socket for you. Of course, I could use my fingers," he continued when that eye wheeled wildly. "But then I'd have a mess on my hands, wouldn't I?"

"Do your worst," the man spat out—but he'd begun to tremble a little. "I'll never betray my queen."

"Bollocks." The shudders and sweat told him this one would be easily and quickly broken. "You'll not only betray her before I'm done with you, you'll do it dancing the hornpipe if I tell you to. But let's just be quick and direct as we've all better things to do."

The man's head jerked back as Cian moved. But instead of going for the face as his quarry anticipated, Cian reached down, gripped the man's cock. And squeezed until there was nothing but screams.

"There's no one else! I'm alone, I'm alone!"

"Be sure." Cian only increased the pressure. "If you lie, I'll find out. And then I'll begin to cut this piece of you off, one inch at a time."

"She sent only me." He was weeping now, tears and snot running down his face. "Only me."

Cian eased the pressure a few fractions. "Why?"

The only answer was raw, rough gasps, and Cian tightened the vise of his fingers again. "Why?"

"One could slip through easily, unnoticed. Un . . . unremarked."

"The logic of that has spared you, at least for the moment, from becoming a eunuch." Cian strolled over, got himself a chair. After placing it in front of the prisoner, he straddled it. And spoke in conversational tones even as the man whimpered. "Now, this is better, isn't it? Civilized. When we're done here, we'll see to those injuries."

"I want water."

"I'm sure you do. We'll get you some—after. So for now, let's talk a bit about Lilith."

It took thirty minutes—and two more sessions of pain—before he was satisfied he knew all the man could tell him. Cian got to his feet again.

The would-be assassin was weeping uncontrollably now. Perhaps from the pain, Cian thought. Perhaps from the belief it was ended.

"What were you before she took you?"

"A teacher."

"Did you have a wife, a family?"

"They were no use but food. I was poor and weak, but the queen saw more in me. She gave me strength and purpose. And when she slaughters you, and these . . . ants who crawl with you, I'll be rewarded. I'll have a fine house, and women of my choosing, wealth and power."

"Promised you all that, did she?"

"That and more. You said I could have water."

"Yes, I did. Let me explain something to you about Lilith." He moved behind the man, whose name he'd never asked, and spoke quietly in his ear. "She lies. And so do I."

He clamped his hands on the man's head and in one fast move, broke his neck.

"What have you done?" Shocked to the pit of her belly, Moira rushed forward. "What have you done?"

"What needed doing. She sent only one—this time. If it upsets your sensibilities, you might want to have your guards take that out of here before I brief you."

"You had no right. No right." Her belly wanted to revolt as it had constantly since he'd begun the torturous interrogation. "You murdered him. What makes you any different from him that you would kill him without trial, without sentence?"

"The difference?" Coolly, Cian lifted his brows. "He was still mostly human."

"Is it so little to you? Life? Is it so little?"

"On the contrary."

"Moira. He's right." Blair moved between them. "He did what had to be done."

"How can you say that?"

"Because I'd have done the same. He was Lilith's dog, and if he'd escaped, he'd have tried again. If he couldn't get to you, he'd kill whoever he could."

"A prisoner of war—" Moira began.

"There are no prisoners in this," Blair interrupted. "On either side. If you'd locked him up, you'd take men out of training, off patrol, to guard him. He was an assassin, a spy sent behind lines during wartime. And mostly human is generous," she added with a glance at Cian. "He'd never be human again. If it had been a vampire in that chair, you'd have staked him without thought or hesitation. This isn't any different."

A vampire didn't leave its body broken on the floor, Moira thought, still chained to a chair.

Moira turned to one of the guards. "Tynan, remove the prisoner's body. See that it's buried."

"Majesty."

She saw Tynan's quick glance at Cian—and recognized the steely approval in the look.

"We'll go back to the parlor," she continued. "No one has eaten. You can . . . brief us while we do."

"Lone gunman," Cian said, and wished almost wistfully for coffee.

"Makes sense." Blair helped herself to eggs and a thick slice of fried ham.

"Why?" Moira addressed the question to Blair.

"Okay, they've got some half-vamps trained for combat." She nodded at Larkin. "Likc the ones Larkin and I dealt with that day at the caves, but it takes time and effort. And it takes a lot of work and will to keep one in thrall."

"And if the thrall is broken?"

"Insanity," Blair said briefly. "Total breakdown. I've heard stories of half-vamps gnawing off their own hand to get free and back to their maker."

"He was doomed before he came here," Moira murmured.

"From the minute Lilith got her hands on him, yeah. My take on this was it was supposed to be a quick hit, suicide mission. Why waste more than one? Things go right, you only need one."

"Yes, one man, one arrow." Moira considered it. "If he's skilled enough and fortunate enough, the circle is broken, Geall is without a ruler only moments, really, after it regains one. It would have been a good and efficient strike."

"There you go."

"But why did he wait until we were back? Why not try for me at the stone?"

"He didn't get there in time," Cian said simply. "He misjudged the distance he had to travel, and arrived after it was done. You were closed in by people on your way back, and he wasn't able to get a clear shot. So he joined the parade, so to speak, and bided his time."

"Eat something." Hoyt dished food onto Moira's plate himself. "So Lilith knew that Moira would go to the stone today."

"She has her ear to the ground," Cian confirmed. "Whether or not she'd planned to send someone to try to disrupt the ritual, and the result before Blair tangled with Lora is debatable. She was pissed," he said. "Wild, according to our late, unlamented archer. As I've said before, her relationship with Lora is strange and complicated, but very deep, very sincere. She ordered an archer chosen for this while she was still half-crazed. Sent him on horseback for speed—and they have only a limited number of horses."

"And how is the little French pastry?" Blair wondered.

"Scarred and screaming when the man left, and being tended to by Lilith personally."

"More important," Hoyt broke in, "where is Lora, and where are the rest of them?"

"Our informant, while handy with a bow, wasn't particularly observant or astute. The best I could get puts Lilith's main base a few miles from the battlefield. He described what seems to be a small settlement, overlooked by a good-sized farm with several cottages and a large stone manor house, where I'd say the gentry who owned the land lived. She's in the manor house."

"Ballycloon." Larkin looked at Moira, saw her face was very pale, her eyes very dark. "It must be Ballycloon, and the O Neills's land. The family we helped the day Blair and I were checking the traps, the day Lora ambushed her, they were coming from near Drombeg, and that's just a bit west of Ballycloon. We would have gone farther east, to check the last trap, but . . ."

"I was hurt," Blair finished. "We went as far as we could. And lucky for us. If she'd already made her base when we dropped in, we'd have been seriously outnumbered."

"And seriously dead," Cian added. "They moved in the night before your altercation with Lora."

"There would have been people there still, or on the road." It knotted Larkin's stomach to think of it. "And the O Neills themselves. I don't know if they've reached safety. How can we know how many . . ."

"We can't," Blair said flatly.

"You, you and Cian, you thought we should move everyone out, force them out if necessary, from all the villages and farms around the battleground. Burn the houses and cottages behind them so Lilith and her army would have no shelter. I thought it was cold and cruel of her. Heartless. And now . . .

"It can't be changed. And I couldn't, wouldn't," Moira corrected, "have ordered homes burned. Perhaps it would have been wiser, and stronger, to do just that. But those whose homes we destroyed would have lost the heart they need to fight. So it's done this way."

She had no appetite for the food on her plate, but she picked up her tea to warm her hands. "Blair and Cian know strategy, as Hoyt and Glenna know magic. But you and I, Larkin, we know Geall and its people. We would have broken their hearts and their spirits."

"They'll burn what they don't need or want," Cian told her.

"Aye, but it won't be our hands that light the torch. That will matter. So we believe we know where they are. Do we know how many?"

"He started out with multitudes, but he was lying. He didn't know," Cian said. "However much Lilith may use mortals, she wouldn't count them in her inner circle, or trust any with salient information. They're food, they're servants, they're entertainment."

"We can look." Glenna spoke for the first time. "Hoyt and I, now that we have a general area, can do a locator spell. We should be able to get harder data. Some idea of the numbers. We know from Larkin's trip to the caves and his look at their arsenal they were armed for a thousand or more."

"We'll look." Hoyt laid his hand over Glenna's. "But what I think Cian isn't saying is whatever the numbers they have, whatever we have, in the end they'll have more. Whatever weapons they have will be more. Lilith has had decades, perhaps centuries, to plan this moment. We've had months."

"And still we'll win."

Cian lifted a brow at Moira's statement. "Because you're good and they're evil?"

"No, and there's nothing so simple as that. You yourself are proof of that, for you're neither like her nor like us, but something else altogether. We'll win because we'll be smarter, and we'll be stronger. And because she has no one like the six of us standing with her."

She turned from him to his brother. "Hoyt, you are the first of us. You brought us together."

"Morrigan chose us."

"She, or fate, selected us," Moira agreed. "But it was you who began the work. It's you who believed, who had the power and the strength to forge this circle. So do I believe it. I rule Geall, but I don't rule this company."

"Nor do I."

"No, none of us do. We must be as one, for all our differences. So we look to each other for what we need. I'm far from the strongest warrior here, and my magic is but a shadow. I don't have Larkin's skills, nor the steeliness of mind to kill in cold blood. What I have is knowledge and authority, so I offer those."

"You have more," Glenna told her. "A great deal more."

"I will have more, before it's done. There are things I must do." She got to her feet. "I'll return to work on whatever is necessary as soon as I'm able."

"Pretty royal," Blair commented after Moira left the room.

"Carrying a lot of weight with it." Glenna turned to Hoyt. "Agenda?"

"Best to see what we can of the enemy. Then I'm thinking fire. It's still one of our most formidable weapons, so we should charm more swords."

"Risky enough to put swords in some of the hands we're training," Blair put in. "Much less flaming ones."

"You'd be right." Hoyt considered, nodded. "It will be up to us then, won't it, to decide who'll be—what is it?—issued that sort of weapon. Good men should be placed in positions as close to Lilith's base as we can manage. They'd need shelter that's safe after sunset."

"It's barracks you're meaning. There are cottages and cabins, of course." Larkin narrowed his eyes in thought. "Other shelters can be built in the daylight hours if need be. There's an inn as well, between her base and the next settlement."

"Why don't we go take a look?" Blair shoved her plate aside. "You and Glenna can look your way, and Larkin and I can do a fly-by. You up for the dragon?"

"I am." He smiled at her. "Especially when you're doing the riding."

"Sex, sex, sex. The guy's a machine."

"On that note," Cian said dryly, "I'm going to bed."

With a quick squeeze of Glenna's hand, Hoyt murmured, "A moment," then followed his brother.

"I need a word with you."

Cian flicked him a glance. "I've had my quota of words this morning."

"You'll have to swallow a few more. My rooms are closer, if you would. I'd prefer this private."

"Since you'd just dog me to my room and pester me until I want to rip your tongue out, your rooms will do."

Servants bustled on the route between the parlor and bedchambers. Preparations for the feasting, Cian thought, and wondered if it was Hoyt's talk of fire that put him in mind of Nero and his fiddle.

Hoyt stepped into a chamber, then immediately threw out an arm to block Cian from entering. "The sun," was all he said, then moved quickly to pull the coverings over the windows.

The room plunged into gloom. Without thinking, Hoyt gestured toward a brace of candles. They flared into light.

"Handy bit of business that," Cian commented. "I'm out of practice lighting tinderboxes."

"It's a basic skill, and one you'd have yourself if you'd ever put your mind and time into honing your power."

"Too tedious. Is that whiskey?" Cian moved straight to a decanter, and poured. "Oh, such sobriety and disapproval." He read his brother's expression clearly as he took the first warm sip. "I'll remind you that it's the end of my day—well past it, come to that."

He glanced around, began to wander. "Smells female. Women like Glenna always leave something of themselves behind to remind a man." Then he dropped down into a chair, slouching, stretching out his legs. "Now, what is it you're bound and determined to bore me with?"

"There was a time you enjoyed, even sought my company."

Cian's shoulders moved in something too lazy to be called a shrug. "I suppose that means nine hundred years of absence doesn't make the heart grow fonder."

Regret showed on Hoyt's face before he turned away to add turf to the fire. "Are you and I to be at odds again?"

"You tell me."

"I wanted to speak with you alone about what you did with the prisoner."

"More humanity heard from. Yes, yes, I should have patted his head so he could stand trial, or before the tribunal, whatever goes for the name of justice in this place. I should've invoked the sodding Geneva Convention. Well, bollocks."

"I don't know this convention, but there could be no trial, no tribunal on such a matter at such a time. That's what I'm saying, you great irritating idiot. You executed an assassin, as I would have done—but with more tact and, well, stealth."

"Ah, so you'd have slithered down to whatever cage they put him in and put a knife between his ribs." Cian raised his eyebrows. "That's all right then."

"It's not. None of it's all right. It's a bloody nightmare is what it is, and we're all having it. I'm saying you did the necessary. And that for his trying to kill Moira, whom I love as I did my own sisters, and for putting an arrow in you, I'd have done for him. I've never killed a man, for these things we've ended these past weeks haven't been men, but demon. But I'd have killed this one if you hadn't been there ahead of me."

Hoyt paused, caught his breath if not his composure. "I wanted to say as much to you so you'd know my feelings on it. But it seems I waste both our time as you couldn't give a damn in hell what my feelings are."

Cian didn't move. His only change was to shift his gaze from his brother's furious face down to the whiskey in his hand. "I do, as it happens, give several damns in hell what your feelings are. I wish I didn't. You've stirred things in me I'd calmed too long ago to remember. You've slapped family in my face, Hoyt, when I'd buried it."

Crossing over, Hoyt took the chair that faced his brother's. "You're mine."

Now when Cian lifted his eyes to his brother's they were empty. "I'm no one's."

"Maybe you weren't, from the time you died until the time I found you. But it's no longer true. So if you give those damns, I'm saying to you I'm proud of what you're doing. I'm saying I know it's harder for you to do this thing than any of us."

"Obviously, as demonstrated, killing vampires or humans isn't difficult for me."

"Do you think I don't see how some of the servants melt away when you're near? That I didn't see Sinann rush to take her child, as if you might have snapped its neck as you did the assassin's? These insults to you don't go unnoticed."

"Some aren't insulted to be feared. It doesn't matter. It doesn't," he insisted when Hoyt's face closed up. "This is a fingersnap of time for me. Less. When it's done, unless I get a lucky stake through the heart, I'll go my way."

"I hope your way will bring you, from time to time, to see me and Glenna."

"It may. I like to look at her." Cian's grin spread, slow and easy. "And who knows, she may eventually come to her senses and realize she chose the wrong brother. I've nothing but time."

"She's mad for me." His tone easy again, Hoyt reached over, took Cian's glass of whiskey and had a sip himself.

"Mad is what she'd have to be to put her lot in with you, but women are odd creatures. You're fortunate in her, Hoyt, if I've failed to mention it before."

"She's the magic now." He passed the glass back. "I'd

have none that mattered without her. My world turned when she came into it. I wish you had . . ."

"That isn't written in the book of fate for me. The poet's may say love's eternal, but I can tell you it's a different matter when you've got eternity, and the woman doesn't."

"Have you ever loved a woman?"

Cian studied his whiskey again, and thought of the centuries. "Not in the way you mean. Not in the way you have with Glenna. But I've cared enough to know it's not a choice I can make."

"Love is a choice?"

"Everything is." Cian tossed back the last of the whiskey, then set the empty glass aside. "Now, I choose to go to bed."

"You chose to take that arrow for Moira today," Hoyt said as Cian started for the door.

Cian stopped, and when he turned his eyes were wary. "I did."

"I find that a very human sort of choice."

"Do you?" And the words were a shrug. "I find it merely an impulsive—and painful—one."

He slipped out to make his way to his own room on the northern side of the castle. Impulse, he thought again, and, he could admit to himself, an instant of raw fear. If he'd seen the arrow fly a second later, or moved with a fraction less speed, she'd be dead.

And in that instant of impulse and fear, he'd seen her dead. The arrow still quivering as it pierced her flesh, the blood spilling the life out of her onto her dark green gown and the hard gray stones.

He feared that, feared the end of her, where she would be beyond him. Where she would go to a place he couldn't see or touch. Lilith would have taken one last thing from him with that arrow, one last thing he could never regain.

For he'd lied to his brother. He had loved a woman, despite his best—or worst—intentions, he loved the new-crowned queen of Geall.

Which was ridiculous, and impossible, and in time

something he'd get over. A decade or two and he'd no longer remember the exact shade of those long gray eyes. That quiet scent she carried would no longer tease his senses. He'd forget the sound of her voice, the look of that slow, serious smile.

Such things faded, he reminded himself. You had only to allow it.

He stepped into his own room, closed and bolted the door.

The windows were covered, and no light was lit. Moira, he knew, had given very specific orders on how his housekeeping should be done. Just as she'd specifically chosen that room, a distance from the others, as it faced north.

Less sunlight, he mused. A considerate hostess.

He undressed in the dark, thought fleetingly of the music he liked to play before sleep, or on wakening. Music, he thought, that filled the silence.

But this time and place didn't run to CD players, or cable radio or any damn thing of the sort.

Naked, he stretched out in bed. And in the absolute dark, the absolute silence, willed himself to sleep.

Chapter 4

Moira stole the time. She escaped from her women, from her uncle, from her duties. She was already guilty, already worried she'd be a failure as a queen because she so craved her solitude.

She would have bartered two days' food, or two nights' sleep, for a single hour alone with her books. Selfish, she told herself as she hurried away from the noise, the people, the questions. Selfish to wish for her own comfort when so much was at stake.

But while she wouldn't indulge herself with books in some sunny corner, she would take the time to make this visit.

On this day she was made queen, she wanted, and she needed, her mother. So hiking up her skirts, she went as fast as she was able down the hill, then through the little gap in the stone wall that bordered the graveyard.

Almost instantly she felt quieter of heart.

She went first to the stone she'd ordered carved and set when she'd returned to Geall. She'd set one herself for King in Ireland, in the graveyard of Cian and Hoyt's ancestors. But she'd vowed to have one done here, in honor of a friend.

After laying a handful of flowers on the ground, she stood and read the words she'd ordered carved in the polished stone.

King
This brave warrior lies not here
but in a faraway land.
He gave his life for Geall,
and all humankind.

"I hope you would like it, the stone and the words. It seems so long ago since I saw you. It all seems so long, and still hardly more than a hand clap. I'm sorry to tell you Cian was hurt today, for my sake. But he's doing well enough. Last night we spoke almost as friends, Cian and I. And today, well, not altogether friendly. It's hard to know."

She laid a hand on the stone. "I'm queen now. That's hard to know as well. I hope you don't mind I put this monument here, where my family lies. For to me, that's what you were for the short time we had. You were family. I hope you're resting now."

She stepped away, then hurriedly back again. "Oh, I meant to say, I'm keeping my left up, as you taught me." By his grave she lifted her arms in a boxing stance. "So, for all the times I don't get a fist in my face, thank you."

With the rest of the flowers in the crook of her arm, she picked her way through the long grass, the stones, to the graves of her parents.

She laid flowers at the base of her father's stone. "Sir. I hardly remember you, and I think the memories—most of them—that I have are ones mother passed to me. She loved you so, and would speak of you often. I know you were a good man, for she wouldn't have loved you otherwise. And all who speak of you say you were strong and kind, and quick to laugh. I wish I could remember the sound of that, of your laugh."

She looked over the stones now, to the hills, the distant mountains. "I've learned you didn't die as we always thought, but were murdered. You and your young brother. Murdered by the demons who are even now in Geall, preparing for war. I'm all that's left of you, and I hope it's enough."

She knelt now, between the graves, to lay the rest of the flowers over her mother. "I miss you, every day. I had to go far away, as you know, to come back stronger. *Mathair.*"

She closed her eyes on the word, and on the image it brought to her, clear as life.

"I didn't stop what was done to you, and still I see that night as if behind a mist. Those that killed you have been punished, one by my own hand. It was all I could do for you. All I can do is fight, and lead my people to fight. Some of them to their death. I wear the sword and the crown of Geall. I will not diminish it."

She sat awhile, with just the sound of the breeze through the tall grass and the shifting lights of the sun.

When she rose, turned toward the castle, she saw the goddess Morrigan standing at the stone wall.

The god wore blue today, soft and pale and trimmed in deeper tones. The fire of her hair was unbound to lay flaming over her shoulders.

Her hands empty of flowers, her heart heavy, Moira walked through the grass to meet her.

"My lady."

"Majesty."

Puzzled by Morrigan's bow, Moira clasped her hands together to keep them still. "Do gods acknowledge queens?"

"Of course. We made this place and deemed those of your blood would rule and serve it. We're pleased with you. Daughter." Laying her hands lightly on Moira's shoulders, she kissed both her cheeks. "Our blessings on you."

"I would rather you bless my people, and keep them safe."

"That is for you. The sword is out of its scabbard. Even

when it was forged, it was known that one day it would sing in battle. That, too, is for you."

"She's already spilled Geallian blood."

Morrigan's eyes were as deep and calm as a lake. "My child, the blood Lilith has spilled would make an ocean."

"And my parents are only drops in that sea?"

"Every drop is precious, and every drop serves a purpose. Do you lift the sword only for your own blood?"

"No." Shifting, Moira gestured. "There's another stone here, standing for a friend. I lift the sword for him and his world, and for all the worlds. We're all a part of each other."

"Knowing this is important. Knowledge is a great gift, and the thirst to seek it even greater. Use what you know, and she will never defeat you. Head and heart, Moira. You are not made to give greater weight to one than the other. Your sword will flame, I promise you, and your crown will shine. But what you hold inside your head and your heart is the true power."

"It seems they're full of fear."

"There's no courage without fear. Trust and know. And keep your sword at your side. It's your death she wants most."

"Mine? Why?"

"She doesn't know. Knowledge is your power."

"My lady," Moira began, but the god was gone.

The feast required yet another gown and another hour of being fussed over. With so much on her hands, she'd left the matter of wardrobe to her aunt, and was pleased to find the gown beautiful and the watery blue color flattering. She enjoyed pretty gowns and taking a bit of time to look her best.

But it seemed she was being laced into a new one every time she turned around, and subjected to the chirping and buzzing of her women half the day.

She could admit she missed the freedom of the jeans

and roomy shirts she'd worn in Ireland. Beginning the next day, however it shocked the women, she would dress as best suited a warrior preparing for battle.

But for tonight, she'd wear the velvets and silks and jewels.

"Ceara, how are your children?"

"Well, my lady, and thank you." Standing behind Moira, Ceara continued to work Moira's thick hair into silky braids.

"Your duties and your training keep you from them more than I would wish."

Their eyes met in the mirror. Moira knew Ceara to be a sensible woman, the most centered, in her opinion, of the three that waited on her.

"My mother tends them, and is happy to do so. The time I take now is well spent. I'd rather lose these hours with them than see them harmed."

"Glenna tells me you're very fierce in hand-to-hand."

"I am." Ceara's face tightened with a grim smile. "I'm not skilled with a sword, but there's time yet. Glenna's a good teacher."

"Strict," Dervil piped in. "Not as strict as the lady Blair, but demanding all the same. We run, every day, and fight and tumble and carve stakes. And end each day with weary legs, bruises and splinters."

"Better to be weary and bruised than dead."

At Moira's flat comment, Dervil flushed. "I meant no disrespect, Majesty. I've learned a great deal."

"And are, I'm told, becoming a demon with a sword. I'm proud. And you, Isleen, are said to have a good hand with a bow."

"I do." Isleen, the youngest of the three flushed with the compliment. "I like it better than the fighting with fists and feet. Ceara always knocks me down."

"When you squeal like a mouse and flutter your hands, anyone could knock you down," Ceara pointed out.

"Ceara's taller, and her arms longer than yours, Isleen. So," Moira said, "you have to learn to be faster, and sneakier.

I'm proud of all of you, for every bruise. Tomorrow, and every day after, for no less than an hour each day, I'll be training with you."

"But, Majesty," Dervil began, "you can't—"

"I can," Moira interrupted. "And I will. I'll expect each of you, and the other women to do their best to knock *me* down. It won't be easy." She stood when Ceara stepped back. "I've learned a great deal as well." She lifted her crown, placed it on her head. "Believe me when I tell you I can knock the three of you, and any else who comes, on your arse."

She turned, resplendent in shimmering blue velvet.

"Any who puts me on mine, or bests me with bare hands or any weapon will be given one of the silver crosses Glenna and Hoyt has charmed. This is my best gift. Tell the others."

It was, Cian thought, like walking into a play. The great hall was the stage, and festooned with banners, enlivened with flowers, blazing with candles and firelight. Knights and lords and ladies were decked in their very best. Doublets and gowns, jewels and gold. He spotted several men and women sporting footwear with the long and pointed upturned toes that he recalled were fashionable when he'd been alive.

So, he thought, even regrettable styles spanned worlds.

Food and drink were so plentiful he imagined the long tables groaned under the platters and pitchers. There was music, bright and lively, from a harper. The talk he overheard ran the gamut. Fashion, politics, sexual gossip, flirtations and finance.

Not so different altogether, he mused, from his own nightclub back in New York. The women wore less there, of course, and the music was louder. But the core of it hadn't changed overmuch through the centuries. People still liked to gather together over food and drink and music.

He thought of his club again, and asked himself if he

missed it. The nightly surge, the sounds, the press of people. And realized he didn't, not in the least.

Very likely, he decided, he'd been growing bored and restless, and would have moved on shortly in any case. It had only taken his brother's sweep through time and space, having Hoyt land—more or less—on his doorstep to up the timetable.

But without Hoyt and his mission from the gods, moving out would have meant a change of name and location, a shifting of funds. Complicated, time-consuming—and interesting. Cian had had more than a hundred names and a hundred homes, and still found the forming of them interesting.

Where might he have gone? he wondered. Sydney perhaps, or Rio. It might have been Rome or Helsinki. It was only a matter, essentially, of sticking a pin in a map. There were few places he hadn't been already, and none he couldn't have made his base if he chose.

In his world, in any case. Geall was a different matter. He'd lived through this sort of fashion and culture once, and had no desire to repeat himself. His family had been gentry, and so he'd attended his share of high-flown feasts.

All in all he'd have preferred a snifter of brandy and a good book.

He didn't intend to stay long, and had come only because he knew someone would come looking for him. While he was confident he could have avoided whoever had come hunting him, he would never avoid the haranguing Hoyt would subject him to the next day.

Easier altogether to put in an appearance, toast the new queen, then slip away.

He had drawn the line at wearing the formal doublet and accessories that had been delivered to his room. He might have been stuck in a medieval timeline, but he'd be damned if he'd dress for it.

So he wore black, pants and sweater. He hadn't packed a suit and tie for this particular journey.

Still he smiled with some warmth at Glenna who drifted

up to him in emerald green, in what he thought had been termed a *robe deguisee* at one time. Very formal, very elegant, and showcasing her very lovely breasts with its low and rounded neckline.

"Now here's a vision I prefer to any goddess."

"I almost feel like one." She spread her arms so the full bell sleeves swayed. "Heavy though. It must be ten pounds of material. I see you went for a less weighty ensemble."

"I believe I'd stake myself before I squeezed into one of those getups again."

She had to laugh. "Can't blame you, but I'm getting a kick out of seeing Hoyt all done up. For me—maybe for you after all this time—it's like a costume ball. Moira chose regal black and gold for the house sorcerer. It suits him, as your more contemporary choice does you. Still, this whole day has been like a very strange dream."

"I was thinking a very strange play."

"Yeah, that works. Whatever, tonight's feasting is a short and colorful respite. We managed to do some scouting today, Hoyt and I magically, Larkin and Blair with the fly-over. We'll fill you in when—"

She broke off at the sound of trumpets.

Moira made her entrance, the train of her gown flowing behind her, her crown flaming in the light of a hundred candles.

She glowed, as queens should, as women could.

As his unbeating heart tightened in his chest, Cian thought: Bloody, buggering hell.

He had no choice but to join the others at the high table for the feast. Leaving beforehand would have been an overt insult—not that he minded that overmuch—but it would have drawn attention. So he was stuck again.

Moira sat at the center of the table, flanked by Larkin and her uncle. Cian, at least, had Blair beside him, who was both an informative and entertaining companion.

"Lilith hasn't burned anything yet, which was a surprise," she began. "Probably too busy nursing Fifi. Oh, question. The French bitch has been around about four hundred years, right? And you more than double that. How come both of you still have accents?"

"And why is it Americans believe everyone should speak as they do?"

"Good point. Is this venison? I think it's venison." She took a bite. "It's not too bad."

She wore siren red, which left a portion of her strong shoulders bared. Her short cap of hair was unadorned, but there were ornate gold medallions, nearly big as a baby's fist, dangling from her ears.

"How do you hold your head up with those earrings?"

"Suffering for fashion," she said easily. "So they've got horses," she continued. "A couple of dozen in various paddocks. Might be more stabled. I figure why not have Larkin put down, and we could run the horses off. Just make a nuisance of ourselves. Maybe—if I can talk him into it—light a few fires. Vamps stay inside, they burn. Come out, they burn."

"Good thinking. Unless, of course, she had guards posted inside, with bows."

"Well, yeah, like I didn't think of that. I figure I'll wing a few flaming arrows down, get their attention. I pick my target—cottage nearest the biggest paddock. Gotta be some troops in there, stands to reason. Imagine my surprise and chagrin when the arrows bump off the air, like it was a wall."

His eyes narrowed as he shifted to face her. "Are you talking force field? What is this, bloody *Star Trek*?"

"That's what I said." In tune with him, Blair punched his shoulder. "She's got that wizard of hers, that Midir, working overtime by my guess. And their base camp's in a protective bubble. Larkin flew down, to get a closer look, and we both got a jolt. Like an electric shock. Pisser."

"Yes, it would be."

"Then the man himself comes out—from the big house, the manor house? Creepy-looking guy, let me say. Flying black robes, lots of silver hair. He just stands there, so we're looking down at him, he's looking up at us. Finally, I get it.

Mexican standoff. We can't get anything through, but neither can they. When the shield's up, they're locked down, we're locked out. Good as a freaking fortress. Better."

"She knows how to make the best use of the people she brings in," Cian mused.

"Looks that way. So I was lowered to making rude gestures, just so it wasn't a waste of time. She'd lower the shield at night, wouldn't she?"

"Possibly. Even if they brought enough food with them, the nature of the beast is to hunt. She wouldn't want her troops to get stale, or too edgy."

"So, maybe we can make a night run at it. I don't know. Something to think about. That's haggis, isn't it?" She wrinkled her nose. "I'm skipping that." She leaned a little closer to him, lowered her voice. "Larkin says the word's gone out on how you dealt with the guy who tried to kill Moira. You've got the castle guards and the knights behind you on that one."

"It hardly matters."

"You know better than that. You get what's essentially going to be this army's first line not just accepting you, but respecting you, it matters. Sir Cian."

He winced, visibly. "Just don't."

"Kind of rings for me. This Jell-O sort of thing is a little gritty. Do you know what it is?"

Cian waited, deliberately, until she'd taken a second bite. "Jellied internal organs—likely pig."

When she choked, the laugh just rolled out of him.

It was such a strange sound, Moira thought. To hear him laugh. Strange, a little wicked, and very appealing. She'd made a misstep with the clothes she'd sent for him. He was too much a creature of his own time—or what had come to be his own time—to put on garb from hers.

But he'd come, and she hadn't been sure he would. Not that he'd spoken a word to her. Not a single word.

He'd killed for her, she thought, but didn't speak to her.

So she would put him out of her mind, as he'd so obviously put her out of his.

She only wished the evening would end. She wanted her bed, she wanted sleep. She wanted to peel off the heavy velvet and slide blissfully—for one night—into the dark.

But she had to make a show of eating, despite her lack of appetite. She had to make a pretense, at least, of paying attention to conversations even though her eyes wanted to close.

She'd had too much wine, felt too warm. And there were hours yet before she could lay down her head.

Of course, she had to stop, to smile, and to drink every time one of the knights was moved to toast her. At the rate they were moving, her head would likely spin right off the pillow.

It was with huge relief that she was finally able to announce the dancing could begin.

She had to stand for the first set, as it was expected of her. And found she felt better for moving, for the music.

He didn't dance, of course, but only sat. Like a dyspeptic king, she thought, foolishly irritated because she'd *wanted* to dance with him. His hands on her hands, his eyes on her eyes.

But there he sat, gazing down on the masses and sipping his wine. She spun with Larkin, bowed to her uncle, clasped hands with Hoyt.

And when she looked back again, Cian was gone.

He wanted air, and more, he wanted the night. The night was still his time. What lived inside the mask of a man would always crave it, and always seek it.

He went up, and out, where the dark was thick and the music from the hall only a silvery echo. Clouds had rolled over the moon, and the stars were smothered by them. Rain would come before morning; he could already smell it.

Below, there were torches to light the courtyards, and guards stood at post at the gates, on the walls.

He heard one of them cough and spit, and the quick flap of the flags overhead in a sudden kick of wind. He could hear, if he tuned himself to it, the rustle of mice in their nest tucked in a gap of the stones, or the papery swish of the wings of a bat that circled overhead.

He could hear what others didn't.

He scented human—that salt on the flesh, and the rich run of blood beneath it. There was a part of him—always—that burned a little with the need. To hunt, to kill, to feed.

That burst of blood in the mouth, in the throat. The sheer life of it that could never be tasted in what came in cool packs of plastic. Hot, he remembered, always hot, that first taste. It heated all the places that were cold and dead, and for that moment, life—or its shadow—stirred inside that cold and that dead.

It was good to remember, now and then, the unspeakable pleasure of it. Good to remember what he pit his will against. Vital to remember what it was those they fought craved.

The humans did not, could not. Not even Blair who understood more than most.

Still they would fight, and they would die. More would come behind them to fight, and to die. Some would run, of course—some always did. Some would break with fear and simply stand and be slaughtered, like rabbits caught in a jacklight.

But most wouldn't run, wouldn't hide, wouldn't freeze in terror. In all the years he'd watched humans live and die, he knew when their backs were pressed hardest to the wall, they fought like demons.

If they won, they would end up romanticizing the whole business, songs and stories. Old men would sit by fires years from now and speak of the glory days while they showed their scars.

And others of them would wake in cold sweats from reliving the horror of war in their dreams.

If he lived, what would it be for him? he wondered. Glory days or nightmares? Neither, he thought, for he wasn't human enough to spend his time on what was over and done.

If Lilith managed to end him, well, true death was an experience he'd yet to have. It might be interesting.

And because he heard what others didn't, he caught the footsteps on the stone stairs. Moira's footsteps, as he knew her gait as well as her scent.

He nearly melted back into the shadows, then cursed himself for being a coward. She was only a woman, only a human. She could and would be nothing more to him.

When she stepped out, he heard her sigh once, long and deep as if she'd just shed some enormous weight. She moved to the stone rail, tipped her head back, closed her eyes. And breathed.

Her face was flushed from the heat of the fire, the exertion of the dance, but there were shadows of fatigue haunting her eyes.

Someone had worked slender braids through her long hair, so the weaving of them with their thin ropes of gold rippled through the rain of glossy brown.

He saw the minute she sensed she wasn't alone. The sudden stiffening in her shoulders, and the slide of her hand into the folds of her gown.

"If you've a stake tucked in there," he said, "I'd as soon you didn't point it in my direction."

Though her shoulders didn't relax, her hand dropped to her side as she turned. "I didn't see you. I wanted some air. It's so warm inside, and I've drunk too much."

"More that you didn't eat enough. I'll leave you to your air."

"Oh, stay. I'm only taking a moment, then you can have the damned air to yourself again." She pushed at her hair, then cocked her head.

He got a good look at her face now, her eyes, and thought, yes, indeed, the little queen was on the way to being plowed.

"Do you come out here to think deep thoughts? I can't decide if deep thoughts require space like this, or are better turned over in confines. I imagine you have many thoughts, with all that you've seen."

She stumbled a little, laughed a little when he caught her arm. And immediately released it.

"You're so careful not to touch me," she commented. "Unless you're saving me from death or injury. Or bashing at me in training. I find that interesting. You're a man of interests, how do you find it?"

"I don't."

"Except for that one time," she continued as if he hadn't spoken, and moved a step closer. "That one time you touched me good and proper. You put your hands on me then, and your mouth. I've wondered about that."

He very nearly took a step in retreat, and the realization of it mortified him. "It was meant to teach you a lesson."

"I'm a scholar, and I do love my lessons. Give me another then."

"The wine's made you foolish." He was annoyed with the stiff and pompous sound of his own voice. "You should go in, have your ladies take you to your bed."

"It has made me foolish. I'll be sorry for it tomorrow, but well, that's tomorrow, isn't it? Oh, what a day this has been for me." She did a slow turn that had her skirts swaying over the stones. "Was it only this morning I walked to the stone? How could it be only this morning? I feel I've carried that sword and the stone with it through this day. Now I'm setting them down, until tomorrow, I'm setting them down. I'm the worse for drink, and what of it?"

She stepped closer yet, and pride wouldn't let him back away.

"I'd hoped you'd dance with me tonight. I hoped, and I wondered what it would be like to have you touch me when it wasn't in a fight or out of manners or mistake."

"I wasn't in the mood for dancing."

"Oh, and you're full of moods, you are." She watched his face carefully, studying him, he thought, as she might the pages of a book. "And sure, so am I. I was in an angry mood when you kissed me before. And a little frightened around it. I'm not angry or frightened now. But I think you are."

"Now you're adding ridiculous to foolish."

"Prove it then." She closed that last bit of distance, tipped up her face to his. "Teach me a lesson."

He could hardly be damned for it. He'd been damned long before. He wasn't gentle; he wasn't tender. But yanked her against him and nearly off her feet before his mouth swooped down to plunder hers.

He tasted the wine and the warmth—and a recklessness he hadn't anticipated. That, he knew, was his mistake.

She was ready for him this time. Her hands were in his hair, her mouth open and avid. She didn't melt against him in surrender, or shudder from the onslaught. She strained for more.

Need clawed at him, one more demon sent to torture him.

She wondered the air between them didn't smoke, wondered how it was both of them didn't simply erupt into flame. This was fire, in the blood, in the bone.

How had she lived all of her life without it?

Even when he released her, pushed her back, it stayed inside her like a fever.

"Did you feel that?" Her whisper was full of wonder. "Did you feel that?"

The taste of her was inside him now, and everything in him craved more of her. So he didn't answer, didn't speak at all. He slipped into the dark and was gone before she could take another breath.

Chapter 5

She awoke early and energized. All through the day before she'd dragged such weight with her, as if it had been shackled to her leg. Now that chain was broken. It didn't matter that rain poured out of moody gray skies that smothered even a hint of sun. She had the light inside her again.

She dressed in what she thought of as her Irish clothes—jeans and a sweatshirt. The time for ceremony and decorum was past, and sensibilities be damned until she could spend time soothing them again.

She might be a queen, she thought as she twisted her hair into a long, single braid, but she would be a working one.

She would be a warrior.

She laced on her boots, strapped on her sword. This woman Moira saw in the looking glass, she recognized and approved of. She was a woman with purpose, and power, and knowledge.

Turning, she studied the room. The queen's chamber, she thought. Once her mother's sanctuary, and now hers. The bed was wide and beautifully draped in deep blue velvet and frothy snow-white lace, for her mother had loved the soft and the pretty. The posts were thick, polished Geallian oak, and deeply carved with Geall's symbols. Paintings that graced the walls were also of Geall, its fields and hills and forests.

On a table near the bed stood a small portrait in a silver frame. Moira's father had watched over her mother every night—now he would watch over his daughter.

She glanced over toward the doors that led to her mother's balcony. The drapes were still pulled tight there, and she would leave them that way. At least for now. She wasn't ready to open those doors, to step out on the stones where her mother had been slaughtered.

Instead, she would remember the happy hours she'd spent with her mother in this chamber.

She went out, making her way to the door of Hoyt and Glenna's chamber where she knocked. Because it took several moments, she remembered the hour. She'd nearly stepped away again, hoping they hadn't heard her knock when the door opened.

Hoyt was still pulling on his robes. His long dark hair was tousled, and his eyes heavy with sleep.

"Oh, I beg your pardon," she began. "I didn't think—"

"Has something happened? Is something wrong?"

"No, no, nothing. I didn't think how early it was. Please, go back to your bed."

"What is it?" Glenna moved into view behind him. "Moira? Is there a problem?"

"Only with my manners. I was up and about early, and wasn't considering others would still be abed, especially after last night's festivities."

"It's all right." Glenna laid a hand on Hoyt's arm, signaling him to step aside. "What did you need?"

"Only a private word with you. The truth of the matter is I was going to ask if you'd have breakfast with me in my mother's—in my sitting room, so I could speak with you about something."

"Give me ten minutes."

"Are you certain? I don't mind waiting until later in the day."

"Ten minutes," Glenna repeated.

"Thank you. I'll see food's prepared."

"She looks . . . ready for something," Hoyt commented when Glenna went to the bowl and basin to wash.

"Or other." Glenna dipped her fingers into the water, focused. She might not be able to take a shower, but she'd be damned if she'd wash in cold water.

She did the best she could with what she had as Hoyt beefed up the fire. Then, giving into vanity, she did a subtle glamour.

"It might be she just wants to talk about today's training schedule." Glenna fixed on earrings she'd have to remember to take off for training. "I told you she's offered a prize—one of our crosses—to any of the women who takes her down in a match today."

"It was clever of her to offer a prize, but I wonder if it would be the best use of the cross."

"There were nine of them," Glenna reminded him as she dressed. "Five for us, and King's, of course, making six. The two we agreed to give to Larkin's mother and pregnant sister. There's a purpose for the ninth. This may be it."

"We'll see what the day brings." He smiled as she pulled a gray sweater over her head. "How is it, *a ghrá*, that you look lovelier every morning?"

"You've got love in your eyes." She turned into his arms when he moved to her—and looked wistfully at the bed. "Rainy morning. It'd be nice to snuggle in for an hour and have my way with you." She tipped her head up for a kiss. "But it looks like I'm having breakfast with the queen."

Moira was, as was her habit, sitting by the fire with a book when Glenna entered. Moira looked up, smiled sheepishly.

"Shame on me, taking you from your husband and your warm bed at such an hour."

"Queen's privilege."

With a laugh, Moira gestured to a chair. "The food will

be along. One day, if the seeds I brought and potted thrive, I'll be able to have the orange juice in the mornings. I miss the taste of it."

"I'd kill for coffee," Glenna admitted. "Then again, in a way, I am. For coffee, apple pie, TiVo and all things human." She sat and studied Moira. "You look good," she decided. "Rested, and as Hoyt said, ready."

"I am. Yesterday, there was so much inside my head and my heart, so it was all so very heavy. The sword and the crown were my mother's, and only mine now because she's dead."

"And you've had no time to grieve, not really."

"I haven't, no. Still, I know she would want me to do as I have, for Geall, for all, and not close myself off somewhere to mourn for her. And I had fear as well. What manner of queen would I be, and at such a time."

With some satisfaction, Moira looked down at her rough pants and boots. "Well, I know what manner of queen I'll try to be. Strong, even fierce. There's no time to sit on a throne and debate matters. Politics and protocol, they'll have to wait, won't they? We've had our ceremony and our celebration, and they were needed. But now it's time for the dirt and the sweat of it."

She got to her feet when the food was brought in. She spoke to the young boy—still sleepy around the edges—and the serving girl who was with him.

Spoke easily, Glenna noted. Called them both by name as the food and dishes were laid out. And while they both looked puzzled by their queen's choice of dress, Moira ignored it, dismissing them with thanks—and orders she and her guest not be disturbed.

When they sat together, Glenna noticed that Moira, who'd picked at her food for days, ate with an appetite to rival Larkin's.

"It'll be muddy and miserable for training today," Moira began, "and that's good, I'm thinking. Good discipline. I wanted to say that while I'll be participating, and likely every day now, you and Blair are still in charge of the thing. I want everyone to see that I'm training, just like the rest. That I'll get dirty and bruised."

"Sounds like you're looking forward to it."

"By the gods, I am." Moira scooped up eggs she'd coached the cooks to prepare as Glenna often had. Scrambled up with chunks of ham and onion right in them. "Do you remember when Larkin and I first came through the Dance to Ireland? I could plant an arrow anywhere I liked, nine of ten, but any one of you could plant *me* on my arse without half trying."

"You always got up."

"Aye, I always got up. But I'm not so easy to plant these days. That's something I want everyone to see as well."

"You showed them a warrior when you fought and killed the vampire."

"I did. Now I'll show them a soldier who takes her lumps. And there's more I want of you."

"I thought there was." Glenna poured them both more tea. "Spill it."

"I've never explored the magic I have. It isn't much of a thing, as you've seen yourself. A bit of a healing gift, and a kind of power that can be opened and reached by others with more. As you and Hoyt have done. Dreams. I've studied dreams, read books on their meanings. And books on magic itself, of course. But it seemed to me there was no real purpose for what I had other than to offer some ease to someone in pain. Or a way of knowing which direction to take to find a buck when hunting. Little things. Small matters."

"And now?"

"And now," Moira said with a nod. "I think there's a purpose, and there's a need. I think I need all I have, all I am. The more I know what's in me, the better I use it. When I touched the sword, when I put my hand on its hilt, it poured into me. The knowing that it was mine, had always been mine. And a power with it, like a strong wind, just blowing into me. More through me, I think. Do you know?"

"Exactly."

Nodding again, Moira continued to eat. "I've neglected this because it wasn't a particular interest. I wanted to read and to study, to hunt with Larkin, to ride."

"To do the things a young woman enjoys," Glenna interrupted. "Why shouldn't you have done what you liked to do? You didn't know what was coming."

"I didn't, no. I wonder, if I'd looked deeper, if I might have."

"You couldn't have saved your mother, Moira," Glenna said gently.

Moira looked up, her eyes very clear. "You see my thoughts so easily."

"I think because in your place, I'd have the same ones. You couldn't have saved her. More—"

"Weren't meant to," Moira finished. "I'm coming around to that, inside my heart. But if I'd explored what I have, I might have seen something of what was coming. For whatever difference it would have made. Like Blair, I've seen the battleground in dreams. But unlike her, I didn't face it. I turned away. That's done, too. I'm not . . . wait." She searched for the phrase. "Beating myself up? Right?"

"Yeah, that's right."

"I'm not beating myself up over it. I'm after changing it. So I'm asking, if you can make the time to help me hone whatever I might have, the way I've honed my fighting skills."

"I can. I'd love to."

"I'm grateful."

"Don't be grateful yet. It'll be work. Magic's an art, and a craft. And a gift. But comparing it to your physical training isn't far off. It's also, well, like a muscle." Glenna tapped a hand on her biceps. "You have to exercise it, and build it. Like medicine it's said we practice magic, so it's never done."

"Every weapon I take into battle is another strike against the enemy." Brows lifted, Moira flexed her arm. "So I'll build that muscle as I have this one, strong as I can.

I want to crush her, Glenna. More than defeat her, to crush her. For so many reasons. My parents, King. Cian," she added after a pause. "He'd dislike that, wouldn't he, knowing I think of him as a victim?"

"He doesn't see himself that way."

"He doesn't, refuses to. It's why he thrives, in his way. He's made his . . . I can't say peace as he's not a peaceful sort, is he? But he's accepted his lot. I suppose, in some sort of way, he's embraced it."

"I'd say you have his number, as much as any could."

Moira hesitated now, making a business of rearranging the food left on her plate. "He kissed me again."

"Oh. Oh." And after a pause. "Oh."

"I made him."

"Not to belittle your charm or powers, I don't think anyone can make Cian do much of anything he doesn't want to do."

"Could be he wanted to, but he wasn't going to until I pushed him into it. I'd had a bit to drink."

"Hmm."

"I wasn't the worse for it," Moira said with a laugh that had some nerves at the edges. "Not really. Just a little looser in my manners, so to speak, and more determined in my mind. I wanted air and some quiet, so I went up, out on one of the battlements. There he was."

She pictured it again. "He might have gone anywhere, and sure I could have gone somewhere else. But neither of us did, so we both ended up in the same place, at the same time. In the night," she said quietly. "With the music and the lights barely reaching us."

"Romantic."

"I suppose it was. With the rain that would come before dawn just beginning to scent the air, and the thin slice of moon very white against the sky. There's a mystery to him I keep wanting to pick at until I find the pieces of it."

"You wouldn't be human if you didn't find him fascinating," Glenna said. They both knew what she hadn't said. He wasn't. He wasn't human.

"He was being all stiff, the way he can be with me, and it was irritating. And well, I'll admit, challenging. At the same time . . . It comes in me sometimes, when I'm with him. The way knowledge does, or magic. Something rising."

She pressed a hand to her belly, then drew it upward toward her heart. "Just . . . pulling up from the center of me. I never had strong feelings, in this way, for a man. Little flutters of them, you know? Comfortable and interesting, but not strong and hot. There's something about him that compels me. He's so . . ."

"Sexy," Glenna finished. "At the outrageous level."

"I wanted to know if it would be like it had been the other time, the only time, when we'd both been so angry and he'd taken hold of me. I told him to do it again, and wouldn't take no for an answer."

She cocked her head now, as if puzzling it out. "Do you know, I think I made him nervous. Seeing him flustered a bit, and trying not to be, that was as intoxicating to me as the wine had been."

"God yes." On a long breath, Glenna picked up her tea. "It would be."

"And when he kissed me it was like the other time, only more. Because I was waiting for it. For that moment, he was as much caught as I was. I knew it."

"What are you looking for from him, Moira?"

"I don't know. Perhaps just that heat, just that power. That pleasure. Is it wrong?"

"I can't say." But it worried her. "He'd never be able to give you more. You have to understand that. He wouldn't stay here, and even if he did, for a time, you could never have a life with him. You're stepping onto dangerous ground."

"Every day from now till Samhain is dangerous ground. I know what you're saying is good, solid sense, but still in my mind and heart I want. I need to let them both settle a bit before I know what should be done about it next. But I do know that I don't want to go into battle stepping back from this only because I'm afraid of what it could be, or what it couldn't."

After a moment's debate, Glenna sighed. "It may be good solid sense, but I very much doubt I'd take my own advice if I were in your place."

Reaching over, Moira took Glenna's hand. "It helps, being able to talk to another woman. Just to be able to say what's in my mind and heart to another woman."

In another part of Geall, in a house shrouded against even the weak and watery light, two other females sat and talked.

It was the end of their day, not the beginning, but they shared a quiet meal.

Quiet because the man they were draining was beyond protest or struggle.

"You were right." Lora leaned back, delicately dabbing blood from her lips with a linen cloth. The man had been chained to the table between them as Lilith wanted her injured companion to sit, to eat, rather than lie in bed and sip from cups. "Getting up, having a civilized kill was what I needed."

"There, you see." Pleased, Lilith smiled.

Lora's face was still badly burned. The holy water that bitch of a demon hunter had hurled at her had wreaked terrible damage. But Lora was healing, and the good fresh meal would help her get her strength back.

"I wish you'd eat a little more though."

"I will. You've been so good to me, Lilith. And I failed you."

"You didn't. It was a good plan, and nearly worked. It's you who paid such a high price for it. I can't stand to think of the pain you were in."

"I would have died without you."

They had been lovers and friends, competitors and adversaries. They had been everything to each other for four centuries. But Lora's injuries, the near end of her, had brought them closer than they'd ever been.

"Until you were hurt, I didn't know how much I loved

and needed you. Here now, sweetheart, just a little more."

Lora obeyed, taking the man's limp arm, sinking her fangs into the wrist.

Before the burns, she'd been pretty, a youthful blonde with a swaggering style. Now her face was raw and red, riddled with half-healed wounds. But the glassy glaze of pain had faded from her blue eyes, and her voice was coming back strong again.

"It was wonderful, Lilith." She sat back again. "But I just can't drink another drop."

"Then I'll have it taken away, and we'll sit by the fire for a bit before bed."

Lilith rang a little gold bell, signaling one of the servants to clear. The leftovers, she knew, would hardly go to waste.

She rose to help Lora across the room where she'd already had pillows and a throw placed on the sofa.

"More comfortable than the caves," Lilith commented. "But still I'll be glad to be out of this place, and into proper accommodations."

She settled Lora before she sat, regal in her red gown, her hair piled high and gold as she'd wanted to add a touch of glamour to the evening.

Her beauty hadn't diminished in the two thousand years since her death.

"Do you have pain?" she asked Lora.

"No. I feel almost myself. I'm sorry I behaved so childishly yesterday morning, when that bitch flew over on her ridiculous dragon-man. Seeing her again just brought it all flooding back, all the fear, the agony."

"We gave her a surprise though, didn't we?" Soothing, Lilith smoothed the throw, tucking it around Lora. "Imagine her shock when her arrows met Midir's shield. You were right to talk me out of killing him."

"The next time I see her, I won't weep and hide under the covers like a frightened child. The next time I see her, she dies, by my hand. I swear it."

"Do you still have a yearning to change her, for a playmate?"

"I'd never give that whore such a gift." Lora's mouth tightened on a snarl. "She'll get only death from me." Then with a sigh, Lora laid her head on Lilith's shoulder. "She would never have been what you are to me. I thought to have a bit of fun with her. And I thought she'd be entertaining for both of us in bed—all that energy and violence inside her was so appealing. But I could never have loved her as I love you."

She tilted her head up now so their lips met in a long, soft kiss. "I'm yours, Lilith. Eternally."

"My sweet girl." Lilith pressed another kiss to Lora's temple. "Do you know when I first saw you, sitting alone on the dark, damp streets of Paris, weeping, I knew you'd belong to me."

"I thought I loved a man," Lora murmured. "And he loved me. But he used me, spurned me, tossed me aside for another. I thought my heart was broken. Then you were there."

"Do you remember what I said to you?"

"I will never forget. You said, 'My sweet, sad girl, are you all alone?' I told you my life was over, that I would be dead of grief by morning."

Lilith laughed, stroked Lora's hair. "So dramatic. How could I resist you?"

"Or I you. You were so beautiful—like the queen you are. You wore red, as you do tonight, and your hair so bright, all curls. You took me to your house, and fed me bread and wine, and listened to my sad tale and dried my tears."

"So young and charming you were. So sure this man who had cast you aside was all you could ever want."

"I don't remember his name now. Or his face."

"You came so willingly into my arms," Lilith murmured. "I asked if you would wish to stay young and lovely forever, if you would wish to have power over men like the one who hurt you. You said yes, and yes again. Even when I tasted you, you held tight to me and said again, yes and yes."

Hints of red stained the whites of Lora's eyes as she remembered that magnificent moment. "I'd never known such a thrill."

"When you drank from me, I loved you as I had no other."

"And when I lived again, you brought him to me, so I could have the one who scorned me for my first kill. We shared him, as we've shared so much."

"When Samhain comes, we will share all there is."

While the vampires slept, Moira stood on the playing field. She was filthy and drenched. Her hip throbbed from a blow that had slipped past her guard, and her breath was still wheezing out of her lungs from the last bout.

She felt wonderful.

She held out a hand to help Dervil to her feet. "You did very well," Moira told her. "You nearly had me."

Wincing, Dervil rubbed her ample rump. "I think not."

Hands on hips, her head covered with a wide-brimmed and now sodden leather hat, Glenna surveyed both of them. "You stayed on your feet longer this time, and got back on them quicker." She nodded approval at Dervil. "Improvement. From what I'm told there are several men on the other side of this field that you could take."

"There are several men on the other side of the field she *has* taken," Isleen called out, and got a number of bawdy laughs.

"And I know what to do with them when I take them," Dervil retorted.

"Put some of that energy into your next match," Glenna suggested, "and you might win it instead of ending up in the mud. Let's finish up with some archery practice, and call this a day."

Even as the women responded with relief that the session was nearly done, Moira waved a hand. "I haven't yet met Ceara in hand-to-hand. I've been saving what I'm told is the best for last. So I can retire full champion from the field."

"Cocky. I like it." Blair spoke as she moved through the rain and the mud. "Weapon details moving along," she added. "We've kicked production up a notch." She tipped back her head. "Let me tell you, this rain feels great after a couple hours with an anvil and forge. So, what's the score here?"

"Moira's taken all comers with sword and hand-to-hand. She's challenged Ceara here to a bout before we finish up with bows."

"Good enough. I can take a group to the targets while you finish up here."

There was immediate and vocal protest from the women who were eager to watch the last match.

"Blood-thirsty." Blair nodded approval. "I like that, too. All right, ladies, give them room. Who's your money on?" she murmured to Glenna as the two women squared off.

"Moira's hot, and motivated. She's just plowed through the field today. I'd have to put my money on her."

"I'll take Ceara. She's tricky, and she's not afraid to take a hit. See," she added when Ceara went sprawling facedown in the mud, and sprang up again to charge.

She feinted, pivoting at the last minute, then swept up a foot to catch Moira mid-body. The queen shot back from the hit, managed to catch her balance and duck the next blow. She came up hard, flipped Ceara over her shoulder. But when she spun around, Ceara wasn't flat on her back, but had pumped off her own hands, and striking out with her feet, kicked Moira into the mud.

Moira was up quickly, and with a light in her eyes. "Well now, your reputation hasn't been exaggerated, I see."

"I'm after the prize." Ceara crouched, circled. "Be warned."

"Come get it then."

"Good fight," Blair commented as fists and feet and bodies flew. "Ceara, keep your elbows up!"

Glenna jabbed Blair with her own. "No coaching from

the peanut gallery." But she was smiling, not just because it was a good, strong fight, but because the rest of the women were shouting and calling out advice.

They'd made themselves a unit.

Moira fell back, scissored out her legs and swept Ceara's from under her. But when she rolled up again to pin her opponent, Ceara thrust up and flipped Moira over her head.

There were several sounds of sympathy as Moira landed with a bone-rattling thud. Before she could shove up again, Ceara was straddling her, an elbow to Moira's throat, and a fist to her heart.

"You're staked."

"Damn me, I am. Get off me, gods' pity, you're crushing my lungs."

She sucked in breath as she struggled to push her still vibrating body into a sitting position. Ceara simply dropped down to sit in the mud beside her, and the two of them panted and eyed each other.

"You're a great bitch in battle," Moira said at length.

"The same to you, with all respect, my lady. I've bruises on top of my bruises now, and knots on top of those."

Moira swiped some of the mud from her face with her forearm. "I wasn't fresh."

"That's true, but I could take you fresh as well."

"I think you're right. You won the prize, Ceara, and won it fair. I'm proud to have been bested by you."

She offered her hand, and after shaking it, raised it high. "Here's the champion of the hand-to-hand."

There were cheers, and in the way of women, hugs. But when Ceara offered a hand to help Moira to her feet, Moira waved her off. "I'm just going to sit here another minute, catch my breath. Go on, get your bow. And with that you nor any will best me."

"It couldn't be done if we had a thousand years. Your Majesty?"

"Aye? Oh God, I won't sit easy for a week," she added, rubbing her sore hip.

"I've never been prouder of my queen."

Moira smiled to herself, then simply sat quiet, taking stock of her aches and pains. Then her gaze was drawn up to the spot where she'd stood with Cian the night before.

And there he was, standing in the gloom and the rain, looking down at her. She could feel the force of him through the distance, the allure he exuded, she thought, as other men never could.

"So what are you looking at?" she said to herself. "Is it amusing to you to see me on my arse in the mud?"

Probably, she decided, and who could blame him? She imagined she made quite the picture.

"We'll have a match of our own, I'm thinking, sooner or later. Then we'll see who bests who."

She pushed herself to her feet, gritted her teeth against the need to limp. So she could walk away steady, and without a backward glance.

Chapter 6

After scraping off an acre of mud, Moira joined the others for a strategy session. She walked in at that tenuous point between discussion and argument.

"I'm not saying you can't handle yourself." Larkin's tone as he addressed Blair had taken on that last ragged edge of patience. "I'm saying Hoyt and I can manage this."

"And I'm saying three would get it done faster than two."

"What would that be?" Moira asked.

The answer came from several sources, with steadily rising voices.

"I can't make much of that out." She held up a hand for peace as she took her seat at the table. "Am I understanding that we're after sending a party out to set up a base near the battlefield, scouting as they go?"

"With the first troops moving out behind them, in the morning," Hoyt finished. "We have locations marked where shelter can be found. Here," he said, tapping the map spread out on the table. "A day's march east. Then another, a day's march from that."

"But the fact is, with Lilith dug in here." Blair laid her fist on the map. "She's taken the advantage of primo location and facilities. We can crisscross our bases, establish a kind of jagged front line. But we need to start moving troops, and we need to secure bases for them before we send them out. Not only along the route, but at the best points near the valley."

"True enough." Considering, Moira studied the map. She saw how it was meant to work, with daylight jumps from position to position. "Larkin can cover the distance faster than any—we'd agree on that?"

"The way things are. But if we recruited other dragons—"

"Blair, I've said that can't be."

"Dragons?" Moira held up a hand again to silence Larkin's interruption. "What do you mean?"

"When Larkin shape-shifts he can communicate, at least on a rudimentary level, with what he becomes," Blair began.

"Aye. And?"

"So if he calls other dragons when he's in that form, why couldn't he convince some of them to follow him—with riders?"

"They're peaceful, gentle creatures," Larkin interrupted. "They shouldn't be drawn into something like this where they could be harmed."

"Wait, wait." Rolling it over in her mind, Moira sat back. "Could it be done? I've seen some take a baby in as a kind of pet from time to time, but I've never heard of anyone riding a full-grown dragon except in stories. If it could be done, it would allow us to travel swiftly, and even by night. And in battle . . ."

She broke off when she saw Larkin's expression. "I'm sorry, truly. But we can't be sentimental about it. The dragon is a symbol of Geall, and Geall needs its symbols. We ask our people, our women, the young ones, the old ones, to fight and to sacrifice. If such a thing could be done, it should be done."

"I don't know if it can be."

Moira knew when Larkin was being mule-headed. "You'll need to try. We love our horses, too, Larkin," Moira reminded him. "But we'll ride them into this. Now, Hoyt, would you tell me plain, is it best for you and Larkin to go on your own, or for the three of you to do this?"

He looked pained. "Well, you've put me between the wolf and the tiger, haven't you? Larkin's concerned that Blair's not fully recovered from the attack."

"I'm good to go," she insisted, then punched Larkin—not so lightly—in the arm. "Want to go one-on-one with me, cowboy, and find out?"

"Her ribs still pain her by end of day, and the shoulder that was hurt is weak yet."

"I'll show you weak."

"Now, now, children." Glenna managed to sound light and sarcastic. "I'm going to stick my neck into this. Blair's fit for duty. Sorry, honey," she said to Larkin, "but we really can't keep her on the disabled list."

"It would be best if she went." Hoyt sent a look of sympathy toward Larkin. "With three, we shouldn't need to be gone more than a day. The first troops could be sent out at first light, and make their way to the first post."

"That leaves three of us here to continue to work and train and prepare." Moira nodded. "This would be best. Would you think Tynan should lead those first troops, Larkin?"

"Do you ask as a sop to my wounded pride, or because you want my opinion of it?"

"Both."

She charmed a reluctant laugh out of him. "Then, aye, he'd be the one for it."

"We should get started." Blair glanced around the table. "With the time Larkin can make in the air, we'd be able to set up the first base, maybe the first two, before nightfall."

"Take whatever you need," Moira told them. "I'll speak to Tynan, and have him lead the first troops out at dawn."

"She'll be expecting you." Cian spoke for the first time since Moira had entered. "If Lilith hasn't thought of this move, one of her advisors would have. She'll have troops posted to intercept and ambush."

Blair nodded. "Figured that. It's why we're better with three, and coming from the air. They won't take us by surprise, but we might just take them."

"Better chance of that if you come from this direction." He got up to come around to the map and illustrate. "Circle around, come at the first location from the east or the north. More time, of course, but they'd likely be watching for you from this direction."

"Good point," Blair acknowledged, then gave Larkin a considering frown. "Hoyt and I could put down, out of sight, and send our boy here to get the lay. Maybe as a bird, or some animal they wouldn't think twice about seeing in the area. Have to take extra provisions," she added, "the way he burns up the fuel with the changes, but better safe than otherwise."

"Keep it small," Cian warned Larkin. "If you go as a deer or any sort of game, they might shoot you for sport or an extra meal. They'll be bored by this time, I'd imagine. If the weather there's as it's been here today, they'll likely be inside or under shelter. We don't care to be drenched any more than humans do."

"Okay, we'll work it out." Blair got to her feet. "Any magic tricks up your sleeve," she said to Hoyt, "don't forget to pack them."

"Be careful." Glenna fussed with Hoyt's cloak as they stood at the gates.

"Don't worry."

"Goes with the territory." She held both hands on his cloak as she looked up into his eyes. "We've stuck pretty tight together since this started, you and I. I wish I were going with you."

"You're needed here." He touched her cross, then his own. "You'll know where I am, and how I am. Two days, at most. I'll come back to you."

"Make damn sure of it." She pulled him to her, kissed him hard and long while her heart trembled. "I love you. Be safe."

"I love you. Be strong. Now go inside, out of the rain."

But she waited while Larkin shimmered into the dragon, then Hoyt and Blair loaded on the packs and weapons. She waited while they vaulted on the dragon's back, and rose up, flying through the gray curtain of rain.

"It's hard," Moira said from behind her, "to be the one who waits."

"Horrible." She reached back, took a strong grip on Moira's hand. "So keep me busy. We'll go in, have our first lesson." They turned, walked away from the gates. "Do you remember when you first knew you had power?"

"No. It wasn't definite, as it was with Larkin. It was more that I sometimes knew things. Where to find something that was lost. Or where someone was hiding if we were playing a game. But it always seemed it could have been as much luck, or just good sense as anything else."

"Was your mother gifted?"

"She was. But softly, if you understand me. A kind of empathy, you could say. A gift for growing things." Idly she tossed her braid behind her shoulder. "You've seen the gardens here, and those were her doing. If she was able to attend a birth or help at a sick bed, she could bring comfort and ease. I thought of what she had, and what I have, as a kind of woman's magic. Empathy, intuition, healing."

They stepped through the archway, moved to the stairs. "But since I began to work with you and Hoyt, I felt more. Like a stirring. It seemed to me it was a kind of echo, or reflection of the stronger power both of you have. Then I took hold of the sword."

"A talisman, or conduit," Glenna speculated. "Or more simply a key that opened a door to what was already in you."

She led the way into the room where she and Hoyt worked. It wasn't so different from the tower room in Ireland. Bigger, Moira thought, and with an arched doorway that led to one of the castle's many balconies.

But the scents were the same, herbs and ash and something that was a mix of floral and metallic. A number of Glenna's crystals were set around on tables and chests. As much Moira supposed for aesthetics as for magical purposes.

There were bowls and vials and books.

And crosses—silver, wood, stone, copper—hung at every opening to the outside.

"Damp and chilly in here," Glenna commented. "Why don't you light the fire?"

"Oh, of course." But when Moira started across to the wide stone hearth, Glenna laughed and grabbed her hand.

"No, not like that. Fire. It's elemental, one of the basic skills. To practice magic, we utilize the elements, nature. We respect them. Light the fire from here, with me."

"I wouldn't know how to begin."

"With yourself. Mind, heart, belly, bone and blood. See the fire, its colors and shapes. Feel the heat of it, smell the smoke and burning turf. Take that from your mind, from inside you, and put it in the hearth."

Moira did as she was told, and though she felt something ripple along her skin, the turf remained quiet and cold.

"I'm sorry."

"No. It takes time, energy and focus. And it takes faith. You don't remember taking your first steps, pulling yourself up with your mother's skirts or on a table, or how many times you fell before you stood. Take your first step, Moira. Hold out your right hand. Imagine the fire lighting inside you, hot, bright. It flows out, up from your belly, through your heart, down your arm to your fingertips. See it, feel it. Send it where you will."

It was almost a trance, Glenna's quiet voice and that building of heat. A stronger ripple now, under her skin, over it. And a weak tongue of flame spurted along a brick of turf.

"Oh! It was a flash inside my head. But you did most of it."

"A little of it," Glenna corrected. "Just a little push."

Moira blew out a long breath. "I feel I've run up a mountain."

"It'll get easier."

Watching the fire catch hold, Moira nodded. "Teach me."

By the end of two hours, Moira felt as though she'd not only climbed a mountain, but had fallen off one—on her head. But she'd learned to call and somewhat control two of the four elements. Glenna had given her a list of simple spells and charms to practice on her own.

Homework, Glenna had called it, and the scholar in Moira was eager to apply herself to it.

But there were other matters to be seen to. She changed to more formal attire, fixed the mitre of her office on her head, and went to meet with her uncle regarding finance.

Wars cost coin.

"Many had to leave their crops unharvested," Riddock told her. "Their flocks and herds untended. Some will surely lose their homes."

"We'll help them rebuild. There will be no tax or levy imposed for two years."

"Moira—"

"The treasury will stand it, Uncle. I can't sit on gold and jewels, no matter what their history, while our people sacrifice. I would melt the royal crown of Geall first. When this is done, I will plant crops. Fifty acres. Another fifty for grazing. What comes from it will be given back to those who fought, the families of any who perished or were injured serving Geall."

He rubbed his own aching head. "And how will you know who has served and who has hidden themselves away?"

"We'll believe. You think I'm naive and softhearted. Perhaps I am. Some of that will be needed from a queen when this is done. I can't be naive and softhearted now, and I must push and prod and ask my people to give and give. I ask a great deal of you. You're here, while strangers turn your home into a barracks."

"It's nothing."

"It's very much, and won't be the last I ask of you. Oran marches tomorrow."

"He's spoken to me." There was pride in Riddock's voice, though his eyes were heavy with sorrow. "My younger son is a man, and must be a man."

"Being yours he could be no less. For now, even as troops begin to march, work has to continued here. Weapons must be forged, people must be fed and housed. Trained. Whatever is required you have leave to spend. But . . ." She smiled now, thinly. "If any merchant or craftsman seeks too heavy a profit, he will have an audience with the queen."

Riddock returned her smile. "Very well. Your mother would be proud of you."

"I hope she would. I think of her every day." She rose, and the gesture brought him to his feet. "I must go to my aunt. She's so good to stand as chantelain these weeks."

"She enjoys it."

"I wonder that she could. The kitchens, the laundry, the sewing, the cleaning. It's beyond my ken with so many to tend. I'd be lost without her."

"She'll be pleased to hear it. But she tells me you come, every day, to speak with her, and to tour those kitchen, the laundry. Just as I'm told you go speak to the smithies, the young ones you have carving stakes. And today you trained with the other women."

"I never thought my office would be an idle one."

"No, but you need rest, Moira. Your eyes are shadowed."

She told herself to ask Glenna to teach her to do a glamour. "There's time enough to rest when this is done."

She spent an hour with her aunt going over household accounts and duties, then another speaking with some of those who performed those duties.

When she started toward the parlor with the idea of a light meal and a vat of tea, she heard Cian's laugh.

It relieved her to know he was keeping Glenna company, but she wondered if she herself had the energy to deal with him after such a long day.

She caught herself turning away, felt a quick flare of anger. Did she need a headful of wine just to sit comfortably in the same room with him? What sort of coward was she?

Straightening her spine, she strode in to see Glenna and Cian sitting by the fire with fruit and tea.

They looked so easy with each other, Moira thought. Did Glenna find it comforting or strange that Cian looked so like his brother? Little differences, of course. That cleft in Cian's chin his brother lacked. And his face was leaner than Hoyt's, his hair shorter.

There was his posture, and his movements. Cian always seemed at his ease, and walked with a near animal fluidity.

She liked watching him move, Moira admitted. He always put her in mind of something exotic—beautiful in its way, and just as lethal.

He knew she was there, she was sure. She'd yet to see anything or anyone come up on him with him unaware. But he continued to slouch in the chair where most men would rise when a woman—much less a queen—entered the room.

It was like his shrug, she thought. A deliberate carelessness. She wished she didn't find that so appealing as well.

"Am I interrupting?" she asked as she crossed the room.

"No." Glenna shifted to smile at her. "I asked for enough for three, hoping you'd have time. Cian's just been entertaining me with stories of Hoyt's exploits as a child."

"I'll leave you ladies to your tea."

"Please don't go." Before he could rise, Glenna took his arm. "You've been working hard to keep me from worrying."

"If you knew it, I wasn't working hard enough."

"You gave me a breather, and it's appreciated. Now, if everything's gone as planned, they should be at the projected base. I need to look." Her hand was steady as she poured tea for Moira. "I think it would be better if we all looked."

"Can you help them if . . ." Moira let it trail off.

"Hoyt's not the only one with magic up his sleeve. But I'll be able to see more clearly, and help if necessary if the two of you work with me. I know you've had a long one, Moira."

"They're my family as well."

With a nod, Glenna rose. "I brought what I thought I'd need." She retrieved her crystal globe, some smaller crystals, some herbs. These she arranged on the table between them. Then she took off her cross, circled the ball with its chain.

"So." She kept her voice light, placed her hands over the ball. "Let's see what they're up to."

It had rained across Geall, making the trip a small misery. They'd circled wide, coming down nearly a quarter mile east of the farm they intended to use for a base. Its location was prime, nearly equidistant from the land Lilith now occupied and the field of battle.

Because it was, Cian's assumption that it would be laid for ambush rang true.

The two riders dismounted from the dragon's back, then off-loaded packs and supplies. There was some cover—the low stone wall separating the fields, and the scatter of trees that ran with it.

Nothing stirred in the rain.

Dragon turned to man, and Larkin scooped both hands through his dripping hair. "Filthy day all in all. You saw the goal right enough?"

"Two-story cottage," Blair answered. "Three outbuildings, two paddocks. Sheep. No smoke or sign of life, no horses. If they're there, they'd have guards posted, a couple in each building, most likely. Taking shifts while the others sleep. They'd need food, so they may have prisoners. Or if they're traveling light, they'd have what they need in canteens—water bags."

"I could risk a look," Hoyt said. "If she sent along any with power though, they could sense it, and us."

"Simpler if I take a run at it." Larkin paused to crunch into an apple. The long trip had hunger gnawing at his belly. "They wouldn't put up the shield, as they have around their main base. Not if they're hoping to snatch some of us if and when we come along."

"Go in small," Blair reminded him. "Cian had a good point about that."

"Aye, well." He stuffed some bread in his mouth. "A mouse is small enough and worked before. It'll take longer than it would as wolf or deer." He slipped off his cross. "You'll need to keep this for me."

"I hate this part." Blair took the cross. "I hate you going in without a weapon or shield."

"Have a little faith." He cupped her chin, kissed her. Then stepping back changed into a small field mouse.

"Can't believe I just kissed that," Blair muttered, then closed her hand tight over his cross as the mouse streaked across the grass. "Now we wait."

"Best if we take precautions. I'll cast a circle."

Larkin was nearly to the first outbuilding when he spotted the wolf. It was large and black, crouched in a thicket of berries. It paid no mind to him while its red eyes scanned the field and the road to the west. Still, he gave it a wide berth before squirming under the doorway.

It was a rough stable, and there were two horses in the stalls. And two vampires seated on the floor having a game of dice. The mouse cocked its head in some surprise. Larkin hadn't considered vampires would game. The wolf, he deduced, was their outlook. A signal from it, and they'd come to action. But for now, they were too involved in the dice to notice a small mouse.

There were swords, and two full quivers with bows. Inspired, he dashed over to where the bows rested against a stall. And busily gnawed at the strings.

One vampire was cursing his fellow's luck when Larkin scrambled out again.

He found similar setups in each building, with the main body of the troop in the cottage. Though he smelled blood, he saw no human. In the cottage, four vampires slept in the loft while five others kept watch.

He did what could be done by a mouse to sabotage, then hurried away again.

He found Hoyt and Blair where he'd left them, sitting now on a damp blanket in a circle that simmered low. "Fifteen by my count," he told them. "And a wolf. We'd need to get past that one for any chance at taking the others by surprise."

"Have to be quiet then." Blair picked up a bow. "And from downwind. Hoyt, if Larkin can give me the exact position, is there a way you can help me see it?"

"I can give you the exact position," Larkin said before Hoyt spoke, "because we'll be going together now. You won the round to come, but you won't go into that nest of demons alone."

"She won't, no. Of the three of us, you've the best hand with a bow, so you'll take the shot," Hoyt told Blair. "But we'll be covering your flank while you're at it. I'll do what I can to help you get a clear shot."

"No point in arguing that one moves faster and quieter than three? Didn't think so," Blair said when she met stony silence. "Let's move out then."

They had to circle widely to keep out of sight, and prevent their scent from carrying. But when they came up behind the wolf, Blair shook her head. "I don't think I can get the heart from here. Moira, maybe, but I'm not that good. Gonna take more than one shot."

She thought it over, saw how it could best be done.

"You take the first one," she whispered to Larkin. "Get as close as you can. If it rears or rolls, shifts around, I can take it. One, two," she added, using her fingers. "Has to be fast, has to be quiet."

He nodded, pulled an arrow from the quiver, notched it in his bow. It was a long shot for him, and the angle poor. But he took aim, breathed out, breathed in. And let the arrow fly.

It took the wolf between the shoulder blades, and its body jerked up. Blair's arrow struck home.

"Nice work," she said as black smoke and ash flew.

Hoyt started to speak, then Glenna's voice sounded in his head as clearly as if she'd been standing beside him.

Behind you!

He spun, pivoted. A second wolf leaped, its body slamming Hoyt aside, knocking him to the ground as it fell on Larkin. Man and wolf grappled, an instant only. Even as Blair drew her sword, and Hoyt his, the wolf was rolled beneath a bear.

The bear's claws swiped, slicing deep across the throat. There was a gush of blood. The bear collapsed on the black ash, and became a man again.

Blair dropped to her knees, running her hands frantically over Larkin. "Are you bit? Are you bit?"

"No. Scratched up here and there. No bites. Ah, the stench of that one." Out of breath, he pushed to his elbows, looked down in disgust at his bloody shirt. "Ruined a good hunting tunic." He looked over at Hoyt. "All right then?"

"I might not have been. Glenna. They must be watching. I heard her in my head." Hoyt held out a hand to help Larkin to his feet. "If you wear that, they'll smell us a half league away. You'll need to . . . wait, wait." And his smile came slow and grim. "I've an idea."

The black wolf crouched over the bloody figure, and from outside the rear of the stables, sent out a low howl. In moments, a vampire armed with a battle-ax opened the door.

"What do we have here?" He glanced over his shoulder. "One of the wolves brought us a present."

Facedown, Hoyt let out a quiet moan.

"It's still alive. Let's get it inside. No need to share it with the others, right? I could use something fresh for a change."

As they stepped out, the second spared the wolf a brief grin. "Yeah, good dog. Let's just have a—"

He exploded into ash as Blair rammed the stake through

his back and into his heart. The second didn't have time to lift his ax before Hoyt sprang off the ground and sliced his sword through its neck.

"Yeah, good dog." Blair mimicked the vampire, and added a quick ruffle of Larkin's fur. "I say we stick with a winner, use the same gambit on the next outbuilding."

They had nearly identical results with the second building, but on the third, only one came out. It was obvious by the way he glanced surreptitiously back at his post that he intended to keep the unexpected meal for himself. When he rolled Hoyt over, the unexpected meal put a stake through his heart.

Using hand signals now, Blair indicated she would go in first, with Hoyt covering her.

Quick and quiet, she thought as she slipped inside. She saw the other guard had made himself a cozy nest with blankets and was taking an afternoon nap in what she thought was a dovecote.

He was actually snoring.

She had to bite back the half a dozen smart remarks that trembled on her tongue, and simply staked him while he slept.

She blew out a long breath. "I don't mean to complain, but this is almost embarrassing, and a little bit boring."

"You're disappointed we're not fighting for our lives?" Hoyt asked.

"Well, yeah. Some."

"Take heart." Larkin stepped in, surveyed the area. "There are nine in the cottage, where we'll be severely outnumbered."

"Ah, thanks, honey. You always know just what to say to perk me up." She hefted the battle-ax she'd taken from the first kill. "Let's go kick some ass."

Bellied down behind a water trough, Blair and Hoyt studied the cottage. The wounded man/wolf gambit wasn't going to work here, and the alternate they'd agreed on was risky.

"He's already gone through a lot of changes," Blair murmured. "It starts taking a toll."

"He ate four honey cakes."

She nodded, hoping it was fuel enough as the dragon landed lightly on the thatched roof. Larkin shimmered free of it, then picked up the scabbard and the sheath for his stake. He signaled down to them before swinging down to peer in one of the second-story windows.

Apparently, Blair thought, he didn't have to change into a monkey to climb like one. Larkin held up four fingers.

"Four up, five down." She moved into a crouch. "Ready?"

Keeping low, they rushed to either side of the doorway. As agreed, she counted to ten. Then kicked in the door.

With the battle-ax, she decapitated the one on her right, then used the staff of it to block the hack of a sword. Out of the corner of her eye she saw a ball of fire flash into Hoyt's hand. Something screamed.

From overhead, Larkin and a vampire flew off the loft to land hard on the floor. She tried to hack her way to him, took a hard kick in her healing ribs. The pain and the force knocked her back into a table that broke beneath her weight.

She used the splintered leg to dust the one that leaped on her. Then she threw the makeshift stake, striking one that rushed Hoyt from behind. She missed the heart, swore and shoved herself breathlessly to her feet.

Hoyt thrust out with a back kick that made her warrior's heart sing. When the vampire fell, Larkin finished it with a sword clean through the throat.

"How many?" Blair shouted. "How many?"

"I took two," Hoyt said.

"Four, by the gods." Even as he grinned, he was grabbing Blair's arm. "How bad?"

"Off my game. Caught my ribs. I only got two. There's another left."

"Gone out the window above. Here, sit, sit. Your arm's bleeding as well."

"Shit." She looked down, saw the gash she hadn't felt. "Shit. Your nose is bleeding, mouth, too. Hoyt?"

"A few nicks." He limped toward them. "I don't think we'd need worry overmuch about the one that escaped. But I'll be doing a spell to revoke any invitation. Let me see what I can do for your arm."

"Spell first." Breathing through her teeth, she looked at Larkin. "Four, huh?"

"It seems two of them were mating, and distracted with it when I came through the window. So I had them both with one blow."

"Maybe we should only count that as one."

"Oh, no, we won't." He finished tying a field dressing on her wounded arm, swiped blood from under his own nose. "Jesus, I'm starving."

It made her laugh, and despite her aching ribs, she wrapped her arms around him to hug.

"They're fine." Glenna let out a shuddering breath. "A little battered, a little bloody, but fine. And safe. Sorry, sorry. But watching it like this, not being able to help . . . I'm just going to have a short breakdown."

As promised, she buried her face in her hands and wept.

Chapter 7

Escaping, Cian left Glenna to Moira. In his experience, women dealt best with women's tears. His own reaction to what they'd seen in the crystal hadn't been fear, or relief, but sheer and simple frustration.

He'd been delegated to do no more than watch while others fought. Cozied in the bloody parlor with women and teacups, like someone's aged grandfather.

While the training sessions were some level of entertainment, he hadn't had a good fight since they'd left Ireland. Hadn't had a woman in longer than that. Two very satisfying ways of releasing tension and energy had been denied to him—or he was denying them to himself.

Hardly a wonder, he thought, he was tied up in nasty knots over a pair of steady gray eyes.

He could seduce a serving girl, but that was fraught with complications and probably not worth the time or effort. He could hardly pick a fight with one of the very handy humans, which was too damn bad.

If he went out on a hunt he could likely scare up at least one or two of Lilith's troops. But he couldn't rev himself up to go out into the endless rain on the chance of a lucky kill.

At least back in his own time, his own world, he'd had work to occupy him. Women if he wanted one, of course, but work to pass the time. The endless time.

With none of those options available to him, he closed himself in his room. He fed, and he slept.

And he dreamed as he hadn't dreamed in decades and more of hunting human.

The strong and salty scent of them stung the air, rising as even their puny and smothered instincts warned them they were prey.

It was a seductive and primitive perfume to stir needs in the belly and in the blood.

She was only a whore, working the alleyways of London. Young though, and fair enough despite her trade, which told him it was unlikely she'd been at it very long. As the aroma of sex clung to her, he knew she'd made a few coppers that night.

He could hear tinny music and the raucous, drunken laughter from some gin parlor, and the clopping of a carriage horse moving away. All distant—too distant for her human ears to catch. And too distant for her human legs to run, if she tried.

She hurried through the thick yellow fog, quickening her pace with nervous glances over her shoulder as he deliberately allowed her to hear his footsteps behind her.

The smell of her fear was intoxicating—so fresh, so alive.

It was so easy to catch her, to cover the squeak of her mouth with his hand—to cover the rabbit-rapid jump of her heart with the other.

So amusing to see her eyes take in his face, young and handsome—the expensive clothing—and go sly, go coy, as he eased his hand from her mouth.

"Sir, you frighten a poor girl. I thought you be a brigand."

"Nothing of the sort." The cultured accent he used was

in direct opposition to squawking cockney. "Simply in need of a little comfort, and willing to pay your price."

With a flutter and a giggle, she named one he knew would be double her usual rate. "For that I think you should make me very comfortable."

"I'm sorry to ask for pay from such a fine and handsome gentleman, but I have to earn my keep, I do. I have a room nearby."

"We won't need it."

"Oh!" She laughed when he pulled up her skirts. "Here, is it?"

With his free hand he yanked down her bodice, covered her breast. He needed to feel her heart, beating, beating, beating. He drove into her, pumping hard so that her bare buttocks slapped against the damp stone wall of the alley. And he saw the shock and surprise in her eyes that he could give her pleasure.

That beat beneath his hand quickened, and her breath went short and expelled on gasps and moans.

He let her come—a small gesture—and let her dazed and sleepy eyes meet his before he showed his fangs.

She screamed—just a quick, high sound he cut off when he sank his fangs into her throat. Her body convulsed, bringing him to a very satisfactory orgasm as he fed. As he killed.

That beating under his hand slowed, stilled. Stopped.

Replete and sated, he left her in the alley with the rats, the price she'd named tossed carelessly beside her. And he strolled away to be swallowed by the thick yellow fog.

He woke in the here and now on an oath. The dream memory had awakened appetites and passions long suppressed. He almost, almost, tasted her blood in his throat, almost smelled the richness of it. In the dark, he trembled a little, an addict in withdrawal, so forced himself to get up and drink what he allowed himself as substitute for human.

It will never satisfy you. It will never fill you. Why do you struggle against what you are?

"Lilith." He said it softly. He recognized the voice in his

head, understood now who and what had put that dream into his mind.

Had it even been his memory? It seemed false now that he was steadier, like a stage play he'd stumbled into. But then he'd killed his share of whores in alleys. He'd killed so many, who could remember the details?

Lilith shimmered into the dark. Diamonds glittered at her throat, her ears, her wrists, even in her luxurious hair. She wore a gown of regal blue trimmed in sable, cut low to highlight the generous mounds of her breasts.

She'd gone to some trouble with her dress and appearance, Cian thought, for this illusionary visit.

"There's my handsome boy," she murmured. "But you look tense and tired. Hardly a wonder with what you've been up to." She wagged her finger playfully. "Naughty of you. But I blame myself. I wasn't able to spend those formative years with you, and as the twig is bent."

"You deserted me," he pointed out. Though he didn't need them, he lighted candles. Then poured himself a cup of whiskey. "Killed me, changed me, set me on my brother, then left me broken at the bottom of the cliffs."

"Where you let him toss you. But you were young, and rash. What could I do?" She tugged her bodice lower to show him the scar of the pentagram. "He burned me. Branded me. I was no good to you."

"And after? The days and months and years after." Odd, he thought, odd to realize he had this resentment, even this hurt buried inside him. Like a child tossed aside by its mother. "You made me, Lilith, birthed me, then left me with less sentiment than an alley cat leaves a deformed kitten."

"You're right, you're right. I can't argue." She wandered the room, lazy sweeps that had the skirts of her gown brushing through a table. "I was careless with you, darling boy. And what did I do but take out my temper for your brother on you. Shame on me!"

Those pretty blue eyes twinkled with merriment, and the curve of her lips was charmingly female. "But you did so well for yourself—initially. Imagine my shock when Lora told me the rumors I'd heard were true, and you'd stopped hunting. Oh, she sends her regards, by the way."

"Does she? I imagine she's a pretty sight at the moment."

Lilith's smile faded, and a hint of red showed in her eyes. "Careful there, or when the time comes it won't just be that fucking demon hunter I rip to pieces."

"Think you can?" He slouched into a chair with his whiskey. "I'd wager you on that, but you wouldn't be able to pay up, being a pile of ash at the end of it."

"I've seen the end of it, in the smoke." She came to him, leaning over the chair—so real he could almost smell her. "This world will burn. I'll have no need of it. Every human on this foolish island will be slaughtered, screaming and drowning in their own blood. Your brother and his circle will die most horribly. I have seen it."

"Your wizard would hardly show you otherwise," Cian said with a shrug. "Were you always so gullible?"

"He shows me *truth*!" She shoved away, her gown sweeping in a furious arch. "Why do you persist in this doomed adventure? Why do you oppose the one who gave you the greatest gift? I came here to offer you a truce—a private and personal agreement, just between you and me. Step away from this, my darling, and you have my pardon. Step away and come to me, and you have not only my pardon but a place at my side come the day. Everything you hunger for and have denied yourself I'll lay at your feet—in repentance for abandoning you when you needed me."

"So, I just go back to my time, my world, and all's forgiven?"

"I give you my word on it. But I'll give you much, much more if you come to me. To me." She purred it, molding her breasts with her hands. "Remember what we shared that night? The spark, the heat of it?"

He watched her run her hands over her body, white against red. "I remember, very well."

"We can have that again, and more. You'll be a prince in

my court. And a general, leading armies instead of slogging through the muck with humans. You'll have your pick of worlds and all their pleasures. An eternity of desires met."

"I remember you promising something along those lines before. Then I was alone, broken and lost, with the graveyard dirt barely washed off me."

"And so this is my penance. Come now, come. You have no place here, Cian. You belong with your own kind."

"Interesting." He tapped his fingers on the side of his cup. "So, all I need do is take your word that you'll reward me rather than torturing and ending me."

"Why would I destroy my own creation?" she replied in reasonable tones. "And one who's proven himself to be a strong warrior?"

"For spite, of course, and because your word is as much an illusion as your appearance here. But I'll give you mine on one vital matter, Lilith, and my word is as hard and as bright as those diamonds you're wearing. It will be I who comes for you. It will be I who does for you."

He picked up a knife and slashed it over his own palm. "I swear it to you, in blood. Mine will be the last face you see."

Fury tightened her face. "You've damned yourself."

"No," he murmured when her image vanished. "You damned me."

It was deep night, and he was done with sleep.

At least at such an hour he could wander where he liked without bumping into servants or courtiers or guards. He'd had enough of company—human and vampire. Still he needed distraction, movement, something to clear away the bitter dregs of the dream, and the visitation that followed it.

He admired the architecture of the castle—something a few steps up, and over into fantasy than what would have been usual when he was alive. It was storybook, inside and out, he mused, with the shifting lights of torches rising from their dragon sconces, the tapestries of faeries and festivals, the polished, jewel-toned marble.

Of course, it hadn't been built as a fortress, but more as a lavish home. Fit, most certainly, for a queen. Until Lilith, Geall had existed in peace and so could focus its energies and intellects on art and culture.

He could, in the quiet and dark, take time to study and admire the art—the paintings and tapestries, the murals and carvings. He could drift through the dark with the perfume of hothouse flowers sweetening the air or wander to the library to peruse the tall shelves.

Since its creation, Geall had been a land for art and books and music rather than warfare and weaponry. How apt, how cold, that both gods and demons should select such a place for bloody war.

The library, as Moira had indicated when falling in love with his own, was a quiet cathedral of books. He'd passed some of his time with a few of them already, and had been both interested and entertained that the stories he'd found there weren't so different from ones written in his own lifetime.

Would Geall, if it survived, produce its own Shakespeare, Yeats, Austen? Would its art go through revivals and renaissance and offer its version of Monet or Degas?

A fascinating thought.

For now, he was too restless, too edgy to settle himself down with a book, and instead moved on. There were rooms he'd yet to explore, and by night he could go wherever he wanted.

As he walked through shadows, the rain drummed steadily.

He moved through what he supposed had been a kind of formal drawing room and was now serving as an armory. He lifted a sword, testing its weight, its balance, its edge. Geall's craftsmen might have devoted their time, previously, to arts, but they knew how to forge a sword.

Time would tell if it would be enough.

Without aim, he turned and stepped into what he saw was a music room.

A gilded harp stood elegantly in one corner. A smaller

cousin, shaped just as a traditional Irish harp, graced a stand nearby. There was a monochord—an early forefather of the piano—enhanced with lovely carving on its soundbox.

He plucked its string idly, pleased its sound was true and clear.

There was a hurdy-gurdy, and when he turned its shaft, slid the bow over its strings, it sang with the mournful music of bagpipes.

There were lutes and pipes, all beautifully crafted. There was comfortable seating, and a pretty hearth from the local marble. A fine room, he mused, for musicians and those who appreciated the art.

Then he saw the vielle. He lifted it. It's body was longer than the violin that would come from it, and it held five strings. When the instruments had been popular, he'd had no interest in such matters. No, he'd been for killing whores in alleyways.

But when a man has eternity, he needs hobbies and pursuits, and years to study them.

He sat with the vielle over his lap, and began to play.

It came back to him, the notes, the sounds, and calmed him as it was said music could do. With the rain as his accompaniment, he let himself fall into the music, drifted away on the tears of it.

She would never have come upon him without him being aware otherwise.

She'd heard it, the quiet sobbing of music as she'd made her own wanderings. She'd followed it like a child follows a piper, then stood just inside the doorway, stunned and enchanted.

So, Moira thought, this is how he looks when he's peaceful, and not just pretending to be. This is how he might have looked before Lilith had taken him, a little dreamy, a little sad, a little lost.

All that had stirred and risen inside her for him seemed to come together inside her heart as she saw him unmasked. Sitting alone, she thought, seeking the comfort of music. She wished she had Glenna's skill with paints or chalk, for she would have drawn him like this. As few, she was sure, had ever seen him.

His eyes were closed, his expression, she would have said, caught somewhere in the misty place between melancholy and contentment. Whatever his thoughts, his fingers were skilled on the strings, long and lean, seducing the instrument into wistful music.

Then it stopped so abruptly she let out a little cry of protest as she stepped forward with her candle. "Oh please, continue, won't you? Sure it was lovely."

He had preferred she come at him with a knife than that innocent, eager smile. She wore only nightrobes, white and pure, with her hair unbound to fall like the rain over her shoulders. The candlelight shifted over her face, full of mystery and romance.

"The floors are cold for bare feet," was all he said, and rose to set the instrument down.

The dreamy look was gone from his eyes, so they were cool again. Frustrated, she set the candle down. "They're my feet, after all. You never said you played."

"There are a lot of things I never said."

"I have no skill at all, to the despair of my mother and every teacher she hired to school me in music. Any instrument I picked up would end by making a sound like a cat being trod on."

She reached over, ran her hand over the strings. "It seemed like magic in your hands."

"I've had more years to learn what interests me than you've been alive. Many times more years."

She looked up now, met his eyes. "True enough, but the time doesn't diminish the art, does it? You have a gift, so why not accept a compliment on it with some grace?"

"Your Majesty." He bowed deeply from the waist. "You honor my poor efforts."

"Oh bugger that," she snapped and surprised a choked laugh out of him. "I don't know why you look for ways to insult me."

"A man must have a hobby. I'll say good night."

"Why? This is your time, isn't it, and you won't seek your bed. I can't sleep. Something cold." She hugged her elbows, shivered once. "Something cold in the air woke me." Because she was watching him, she caught the slight change in his eyes. "What? What do you know? Has something happened. Larkin—"

"It's nothing to do with that. He and the others are well enough as far as I know."

"What then?"

He debated for a moment. His personal desire to be away from her couldn't outweigh what she should know. "It's too cold in here for nighttime confessions."

"Then I'll light the fire." She walked to the hearth, picked up the tinderbox that rested there. "There was always whiskey in that painted cabinet there. I'd have some."

She didn't have to see to know he'd lifted a brow, a gesture of sarcasm, before he crossed to the cabinet.

"Did your mother always fail to teach you that it would be considered improper for you to be sharing a fire and whiskey alone with a man, much less one who is not a man, in the middle of the night?"

"Propriety isn't an immediate concern of mine." She sat back on her haunches, watching for a moment to be sure the turf caught. Then she rose to go to a chair, and held out her hand for the whiskey. "Thanks for that." She took the first swallow. "Something happened tonight. If it concerns Geall, I need to know."

"It concerns me."

"It was something to do with Lilith. I thought it was just my own fears, creeping in while I slept, but it was more than that. I dreamed of her once, more than a dream. You woke me from it."

And had been kind to her after, she remembered. Reluctant, but kind.

"It was something like that," she continued, "but I didn't dream. I only felt . . ."

She broke off, her eyes widening. "No, not just felt. I heard you. I heard you speaking. I heard your voice in my head, and it was cold. *It will be I who does for you.* I heard you say that, so clearly. As I was waking, I thought I would freeze to death if you spoke so cold to me."

And had felt compelled to get out of bed, she thought. Had followed his music to him. "Who was it?"

Later, he decided, he might try to puzzle out how she could hear, or feel, him speak in her dreams. "Lilith."

"Aye." Her eyes on the fire, Moira rubbed a hand up and down her arms. "I knew. There was something dark with the cold. It wasn't you."

"You could be sure?"

"You have a different . . . hue," she decided. "Lilith is black. Thick as pitch. You, well, you're not bright. It's gray and blue. It's twilight in you."

"What is this, an aura thing?"

The chilly amusement in his tone had a flush creeping up her neck. "It's how I see sometimes. Glenna told me to pursue it. She's red and gold, like her hair—if you have an interest in it. Was it a dream? Lilith?"

"No. Though she sent me one that may have been a memory. A whore I fucked and killed in the filth of a London alley." The way he lifted his glass and drank was a callous punctuation to the words. "If it wasn't that particular one, I fucked and killed others, so it hardly matters."

Her gaze never wavered from his. "You think that shocks me. You say it, and in that way, to put something cruel between us."

"There's a great deal of cruelty between us."

"What you did before that night in the clearing in Ireland when you first saved my life isn't between us. It's behind you. Do you think I'm so green I don't know you've had all manner of women, and killed all manner of them as well? You only insult me, and your own choices since by pushing them into the now."

"I don't understand you." What he didn't understand he usually pursued. Understanding was another kind of survival.

"Sure it's not my fault, is it? I make myself plain in

most matters. If she sent you the dream, true or not, it was to disturb you."

"Disturb," he repeated and moved away toward the fire. "You are the strangest creature. It excited me. And it unnerved me, for lack of a better term. That was her purpose, and she succeeded very well."

"And having served her purpose, dug into some vulnerability in you, she came to you. The apparition of her. As Lora did with Blair."

He turned back, holding the whiskey loosely in one hand. "I got an apology, centuries overdue, for her abandonment of me when I was only days into the change, and near dead from Hoyt tossing me off a cliff."

"Perhaps tardiness is relative, given the length of your existence."

Now he did laugh, couldn't stop himself. It was quick and rich and full of appreciation. "Aye, the strangest creature, with a sharp wit buried in there. She offered me a deal. Are you interested to hear it?"

"I am, very interested."

"I have only to walk away from this. You and the others, and what comes on Samhain. I do that, and she'll call it quits between her and me. Better, if I walk away from you, and into her camp, I'll be rewarded handsomely. All and anything I can want, and a place at her side. Her bed as well. And any others I can to take to mine."

Moira pursed her lips, then sipped more whiskey. "If you believe that, you're greener than you think me."

"I was never so green as you."

"No? Well, which of the two of us was green enough to sport with a vampire and let her sink fangs into him?"

"Hah. You've got a point. But then you've never been a randy young man."

"And women, of course, have no interest in carnal matters. We much prefer to sit and do our needlework with prayers running through our heads."

His lips twitched before he shook his head. "Another point. In any case, no longer being a randy young man or with any sprig of green left in me, I'm fully aware Lilith would imprison and torture me. She could keep me alive, as it were, for . . . well, ever. And in unspeakable pain."

He considered it now, his thoughts sparked by the brief debate with Moira. "Or, more likely, she'd keep her word—on sex and other rewards—for as long as it suited her. She would know I'd be useful to her, at least until Samhain."

In agreement, Moira nodded. "She would bed you, lavish gifts on you. Give you position and rank. Then, when it was done, she'd imprison and torture you."

"Exactly. But I have no intention of being tortured for eternity, or being of use to her. She killed a good man I had affection for. If for nothing else, I owe her for King."

"She would have been displeased by your refusal."

He sent Moira a bland look. "You're the queen of understatement tonight."

"Then let me also be the mistress of intuition and say you told her you would make it your mission to destroy her."

"I swore it, in my own blood. Dramatic," he said, glancing at the nearly healed wound on his hand. "But I was feeling theatrical."

"You make light of it. I find it telling. You need her death by your own hands more than you'll say. She doesn't understand that, or you. You need it not just for retribution, but to close a door." When he said nothing, she cocked her head. "Do you think it odd I understand you better than she? Know you, better than she could."

"I think your mind is always working," he replied. "I can all but hear the wheels. It's hardly a surprise you're not sleeping well these past days with all the bloody noise that must go on inside that head of yours."

"I'm frightened." His eyes narrowed on her face, but she wouldn't meet them now. "Frightened to die before I've really lived. Frightened to fail my people, my family, you and the others. When I feel that cold and dark as I did tonight, I know what would become of Geall if she wins this.

Like a void, burned out, hulled, empty and black. And the thought of it frightens me beyond sleep."

"Then the answer must be she can't win."

"Aye. That must be the answer." She set the whiskey aside. "You'll need to tell Glenna what you told me. I think it would be harder to get the answer if there are secrets among us."

"If I don't tell her, you will."

"Of course. But it should come from you. You're welcome to play any of the instruments you like whenever you're moved to. Or if you'd rather be private, you could take any you like to your room."

"Thank you."

She smiled a little as she got to her feet. "I think I could sleep for a bit now. Good night."

He stayed as he was as she retrieved her candle and left him. And stayed hours longer in the fire-lit dark.

In the raw, rainy dawn Moira stood with Tynan as he and the handpicked troops prepared to set out.

"It'll be a wet march."

Tynan smiled at her. "Rain's good for the soul."

"Then our souls must be very healthy after these last days. They can move about in the rain, Tynan." She touched her fingers lightly to the cross painted on his breastplate. "I wonder if we should wait until this clears before you start this journey."

With a shake of his head, he looked beyond her to the others. "My lady, the men are ready. Ready to the point that delay would cut into morale and scrape at the nerves. They need action, even if it's only a long day's march in the rain. We've trained to fight," he continued before she could speak again. "If any come to meet us, we'll be ready."

"I trust you will." Had to trust. If not with Tynan, whom she'd known all of her life, where would she begin? "Larkin and the others will be waiting for you. I'll expect their return shortly after sunset, with word that you arrived safe and have taken up the post."

"You can depend on it, and on me. My lady." He took both her hands.

Because they were friends, because he was the first she would send out, she leaned up to kiss him. "I do depend." She squeezed his fingers. "Keep my cousins out of trouble."

"That, my lady, may be beyond my skills." His gaze shifted from her face. "My lord. Lady."

With her hands still caught in Tynan's, Moira turned to Cian and Glenna.

"A wet day for traveling," Cian commented. "They'll likely have a few troops posted along the way to give you some exercise."

"So the men hope." Tynan glanced over to where nearly a hundred men were saying goodbye to their families and sweethearts, then turned back so his eyes met Cian's. "Are we ready?"

"You're adequate."

Before Moira could snap at the insult, Tynan roared out a laugh. "High praise from you," he said and clasped hands with Cian. "Thank you for the hours, and the bruises."

"Make good use of them. *Slán leat*."

"*Slán agat*." He shot Glenna a cocky grin as he mounted. "I'll send your man back to you, my lady."

"See that you do. Blessed be, Tynan."

"In your name, Majesty," he said to Moira, then wheeled his mount. "Fall in!"

Moira watched as the scattered men formed lines. And watched in the rain as her cousin Oran and two other officers rode out, leading her foot soldiers to the first league toward war.

"It begins," she murmured. "May the gods watch over them."

"Better," Cian said, "if they watch over themselves."

Still he stood as she did until the first battalion of Geall's army was out of sight.

Chapter 8

Glenna frowned over her tea as, with Moira's prodding, Cian related his interlude with Lilith. The three of them took the morning meal together, in private.

"Similar to what happened with Blair then, and with me back in New York. I'd hoped Hoyt and I had blocked that sort of thing."

"Possibly you have, on humans," he added. "Vampire to vampire is likely a different matter. Particularly—"

"When the one intruding is the sire," Glenna finished. "Yes, I see. Still, there should be a way to shut her out."

"It's hardly worth your time and energies. It's not a problem for me."

"You say that now, but it upset you."

He glanced at Moira. "Upset is a strong word. In any case, she left in what we'll call a huff."

"Something good came out of it," Glenna continued. "For her to come to you, try to deal, she can't be as confident as she'd like to be."

"On the contrary, she believes, absolutely, that she'll win. Her wizard's shown her."

"Midir? You said nothing of this last night."

"It didn't come up," Cian said easily. In truth, he'd thought long and hard before deciding it should be told. "She claims he's shown her victory, and in my opinion, she believes. Any losses we've dealt her thus far are of little importance to her. Momentary annoyances, slaps to the pride. Nothing more."

"We make destiny with every turn, every choice." Moira kept her eyes level with Cian's. "This war isn't won until it's won, by her, by us. Her wizard tells her, shows her, what she wants to hear, wants to see."

"I agree," Glenna said. "How else would he keep his skin intact?"

"I won't say you're wrong, either of you." With a careless shrug, Cian picked up a pear. "But that kind of absolute belief can be a dangerous weapon. Weapons can be turned against the one who holds them. The deeper we prick under her skin, the more reckless she might be."

"Just what do we use for the needle?" Moira demanded.

"I'm working on that."

"I've something that may work." Glenna narrowed her eyes as she stirred her tea. "If her Midir can open the door for her to come into your head, Cian, I can open it, too. I wonder how Lilith would like a visit."

Biting into the pear, Cian sat back. "Well now, aren't you the clever girl?"

"Yes, I am. I'll need you. Both of you. Why don't we finish off breakfast with a nice little spell?"

It wasn't little, and it wasn't nice. It took Glenna more than an hour to prepare her tools and ingredients.

She ground flourite, turquoise, set them aside. She gathered cornflower and holly, sprigs of thyme. She scribed candles of purple, of yellow. Then set the fire under her cauldron.

"These come from the earth, and now will mix in water." She began to sprinkle her ingredients into the cauldron.

"For dreaming words, for sight, for memory. Moira, would you set the candles in a circle, around the cauldron?"

She continued to work as Moira set the candles. "I've actually been thinking about trying this since what happened with Blair. I've been working it out in my head how it might be done."

"She's hit you hard every time you've used magic to look into her bases," Cian reminded her. "So be sure. I wouldn't enjoy having Hoyt try to toss me off a cliff again because I let something happen to you."

"It won't be me—at least not front line." She brushed her hair back as she looked over at him. "It'll be you."

"Well then, that's perfect."

"It's risky, so you're the one who has to be sure."

"Well, it's the guts and glory business, isn't it?" He moved forward to peer into the cauldron. "And what will I be doing?"

"Observing, initially. If you choose to make contact . . . it'll be up to you, and I'll need your word that you'll break it off if things get dicey. Otherwise, we'll yank you back—and that won't be pleasant. You'll probably have the mother of all headaches, and a raging case of nausea."

"What fun."

"Fun's just beginning." She walked over, unlocked a small box. Then held up a small figure carved in wax.

Cian's brows shot up. "A strong likeness. You are clever."

"Sculpting's not my strongest skill, but I can handle a poppet." Glenna turned the figure of Lilith around so Moira could see. "I don't generally make them—it's intrusive, and dangerous to the party you've captured. But the harm-none rule doesn't apply to undead. Present company excepted."

"Appreciated."

"There's just one little thing I need from you."

"Which is."

"Blood."

Cian did nothing more than look resigned. "Naturally."

"Just a few drops, after I bind the poppet. I have nothing of hers—hair, nail clippings. But you mixed blood, once upon a time. I think it'll do the job." She hesitated, twisting the chain of her pendant around her fingers. "And maybe this is a bad idea."

"It's not." Moira set the last candle. "It's time we push into her mind, as she's pushed into all of ours. It's a good, hot needle under the skin, if you're asking me. And Cian deserves to give her a taste of her own."

She straightened. "Will we be able to watch?"

"Thirsty for some vengeance yourself?" Cian questioned.

Moira's eyes were cold smoke. "Parched. Will we?"

"If all goes as it should." Glenna took a breath. "Ready for some astral projection?" she asked Cian.

"As I'll ever be."

"Step inside the circle of candles, both of you. You'll need to achieve a meditative state, Cian. Moira and I will be your watchers, and the observers. We'll hold your body to this plane while your mind and image travel."

"Is it true," Moira asked her, "that it helps hold a traveling spirit to the safety of its world if it carries something from someone of it?"

Glenna pushed at her hair again. "It's a theory."

"Then take this." She tugged off the band of beads and leather that bound her braid. "In case the theory's true."

After giving it a dubious frown, Cian shoved it in his pocket. "I'm armed with hair trinkets."

Glenna picked up a small bowl of balm. "Focus, open the chakras," she said as she rubbed the balm on his skin. "Relax your body, open your mind."

She looked at Moira. "We'll cast the circle. Imagine light, soft, blue light. This is protection."

While they cast, Cian focused on a white door. It was his habitual symbol when he chose to meditate. When he was ready, the door would open. And he would go through it.

"He has a strong mind," Glenna told Moira. "And a great deal of practice. He told me he studied in Tibet.

Never mind," she said with a wave of her hand. "I'm stalling. I'm a little nervous."

"Her wizard isn't any stronger than you. What he can do, you can do."

"Damn right. Gotta say though, I hope to hell Lilith is sleeping. Should be, really should be." Glenna glanced at the window at the thinning rain. "We're about to find out."

She'd left an opening in the poppet, and prepared to fill it with grains of graveyard dirt, rosemary and sage, ground amethyst and quartz.

"You have to control your emotions for the binding, Moira. Set aside your hatred, your fear. We desire justice and sight. Lilith can be harmed, and we can use magic to do so, but Cian will be a conduit. I wouldn't want any negativity to backwash on him."

"Justice then. It's enough."

Glenna closed the poppet with a plug of wax.

"We call on Maat, goddess of justice and balance to guide our hand. With this image we send magic across air, across land." She placed a white feather against the doll, wrapped it in black ribbon. "Give the creature whose image I hold, dream and memory ancient and old."

She handed the ritual knife to Moira, nodded.

"Sealed by blood she shed, bound now with these drops of red."

Cian showed no reaction when Moira lifted his hand to draw the knife over his palm.

"Mind and image of the life she took joins her now so he may look. And while we watch we hold him safe in hand and heart until he chooses to depart. Through us into her this magic streams. Take our messenger into her dream. Open doors so we may see. As we will, so mote it be."

Glenna held the poppet over the cauldron, and releasing it, left it suspended on will and air.

"Take his hand," she said to Moira. "And hold on."

When Moira's hand clasped his, Cian didn't go through the door. He exploded through it. Flying through a dark even his eyes couldn't conquer, he felt Moira's hand tighten strong on his. In his mind, he heard her voice, cool and calm.

"We're with you. We won't let go."

There was moonlight, sprinkling through the dark to bring blurry smears of shape and shadow. There were scents, flowers and earth, water and woman.

Humans.

There was heat. Temperature meant little to him, but he could feel the shift of it from the damp chill he'd left behind. A baking heat, eased only a little by a breeze off the water.

Sea, he corrected. It was an ocean with waves lapping at the sugar of sand. And there were hills rising up from the beach. Olive trees spread over the terraces of those hills. And on one of the rises—the highest—stood a temple, white as the moonlight with its marble columns overlooking that ocean, the trees, gardens and pools.

Overlooking, too, the man and woman who lay together on a white blanket edged in gold on the sparkling sand near the play of white foam.

He heard the woman's laugh—the husky sound of a roused woman. And knew it was Lilith, knew it was Lilith's memory, or her dream he'd fallen into. So he stood apart, and watched as the man slid the white robe from her shoulders, and bent his head to her breasts.

Sweet, so sweet, his mouth on her. Everything inside her ebbed and flowed, as the tide. How could it be forbidden, the beauty of this? Her body was meant for his. Her spirit, her mind, her soul had been created by the gods as the mate for his.

She arched, offering, with her fingers combing gently through his sun-kissed hair. He smelled of the olive trees, and the sunlight that ripened their fruit.

Her love, her only. She murmured it to him as their lips met again. And again, with a hunger that built beyond bearing.

Her eyes were full of him when at last his body joined with hers. The pleasure of it brought tears glimmering, turned her sighs to helpless gasps.

Love swarmed through her, pounded in her heart, a thousand silken fists. She held him closer, closer, crying out her joy with an abandon that dared even the gods to hear.

"Cirio, Cirio." She cradled his head on her breast. "My heart. My love."

He lifted his head, brushing at her gilded hair. "Even the moon pales against your beauty. Lilia, my queen of the night."

"The nights are ours, but I want the sun with you—the sun that gilds your hair and skin, that touches you when I cannot. I want to walk beside you, proud and free."

He only rolled onto his back. "Look at the stars. They're our torches tonight. We should swim under them. Bathe this heat away in the sea."

Instantly pique hardened the sleepy joy from her face. "Why won't you speak of it?"

"It's too hot a night for talk and trouble." He spoke carelessly as he sifted sand through his fingers. "Come. We'll be dolphins and play."

But when he took her hands to pull her up she drew them away with a sharp, sulky jerk. "But we *must* talk. We must plan."

"My sweet, we have so little time left tonight."

"We could have forever, every night. We have only to leave, to run away together. I could be your wife, give you children."

"Leave? Run away?" He threw back his head with a laugh. "What foolishness is this? Come now, come, I have only an hour left. Let's swim awhile, and I'll ride you on the waves."

"It's not foolishness." This time she slapped his hand away. "We could sail from here, to anywhere we wished. Be together openly, in the sunlight. I want more than a few hours in the dark with you, Cirio. You promised me more."

"Sail away, like thieves? My home is here, my family. My duty."

"Your coffers," she said viciously. "Or your father's."

"And what of it? Do you think I would smear my family name by running away with a temple priestess, living like paupers in some strange land?"

"You said you could live on my love alone."

"Words are easy in the heat. Be sensible." His tone cajoling, he skimmed a finger down her bare breast. "We give each other pleasure. Why does there need to be more?"

"I *want* more. I love you. I broke my vows for you."

"Willingly," he reminded her.

"For love."

"Love doesn't feed the belly, Lilia, or spend in the marketplace. Don't be sad now. I'll buy you a gift. Something gold like your hair."

"I want nothing you can buy. Only freedom. I would be your wife."

"You cannot. If we attempted such madness and were caught, we'd be put to death."

"I would rather die with you than live without you."

"I value my life more, it seems, than you value either of ours." He nearly yawned, so lazy was his voice. "I can give you pleasure, and the freedom of that. But as for a wife, you know one has already been chosen for me."

"You chose me. You said—"

"Enough, enough!" He threw up his hands, but seemed more bored by the conversation than angry. "I chose you for this, as you chose me. You were hungry to be touched. I saw it in your eyes. If you've spun a web of fantasy where we sail off, it's your own doing."

"You pledged yourself to me."

"My body. And you've had good use of it." He belted on his robes as he rose. "I would have kept you as mistress, happily. But I have no time or patience for ridiculous demands from a temple harlot."

"Harlot." The angry flush drained, leaving her face

white as the marble columns on the hillside. "You took my innocence."

"You gave it."

"You can't mean these things." She knelt, clasping her hands like a woman at prayer. "You're angry because I pushed you. We'll speak no more of it tonight. We'll swim, as you said and forget all these hard words."

"It's too late for that. Do you think I can't read what's in your mind now? You'll nag me to death over what can never be. Just as well. We've challenged the gods long enough."

"You can't mean to leave me. I love you. If you leave me, I'll go to your family. I'll tell—"

"Speak of this, and I'll swear you lie. You'll burn for it, Lilia." He bent down, ran a finger over the curve of her shoulder. "And your skin is too soft, too sweet for the fire."

"Don't, don't turn from me. It will all be as you say, as you like. I'll never speak of leaving again. Don't leave me."

"Begging only spoils your beauty."

She called out to him in shock, in terrible grief, but he strode away as if he couldn't hear her.

She threw herself down on the blanket, wildly weeping, pounding her fists. The pain of it was like the fire he'd spoken of, burning through her so that her bones seemed to turn to ash. How could she live with the pain?

Love had betrayed her, and used her and cast her aside. Love had made her a fool. And still her heart was full of it.

She would cast herself into the sea and drown. She would climb to the top of the temple and fling herself off. She would simply die here, from the shame and the pain.

"Kill him first," she choked out as she raged. "I'll kill him first, then myself. Blood, his and mine together. That is the price of love and betrayal."

She heard a movement, just a whisper on the sand, and flung herself up with the joy. He'd come back to her! "My love."

"Yes. I will be."

His hair was black, flowing past his shoulders. He wore long robes the color of the night. His eyes were the same, so black they seemed to shine.

She grabbed up her toga, held it to her breasts. "I am a priestess of this temple. You have no leave to walk here."

"I walk where I will. So young," he murmured as those black eyes traveled over her. "So fresh."

"You will leave here."

"In my time. I've watched you these past three nights, Lilia, you and the boy you waste yourself on."

"How dare you."

"You gave him love, he gave you lies. Both are precious. Tell me, how would you like to repay him for his gift to you?"

She felt something stir in her, the first juices of vengeance. "He deserves nothing from me, neither he nor any man."

"How true. So you'll give to me what no man deserves."

Fear rushed in, and she ran with it. But somehow he was standing in front of her, smiling that cold smile.

"What are you?"

"Ah, insight. I knew I'd chosen well. I am what was before your weak and rutting gods were belched out of the heavens."

She ran again, a scream locked in her throat. But he was there, blocking her way. Her fear had jumped to terror. "It's death to touch a temple priestess."

"And death is such a fascinating beginning. I seek a companion, a lover, a woman, a student. You are she. I have a gift for you, Lilia."

This time when she ran, he laughed. Laughed still when he plucked her off her feet, tossed her sobbing to the ground.

She fought, scratching, biting, begging, but he was too strong. Now it was his mouth on her breast, and she wept with the shame of it even as she raked her nails down his cheek.

"Yes. Yes. It's better when they fight. You'll learn. Their

fear is perfume; their screams music." He caught her face in his hand, forced her to look at him.

"Now, into my eyes. Into them."

He drove himself into her. Her body shuddered, quaked, bucked, from the shock. And the unspeakable thrill.

"Did he take you so high?"

"No. No." The tears began to dry on her cheeks. Instead of clawing, beating, her hands dug into the sand searching for purchase. Trapped in his eyes, her body began to move with his.

"Take more. You want more," he said. "Pain is so . . . arousing."

He plunged harder, so deep she feared she might rend in two. But still her body matched his pace, still her eyes were trapped by his.

When his went red, her heart leaped with fresh fear, and yet that fear was squeezed in a fist of terrible excitement. He was so beautiful. Her human lover pale beside this dark, damning beauty.

"I give you the instrument of your revenge. I give you your beginning. You have only to ask me for it. Ask me for my gift."

"Yes. Give me your gift. Give me revenge. Give me—"

Her body convulsed when his fangs struck. And every pleasure she had known or imagined diminished beside what rushed into her. Here, here was the glory she'd never found in the temple, the burgeoning black power she'd always known stretched just beyond her fingertips.

Here was the forbidden she'd longed for.

It was she, writhing in that pleasure and power, that brought him to climax. And she, without being told, reared up to drink the blood she'd scored from his cheek.

Smiling through bloody lips, she died.

And woke in her bed two thousand years after the dream.

Her body felt bruised, tender, her mind muddled. Where was the sea? Where was the temple?

"Cirio?"

"A romantic? Who would have guessed." Cian stepped out of the shadows. "To call out for the lover who spurned and betrayed you."

"Jarl?" It was the name she'd called her maker. But as dream separated from reality, she saw it was Cian. "So, you've come after all. My offer . . ." But it wasn't quite clear.

"What became of the boy?" As if settling in for a cozy chat, Cian sat on the side of the bed.

"What boy? Davey?"

"No, no, not the whelp you made. Your lover, the one you had in life."

Her lips trembled as she understood. "So you toy with my dreams? What does that matter to me?" But she was shaken, down to the pit of her. "He was called Cirio. What do you think became of him?"

"I think your master arranged for him to be your first kill."

She smiled with one of her sweetest memories. "He pissed himself as Jarl held him out to me, and he sniveled like a child as he begged for his life. I was new, and still had the control to keep him alive for hours—long after he begged for his death. I'll do better with you. I'll give you years of pain."

She swiped out, cursed when her raking nails passed through him.

"Entertaining, isn't it? And Jarl? How long before you did for him."

She sat back, sulking a little. Then shrugged. "Nearly three hundred years. I had a lot to learn from him. He began to fear me because my power grew and grew. I could smell his fear of me. He would have ended me, if I hadn't ended him first."

"You were called Lilia—Lily."

"The pitiful human I was, yes. He named me Lilith when I woke." She twirled a lock of her hair around her finger as she studied Cian. "Do you have some foolish hope that by learning my beginning you'll find my end?"

She tossed the covers aside, rose to walk naked to a silver pitcher.

When she poured the blood into a cup, her hands trembled again.

"Let's speak frankly here," Cian suggested. "It's only you and I—which is odd. You don't sleep with Lora or the boy, or some other choice today?"

"Even I, occasionally, seek solitude."

"All right. So, to be frank. It's strange, isn't it, disorienting, to go back even in dreams to human? To see your own end, own beginning as if it just happened. To feel human again, or as best we can remember it feels to be human."

Almost as an afterthought, she shrugged into a robe. "I would go back to being human."

His brows lifted. "You? Now you surprise me."

"To have that moment of death and rebirth. The wonderful, staggering thrill of it. I'd go back to being weak and blind, just to experience the gift again."

"Of course. You remain predictable." He got to his feet. "Know this. If you and your wizard steer my dreams again, I'll return the favor, threefold. You'll have no rest from me, or from yourself."

He faded away, but he didn't go back. Though he could feel the tugs from Moira's mind, from Glenna's will, he lingered.

He wanted to see what Lilith would do next.

She heaved the cup and what was left of the blood in it against the wall. She smashed a trinket box, pounded holes into the wall with her fists until they bled.

Then she screamed for a guard.

"Bring that worthless wizard to me. Bring him in chains. Bring him— No, wait. Wait." She turned away in an obvious fight for control. "I'll kill him if he crosses paths with me now, then what good will he be to me? Bring me someone to eat."

She whirled back. "A male. Young. Twenty or so. Blond if we have one. Go!"

Alone, she rubbed her temple. "I'll kill him again," she

murmured. "I'll feel better then. I'll call him Cirio, and kill him again."

She snatched her precious mirror from the bureau. And seeing her own face reminded her why she would keep Midir alive. He'd given her this gift.

"There I am," she said softly. "So beautiful. The moon pales, yes, yes, it does. I'm right here. I'll always be here. The rest is ghosts. And here I am."

Picking up a brush, she began to groom her hair, and to sing. With tears in her eyes.

"Drink this." Glenna pushed a cup to Cian's lips, and immediately had it pushed aside.

"I'm fine. I'm not after drinking whiskey, or swooning on you without it."

"You're pale."

His lips quirked. "Part of the whole undead package. Well. That was quite a ride."

Since he refused it, Glenna took a sip of the whiskey herself, then passed it off to Moira. "E-ticket. She didn't sense us," she said to Moira. "I'd like to think my blocks and binding were enough, but I think, in large part, she was just too caught up to feel us."

"She was so young." Moira sat now. "So young, and in love with that worthless prick of a man. I don't know what language they were speaking. I could understand her, strangely enough, but I didn't know the tongue."

"Greek. She started out a priestess for some goddess. Virginity's part of the job description." Cian wished for blood, settled for water. "And save your pity. She was ripe for what happened."

"As you were?" Moira shot back. "And don't pretend you felt nothing for her. We were linked. I felt your pity. Her heart was broken, and moments later, she's raped and taken by a demon. I can despise what Lilith is and feel pity for Lilia."

"Lilia was already half mad," he said flatly. "Maybe the change is what kept her relatively sane all this time."

"I agree. I'm sorry," Glenna said to Moira. "And I got no pleasure out of seeing what happened to her. But there was something in her eyes, in her tone—and God, in the way she ultimately responded to Jarl. She wasn't quite right, Moira, even then."

"Then she might have died by her own hand, or been executed for killing the man who used her. But she'd have died clean." She sighed. "And we might not be here, discussing the matter. It all gives you a headache if you think about it hard enough. I have a delicate question, which is more for my own curiosity than anything else."

She cleared her throat before asking Cian. "How she responded, as Glenna said. Is that not usual?"

"Most fight, or freeze with fear. She, on the other hand, participated after the . . . delicacy escapes me," Cian admitted. "After she began to feel pleasure from the rape. It was rape, no mistake, and no sane woman gains pleasure from being brutalized and forced."

"She was already his before the bite," Moira murmured. "He knew she would be, recognized that in her. She knew what to do to change—to drink from him. Everything I've read has claimed the victim must be forced or told. It must be offered. She took. She understood, and she wanted."

"We know more than we did, which is always useful," Cian commented. "And the episode unnerved her, an added benefit. I'll sleep better having accomplished that. Now it's past my bedtime. Ladies."

Moira watched him go. "He feels. Why do you think he goes to such lengths to pretend he doesn't?"

"Feelings cause pain, a great deal of the time. I think when you've seen and done so much, feelings could be like a constant ache." Glenna laid a hand on Moira's shoulder. "Denial is just another form of survival."

"Feelings loosed can be either balm or weapon."

What would his be, she wondered, if fully freed?

Chapter 9

The rain slid into a soggy twilight that curled a smoky fog low over the ground. As night crept in, no moon, no stars could break through the gloom.

Moira waded through the river of fog over the courtyard to stand beside Glenna.

"They're nearly home," Glenna murmured. "Later than we'd hoped, but nearly home."

"I've had the fires lit in your room and Larkin's, and baths are being prepared. They'll be cold and wet."

"Thanks. I didn't think of it."

"When we were in Ireland, you thought of all the comfort details. Now it's for me." Like Glenna, Moira watched the skies. "I've ordered food for the family parlor, unless you'd rather be private with Hoyt."

"No. No. They'll want to report everything at once. Then we'll be private." She lifted her hand to grip her cross and the amulet she wore with it. "I didn't know I'd be so worried. We've been in the middle of a fight, outnumbered, and I haven't obsessed like this."

"Because you were with him. To love and to wait is worse than a wound."

"One of the lessons I've learned. There have been so many of them. You'd be worried about Larkin, I know. And about Tynan now. He has feelings for you."

Moira understood Glenna didn't mean Larkin. "I know. Our mothers hoped we might make a match of it."

"But?"

"Whatever needs to be there isn't there for me. And he's too much a friend. Maybe having no lover to wait for, no lover to lose, makes it easier for me to bear all of this."

Glenna waited a beat. "But."

"But," Moira said with a half laugh. "I envy you the torture of waiting for yours."

From where she stood Moira saw Cian, the shape of him coming through the gloom. From the stables, she noted. Rather than the cloak the men of Geall would wear against the chill and rain, he wore a coat similar to Blair's. Long and black and leather.

It billowed in the mists as he crossed to them with barely a sound of his boots against the wet stones.

"They won't come any sooner for you standing in the damp," he commented.

"They're nearly home." Glenna stared up at the sky as if she could will it to open and send Hoyt down to her. "He'll know I'm waiting."

"If you were waiting for me, Red, I wouldn't have left in the first place."

With a smile, she tipped her head so it leaned against his shoulder. When he put his arm around Glenna, Moira saw in the gesture the same affection she herself had with Larkin, the kind that came from the heart, through family.

"There," Cian said softly. "Dead east."

"You see them?" Glenna strained forward. "You can see them?"

"Give it a minute, and so will you."

The moment she did, her hand squeezed Moira's. "Thank God. Oh, thank God."

The dragon soared through the thick air, a glimmer of gold with riders on its back. Even as it touched down, Glenna was sprinting over the stones. When he dismounted, Hoyt's arms opened to catch her.

"That's lovely to see." Moira spoke quietly as Hoyt and Glenna embraced. "So many said goodbye today, and will tomorrow. It's lovely to see someone come home to waiting arms."

"Before her, he'd most often prefer coming back to solitude. Women change things."

She glanced up at him. "Only women?"

"People then. But women? They alter universes just by being women."

"For better or worse?"

"Depends on the woman, doesn't it?"

"And the prize, or the man, she's set her sights on." With this, she left his side to rush toward Larkin.

Despite the fact that he was dripping, she hugged him hard. "I have food, drink, hot water, all you could wish. I'm so glad to see you. All of you." But when she would have turned from Larkin to welcome the others, he gripped her hard.

Moira felt her relief spin on its head to fear.

"What? What happened?"

"We should go in." Hoyt's voice was quiet, and tight. "We should go in out of the wet."

"Tell me what happened." Moira drew away from Larkin.

"Tynan's troop was set upon, at the near halfway point."

She felt everything inside her freeze. "Oran. Tynan."

"Alive. Tynan was injured, but not seriously. Six others . . ."

She took Larkin's arm, digging her fingers in. "Dead or captured?"

"Five dead, one taken. Several others wounded, two badly. We did what we could for them."

The cold remained, like ice over her heart. "You have the names? The dead, the wounded, and the other?"

"We have them, yes. Moira, it was young Sean taken. The smithy's son."

Her belly twisted with the knowledge that what the boy faced would be worse than death. "I'll speak to their families. Say nothing to anyone until I've spoken to their families."

"I'll go with you."

"No. No, this is for me. You need to get dry and warm, and fed. It's for me to do, Larkin. It's my place."

"We wrote down the names." Blair took a scrap of paper out of her pocket. "I'm sorry, Moira."

"We knew this would come." She slipped the paper inside her cloak, out of the wet. "I'll come to the parlor as soon as I'm able, so you can tell me the details of it. For now, the families need to hear this from me."

"Lot of weight," Blair declared when Moira walked away.

"She'll bear it." Cian looked after her. "It's what queens do."

She thought it would crush her, but she did bear it. While mothers and wives wept in her arms, she took the weight. She knew nothing of the attack, but told each and every one their son or husband or brother had died bravely, died a hero.

It was what needed to be said.

It was worse with Sean's parents, worse to see the hope in the blacksmith's eyes, the tears of that hope blurring his wife's. She couldn't bring herself to snuff it out, so left them with it, with the prayers that their son would somehow escape and return home.

When it was done, she went to her rooms to put the names into a painted box she would keep now beside her bed. There would be other lists, she knew. This was only the first. And every name of every one who gave his or her life would be written down, and kept in that box.

With it, she put a sprig of rosemary for remembrance, and a coin for tribute.

After closing the box, she buried her need for solitude, for grieving, and went to the parlor to hear how it had been done.

Conversation stopped when she entered, and Larkin rose quickly.

"My father has just left us. I'll go bring him back if you like."

"No, no. Let him be with your mother, your sister." Moira knew her pregnant cousin's husband was to lead tomorrow's troop.

"I'll warm you some food. No, you will eat," Glenna said even as Moira opened her mouth. "Consider it medicine, but you'll eat."

While Glenna put food on a plate, Cian poured a stiff dose of apple brandy into a cup. He took it to her. "Drink this first. You're white as wax."

"With this I'll have color, and a swimming head." But she shrugged, tossed it back like water.

"Have to admire a woman who can take a slug like that." Impressed, he took the empty glass, then went back to sit.

"It was horrible. At least I can admit that here, to all of you. It was horrible." Moira sat down at the table, then pressed her hands to her temples. "To look into their faces and see the change, and know they'll forever be changed because of what you've brought to them. To what's been taken from them."

"You didn't bring it." Anger lashed in Glenna's voice as she slapped a plate down in front of Moira. "You didn't take it."

"I didn't mean the war, or the death. But the news of it. The hardest was the one who was taken prisoner. The smithy's boy, Sean. His parents still have hope. How could I tell them he's worse than dead? I couldn't cut that last thread of hope, and wonder if it would be kinder if I had."

She let out a breath, then straightened. Glenna was right, she would eat. "Tell me what you know."

"They were in the ground," Hoyt began, "as they were when they set upon Blair. Tynan said no more than fifty, but the men were taken by surprise. He told us it seemed they didn't care if they were cut down, but charged and fought like mad animals. Two of our men fell in the first instant, and they gained three horses from us in the confusion of the battle."

"Nearly a third of the horses that went with them."

"Four, maybe five of them took the smithy's son, alive from what those who tried to save him said. They took him off, heading east, while the rest held their line and battled back. They killed more than twenty, and the others scattered and ran as the tide turned."

"It was a victory. You have to look at it that way," Blair insisted. "You have to. Your men took out over twenty vamps on their first engagement. Your casualties were light in comparison. Don't say every death is one too many," she added quickly. "I know that. But this is the reality of it. Their training held up."

"I know you're right, and I've already told myself the same. But it was their victory, too. They wanted a prisoner. No reason else to take one. Their mission must have been to take one alive, whatever the cost of it."

"You're right, no argument. But I don't see that as a victory in their column. It was stupid, and it was a waste. Say five for the prisoner. Those vamps had stayed and fought, they'd have taken more of ours—alive or dead. My take is that Lilith ordered this because she was feeling pissy, or it was impulse. But it was also bad strategy."

Moira ate food she couldn't taste while she considered it. "The way she sent King back to us. It was petty, and vicious. But playful in her way. She thinks these things will undermine us, crush our spirits. How can she know us so little? You've lived half her time," she said to Cian. "You know better."

"I find humans interesting. She finds them . . . tasty at best. You don't have to know the mind of a cow to herd them up for steaks."

"Especially if you've got a whole gang to handle the roping and riding," Blair put in. "Just following your metaphor," she said to Cian. "I hurt her girl, so she needs some payback for that. We took three of her bases—should add we cleared out the second two locations this morning."

"They were empty," Larkin stated. "She hadn't bothered to set traps there, or base any of her troops. Added to that, Glenna told us how you played with her while we were gone."

"Sum of it is, this was tit for tat. But she loses more than we do. Doesn't make it any easier on the families of the dead," Blair added.

"And tomorrow, I send more out. Phelan." Moira reached out for Larkin. "I can't hold him back. I'll speak to Sinann, but—"

"No, that's for me. I expect our father has already talked to her, but I'll see her myself."

She nodded. "And Tynan? His wounds?"

"A gash along the hip. Hoyt treated the wounded. He was doing well when we left them. They're secured for the night."

"Well then. We'll pray for sun in the morning."

She had another duty to see to.

Her women had a sitting room near her own chambers where they could sit and read, or do needlework, or gossip. Moira's mother had made it a cheerful, intensely female space with soft fabrics, many cushions, pots filled with flowering plants.

The fire here was habitually of apple wood for the scent, and there were wall sconces of pretty winged faeries.

When she was crowned, Moira had given her own women leave to make any changes they liked. But the room remained as it had in all her memory.

Her women were there now, waiting for her to retire for the night, or simply dismiss them.

They rose when she entered, and curtseyed.

"We're all women here now. For now, in this place, we're all only women." She opened her arms to Ceara.

"Oh, my lady." Ceara's eyes, already red and swollen from weeping overflowed as she rushed into Moira's embrace. "Dwyn is dead. My brother is dead."

"I'm sorry. I'm so sorry. Here now, here." She led Ceara to a seat, holding her close. And she wept with her as she'd wept with Ceara's mother, and all the others.

"They buried him there, in a field by the road. They couldn't even bring him home. He had no wake."

"We'll have a holy man consecrate the ground. And we'll build a monument to those who fell today."

"He was eager to go, to fight. He turned and waved at me before he marched off."

"You'll have some tea now." Her own eyes red from weeping, Isleen set the pot down. "You'll have some tea, Ceara, and you, my lady."

"Thank you." Ceara mopped at her damp face. "I don't know what I'd have done these past hours without Isleen and Dervil."

"It's good that you have your friends. But you'll have your tea, then you'll go to your family. You'll need your family now. You have my leave for as long as you want it."

"There's something more I want, Your Majesty. Something I ask you to give me, in my brother's name."

Moira waited, but Ceara said nothing more. "Would you ask me to give you my word on something without knowing what I promise?"

"My husband marches tomorrow."

Moira felt her stomach sink. "Ceara." She reached over, smoothed a hand on Ceara's hair. "Sinann's husband marches with the sunrise as well. She carries her third child, and still I can't spare her from his leaving."

"I don't ask you to spare me. I ask you allow me to march with him."

"To—" Stunned, Moira sat back. "Ceara, your children."

"Will be with my mother, and as safe and well as they can be, here, with her. But my man goes to war, and I've trained as he has. Why am I to sit and wait?" Ceara held out her hands. "Peck at needlework, walk in the garden when he goes to fight. You said we would all need to be ready to defend Geall, and worlds beyond it. I've made myself ready. Your Majesty, my lady, I beg your leave to go with my husband on the morrow."

Saying nothing, Moira got to her feet. She moved to the window to look out at the dark. The rain, at last, had stopped, but the mists from it swarmed like clouds.

"Have you spoken with him on this?" Moira asked at length.

"I have, and his first thought was for my safety. But he understands my mind is set, and why."

"Why is it?"

"He's my heart." Ceara stood, laid a hand on her breast. "I wouldn't leave my children unprotected, but trust my mother to do all she can for them. My lady, have we, we women, trained and slogged in the mud all this time only to sit by the fire?"

"No. No, you haven't."

"I'm not the only woman who wants this."

Moira turned now. "You've spoken to others." She looked at Dervil and Isleen. "Both of you want this as well?" She nodded. "I see I was wrong to hold you back. Arrangements will be made then. I'm proud to be a woman of Geall."

For love, Moira thought as she sat to make another list of names. For love as much as duty. The women would go, and fight for Geall. But it was the husbands and lovers, the families inside of Geall that made them reach for the sword.

Who did she fight for? Who was there for her to turn to the night before a battle, to reach for that warmth, for that reason to fight?

The days ticked away, and Samhain loomed like a bloodied ax over her head. And here she sat, alone as she sat alone every night. Would she reach for a book again, or another map, another list? Or would she wander the room again, the gardens and courtyards, wishing for . . .

Him, she thought. Wishing he would put his hands on her again and make her feel so full, so alive, so bright. Wishing he'd share with her what she'd seen in him the night he'd played music and had stirred her heart as truly as he'd stirred her blood.

She'd fought and she'd bled, would fight and bleed again. She would ride into battle as queen, with the sword of gods in her hand. But here she sat in her quiet room, wishing like a blushing maid for the touch and the heat of the only one who'd ever made her pulse quicken.

Surely that was foolish and wasteful. And, it was an insult to women everywhere.

She rose to pace as she considered it. Aye, it was insulting, and small-minded. She sat and wished for the same reasons she'd held back sending the women on the march. Because it was traditional for the man to come to the woman. It was traditional for the man to protect and defend.

Things had changed, hadn't they?

Hadn't she spent weeks in a world and time where women, like Glenna and Blair, held their own—and more—at every turn?

So, if she wanted Cian's hands on her, she'd see that he put them there, and that would be that.

She started to sweep out of the room, remembered her appearance. She could do better. If she was about to embark on seducing a vampire, she'd have to go well armed.

She stripped off her dress. She might have wished for a bath—or oh, the wonderfully hot shower of Ireland—but she made do washing from the basin of scented water.

She creamed her skin, imagined Cian's long fingers skimming over it. Heat was already balling in her belly and throbbing along nerves as she chose her best nightrobe.

Brushing her hair she had a moment to wish she'd asked Glenna to teach her how to do a simple glamour. Though it seemed to her that her cheeks were becomingly flushed, her eyes held a glint. She bit her lips until they hurt, but thought they'd pinked and plumped nicely.

She stood back from the long glass, studied herself carefully from every angle. She hoped she looked desirable.

Taking a candle she left the room with the sheer determination she wouldn't return to it a virgin.

In his room, Cian pored over maps. He was the only one of the circle who'd been denied a look at the battlefield, either in reality or dreams. He was going to correct that.

Time was a problem. Five days' march, well, he could ride it in two, perhaps less. But that meant he'd need a safe place to camp during the daylight.

One of the bases the others had secured would do. Once he'd taken his survey, he could simply relocate in one of those bases until Samhain.

Get out of the bloody castle, and away from its all-too-tempting queen.

There'd be objections—that was annoying. But they could hardly lock him in a dungeon and make him stay put. They'd be leaving themselves in another week or so. He'd just ride point.

He could ride out with the troops in the morning, if the sun stayed back. Or simply wait for sundown.

Sitting back he sipped blood he'd laced with whiskey—his own version of a sleep-inducing cocktail. He could just go now, couldn't he? No arguments from his brother or the others if he just rode off.

He'd have to leave a note, he supposed. Odd to have people who'd actually be concerned for his welfare, and somewhat pleasant though it added certain responsibilities.

He'd just pack and go, he decided, pushing the drink aside. No muss, no fuss. And he wouldn't have to see her again until they caught up to him.

He picked up the band of beaded leather he'd failed to give back, toyed with it. If he left tonight, he wouldn't have to see her, or smell her, or imagine what it would be like to have her under him in the dark.

He had a bloody good imagination.

He got to his feet to decide what gear would be most useful for the journey, and frowned at the knock on his door.

Likely Hoyt, he decided. Well, he just wouldn't mention his plans, and thereby avoid a long, irritating debate on the matter. He considered not answering at all, but silence and a locked door wouldn't stop his brother the sorcerer.

He knew it was Moira the moment his hand touched the latch. And he cursed. He opened the door, intending to send her on her way quickly so he could be on his.

She wore white, thin, flowing white, with something filmy over it that was nearly the same gray as her eyes. She smelled like spring—young and full of promise.

Need coiled inside him like snakes.

"Do you never sleep?" he demanded.

"Do you?" She swept by him, the move surprising him enough that he didn't block it.

"Well, come right in, make yourself at home."

"Thank you." She said it politely, as if his words hadn't dripped with sarcasm. Then she set down her candle and turned to the the fire he hadn't bothered to light.

"Let's see if I can do this. I practiced until my ears all but bled. Don't speak. You'll distract me."

She held out a hand toward the fire. Focused, imagined. Pushed. A single weak flame flickered, so she narrowed her eyes and pushed harder.

"There!" There was absolute delight in her voice when the turf caught.

"Now I'm surrounded by bloody magicians."

Both her hair and her robes fanned out as she turned. "It's a good skill, and I intend to learn more."

"You won't find a tutor in sorcery here."

"No." She brushed back her hair. "But I think in other

things." Walking back to the door, she locked it, then turned to him. "I want you to take me to bed."

He blinked as otherwise he might have goggled. "What?"

"There's not a thing wrong with your hearing, so you heard me well enough. I want to lie with you. I thought I might try being coy or seductive, but then it seemed to me you'd have more respect for plain speaking."

The snakes coiled inside him began to writhe. And bite. "Here's plain speaking. Get out."

"I see I've surprised you." She wandered, running a finger over a stack of books. "That's not easy to do, so as Blair would say, points for me." She turned again, smiled again. "I'm green at this, so tell me, why would a man be angry to have a woman want to lie with him?"

"I'm not a man."

"Ah." She lifted a finger to acknowledge his point. "But still, you have needs, desires. You've desired me."

"A man will put his hand on nearly any female."

"You're not a man," she shot back, then grinned. "More points for me. You're not keeping up."

"If you've been drinking again—"

"I haven't. You know I haven't. But I've been thinking. I'm going to war, into battle. I may not live through it. None of us may. Good men died today, in mud and blood, and left broken hearts behind them."

"And sex reaffirms life. I know the psychology of it."

"That, aye that, true enough. And on a more personal level, I'm damned—I swear it—if I'll die a virgin. I want to *know* what it is. I want to feel it."

"Then order up a subject for stud, Majesty. I'm not interested."

"I don't want anyone else. I never wanted anyone before you, and haven't wanted any but you since I first saw you. It shocked me, that I could have any such feelings for you, knowing what you are. But they're inside me, and they won't leave. I have needs, like anyone. And wiles enough, I think, to overcome your resistance if need be—though you may no longer be a randy young man."

"Found your feet, haven't you?" he muttered.

"Oh, I've always had them. I'm just careful where I step." Watching him, measuring him, she trailed a hand down one of the bedposts. "Tell me, what difference would it make to you? An hour or two. You haven't had a woman in some time, I'm thinking."

He felt like an idiot. Stiff and foolish and needy. "That wouldn't be your concern."

"It might be. I've read that when a man's been denied, we'll say, for a while, it can affect his performance. But you shouldn't worry about that, as I've nothing to compare it to."

"Isn't that lucky for me? Or would be if I wanted you."

Her head cocked, and all he could see on her face was curiosity and confidence.

"You think you can insult me away. I wager—any price you name—that you're hard as stone right now." She moved toward him. "I want so much, Cian, for you to touch me. I'm tired of dreaming of it, and want to feel it."

The ground was crumbling under his feet. Had been, he knew, since the moment she'd walked in. "You don't know what you're asking, what you're risking. The consequences are beyond you."

"A vampire can lie with a human. You won't hurt me." She reached up, drew the cross over her head, set it aside on the table.

"Trusting soul." He tried for sarcasm, but the gesture had moved him.

"Confident. I don't need or want a shield against you. Why do you never say my name?"

"What? Of course, I do."

"No, you don't. You refer to me, but you never look at me and say my name." Her eyes were smoke now, and full of knowledge. "Names have power, taken or given. Are you afraid of what I might take from you?"

"There's nothing for you to take."

"Then say my name."

"Moira."

"Again, please." She took his hand, laid it on her heart.

"Don't do this."

"Cian. There's your name from me. Cian. I think if you don't touch me, if you don't take me, a part of me will die before I ever go to battle. Please." She framed his face in her hands, and saw—at last—what she needed to see in his eyes. "Say my name."

"Moira." Lost, he took her wrist, turned his lips into her palm. "Moira. If I wasn't damned already, this would send me to hell."

"I'll try to take you to heaven first, if you teach me."

She rose to her toes, drawing him down. Her sigh trembled out when his lips met hers.

Chapter 10

He'd believed his will would prevent this. A thousand years, he thought, and sank into her, and the male still deluded itself it could control the female.

She was leading him, and had in her way been leading him to this from the first instant. Now he would take what she offered him, what she demanded from him, however selfish the act. But he would use the skill of a dozen lifetimes to give her what she wanted in return.

"You're foolish, reckless to give up your innocence to such as me." He skimmed a fingertip across her collarbone. "But you won't leave now until you have."

"Virginity and innocence aren't always the same. I lost my innocence before I met you." The night her mother had been murdered, she thought. But memories of that weren't for tonight.

Tonight was for knowing him.

"Should I disrobe for you, or is that for you to do?"

He gave a short, almost pained laugh before resting his brow to hers in a gesture she found surprisingly tender. "In such a hurry," he murmured. "Some things, especially the first time they're tasted, are better savored than gulped."

"There, you see. I've learned something already. When you kiss me, things wake up inside my body. Things I didn't know were sleeping there until you. I don't know what you feel."

"More than I'd like." He combed his fingers through her hair as he'd longed to for weeks. "More than could be good for either of us. This . . ." He kissed her, softly. "Is a mistake." And again, deeper.

Like her scent, her taste was of springtime, of sunlight and youth. He craved the flavor of it, filled himself on it and the quick catch of her breath as he skimmed his teeth lightly, very light, over her bottom lip.

He let his hands plunge into her hair, the long, sleek fall of it, then under it to tease and waken the nerves along her spine.

When she trembled, he brought his hands to her shoulders to slide the robes down and bare that soft flesh for his lips. He could feel the yielding in her as well as the tremors, and when his mouth brushed along her throat, that seductive pulsing of blood under the skin.

She didn't jolt when his teeth grazed there, but stiffened when he brushed his hand over her breast.

No one had ever touched her so intimately. The flash of heat his hands brought her was a shock, as was the knowledge only a thin layer of material was between his hand and her flesh.

Then even that was gone, and her nightrobes pooled around her feet. Her hand came up instinctively to cover herself, but he only took it, nipped his teeth lightly at her wrist while his eyes watched hers.

"Are you afraid?"

"A little."

"I won't bite you."

"No, no, not of that." She turned the hand he held so her palm cupped his cheek. "There's so much happening inside of me. So much new. No one's ever touched me like this." Gathering her courage, she took his other hand, brought it to her breast. "Show me more."

He brushed his thumb over her nipple, watched the shock of pleasure flicker over her face. "Turn that busy mind off, Moira."

It was already as if mists clouded it. How could she think when her body was swimming in sensation?

He lifted her off her feet so that her face was suddenly on level with his. Then his mouth took hers into the heat again.

The bed was beneath her? Had he crossed the room? How had . . . but her mind misted over again as his hands, his mouth, slid like flaming velvet over her body.

She was a feast, and he'd fasted far too long. But still he sampled slowly, lingering over tastes and textures. And with each shiver, each sigh or gasp, she fed his own arousal.

When her curious hands came too close to breaking his control, he caught them in his own, trapping them as he slowly, mercilessly ravished her breasts.

She was building beneath him; he could feel the power filling her, harder, fuller. And when he pushed her to peak, she bowed up, riding it with a strangled cry.

She melted down, her hands going limp under his.

"Oh." The word was a long expulsion of breath. "Oh, I see."

"You think you do." His tongue traced over the thick beat of the pulse in her throat. As she sighed, he glided his hand between her legs, and sliding into the wet heat, showed her more.

Everything went bright. It blinded her, the brilliance of it all but seared her eyes, her skin, her heart. She was nothing but feelings now, a mass of pleasures beyond any possibility. She was the arrow from the bow, and he'd shot her high, on an endless flight.

His hands simply ruled her until she was a hostage to this never-ending need. Half-mad she struggled with his shirt.

"I need—I want—"

"I know." He pulled off his shirt so she could touch and taste him in turn. And let himself glide on the pleasure of her eager explorations. Her breath against his skin, warm and quick, her fingers tracing, then digging. When her hands gripped his hips, he let her help him strip the rest of his clothes away.

And wasn't sure whether to be amused or flattered when her eyes went huge.

"I . . . I didn't realize. I've seen a cock before, but—"

Now he laughed. "Oh, have you now?"

"Of course. Men bathe in the river, and well, and being curious . . ."

"You've spied on them. A man's pride isn't at its, ah, fullest after a bath in a cold river. I won't hurt you."

He'd have to, wouldn't he? she thought. She'd read of such things, and certainly she'd heard the women speak of it. But she wasn't afraid of the pain. She feared nothing now.

So she laid back again, braced for him. But he only began to touch her again, rouse her again, undo her again as if she were a knot of string.

He wanted her drenched, drowning, beyond thought and nerves. That tight and slender body she'd stiffened in anticipation went loose again. Warm and soft again, with that erotic flush of blood spreading under the skin.

"Look at me. Moira *mo chroi*. Look at me. Look into me."

This he could do, with will and control. He could ease that moment, that flash of pain and give her only the pleasure. When those heavy gray eyes blurred, he pierced her. He filled her.

Her lips trembled, and the moan they formed was low and deep. He kept her trapped in his eyes as he began to move, long, slow thrusts that had the thrill of it rippling over her face, over her body.

Even when he released her from the thrall, when she began to move with him, her eyes stayed locked on his. Her heart was raging, a wild drum against his chest, so vital it seemed—for a moment—as if it beat inside him.

She came with a cry of wonder and abandonment. At last, at last, he let his own need take him with her.

She curled up against him, a cat who'd lapped up every drop of cream. He would, he was sure, berate himself later for what he'd done. But for now he was content to wallow a bit.

"I didn't know it could be like that," she murmured. "So enormous."

"Being so well-endowed, I've likely ruined you for anyone else."

"I didn't mean the size of your pride, as you called it." Laughing, she looked up at him, and saw from his lazy smile he'd understood her meaning perfectly. "I've read of the act, of course. Medical books, storybooks. But the personal experience of it is much more satisfying."

"I'm happy to have assisted you in your research."

She rolled over so she could splay herself on him. "I'll need to do considerably more research, I'm thinking, before I know all there is to know. I'm greedy for knowledge."

"Damn you, Moira." he said it with a sigh as he played with her hair. "You're perfect."

"Am I?" Her already glowing cheeks went pinker with pleasure. "I won't argue because I feel so perfect right now. Thirsty though. Is there any water about?"

He nudged her aside, then rose to fetch the jug. She sat up as he poured, and her hair spilled over her shoulders and breasts. He thought if he had a heartbeat, the sight of her like this might stop it.

He handed her the cup, then sat across from her on the bed. "This is madness. You know it."

"The world's gone mad," she replied. "Why shouldn't we have a piece of it? I'm not being foolish, or careless," she said quickly, laying a hand over his. "I have to do so many things, Cian, so many things where there's no choice for me. This was my choice. My own."

She drank, handed him the cup so he could share. "Will

you regret something that gave us pleasure and harmed no one?"

"You haven't thought about what others will think of you for sharing a bed with me."

"Listen to you, worrying about my reputation of all things. I'm my own woman, and I don't need to explain to anyone whose bed I share."

"Being queen—"

"Doesn't make me less a woman," she interrupted. "A Geallian woman, and we're known for making up our own minds. I was reminded of that earlier tonight." Now she rose, picking up her outer robe to wrap it around her.

He thought it was like she wrapped herself in mist.

"One of my ladies, Ceara—do you know who I mean?"

"Ah, tall, dark blond hair. She took you down in hand-to-hand."

"That she did. Her brother was killed today, on the march. He was young, not yet eighteen." It pierced her heart, again. "I went to the sitting room where my ladies gather and found her there when I would have given her leave to be with her family."

"She's loyal, and thinks of her duty to you."

"Not just to me. She asked if I would give her one thing, in her brother's name. One thing." Emotion quivered in her voice before she conquered it. "And that was to march in the morning with her husband. To go from here, from her children, from safety and face whatever might be on the road. She's not the only woman who asks to go. We're not weak. We don't sit and wait, or no longer will. I was reminded of that tonight."

"You'll let her go."

"Her, and any who wish it. In the end, some who may not wish it will be sent. I didn't come to you because I'm weak, because I needed comfort or protection. I came because I wanted you. I wanted this."

She cocked her head, and with a little smile, let the robe fall. "Now it seems I'm wanting you again. Do I need to seduce you?"

"Too late for that."

Her smile widened as she moved toward the bed. "I've heard—and I've read—that a man needs a bit of time between rounds."

"You force me to repeat myself. I'm not a man."

He grabbed her hand, flipped her onto the bed—and under him.

She laughed, tugged playfully at his hair. "Isn't that handy, under the circumstances."

Later, for the first time in too long to remember, Cian didn't slip into sleep in silence, but to the quiet rhythm of Moira's heart.

It was that heart that woke him. He heard the sudden and rapid beat of it even before she thrashed in sleep.

He cursed, remembering only then she wasn't wearing her cross, nor had he taken any of Glenna's precautions against Lilith's intrusion.

"Moira." He took her shoulders, lifting her. "Wake up."

He was on the point of shaking her out of it when her eyes flew open. Instead of the fear he'd expected, he saw grief.

"It was a dream," he said carefully. "Only a dream. Lilith can't touch you in dreams."

"It wasn't Lilith. I'm sorry I woke you."

"You're shaking. Here." He pulled up a blanket, tossed it over her shoulders. "I'll get the fire going again."

"No need. Don't trouble," she said even as he got up. "I should go. It must be nearing dawn."

He simply crouched down, placed the turf in the hearth. "You won't trust me with this."

"It's not that. It's not." She should have gotten up quickly, she realized. Left straight on waking. For now she couldn't seem to move. "It wasn't Lilith, it was just a bad dream. Just . . ."

But her breath began to hitch and heave.

Rather than go to her, he lit the turf, then moved around the room to light candles.

"I can't speak of it. I can't."

"Of course you can. Maybe not to me, but to Glenna. I'll go wake her."

"No. No. No." She covered her face with her hands.

"So." Since he was up, and unlikely to sleep again for now, he poured himself a cup of blood. "Geallian women aren't weak."

She dropped her hands, and the eyes she'd hidden with them went hot with insult. "You bloody bastard."

"Exactly so. Run back to your room if you can't handle it. But if you stay, you'll pull out whatever's knotted up your guts. Your choice." He took a chair. "You're big on choices, so make one."

"You want to hear my pain, my grief? Why not to you then, who it would mean so little to? I dreamed, as I do over and over, of my mother's murder. Every time, it's clearer than it was before. At first, it was so muddled and pale—like I saw it through a smear of mud. It was easier then."

"And now?"

"I could see it."

"What did you see?"

"I was sleeping." Her eyes were huge on his face, and full of pain. "We'd had supper, and my uncle, Larkin, the family had come. A little family party. My mother enjoyed having them every few months. We had music after, and dancing. She loved to dance, my mother. It was late when we went to bed, and I fell asleep so quickly. I heard her scream."

"No one else heard?"

Moira shook her head. "No. She didn't scream, you see. Not out loud. I don't think she screamed out loud. In her head, she did, and I heard it in mine. Just once. Only once. I thought I imagined it, must have imagined it. But I got up, and went down to her room. Just to ease my mind."

She could see it even now. She hadn't bothered with a candle because her heart was beating so fast and hard. She'd simply run from her room and down to her mother's door.

"I didn't knock. I was saying to myself, no, you'll wake her. Just ease inside and see for yourself that she's sleeping.

"But when I opened the door, she wasn't in her bed, she wasn't sleeping. I heard such sounds, such horrible sounds. Like animals, like wolves, but worse. Oh, worse."

She paused, tried to swallow through her dry throat. "The doors to her balcony were open, and the curtains moving with the breeze. I called out for her. I wanted to run to the doors, but I couldn't. My legs felt as if they'd turned to lead. I could barely make one step in front of the other. I can't say it."

"You can. You walked to the door, to the balcony door."

"I saw . . . Oh God, oh God, oh God. I saw her, on the stones. And the blood, so much blood. Those things were . . . I'll be sick."

"You won't." He got up now, crossed to her. "You won't be sick."

"They were ripping at her." And the words tore out of her now. "Ripping at her body. Demons, things of nightmares, tearing at my mother. I wanted to scream, but I couldn't scream. I wanted to run out and beat them off. One, one looked at me. His eyes red, my mother's blood all over his face. My mother's blood. He charged at the door, and I stumbled back. Back, away from her when I should have gone to her."

"She was dead, Moira, you knew it. You'd be dead if you'd stepped out that door."

"I should have gone to her. It leaped at me, and then I screamed, and screamed and screamed. Even when it fell back as if it had struck a wall, I screamed. Then it all went to black. I did nothing but scream while my mother lay bleeding."

"You're not stupid," he said flatly. "You know you were in shock. You know that what you saw was the same as being struck a stunning physical blow. Nothing you could have done would have saved your mother."

"How could I leave her there, Cian? Just leave her

there." Tears spilled from her eyes to slide down her cheeks. "I loved her more than anything in this world."

"Because your mind couldn't cope with what you saw, with what was—to you—impossible. She was already dead, before you came into the room. She was dead, Moira, the moment you heard her scream."

"How can you be sure? If—"

"They were assassins. They would have killed her instantly. What came after was indulgence, but death was the goal."

Now he took her cold hands in his to warm them. "She would have had only a moment to feel afraid, to feel the pain. The rest, she was beyond the rest of it."

She went very still, stared hard into his eyes. "Will you swear to me you believe that?"

"It's not a matter of believing, but knowing. I can swear that to you. If they'd wanted to torture her, they'd have taken her somewhere where they could have taken their time. What you saw was a cover-up. Wild animals, it would have been said. The way it was with your father."

She let out a long breath, then another as she saw the horrible logic of it. "I've been sick at the thought that she might have been alive when I got there. Still alive while they tore at her. It's somehow easier to know she wasn't."

She knuckled a tear away. "I'm sorry I called you a bastard."

"I pissed you off."

"With cool deliberation. I haven't spoken of that night to anyone before this. I couldn't pull it out of me and look at it, speak of it."

"Now you have."

"Maybe now that I have I won't see her the way she was that night. Maybe I'll see her as she was when she was alive, and happy. All those paintings I have inside my head of her, instead of that last one. Would you hold on to me for a bit?"

He sat, put his arm around her, stroked her hair when she rested her head on his shoulder. "I feel better that I've told you. It was kind of you to piss me off so I would."

"Anytime."

"I wish I could stay, just stay here in the dark and quiet. Stay with you. But I need to go and dress. I need to see the troops off at first light."

She tipped her head up. "Will you kiss me good morning?"

He met her lips with his, drew the kiss out until it brought a pang to his belly.

She opened sleepy eyes. "I could feel that one right down to the soles of my feet. I hope that means I'll walk lighter today."

Rising, she reached for her robes. "You could miss me a little these next hours," she told him. "Or just lie when I see you again and say you did."

"If I tell you I missed you, it won't be a lie."

Dressed, she caught his face in her hands for one more kiss. "Then I'll settle for whatever happens to be the truth."

She picked up her candle, went to the door. After shooting him a last quick grin over her shoulder, she unlatched it.

And opened it an instant before Larkin could knock.

"Moira?" His smile was quick and baffled. It faded instantly when he saw the rumpled bed and Cian lazily wrapping a blanket around his waist.

It was wild rage now that had him shoving Moira aside and charging.

Cian didn't bother to block the blow, but took it full on the face. The second fist he caught in his hand an inch before it struck. "You're entitled to one. But that's enough."

"He's entitled to nothing of the sort." Moira had the presence of mind to shut and latch the door. "Strike out again, Larkin, I'll kick your arse myself."

"You fucking bastard. You'll answer for this."

"Undoubtedly. But not to you."

"It will be me, I promise you."

"Stop it. I mean it!"

When Larkin's fists bunched again, Moira had to fight the urge to bean him with a candlestick. "Lord Larkin, as your queen I command you to step back."

"Oh, don't start bringing rank into it," Cian said easily. "Let the boy try to defend his cousin's honor."

"I'll beat you bloody unconscious."

Out of patience, Moira shoved between them. "Look at me. Damn your thick skull, Larkin, look at me. What room are we in here?"

"The bloody buggering bastard's."

"And do you think he dragged me in here by the hair, forced himself on me? You're a numbskull is what you are. I walked here, and I knocked on Cian's door. I pushed myself into this room, into this bed, because it's what I wanted."

"You don't know what—"

"If you dare, if you *dare* to say to me that I don't know what I want I'll beat *you* bloody unconscious." She drilled a finger into his chest to emphasize the point. "I've a right to this private matter, and you've no say in it at all."

"But he—you. It's not proper."

"Bollocks to that."

"It's hardly a surprise your cousin objects to you sleeping with a vampire." Cian moved away from them, picked up his cup. Deliberately he dipped a finger in, licked the blood from it. "Nasty habit."

"I won't have you—"

"Wait." Larkin interrupted Moira's furious spate. "A moment. I'd like to speak with Cian in private. Talk only," he said before Moira could object. "My word on it."

She pushed a hand through her hair. "I don't have time for either of you, and this foolishness. Be men then, and discuss what is none of your business or concern as if I'm addle-brained. I have to dress and speak to the troops who march today."

She strode to the door. "I'll trust you not to kill each other over my private relationships."

She went out, slammed the door.

"Make it quick," Cian snapped. "I'm suddenly weary of humans."

The worst of the temper had faded out of Larkin's face.

"You think I hit you, that I'm angry because of what you are. I would have had the same reaction, done the same to any man I'd found her with like this. She's my girl, after all. It wasn't part of what I was thinking, as I wasn't thinking in any case."

He shifted his feet, blew out a hard breath. "And now that I do, well, it adds a complicated layer to it all. But I don't want you thinking I planted one on you because you're a vampire. The fact is, I don't think of you that way unless, well, unless I think about it. You're a friend to me. You're one of the six of us."

Even as he spoke, the flush of temper came back. "And I'm saying clear, me demanding, here and now, what the sodding hell you were thinking of taking advantage of my cousin has nothing to do with whether or not you have a fucking heartbeat."

Cian waited a moment. "Are you done with that part of the speech?"

"I am, until I have an answer."

With a nod, Cian sat, picked up his cup again. "You put me in a position, don't you? Calling me a friend, and one of you. I may be the first, but I'll never be the second."

"Bollocks. That's a kind of way out of things. I trust you as I trust few others. And now you've seduced my cousin."

Cian let out a snorting laugh. "You're not giving her enough credit. Neither did I." Idly, Cian traced a finger over the beaded leather. "She unraveled me like a ball of yarn. It doesn't excuse not making her leave, but she's persuasive and stubborn. I couldn't— I didn't resist her."

He glanced over at the maps he'd neglected since she'd knocked on the door. "It won't be a problem as I'm leaving tonight. Earlier if the weather cooperates. I want a firsthand look at the battlefield. So she's safe from me, and me from her, until this is over."

"You can't. You can't," Larkin repeated when Cian merely lifted a brow. "If you go like this, she'll think it's because of her. It'll hurt her. If I'm responsible for you planning to leave—"

"I'd decided it before she came here last night. Partially because I'd hoped to keep my hands off her."

Obviously frustrated, Larkin dragged his hands through his hair. "As you didn't make it away quick enough for that, it'll just have to wait. I'll take you there myself, by air, in a few days or whenever it can be done. But we six need to be together."

Calmer, Larkin studied Cian's face. "We need to be one circle. This is bigger than lying with or not lying with each other. And that, now that my blood's cooler, I can say is between the two of you. It's not my place to interfere. But damn it," he continued, "I'm going to ask you one thing. I'm going to ask you as a friend, and as her blood kin standing for her father. Have you feelings for her? True feelings?"

"You play the friendship card handily, don't you?"

"You are my friend, I care for you as I would a brother. That's the truth from me."

"Damn it." Cian slammed down the cup, then scowled at the blood that splattered on the maps. "You humans crowd me with these feelings. You push them at me, and into me without a single thought for how I can survive them."

"How can you survive without them?" Larkin wondered.

"Comfortably. What difference does it make to you what I feel? She needed someone."

"Not someone. You."

"Her mistake," Cian said quietly. "My damnation. I love her, or I would have taken her before this for the sport of it. I love her, or I'd have sent her away from me last night. How, I'm not sure, but I love her otherwise I wouldn't feel so goddamn desperate. And you repeat that to anyone, I'll snap your head from your shoulders, friend or not."

"All right." With a nod, Larkin got to his feet, offered his hand. "I hope you'll make each other as happy as you're able, for as long as you're able."

"Hell." Cian accepted the hand. "What the hell are you doing here at this hour anyway?"

"Oh, I forgot completely. I thought you'd not yet be in bed. I wanted to ask if you'd be willing to let us—my family—mate your stallion with one of our mares. She's in season, and your Vlad would be a fine sire."

"You want to use my horse as stud?"

"I would, yes, if it's no problem for you. I'd have her brought to him this morning."

"Go ahead. I'm sure he'll enjoy it."

"Thanks for that. We'll pay you the standard fee."

"No. No fee. We'll consider this a gesture between friends."

"Between friends then. Thanks. I'll just go and find Moira, and let her break her temper over my head as I deserve." Larkin paused at the door. "Oh, the mare I've in mind for your stallion. She's fetching."

The quick grin, the quick wink as Larkin went out had Cian laughing despite the mess of the morning.

Chapter 11

At Moira's orders, the flags flew at half-staff, and pipers played a requiem in the dawn light. She would do more, if the gods were willing, for those who gave their lives in this war. But for now, this was all that could be done to acknowledge the dead.

Standing in the courtyard, she was torn between grief and pride as she watched the men and women—the warriors—prepare for the long march east. She'd already bid her farewells to her women, and to Phelan, her cousin's husband.

"Majesty." Niall, the big guard who was now one of her trusted captains, stepped before her. "Should I order the gates opened?"

"In a moment. You wish you were going today."

"I serve at your pleasure, my lady."

"Your wishes are your own, Niall, and I understand them. But I need you here a bit longer. You'll have your time soon enough." They would all have their time, she thought. "Your brother and his family? How are they?"

"Safe, thanks to Lord Larkin and the lady Blair. Though my brother's leg is healing, he won't be able to fight on his feet."

"There will be more to this than swinging a sword on the battlefield."

"Aye." His hand closed over the hilt of the blade at his side. "But in truth I'm ready to swing mine."

She nodded. "You will." She drew a breath. "Open the gates."

For the second time she watched her people march away from the safety of the castle. It would be a scene repeated, she knew, until she herself rode through the gates, leaving behind the very old, the very young, the ill and infirm.

"It's a clear day," Larkin said from beside her. "They should reach the first base safely."

Saying nothing, Moira looked over to where Sinann stood, a child in her arms, another in her belly, one more at her skirts. "She never wept."

"She wouldn't send Phelan off with tears."

"They must be like a flood inside her, yet even now she won't let her children see them. If courage of heart is a weapon, Larkin, we'll sweep the enemy out of existence."

When she turned to go he fell into step with her. "There wasn't time," he began, "to speak with you before. Or after."

"Before the ceremony." Her voice was cool as the morning now. "After you invaded my private life."

"I didn't invade it. I was just there, at what was an awkward time for everyone involved. Cian and I resolved matters between us."

"Oh, did you?" Her eyebrows winged up as she spared him a glance. "Hardly surprising, as men will resolve matters between them one way or another."

"Don't take that royal tone with me." He took her arm, drew her toward one of the gardens, and more privacy. "How, I'm asking you, would you expect me to react when I've seen you've been with him?"

"I suppose expecting you to be well-mannered enough to excuse yourself is too much to ask."

"That's damn right. When I think a man of damn near eternal experiences seduces you—"

"It was the other way around. Entirely."

He flushed, scratched his head, turned a frustrated circle. "I don't want to know the details of it, if you don't mind. I've apologized to him."

"And to me?"

"What do you want from me, Moira? I love you."

"I expect you to understand I'm a woman grown, and one capable of making her own decisions about taking a lover. Don't wince at the term," she snapped impatiently. "I can rule, I can fight, I can die if need be, but your sensibilities are bruised at the thought I can have a lover?"

He thought it over. "Aye. But they'll get over it. I only want, more than anything, never to see you hurt. Not in battle, not in the heart. Is that enough?"

Her feathers smoothed out, and her heart softened as it always did with him. "It must be, as I want the same for you. Larkin, would you say that I have a good, strong mind?"

"Almost too much of both at times."

"In my mind, I know that I can't have a life with Cian. In my head I understand that what I've done will one day cause me grief and pain and sorrow. But in my heart I need what I can have with him now."

She brushed her fingers over the leaves of a flowering shrub. The leaves would fall, she thought, with the first frost. Many things would fall.

"When I put my head and heart together, I know, in both, that he and I are better for what we gave to each other. How can you love and turn away?"

"I don' t know."

She looked back toward the courtyard where people were once again going about their business, their routines. Life went on, she mused, whatever fell. They would see that life went on.

"Your sister watched her man ride away from her, and

knows she might never see him alive again. But she didn't weep in front of him, or in front of their children. When she weeps, she'll weep alone. They're her tears to shed. So will mine be, when this ends."

"Will you do something for me?"

"If I can."

He touched her cheek. "When you have tears, will you remember I have a shoulder for you?"

She smiled now. "I will."

When they parted, she went to the parlor where she found Blair and Glenna already discussing the day's schedule.

"Hoyt?" Moira asked as she poured herself tea.

"Hard at work. We had a slew of new weapons finished yesterday." Glenna rubbed tired eyes. "We'll be charming them twenty-four/seven. I'm going to work with some of those who'll be staying here when the rest of us leave. Basic precautions, defensive, offensive tutorials."

"I'll help you with that. And you, Blair?"

"As soon as Larkin's finished playing pimp, we're—"

"I'm sorry, what?"

"He's got a horny mare, and cleared it with Cian to have Vlad give her a bang. She doesn't even get dinner and drinks first. I thought he told you."

"No, we had other matters, and it must have slipped his mind. So he's having Cian's stallion stand as stud." Her smile came slowly. Yes, life went on. "That's a fine thing. Strong and hopeful—and damn clever, too, as he may be starting a brilliant line there. So, that's what he was about, knocking on Cian's door before sunrise."

"He figured if Cian gave the go-ahead, he could—Wait." Blair held up a hand. "Replay. How do you know he knocked on Cian's door before sunrise?"

"Because I was just leaving the room when Larkin arrived." Moira sipped her tea calmly while Blair slanted a look at Glenna, then puffed out her cheeks.

"Okay."

"Aren't you going to berate and damn Cian for seducing an innocent?"

Blair ran her tongue over her teeth. "You were in his room. I don't think luring you in there to look at his etchings is his style."

Moira slapped a hand to the table with satisfaction. "There! I knew a woman would have more sense—and a bit more respect for my own wiles. And you?" She lifted her eyebrows at Glenna. "Have you nothing to say about it?"

"You're both going to be hurt, and you both know it already. So I'll say I hope you're both able to give and take whatever happiness you can, while you can."

"Thanks."

"Are you all right?" Glenna asked. "The first time is often difficult or a little disappointing."

Now Moira smiled fully. "It was beautiful, and thrilling, and more than I imagined. Nothing I'd played through my mind was near the truth of it."

"A guy isn't good at it after a few hundred years' practice," Blair speculated. "He'd be hopeless. And Larkin walked in when . . . he must've flipped."

"He punched Cian in the face, but they've made it up now. As men do when they pound each other. We've agreed that my choice of bedmate is mine, and moved on."

There was a moment of unified silence as all three women rolled their eyes.

"There's little time left before we leave the safety of this place. And, we can hope, plenty of time after Samhain to debate my choices."

"Then I'll move on, too," Blair told her. "Larkin and I—after considerable browbeating by yours truly—are heading out in a couple of hours to see if we can wrangle ourselves some dragons. He's still not sold on the idea, but he's agreed we'll give it a shot."

"If it's possible, it would be a great advantage for us." Propping her chin on her fist, Moira turned it over in her mind. "I think we could cull out those we feel may not be as strong on the field. If they could ride . . . archers in the air."

"Flaming arrows," Blair said with a nod. "Their aim doesn't have to be on the money."

"As long as they don't shoot the home team," Glenna finished. "There isn't much time left to train, but it's worth the try."

"Fire, aye," Moira agreed. "It's a strong weapon—stronger yet coming from the air. A pity you can't charm the sun onto the tip of an arrow, Glenna, then this would be done."

"I'm going to see if I can move Larkin along." Blair got to her feet, hesitated. "You know, my first time, I was seventeen. The guy, he was in a hurry, and left me thinking at the end: So this is it? BFD. Something to be said for being initiated by someone who knows what he's doing, and has a sense of style."

"There is." Moira's smile was slow and satisfied. "There certainly is." She sensed Blair and Glenna exchange another look over her head, so continued to drink her tea as Blair left the room.

"Do you love him, Moira?"

"I think there's a part of me, inside me, that's waited all my life to feel what I feel for him. What my mother felt for my father in the short time they had. What I know you feel for Hoyt. Do you think I only imagine it's love because of what he is?"

"No, no, I don't. I have strong, genuine feelings for him myself. They have everything to do with who he is. But, Moira, you know you won't be able to have a life with him. That is because of what he is. What neither of you can change any more than the sun can fly on an arrow."

"I listened to everything he and Blair have told us about . . . we'll say his species." And read, Moira thought, countless volumes of fact and lore. "I know he'll never age. He'll be forever as he was in that moment before he was changed. Young and strong and vital. I will change. Grow old, frailer, gray and lined. I'll have sickness, and he never will."

She rose now to walk to a window and the slant of sunlight. "Even if he loved as I love, it's no life for either of us. He can't stand here as I am now and feel the sun warm on my face. All we'd have is the dark. He can't have children. So I won't be able to take away from this even that much of him. I might think, just a year together, or five, or ten. Just that much. I might think and wish for that," she murmured. "But however selfish my own needs might be, I have a duty."

She turned back. "He could never stay here, and I can never go."

"When I fell in love with Hoyt, and believed that we'd never be able to be together, it broke my heart every day."

"But still, you loved him."

"But still I loved him."

Moira stood with the sun slanting at her back, glinting on her crown. "Morrigan said this is the time of knowing. I know my life would be less if I didn't love him. The more life, the longer and harder we'll fight to keep it. So, I have another weapon inside me. And I'll use it."

Moira discovered a long day of teaching children and the old how to defend themselves and each other from monsters was more tiring than hours of sweaty physical training. She hadn't known how hard it would be to tell a child that monsters were real after all.

Her head ached from the questions, and her heart was bruised from the fear she'd seen.

She stepped out into the garden for some air, and to check the sky, again, for Larkin and Blair's return.

"They'll be back before sunset."

She whirled at the sound of Cian's voice. "What are you doing? It's still day."

"Shade's deep here this time of day." Still, he leaned back against the stones, well out of direct light. "It's a pretty spot, a quiet one. And sooner or later, you end up here for a few minutes."

"So, you've studied my habits."

"It passes the time."

"Glenna and I have been with the children and the old

ones, teaching them how to defend themselves if there's an attack here after we leave. We can't spare many of the able-bodied to hold the castle."

"The gates stay locked. Hoyt and Glenna will add a layer of protection. They'll be safe enough."

"And if we lose?"

"There'll be nothing they can do."

"I think there's always something, if you put choice and a weapon in someone's hands." She walked toward him. "Did you come here to wait for me?"

"Yes."

"Now that I'm here, what do you choose to do?"

He stayed where he was, but she could see the war inside him. Though the air suddenly seemed to lash and swirl with that battle, she stood calmly, her eyes grave and patient.

He took her with both hands, a quick and violent jerk that slammed her body to his. His mouth was ravenous.

"A fine choice," she managed when she could speak again.

Then his lips were assaulting hers again, stealing both breath and will.

"Do you know what you've let loose here?" he demanded. Before she could speak, he turned, gripped her hands to drag her up onto his back.

"Cian, what—"

"You'd better hold on," he ordered, interrupting her baffled laugh.

He leaped up. Her arms tightened around his neck as she gasped. He'd simply soared up, more than ten feet in the air from a stand, and was scaling the walls.

"What are you doing?" She risked a look down, felt her stomach shudder at the drop. "You could have warned me you'd lost your bloody mind."

"I lost it when you walked into my room last night." Now he swung through the window, flicked the drapes shut behind him and plunged them into the dark. "This is the price you pay for it."

"If you'd wanted to come back inside, there are doors—"

She let out a quick cry of alarm when he swooped her up. It felt as though she was flying through the air, blind in the dark. Her next cry was of stunned excitement as she found herself under him on the bed, and his hands tugged aside clothes to take flesh.

"Wait. Wait. I can't think. I can't see."

"Too late for both." His mouth silenced her, and his hands drove her to a hard, violent crest.

Her body strained beneath his, and he knew she was reaching, reaching for the burning tip of that crest. Her breath sobbed against his lips as she reached it, and her body went limp.

He gripped her wrists in his hand, pulling her arms over her head. She was one long line of surrender now, and he sheathed himself in her.

She would have cried out again, but she had no voice. No sight, and with her hands captured, no hold. She could do nothing but feel as he plunged himself into her, battering her body with dark, desperate pleasure until she was writhing, then rising, then recklessly matching him beat for violent beat.

This time the hot tip of the crest shattered her.

She lay, scorched skin over melted bones, unable to move even when he left her to light the fire and candles.

"Choice isn't always an issue," he said, and she thought she heard liquid being poured into a cup. "Nor is it a weapon."

She felt the cup bump against her hand, and managed to open her heavy eyes. She made some sound, took the cup, but wasn't at all sure she could swallow any water.

Then she saw the raw red burn on his hand. She pushed up quickly, nearly sloshing water over the rim. "You've burned yourself. Let me see. I—" And she did see, that the mark was the shape of a cross.

"I would have taken it off." Hurriedly, she pushed the cross and chain under her bodice.

"Small price to pay." He lifted her wrist, noted the faint bruising. "I have less control with you than I'd like."

"I like that you have less. Give me your hand. I have a little skill with healing."

"It's nothing."

"Then give me your hand. It's good practice for me." She held hers out expectantly. After a moment he sat beside her, laid his hand in hers.

"I like that you have less," she said again, drawing his eyes to hers. "I like knowing I can be wanted that much, that there's something in me that pulls something in you enough that something strains, nearly snaps."

"Dangerous enough when you're dealing with a human. When a vampire's control snaps, things die."

"You'd never hurt me. You love me."

His face went carefully blank. "Sex rarely has anything to do with—"

"Being inexperienced doesn't make me stupid, or gullible. Is it better?"

"What?"

She smiled at him. "Your hand. The redness has eased."

"It's fine." He drew it away. In fact there was no longer any burning. "You learn quickly."

"I do. Learning is a passion for me. I'll tell you what I've learned of you, when it comes to me. You love me." Her lips were softly curved as she brushed at his hair. "You might have taken me last night—in fact you would have, with less resistance—if it had been just for sex. If it had been only need, only sex, you wouldn't have taken me with such care, or trusted me enough to sleep awhile with me."

She held up a finger before he could speak. "There's more."

"With you, there tends to be."

She rose, straightening her clothes. "When Larkin came in, you did nothing to stop him from striking you. You love me, so you were guilty about taking what you saw as my innocence. You love me, so you've watched me enough to know one of my favorite places. You waited for me there, then you brought me here because you needed me. I pull at you, Cian, as you pull at me."

She watched him as she sipped water. "You love me, as I love you."

"To your peril."

"And yours," she said with a nod. "We live in perilous times."

"Moira, this can never—"

"Don't tell me never." Passion vibrated in her voice and turned her eyes to hellsmoke. "I know. I know all about never. Tell me today. Between you and me let it be today. I have to fight for tomorrow, and the day after and into always. But with this, with you, it's just today. Every today we can have."

"Don't cry. I'd rather have the burn than the tears."

"I won't." She shut her eyes for a moment, and willed herself to keep her word. "I want you to tell me what you've shown me. I want you to tell me what I see when you look at me."

"I love you." He came to her, gently touched her face with his fingertips. "This face, those eyes, all that's inside them. I love you. In a thousand years I've never loved another."

She took his hand, pressed her lips to it. "Oh! Look. There's no burn now. Love healed you. The strongest magic."

"Moira." He kept her hand in his, then laid hers against his chest. "If it beat, it would beat for you."

Tears stung her eyes again. "Your heart may be still, but it isn't empty. It isn't silent because it speaks to me."

"And that's enough?"

"Nothing will ever be enough, but it will do. Come, we'll—"

She broke off when she heard shouting from outside. Turning, she rushed to the window, drew back one of the drapes. Her hand went to her throat. "Cian, come look. The sun's low enough. Come look."

The sky was full of dragons. Emerald and ruby and

gold, their sleek bodies soared above the castle like flashing jewels in the softening light. And their trumpeting calls were like a song.

"Have you ever seen anything so beautiful?"

When his hand laid on her shoulder, Moira reached up, clasped it. "Listen how the people cheer them. Look at the children running and laughing. It's the sound of hope, Cian. The sound, the sight."

"Getting them here, and getting them to be ridden, and to respond in battle like warhorses, two different matters, Moira. But yes, it's a beautiful sight, and a hopeful sound."

She watched as they began to land. "In all your years, I imagine there's little you haven't done."

"Little," he agreed, then had to smile. "But no, I've never ridden a dragon. And yeah, damn right I want to. Let's go down."

There was still enough sunlight that he needed the bloody cloak in open spaces. But despite it, Cian discovered he could still be enchanted and surprised—when he looked into a young dragon's golden eye.

Their sinuous bodies were covered in large, jewel-toned scales that were smooth as glass to the touch. Their wings were like gossamer, and kept close into the body when they grazed along the ground. But it was the eyes that captivated him. They seemed to be alive with interest and intelligence, even humor.

"Figured the younger ones would be easier to train," Blair said to him as they stood, watching. "Larkin's best at communicating with them, even in his regular form. They trust him."

"Which is making it harder on him to use them in battle."

"Yeah, my guy's a softie, and we went around and around about it. He was hoping to convince everyone we could use them for transportation only. But they could make a hell of a difference on the field. Or above it. Still, I have to admit, I get a little twinge at the idea myself."

"They're beautiful—and unspoiled."

"We're going to change the second part." Blair let out a sigh. "Everything's a weapon," she murmured. "Anyway, want to go up?"

"Bet your ass."

"First flight's with me. Yeah, yeah," she said when she saw the objection on his face. "You pilot your own plane, ride horses, leap tall buildings in a single bound. But you've never ridden a dragon, so you're not going solo yet."

She walked slowly toward one of ruby and silver. She'd ridden it back, and still held out her hand so it would test her scent. "Go ahead, let her get acquainted."

"Her?"

"Yeah, I checked out the plumbing." Blair grinned. "Couldn't help it."

Cian laid his hand on the dragon's side, worked his way slowly to the head. "Well now, aren't you a gorgeous one." He began to murmur to her in Irish. She responded with what could only be termed a flirtatious swish of her tail.

"Hoyt's got the same way with them you do." Blair nodded toward where Hoyt was stroking sapphire scales. "Must be a family trait."

"Hmm. Now why is it that Her Majesty there is mounting one by herself?"

"She's ridden a dragon before. That is, she's ridden Larkin in dragon form, so she knows the ropes. Not all she's riding lately."

"Beg your pardon?"

"Just saying. You two look a lot more relaxed than either of you did yesterday." She gave him a wide, toothy grin, then swung onto the dragon. "Alley-oop."

He mounted the same way he'd scaled the walls. With an easy and fluid leap. "Sturdy," Cian commented. "More comfortable than they look. Not so very different from horseback all in all."

"Yeah, if you're talking Pegasus. Anyway, you don't give them a little kick like a horse or cluck. You just—"

Blair demonstrated by leaning down on the dragon's

neck, gliding a hand over its throat. With a sound like silk billowing, it spread its wings. And it rose up into the sky.

"Live long enough," Cian said behind Blair, "you do every damn thing."

"This has got to be one of the best. There are still logistics. The care and feeding, dragon poop."

"I bet it'll make the roses bloom."

She threw back her head and laughed. "Could be. We've got to train them, and their riders. But these beauties catch on fast. Watch." She leaned to the right, and the dragon swerved gently to follow her direction.

"A bit like riding a motorcycle."

"Some of that principle. Lean into the turns. Look at Larkin. That showoff."

He was riding a huge gold, and doing fancy loops and turns.

"Sun's nearly set," Cian commented. "Give it a few minutes, so I won't fry, and we'll give him a run for his money."

Blair shot a look over her shoulder. "You got it. Going to say something."

"When did you not?"

"She's carrying the weight of the fricking world. If what you two have going lightens that a little, I'm for it. Being with Larkin shifted some of mine, so I hope it's working for the two of you."

"You surprise me, demon hunter."

"I surprise myself, vampire, but there it is. Sun's down. You ready to rock?"

With enormous relief, he shoved back the hood of the cloak. "Let's show your cowboy some real moves."

Chapter 12

Davey had been Lilith's for nearly five years. She'd slaughtered his parents and younger sister one balmy summer night in Jamaica. The off-season vacation package—airfare, hotel and continental breakfast included—had been a surprise thirtieth birthday gift from Davey's father to his wife. Their first night there, giddy with holiday spirit and the complimentary glasses of rum punch, they had conceived a third child.

They were, of course, unaware of this, and had things gone differently the prospect of a new baby would have put the skids on tropical vacations for some time to come.

As it was, it was their last family holiday.

It had been during one of Lilith's brief and passionate estrangements from Lora. She'd chosen Jamaica on a whim, and entertained herself picking off locals and the occasional tourist. But she'd grown tired of the taste of the men who trolled the bars.

She wanted some variety—something a little fresher and sweeter. She found just what she was looking for with the young family.

She'd ended the mother's and little girl's giggling moonlight walk along the beach swiftly and viciously. Still she'd been impressed with the woman's panicked and ineffectual struggle, and her instinctive move to protect the child. As they'd satisfied her hunger, she might have left the man and boy splashing unaware in the surf down the beach. But she'd wanted to see if the father would fight for the son. Or beg, as the mother had begged.

He had—and had screamed at the boy to run. Run, Davey, run! he'd shouted. And his terror for his son enriched his blood to make the kill all the sweeter.

But the boy hadn't run. He'd fought, too, and that had impressed her more. He'd kicked and he'd bitten, and had even tried to leap on her back to save his father. It was the wildness of his attack combined with his angelic face that had decided her on changing him rather than draining him and moving on.

When she had pressed his mouth to her bleeding breast, she had felt something stirring inside her that had never stirred for another. The almost maternal sensation had fascinated and delighted her.

So Davey became her pet, her toy, her son, her lover.

It pleased her how quickly, how naturally he'd taken to the change. When she and Lora had reconciled, as they always did, Lilith had told her Davey was their vampiric Peter Pan. The little boy, eternally six.

Still like any boy of six, he needed to be tended to, entertained, taught. Only more so, in Lilith's opinion, as her Davey was a prince. As such, he had both great privilege, and great duty.

She considered this specific hunt to be both.

He quivered with excitement as she dressed him in the rough clothes of a peasant boy. It made her laugh to see his eyes so bright as she added to the game by smearing some dirt and blood on his face.

"Can I see? Can I look in your magic mirror and see myself? Please, please!"

"Of course." Lilith sent a quick and amused look toward

Lora—adult to adult. Picking up the game, Lora shuddered as she picked up the treasured mirror.

"You look terrifying," Lora told Davey. "So small and weak. And . . . *human*!"

Carefully taking the mirror, Davey stared at his reflection. And bared his fangs. "It's like a costume," he said, and giggled. "I get to kill one all by myself, right, Mama? All by myself."

"We'll see." Lilith took the mirror, and bent down to kiss his filthy cheek. "You have a very important part to play, my darling. The most important part of all."

"I know just what to do." He bounced up and down on his toes. "I practiced and practiced."

"I know. You've worked very hard. You're going to make me so proud."

She put the mirror aside, facedown, forcing herself not to take a peek at herself. Lora's burns were still raw and pink, and her reflection so distressing that Lilith only looked into the charmed mirror when Lora was out of the room.

At the knock at the door, she turned. "That will be Midir. Let him in, Davey, then go out and wait with Lucian."

"We're going soon?"

"Yes. In just a few minutes."

He raced to the door, then stood, shoulders straight while the sorcerer bowed to him. Davey marched out, her little soldier, leaving Midir to shut the door behind him.

"Your Majesty. My lady."

"Rise." Lilith gave a careless wave of the hand. "As you see, the prince is prepared. Are you?"

He stood, his habitual black robes whispering with the movement. His face was hard and handsome, framed by his flowing mane of silver hair. Eyes, rich and black, met Lilith's cool blue.

"He will be protected." Midir glanced toward the large chest at the foot of the bed, and the silver pot that stood opened on it. "You used the potion, as I instructed."

"I did, and it's your life, Midir, if it fails."

"It will not fail. It, and the chant I will use, will shield him from wood and steel for three hours. He will be as safe as he would be in your arms, Majesty."

"If not, I'll kill you myself, as unpleasantly as possible. And to make certain of it, you'll go with us on this hunt."

She saw, for just a moment, both surprise and annoyance on his face. Then he bowed his head, and spoke meekly. "At your command."

"Yes. Report to Lucius. He'll see you mounted." She turned away in dismissal.

"You shouldn't worry." Lora crossed to Lilith, slipped her arms around her. "Midir knows it's his life if any harm comes to our sweet boy. Davey needs this, Lilith. He needs the exercise, the entertainment. And he needs to show off a bit."

"I know, I know. He's restless and bored. I can't blame him. It'll be fine, just fine," she said as much to assure herself. "I'll be right there with him."

"Let me go. Change your mind and let me go with you."

Lilith shook her head, brushed a kiss over Lora's abused cheek. "You're not ready for a hunt. You're still weak, sweetheart, and I won't risk you." She took Lora's arms, gripped tight. "I need you on Samhain—fighting, killing, gorging. On that night, when we've flooded that valley with blood, taken what's ours by right, I want you and Davey at my side."

"I hate the wait almost as much as Davey."

Lilith smiled. "I'll bring you back a present from tonight's little game."

Davey rode pinion with Lilith through the moonstruck night. He'd wanted to ride his own pony, but his mama had explained that it wasn't fast enough. He liked going fast, feeling the wind, flying toward the hunt and the kill. It was the most exciting night he could remember.

It was even better than the present she'd given him on

his third birthday when she'd taken him through the summer night to a Boy Scout camping ground. And that had been such *fun*! The screaming and the running and the crying. The *chomp, chomp, chomp*ing.

It was better than hunting the humans in the caves, or burning a vampire who'd been bad. It was better than anything he could remember.

His memories of his human family were vague. There were times he woke from a dream and for a moment was in a bedroom with pictures of race cars on the walls and blue curtains at the windows. There were monsters in the closet of the bedroom, and he cried until she came.

She had brown hair and brown eyes.

Sometimes he would come in, too, the tall man with the scratchy face. He'd chase the monsters away, and she would sit and stroke his hair until he fell asleep again.

If he tried very hard, he could remember splashing in the water, and the feel of the wet sand going gooshy under his feet and the man laughing as the waves splashed them.

Then he wasn't laughing, he was screaming. And he was shouting: Run! Run, Davey, run!

But he didn't try very hard, very often.

It was more fun to think about hunting and playing. His mother let him have one of the humans for a toy, if he was very, very good. He liked best the way they smelled when they were afraid, and the sounds they made when he started to feed.

He was a prince, and could do anything he wanted. Almost.

He would show his mother tonight that he was a big boy now. Then there would be no more almost.

When they stopped the horses, he was almost sick with the thrill of what was to come. They would go on foot from here—and then it would be his turn. His mother held tight to his hand, and he *wished* she wouldn't. He wanted to march like Lucius and the other soldiers. He wanted to carry a sword instead of the little dagger hidden under his tunic.

Still, it was fun to go so fast, faster than any human, across the fields toward the farm.

They stopped again, and his mother crouched down to him to take his face in her hands. "Do just the way we practiced, my sweet boy. You'll be wonderful. I'll be very close, every minute."

He puffed out his chest. "I'm not afraid of them. They're just food."

Behind him Lucius chuckled. "He may be small, Your Majesty, but he's a warrior to the bone."

She rose, and her hand stayed on Davey's shoulder as she turned to Midir. "Your life," she said quietly. "Begin."

Spreading his arms in the black robes, Midir began his chant.

Lilith gestured so that the men spread out. Then she, Lucius and Davey moved closer to the farm.

One of the windows showed the flickering glow of a fire banked for the night. There was the smell of horses closed inside the stable, and the first hints of human. It stirred hunger and excitement in Davey's belly.

"Be ready," she told Lucius.

"My lady, I would give my life for the prince."

"Yes, I know." She laid a hand briefly on Lucius's arm. "That's why you're here. All right, Davey. Make me proud."

Inside the farmhouse, Tynan and two others stood guard. It was nearly time to wake their relief, and he was more than ready for a few hours' sleep. His hip ached from the wound he'd suffered during the attack on their first day's march. He hoped when he was able to close his gritty eyes he wouldn't see the attack again.

Good men lost, he thought. Slaughtered.

The time was coming when he would avenge those men on the battlefield. He only hoped that if he died there, he fought strong and brave first and destroyed a like number of the enemy.

He shifted his stance, preparing to order the relief watch when a sound brought his hand to the hilt of his sword.

His eyes sharpened; his ears pricked. It might have been a night bird, but it had sounded so human.

"Tynan."

"Yes, I hear it," he said to one of the others on guard.

"It sounds like weeping."

"Stay alert. No one is to . . ." He trailed off as he spotted a movement. "There, near the northmost paddock. Do you see? Ah, in the name of all the gods, it's a child."

A boy, he thought, though he couldn't be sure. The clothes covering him were torn and bloody, and he staggered, weeping, with his thumb plugged into his mouth.

"He must have escaped some raid near here. Wake the relief, and stay alert with them. I'll go get the child."

"We were warned not to step outside after sundown."

"We can't leave a child out there, and hurt by the look of him. Wake the relief," Tynan repeated. "I want an archer by this window. If anything out there moves but me and that child, aim for its heart."

He waited until the men were set, and watched the child fall to the ground. A boy, he was nearly sure now, and the poor thing wailed and whimpered pitifully as it curled into a ball.

"We could keep an eye on him until morning," one of the others on duty suggested.

"Are Geallian men so frightened of the dark they'd huddle inside while a child bleeds and cries?"

He shoved the door open. He wanted to move quickly, get the child inside to safety. But he forced himself to stop his forward rush when the boy's head came up and the round little face froze in fear.

"I won't hurt you. I'm one of the queen's men. I'll take you inside," he said gently. "It's warm, and there's food."

The boy scrambled to his feet and screamed as if Tynan had hacked him with a sword. "Monsters! Monsters!"

He began to run, limping heavily on his left leg. Tynan dashed after him. Better to scare the boy than to let him get away and very likely be a snack for some demon. Tynan caught him just before the boy managed to scramble over the stone wall bordering the near field.

"Easy, easy, you're safe." The boy kicked and slapped and screamed, shooting fresh pain into Tynan's hip. "You need to be inside. No one's going to hurt you now. No one . . ."

He thought he heard something—chanting—and tightened his grip on the child. He turned, ready to sprint back for the house when he heard something else, something that came from what he held in his arms. It was a low, feral growl.

The boy grinned, horribly, and went for his throat.

There was something beyond agony, and it took Tynan to his knees. Not a child, not a child at all, he thought as he fought to free himself. But the thing ripped at him like a wolf.

Dimly he heard shouts, screams, the thud of arrows, the clash of swords. And the last he heard was the hideous sound of his own blood being greedily drunk.

They used fire, tipping arrows with flame, and still, nearly a quarter of their number were killed or wounded before the demons fell back.

"Take that one alive." Lilith delicately wiped blood from her lips. "I promised Lora a gift." She smiled down at Davey who stood over the body of the soldier he'd killed. It swelled pride in her that her boy had continued to feed even when troops had dragged the body, with the prince clinging to it, away from the battle.

Davey's eyes were red and gleaming, and his freckles stood out like gold against the rosy flush the blood had given his cheeks.

She picked him up, held him high over her head. "Behold your prince!"

The troops who hadn't been destroyed in the brief battle knelt.

She lowered him to kiss him long and deep on his mouth.

"I want more," he said.

"Yes, my love, and you'll have more. Very soon. Toss that thing on a horse," she ordered with a careless gesture toward Tynan's body. "I have a use for it."

She mounted, then held out her arms so that Davey could leap into them. With her cheek rubbing against his hair, she looked down at Midir.

"You did well," she said to him. "You can have your choice of the humans, for whatever purposes you like."

The moonlight shone on his silver hair as he bowed. "Thank you."

Moira stood in the brisk wind and watched dragons and riders circle overhead. It was a stunning sight, she thought, and would have sent her heart soaring under any other circumstances. But these were military maneuvers, not spectacle.

Still, she could hear children calling out and clapping, and more than a few of them pretending they were dragon or rider.

She smiled a greeting when her uncle strode over to watch beside her. "You're not tempted to fly?" she asked him.

"I leave it for the young—and the agile. It's a brilliant sight, Moira. And a hopeful one."

"The dragons have lifted the spirits. And in battle, they'll give us an advantage. Do you see Blair? She rides as if she was born on the back of one."

"She's hard to miss," Riddock murmured as Blair drove her mount toward the ground at a dizzying speed, then swept up again.

"Are you pleased she and Larkin will marry?"

"He loves her, and I can think of no other who suits him so well. So aye, his mother and I are pleased. And will miss him every day. He must go with her," Riddock said before Moira could speak. "It's his choice, and I feel—in my heart—it's the right choice for him. But we'll miss him."

Moira leaned her head against her uncle's arm. "Aye, we will."

She would be the only one to remain, she thought as she went inside again. The only one of the first circle who would remain in Geall after Samhain. She wondered how she would be able to bear it.

Already the castle felt empty. So many had already gone ahead, and others were busy with duties she'd assigned. Soon, very soon, she would leave herself. So it was time, she determined, to write down her wishes in the event she didn't return.

She closed herself in her sitting room and sat to sharpen her quill. Then changed her mind and took out one of the treasures she'd brought back with her from Ireland.

She would write this document, Moira determined, with the instrument of another world.

She'd use a pen.

What did she have of value, she wondered, that wouldn't by rights belong to the next who ruled Geall?

Some of her mother's jewelry, certainly. And this she began to disburse in her mind between Blair and Glenna, her aunt and cousin, and lastly, her ladies.

Her father's sword should be Larkin's, she decided, and the dagger he'd once carried would go to Hoyt. The miniature of her father would be her uncle's if she died before him, as her father and uncle had been fast friends.

There were trinkets, of course. Bits of this and that which she gave thought to bequesting.

To Cian she left her bow and quiver, and the arrows she'd made with her own hand. She hoped he'd understand that these were more than weapons to her. They were her pride, and a kind of love.

She wrote it all carefully, sealed it. She would give the document to her aunt for safekeeping.

She felt better having done it. Lighter and clearer in her mind somehow. Setting the paper aside, she rose to face the next task. Moving back into the bedroom, she crossed to the balcony doors. The drapes still hung there, blocking the light, the view. And now she drew them back, let the soft light spill through.

In her mind's eye she saw it again, the dark, the blood, the torn body of her mother and the things that mutilated her. But now she opened the door and made herself walk through them.

The air was cool and moist, and overhead the sky was full of dragons. Streaks and whirls of color riding the pale blue. How her mother would have loved the sight of them, loved the sound of the wings, the laughter of the children in the courtyard below.

Moira walked to the rail, laid her hands on it and felt the sturdy stone. And standing as her mother had often done, she looked out over Geall, and swore to do her best.

She might have been surprised to know that Cian spent a large portion of his restless day doing what she had done. His lists of bequests and instructions were considerably longer than hers and minutely more detailed. But then he'd lived considerably longer and had accumulated a great deal.

He saw no reason for any of it to go to waste.

A dozen times during the writing of it he cursed the quill and wished violently for the ease and convenience of a computer. But he kept at it until he believed he'd spread his holdings out satisfactorily.

He wasn't certain it could all be done as some of it would be up to Hoyt. They'd speak about it, Cian thought. If he could count on anything, he could count on Hoyt doing everything in his considerable power to fulfill the obligation Cian meant to give him.

All in all, he hoped it wouldn't be necessary. A thousand years of existence didn't mean he was ready to give it up. And he damn well didn't intend to go to hell until he'd sent Lilith there before him.

"You were always one for business."

He pushed to his feet, drawing his dagger in one fluid motion as he turned toward the sound of the voice. Then the dagger simply fell out of his limp fingers.

Even after a millennium, there can be shocks beyond imagining.

"Nola." His voice sounded rusty on the name.

She was a child, his sister, just as she'd been when he'd last seen her. Her long dark hair falling straight, her eyes deep and blue. And smiling.

"Nola," he said again. "My God."

"I thought you would say you have no god."

"None that would claim me. How can you be here? Are you here?"

"You can see for yourself." She spread her arms, then did a little turn.

"You lived, and you died. An old woman."

"You didn't know the woman, so I'm as you remember me. I missed you, Cian. I looked for you, even knowing better. For years I looked and I hoped for you and for Hoyt. You never came."

"How could I? You know what I was. Am. You understand that now."

"Would you have hurt me? Or any of us?"

"I don't know. I hope not, but I didn't see any reason to risk it. Why are you here?"

He reached out, but she held up her hand and she shook her head. "I'm not flesh. Only an apparition. Here to remind you that you may not be what you were when you were mine, but you're not what she would have made you."

Because he needed a moment, he bent to pick up the dagger he'd dropped, then sheathed it again. "What does it matter?"

"It does. It will." And apparition or not, her eyes swam as they locked on his. "I had children, Cian."

"I know."

"Strong, skilled, gifted. Your blood, too."

"Were you happy?"

"Oh, aye. I loved a man, and he loved me. We had those children, and lived a good life. And still my brothers left a place in my heart I could never fill. A little ache inside.

I would see you, and Hoyt, sometimes. In the water, or the mist, or the fire."

"There are things I've done I wouldn't have you see."

"I saw you kill, and feed. I saw you hunt humans as you'd once hunted deer. And I saw you stand by my grave in the moonlight and lay flowers on it. I saw you fight beside the brother we both love. I saw my Cian. Do you remember how you'd pull me up on your horse and ride and ride?"

"Nola." He rubbed his fingers over his brow. He hurt too much to think of it. "We're both dead."

"And we both lived. She came to my window one night."

"She? Who?" Inside him, he went cold as winter. "Lilith."

"We're both dead," Nola reminded him. "But your hands go to fists and your eyes go sharp as your dagger. Would you still protect me?"

He walked to the fire, kicked idly at the simmering turf. "What happened?"

"It was more than two years after Hoyt left us. Father had died and mother was ill. I knew she would never be strong again, that she would die. I was so sad, so afraid. I woke from sleep in the dark, and there was a face at my window. So beautiful. Golden hair and a sweet smile. She whispered to me, called me by name. 'Ask me in,' she said, and promised me a treat."

Nola tossed back her hair, and her face was full of disdain. "She thought since I was only a girl, the youngest of us, I'd be foolish, I'd be easy to trick. I went to the window, and I looked in her eyes. There's power in her eyes."

"Hoyt must have told you not to take such risks. He must have—"

"He wasn't there, and neither were you. There was power in me as well. Have you forgotten?"

"No. But you were a child."

"I was a seer, and the blood of demon hunters was in my veins. I looked in her eyes and I told her it was my blood who would end her. My blood who would rid the worlds of her. And for her there would be no eternity in hell, or anywhere. Her damnation would be an end of all. She would be dust, and no spirit would survive."

"She wouldn't have been pleased."

"Her beauty remains even when she shows her true self. That's another power. I held up Morrigan's cross, that I wore always around my neck. The light flashed from it, like a sunbeam. She was screaming when she ran."

"You were always fearless," he murmured.

"She never came back while I lived, and never came again until you and Hoyt went home together. You're stronger than you were without him, and he with you. She fears that, hates that. Envies that."

"Will he live through this?"

"I can't know. But if he falls, it will be as he lived. With honor."

"Honor's cold comfort when you're in the ground."

"Then why do you hold your own?" she demanded with a whip of impatience in her voice. "It's honor that brings you here. Honor that you'll carry into battle along with your sword. She couldn't drain it out of you, and just the little she left was enough for you to draw on again. You made this choice. You've still more to make. Remember me."

"Don't. Don't leave."

"Remember me," she repeated. "Until we see each other again."

Alone, he sat, lowering his head into his hands. And remembered far too much.

Chapter 13

For the most part, Cian avoided the tower room where Hoyt and Glenna worked their magicks. Such things often involved considerable light, flashes, fire and other elements unfavorable to vampires.

But in a way he hadn't—or hadn't admitted to in centuries—he needed his brother.

He noted before he knocked that one or both of his magically inclined relations had taken the precaution of drawing protection symbols on the tower door to keep the curious out. He'd have preferred to stay out himself, but he knocked.

When Glenna answered, there was a dew of sweat on her skin. Her hair was bundled up, and she'd stripped down to a tank and cotton pants. Cian lifted a brow.

"Am I interrupting?"

"Nothing physical, unfortunately. It's just viciously hot in here. We're working on a lot of heat and fire magicks. Sorry."

"I'm not bothered much by temperature extremes."

"Oh. Right." She closed the door behind him. "We've

got the windows blocked off—keeping everything contained—so you won't have to worry about the light."

"It's nearly sundown."

He looked over to where Hoyt stood over an enormous copper trough. Hoyt had his hands spread above it, and there was a sensation, even across the room, of more heat, of power and energy.

"He's fire-charging weapons," Glenna explained. "And I've been working on, well, it's a kind of bomb, really. Something we may be able to drop from the air."

"The NSO would love to have you on staff."

"I could be their version of Q." She swiped at her damp brow with the back of her hand. "You want a tour?"

"Actually . . . I wanted to . . . I'll just speak with Hoyt when he's not so involved."

"Wait." It was the first time Glenna could remember seeing Cian flustered. No, not flustered, she thought. Upset. "He needs a break. So do I. If you can stand the heat, just hang out a few more minutes. He's nearly done. I'm going to go get some air."

Cian caught her hand before she turned to go. "Thank you. For not asking."

"No problem. And if it is a problem, I'll be around."

When she went out, Cian leaned against the door. Hoyt remained just as he'd been, hands spread over the silver smoke that rose from the trough. His eyes were darkened as they were when he held his power strong and steady.

It had always been so, Cian thought, since they were children.

Like Glenna, Hoyt had stripped down for work, and wore a white T-shirt and faded jeans. It was odd, even after the past months, to see his brother in twenty-first-century clothing.

Hoyt had never been one for fashion, Cian recalled. But for dignity and purpose. However much they looked alike, they'd approached life from different poles. Hoyt for solitude and study, and he himself for society and business—and the pleasure both brought him.

Still, they'd been close, had understood each other on a level few others could. Had loved each other, Cian thought now, in a way that was as strong and as steady as Hoyt's power.

Then the world, and everything in it, had changed.

So what was he doing here? Looking for answers, for comfort, when he knew there could be neither? None of it could be taken back, not a single act, a single thought, a single moment. It was a foolish waste of time and energy on all counts.

The man who stood like a statue in the smoke wasn't the man he'd known, any more than he was the same man he'd been. Or a man at all for that matter.

Too much time spent with these people, these feelings, these needs made him forget what could never be altered. He pushed away from the door.

"Wait. A moment more."

Hoyt's voice stopped him—and it irritated him to understand Hoyt had known he wasn't simply shifting position but leaving.

Hoyt lowered his hands, and the smoke whisked away.

"Sure we'll go into this well-armed." Hoyt reached into the trough and lifted a sword by the hilt. Spinning, he pointed it toward the hearth. And shot a beam of fire.

"Will you be using one of these?" Hoyt turned the sword in his hand, eying its edge. "You've skill enough not to burn yourself."

"I'll use whatever comes best to hand—and do my best to stay away from those you arm who are considerably less skilled."

"It's not worry over poor swordsmanship that brings you here."

"No."

Since he was here, he'd do what he'd come to do. But he wandered the room first while Hoyt removed the other weapons from the trough. The room smelled of herbs and smoke, of sweat and effort.

"I've chased your woman away."

"I'll find her again."

"Since she's not here, I'll ask you. Are you afraid you'll lose her in this?"

Hoyt laid the last sword on the worktable. "It's my last thought before sleep, my first on waking. The rest of the time I try not to think of it—or let out the part of myself that wants to lock her away safe until this is over."

"She isn't a woman you could lock away, even with your skill."

"No, but knowing that doesn't stop the fear. Are you afraid for Moira?"

"What?"

"Do you think I don't know you're with her? That your heart is with her?"

"A temporary madness. It'll pass." At his brother's quiet, steady look, Cian shook his head. "I've no choice in it, and neither does she. What I am doesn't run to white picket fences and golden retrievers." He waved it away when Hoyt's look turned puzzled. "To home and hearth, brother. I can't give her a life—if I wanted to—and what passes for mine will go on long after hers is ended. And that's not what I've come to tell you."

"Tell me this first. Do you love her?"

It came into him, the truth of it, swirling through his heart and into his eyes. "She is . . . She is like a light for me when I've lived eternally in the dark. But the dark is mine, Hoyt. I know how to survive there, to be content and productive and entertained there."

"You don't say happy."

Frustration snapped into his voice. "I was happy enough before you came. Before you changed everything again, as surely as Lilith had done to me. What would you have me do? Wish for what you have, and will have with Glenna if you live? What good will it do me? Will it start my heart again? Can your magic do that?"

"No. I've found nothing that can take you back. But—"

"Let it be. I am what I am, and I've done more than well enough. I'm not whining about it. She's an experience.

Love is an experience, and I've always sought them out." He dragged his hands through his hair. "Christ. Is there anything to drink in this place?"

"There's whiskey." Hoyt lifted his chin toward a cabinet. "I'll have one as well."

Cian poured whiskey generously into cups, then crossed to where Hoyt drew two three-legged stools together. So Cian sat, and they drank for a few moments in silence.

"I've written out a document, a kind of will, should my luck run out on Samhain."

Hoyt lifted his eyes from his whiskey and met Cian's. "I see."

"I've accumulated considerable property and holdings, assets, personal items. I expect you'll see to them, as I've instructed."

"I will, of course."

"It'll be no small task as they're spread out over the world. I don't keep a great many eggs in one basket. There are passports and other identification papers in the New York apartment, and in safety deposit boxes here and there. If any are useful to you, you're welcome to them."

"Thanks for that."

Cian swirled the whiskey in his glass, kept his eyes on it. "There are some things I'd like Moira to have, if you can get them here."

"I'll get them here."

"I thought to leave the club and the apartment in New York to Blair—and to Larkin. I think they'd suit them better than you."

"They would. They'll be grateful, I'm sure."

Annoyance rose up at his brother's easy and practical tone. "Well, don't let sentiment choke you, as it's more likely I'll be holding a wake for you than you for me."

Hoyt angled his head. "Do you think so?"

"I damn well do. You haven't had three decades and I've had near a hundred. And you never were as good in a fight as me when we were both alive, however many tricks you have up your sleeve."

"But then again, as you said, we aren't what we were, are we?" Hoyt smiled pleasantly. "I'm determined we'll both come through this, but if you fall, well . . . I'll lift a glass to you."

Cian let out a half laugh as Hoyt did just that.

"And would you be wanting pipes and drums as well?"

"Oh, bugger it." Now a wicked gleam came into Cian's eyes. "I'll toss in some fifes for yours, then console your grieving widow."

"At least I won't have to dig a hole for you, seeing as you'll just be dust, but I'll show you the honor of having a stone carved. 'Here doesn't lie Cian, for he's blown off with the wind. He lived and he died, then stayed on like the last annoying guest to leave the ball.' Does that suit you?"

"I'm thinking I'll go back and change some of those bequests, for principle only, seeing as I'll be singing 'Danny Boy' over your grave."

"What's 'Danny Boy'?"

"A cliche." Cian picked up the bottle he'd set on the floor and poured more whiskey into the cups. "I saw Nola."

"What?" Hoyt lowered the cup he'd just lifted. "What did you say?"

"In my room. I saw Nola, spoke with her."

"You dreamed of Nola?"

"Is that what I said?" Cian snapped. "I said I saw her, spoke with her. As awake then as I am now, looking and speaking to you. She was still a child. Jesus, there isn't enough whiskey in the world for this."

"She came to you," Hoyt murmured. "Our Nola. What did she say?"

"She loved me, and you. She missed us. She'd waited for us to come home. Damn it. Goddamn it." He pushed up to pace. "She was a child, exactly as she'd been the last I saw her. It was a lie, of course. She'd grown up, grown old. She'd died and gone to dust."

"And why would she come to you as a grown woman, or an old one?" Hoyt demanded. "She came to you as you remembered her, as you think of her. She gave you a gift. Why are you angry?"

It was fury in him now, fury to wrap tight around the pain. "How can you know what it is to feel this, to have it ripping inside you? She looked the same, and I'm not. She talked of how I'd swing her up on my horse and take her riding. And it was like it was yesterday. I can't have those yesterdays in my head and stay sane."

He turned back. "At the end of this, you'll know you did what you could, what was asked of you—for her, for all of them. If you live, whatever pang you feel at leaving them behind will be balanced out by that knowing, and by the life you make with Glenna. I have to go back where I was. I have to. I can't take this with me and survive it."

Hoyt was quiet a moment. "Was she in pain, afraid, grieving?"

"No."

"And you can't take that with you and survive it?"

"I don't know, that's the plain truth. But I know that one feeling leads to another until you drown in them. I'm half drowned now with what's in me for Moira."

He calmed himself, sat again. "She wore the cross you gave her, Nola did. She said she wore it always, just as you told her. I thought you should know. And I thought you should know she told me Lilith had come back, and tried to lure her into an invitation."

As Cian's had done, Hoyt's hand fisted. "That hell-bitch went for our Nola?"

"She did, and got a boot up the ass for the trouble—metaphorically." He told Hoyt what Nola had said, watched Hoyt's grim face soften a little with pride and satisfaction. "Then she flashed that cross of yours and sent her packing. According to Nola she never came back again, until we did."

"Well now, well. Isn't that interesting. The cross didn't just shield the wearer, it frightened Lilith enough to send her haring off. That, and the prediction we'd end her."

"Which may be why she's so determined to end us."

"Aye. Nola's threat could have added weight to that. Imagine how it must have been for Lilith, being frightened off by a child."

"She wants her own back, no doubt of it. She wants to win this, of course. To set herself up as a kind of god, but under that, it's us. The six of us and the connection between us. She wants us destroyed."

"Hasn't had much luck with that, has she?"

"And what do you think of that? The gods depose, don't they? We've all of us had our close calls, and bled for it. But we're all of us, Lilith included, being driven toward one time and place. The fact of the matter is, I don't care for being led by the nose by gods any more than demons."

Hoyt lifted his brows. "What choice is there?"

"They all talk of choice, but which of us would turn away from this now? It's not just humans who have pride, after all. So, the time clicks away." He rose. "And we'll see what we see on that reckoning day. The sun's well down. I'm going out for air."

He walked to the door, paused to glance back. "She couldn't tell me if you survived it."

Hoyt lifted a shoulder, finished off his whiskey. Then he smiled. " 'Danny Boy,' is it?"

Cian went to see to his horse. Then, though he knew it was risky, saddled Vlad and rode out through the gates. He needed the speed, and the night. Maybe he needed the risk as well.

The moon was past half full now. When that circle was complete, blood—human and demon—would soak the ground.

He hadn't fought in other wars, hadn't seen the point of them. Wars for land, for riches and resources. Wars waged in the name of faith. But this one had come to be his.

No, it wasn't only humans who had pride, or even honor. Or love. So for all of that, this was his. If his luck was in, he'd ride one day again in Ireland—or wherever he chose. And he'd think of Geall with its lovely hills and thick forests. He'd think of the green and the tumbling water, the standing stones, and the fanciful castle on the rise near the river.

He'd think of its queen. Moira, with the long gray eyes and the quiet smile that masked a clever, flexible brain and a deep, rich heart. Who would have believed that after all these lifetimes he would be seduced, bewitched, drowned in such a woman?

He took Vlad leaping over stone walls, galloping over fields where the air was sweet and cool with the night. The moonlight rained down on the stones of her castle, and the windows glowed with candles and lamps. She'd kept her word, he thought, and had hoisted that third flag, so there was claddaugh, dragon, and now the bright gold sun.

He wished, with all that was in him, that she would give Geall, and all the worlds, the sun after the blood spilled.

Maybe he couldn't take all these feelings, these needs and wants with him and survive. But he wanted to take this. When he went back to the dark, he wanted to take this much of her, and have that single glimmer of light through all his nights.

He rode back, and found her waiting, with her bow in her hands and the sword of Geall strapped to her side.

"I saw you ride out."

He dismounted. "Covering my back, were you?"

"We'd agreed none of us would go out alone, particularly after dark."

"I needed it," was all he said, and led the stallion to the stables.

"So it seemed, from the way you were riding. I didn't see any hounds of hell, but it appeared you did. Would you trust one of the stable boys to cool him and settle him for the night? It helps them to have the work, as much as it might help you to have a wild ride."

"There's a scolding under that accommodating tone, Majesty. You do it very well."

"Learned at my mother's knee." She took the reins herself, then passed them with instructions to the boy who came hurrying out from the stables.

When she'd finished, she looked up at Cian. "Are you in a mood?"

"Always."

"I should have said a difficult mood, but the answer might be always to that as well. If you're not, more than usual, I'd hoped you'd have a meal with me. In private. I'd hoped you'd stay with me tonight."

"And if I am in a difficult mood?"

"Then a meal and some wine might sweeten it enough for you to lie with me, and stay with me. Or, we can argue over the food, then go to bed."

"I'd have to have taken a spill from the horse and damaged my brain to turn down that offer."

"Good. I'm hungry."

And furious, he thought with some amusement. "Why don't you get the lecture out of your system. It's liable to give you indigestion."

"I don't have a lecture, and if I did, it's not what would suit me." She walked—regally, he thought—across the courtyard. "What I'd like is to give you a good, strong kick in the ass for taking a chance like that. But . . ."

She drew a long breath, then a second as they entered the castle. "I know what it is to need to get away, to just go for a bit. How it feels you'll rip apart from the pressure inside if you don't. I can go into a book and be quiet in my mind again. You needed the ride, the speed of it. And, I think, there are times you just need the dark."

He said nothing until they'd come to the door of her room. "I don't know how you can understand me that way."

"I've made a study of you." Now she smiled a little, looking up and into his eyes. "I'm a good study. And added to it, you're inside my heart now. You're inside me, so I know."

"I haven't earned you," he said quietly. "That occurs to me now. I haven't earned you."

"I'm not a wage or a prize. I wouldn't care to be earned." She opened the door to her sitting room.

She'd had the fire lit, and the candles. The cold supper and the good wine were already laid out, with flowers from one of the hothouses.

"You've gone to some trouble." He shut the door behind them. "Thank you."

"It was for me, but I'm glad you like it. I wanted a night, just one, where it would be only the two of us. As if none of this was happening. Where we could sit and talk and eat. And where I might drink just a little too much wine."

She laid down her bow and quiver, unhooked her sword. "One night when we don't talk of battles and weapons and strategy. You'd tell me you love me. You wouldn't even have to say it, because I'd see it when you looked at me."

"I do love you. I looked back at the castle, and saw the glow in the windows from these candles. That's how I think of you. A steady glow."

She stepped toward him, took his face in her hands. "And if I think of you as the night, it's the mystery of it, and the thrill. I'll never be afraid of the dark again, because I've seen into it."

He kissed her brow, her temples, then her lips. "Let me pour you the first glass of too much wine."

She sat at the little table and watched him. This was her lover, she thought. This strange and compelling man who carried wars inside him. And she'd have this night with him, the whole of it, and a few hours of peace for them both.

She chose food for his plate, knowing it was a wifely gesture. She'd have that as well, this one night. When he sat across from her, she lifted her glass to his. "*Sláinte.*"

"*Sláinte.*"

"Will you tell me the places you've seen? Where you've traveled? I want to go there in my mind. I studied the maps in your library in Ireland. Your world is so big. Tell me the wonderful things you've seen."

He took her to Italy during the Renaissance, and Japan in the time of samurai, to Alaska during the gold rush, to Amazon jungles and to African plains.

He tried to paint quick snapshots with words, so she could see the variety, the contrasts, the changes. He could all but see her mind opening to take it in. She asked dozens of questions, particularly when something he related expanded or contradicted what she'd read when in his library.

"I've wondered what lies beyond the sea." She propped her chin on her fist as he poured more wine. "Other lands, other cultures. It seems that if we were once a part of Ireland, that there may be parts of Italy and America, Russia, all those wondrous places here, in this world, too. One day . . . I'd like to see an elephant."

"An elephant."

She laughed. "Aye, an elephant. And a zebra and a kangaroo. I'd like to see the paintings from the artists you've seen, and the ones I found in your books. Michelangelo and DaVinci, Van Gogh, Monet, Beethoven."

"Beethoven was a composer. I don't believe he could paint."

"That's right, sure, that's right. The *Moonlight Sonata*, and all those symphonies with numbers. It's the wine muddling it up a bit. I'd like to see a violin, and a piano. And an electric guitar. Do you play any of those?"

"Actually, it's a little known fact that there were six original Beatles. Never mind."

"I know. John, Paul, George and Ringo."

"You've got a memory like that elephant you'd like to see."

"As long as you remember it, it belongs to you. I'll likely never see an elephant, but I'll have orange trees one day. The seeds in the hothouse pots are sprouting." She held her thumb and forefinger up, close together. "That bit of green coming out of the dirt. Glenna tells me the blossoms will be very fragrant."

"Yes, they will be."

"And I took other things."

It amused him to hear the confessional tone in her voice. "So, you've sticky fingers, have you?"

"I thought, if I'm not meant to take them to Geall, they won't go. I took a cutting of your roses. All right, well, three cuttings. I was greedy. And a photograph Glenna took of Larkin and me. And a book. I confess it, I took a book right out of your library. It's a thief I am."

"Which book?"

"It was poems by Yeats. I wanted it particularly because he was Irish it said, and it seemed important I bring something that was written down by an Irishman."

Because you were Irish, she thought. Because the book was yours.

"And the poems were so beautiful and strong," she continued. "I told myself I was going to give it back to you once I'd copied more down, but that's a lie. I'm keeping it."

He laughed, shook his head. "Consider it a gift."

"Thank you, but I'll happily pay you for it." She rose, stepped over to where he sat. "And you may name the price." She sat on his lap, linked her arms around his neck. "He wrote something, your Yeats, that made me think of you, and especially what we have between us tonight. He wrote: 'I spread my dreams at your feet. Tread softly because you tread on my dreams.' "

She combed her fingers through his hair. "You can give me your dreams, Cian. I'll tread softly."

Impossibly moved, he rested his cheek against hers. "You're unlike any other."

"With you, I'm more than I ever was. Will you come out, stand for a while on the balcony with me? I'd like to look at the moon and the stars."

He rose with her, but when he turned, she drew him back. "No, the bedroom balcony."

He thought of her mother, of what she'd seen. "Are you sure?"

"I am. I stood out there today, alone. I want to stand there with you, in the night. I want you to kiss me there so I'll remember it all of my life."

"You'll want a cloak. It's cold."

"Geallian woman are made of sterner stuff."

And when she led the way, when her hand gripped his tight as she opened the balcony doors, he thought, yes, yes, she was.

Chapter 14

He kissed her on the balcony, and she would remember it, all of it. She wouldn't forget the quiet music of the night, the chill in the air, the easy skill of his mouth.

Tonight she wouldn't think of sunrise and the obligations that came with it. The night was his time, and while she was with him, it would be hers.

"You've kissed many women."

He smiled a little, brushed his lips over hers again. "I have."

"Hundreds."

"At least."

Her eyes narrowed. "Thousands."

"Very likely."

"Hmm." She wandered away from him, then turned, leaning back on the stone rail. "I think I'll make a decree, that every man must come and kiss their queen. So I can catch up. At the same time it would be a kind of study, a comparison. I could see how you rate in this particular skill."

"Interesting. I'm afraid you'd find your countrymen sadly lacking."

"Oh? How can you be sure? Have you ever kissed a man of Geall?"

He laughed. "Clever, aren't you?"

"So I'm told." She stayed as she was when he moved to her, when he caged her in by laying his hands on the rail on either side of her. "Does your taste run to clever women?"

"Currently, when their eyes are like night fog, and their hair the color of polished oak."

"Gray and brown. I always thought they were such dull colors, but nothing about me feels dull when I'm with you." She laid a hand on his heart. Though it didn't beat, she saw the pulse of it in his eyes. "I don't feel shy with you, or nervous. I did, until you kissed me."

She pressed her lips to where her hand had laid. "Then I thought, well of course. I should have known. A curtain lifted inside me. I don't think it will ever close again."

"You bring the light inside me, Moira." He didn't say, not to her, not to himself, that when he left her it would go out again.

"The moon's clear tonight, and the stars shine." She laid her hands on his. "We'll leave the drapes open until it's time for sleep."

She went inside with him, into a room shimmering with moonlight and candlelight. She knew what it would be now, the warmth that went to heat, and the heat that went to fire. And all the thrills and sensations that came between.

From somewhere outside an owl called. For its mate, she thought. She knew what it was now to pine for her mate.

She lifted off her circlet, set it aside, then reached up to take off her earrings. When she saw him watching her she realized these small acts, this prelude to disrobing, could arouse.

So she took them off slowly, watching him as he watched her. She took the cross she'd tucked under her bodice, drawing it over her head. This, she knew, was an act of trust.

"I have no ladies. Would you see to my laces?"

She turned her back, lifted her hair.

"I think I'll try to make a zipper. It's a simple thing, really, and makes dressing easier."

"A lot of charm is lost to convenience."

She sent him a smile over her shoulder. "Easy for you to say." But then again, feeling him loosen those laces brought a flutter to her belly. "What invention pleased you the most over your time?"

"Indoor plumbing."

The quickness of his answer made her laugh. "Larkin and I were spoiled, and miss it sorely. I studied the pipes and the tanks. I think I could fashion something like your shower."

"A queen and a plumber." He laid his lips on her shoulder as he eased the material away. "There's no end to your talents."

"I wonder how I'll be as a gentleman's valet." She turned to him. "I like buttons," she said as she began to undo his shirt. "They're sensible, and pretty."

So was she, he thought as she worked her way down efficiently. Then she shoved at her hair.

"I think I should cut this off. Like Blair's. That's sensible, too."

"No. Don't." His belly quivered as her fingers paused on the button of his jeans. His combed down through the length of her hair, from crown to waist. "It's beautiful. The way it falls over your shoulders, spills down your back. It all but glows against your skin."

Charmed, she glanced over toward the long looking glass. And was jolted to see herself standing half dressed. And alone.

She looked away quickly, sent him an easy smile. "Still, it's a great deal of trouble, and—"

"Does it frighten you?"

There was no point pretending she didn't understand

him. "No. It's a bit of a shock is all. Is it hard for you? Not being able to see your reflection?"

"It just is. You adjust. Just another irony. Here, you've got eternal youth, but you won't be able to admire yourself. Still . . ."

He turned her around so they both faced the mirror. Then he lifted her hair, let it fall. When she let out a laugh at watching her hair seem to fly around on its own, he laid his hands on her shoulders.

"There are always ways to amuse yourself," he told her. He lifted her hair again, and this time brushed his lips—and just a hint of teeth—along the nape of her neck.

He heard the quick intake of her breath, saw her eyes widen.

"No, no," he murmured when she started to turn. "Just watch." And trailed his fingers along her skin—bare shoulders, and down to where her loosened bodice clung tenuously to her breasts. "Just feel."

"Cian."

"Did you ever dream of a lover coming to you in the night, in the dark?" He nudged the dress down to her waist then glided his fingertips over her breasts. "Overtaking you. Hands and lips heating your skin."

She lifted her hands to his, needing to feel them. Then flushed and dropped them again as the reflection showed her cupping her own breasts.

Behind her, invisible, he smiled. "You said I didn't take your innocence. You might have been right, but I think I will now. It's . . . succulent, and what I am craves it."

"I'm not innocent," she said, but trembled.

"More than you know." He circled her breasts with his thumbs, moving in slowly until they rubbed stiffened peaks. "Are you afraid?"

"No." And shuddered. "Yes."

"A little fear can add to excitement." He pushed the dress to the floor, leaned close to her ear. "Step out," he whispered. "Now watch. Watch your body."

Fear twisted with arousal so it was impossible for her to

tell them apart. Her body was helpless, her mind transfixed. Hands and lips she couldn't see roamed over her, erotically intimate, lazily possessive. She could see herself quivering, and the startled pleasure on her own face.

The clouds of surrender in her own eyes.

Her phantom lover ran his hands down her, fingers toying, tracing, leaving a trail of shivering flesh. This time when they took her breasts, she covered his hands with hers, shameless.

She moaned for him, and still her eyes stayed on the glass. His scholar would never shut her eyes to new experience, to new knowledge. He could feel her trembles, and the instinctive movement of her hips as pleasure took her over. Candlelight played over her skin and sensation warmed it so it bloomed like a rose.

She moaned again as he trailed his fingers over her belly, and melting into him, hooked her arm back around his neck.

He only teased, skimming his fingers along her thighs, over the most sensitive flesh, hinting, only hinting at what was to come until her breath was sobbing out.

"Take," he murmured. "Take what you want." He gripped her hand, pressed it to his between her thighs. Trapped it there.

She felt her body buck against him, against herself as he stroked her toward a new, towering pleasure. His body was solid behind hers, and his voice murmured words she no longer understood, but in the glass there was only her own form, lost now to its own rising needs.

Release left her breathless, limp and amazed.

He spun her around so quickly she couldn't find her balance, and knew she'd have lost it again in any case when his mouth took hers with a wild urgency. She could only cling, could only give while her heart slammed an anvil beat against his chest.

Of all he'd had and taken and tasted, he'd never known such hunger. A kind of madness of need that could only be met with her. For all his skill, all his experience, he was helpless when she held him against her. As ready and wrecked as she, he pulled her to the floor, and plunged inside her to forge that first desperate link.

He turned her face to the mirror once again as he ravished her, as her body went wild under his strong, thrusting hips. And when she came, quaking, he chained need with will until her heavy eyes opened, met his. Until she saw who had her.

He took her again, building and building until her need paced his own. Then burying his face in her hair, emptied himself into her.

She might have lain there, spent, for the rest of her life, but he lifted her. Simply scooped her up, she realized, and stood with her in his arms all in one effortless motion.

And her heart did a little jig in her chest.

"It's foolish," she said as she nuzzled his neck, "and I'm thinking it's female. But I love it that you're so strong, and that for a moment when we love each other, I make you weak."

"There's a part of me, *mo chroi*, that's always weak when it comes to you."

My heart, he'd called her, and it made her own dance again. "Oh, don't," she said after he'd laid her on the bed and turned to close the drapes. "Not yet. There's so much night left." She rolled off the bed again and grabbed her night robe. "I'm going to get the wine. And the cheese," she decided. "I'm half starving again."

As she ran out he went to the fire, tossed on another brick of turf. He closed his mind to the part of him that asked what he was doing. Every time he was with her, there was another scar to his heart, for the day that would come when he'd never be with her again.

She'd survive it, he reminded himself. And so would he. Survival was something humans and demons had in common. Nothing really died of a broken heart.

She came back, carrying a tray. "We can eat and drink in bed, full of decadence." She set the tray on the bed, and climbed up after it.

"I've certainly given you enough of that."

"Oh?" She brushed back her hair and gave him a slow smile. "And here I was hoping there'd be more to come. But if you've shown me all you know, I suppose we can just begin repeating ourselves."

"I've done things you can't imagine. Things I wouldn't have you imagine."

"Now you're bragging." She made herself say it lightly.

"Moira—"

"Don't be sorry for what's between us, or for what you believe can't be, or shouldn't." Her gaze was clear, direct. "Don't be sorry when you look at me for whatever you might have done in the past. Whatever it was, each time, it was a step to bringing you here. You're needed here. I need you here."

He crossed to the bed. "Do you understand I can't stay?"

"Yes, yes. Yes. I don't want to speak of it, not tonight. Can't we have an illusion for just one night?"

He touched her hair. "I can't be sorry for what's between us."

"That's enough then." Had to be enough, she reminded herself, though with every minute that passed there was something inside her going wild, and wilder still with grief.

She lifted one of the goblets, offered it with a steady hand. When he saw it was blood, he lifted a brow at her.

"I thought you might need it. For energy."

He shook his head and sat on the bed with her. "So, should we talk about plumbing?"

She hadn't been sure what he'd say, but that was the last on any list she might have made. "Plumbing."

"You're not the only one who's made studies. Added to the fact that I was around when that kind of thing was being incorporated into daily life. I have some ideas how you could install some basics."

She smiled and sipped her wine. "Educate me."

They spent considerable time at it, with Moira going off

for paper and ink so they could draw basic diagrams. The fact that he took such an interest in something she imagined people of his time took for granted opened another facet of him for her.

But she realized she shouldn't have been surprised by it, not when she considered the extent of his library in Ireland. And in a house, she remembered, he didn't visit more than once or twice a year.

She understood, too, that he could have been anything he'd wanted. He had a quick, curious mind, clever hands, and from the way he'd played music, the soul of a poet. And a way with business as well, she reminded herself.

In Geall, in her time, he would have been prosperous, she was certain. Respected, even renowned. Other men would have come to him for advice and counsel. Women would have flirted with him at every opportunity.

But she and he would have met, and courted, and loved, she was sure of it. And he would have ruled by her side over a rich and peaceful land.

There would be children, with his beautiful blue eyes. And a boy—at least one boy—with that little cleft in the chin like his father.

And on nights like this, late and quiet, they'd talk of other plans for their family, for their people, for their land.

She blinked herself back when his fingers brushed her cheek.

"You need sleep."

"No." She shook her head, tried to refocus on the diagrams again—to hold off those minutes that drained away her time with him. "My mind was wandering off."

"You'd've been snoring in a minute."

"Well, what a lie. I don't snore." But she didn't argue when he gathered up the papers. She could barely keep her eyes open. "Perhaps we'll rest a little while."

She rose to snuff candles as he moved to close the drapes. But when she moved back toward the bed, he was opening the doors and stepping out.

"For heaven's sake, Cian, you're next to naked." Plucking

up his shirt, she hurried out after him. "At least put this on. You may not mind the cold, but I mind having one of the guards see you standing here in your altogether. It's not proper."

"There's a rider coming."

"What? Where?"

"Due east."

She looked east, but saw nothing. Still, she didn't doubt him. "A single rider?"

"Two, but the second's being led by the first. They're coming at a gallop."

With a nod, she strode back into the bedchamber and began to dress. "The guards are instructed not to pass anyone in. I'll have a look. It may be stragglers. If so, we can't leave them outside the gates and unprotected."

"Invite no one," Cian ordered as he yanked on his jeans. "Even if they're known to you."

"I won't, and neither will any of the guards." With a small pang of regret, she put on her circlet and became queen again. And as queen, she lifted her sword.

"It'll be stragglers," she said. "In need of food and shelter."

"And if not?"

"Then they've ridden a long way to die."

When she stood at the post on top of the wall she could see the riders, or the shape of them. Two as Cian had said, with the first leading the second horse. They wore no cloaks though there was a chill in the air, and a hint of the first frost.

She glanced at Niall who'd been awakened when the guards had spotted the riders. "I'll want a bow."

Niall gestured to one of the men, took a bow and quiver from him. "Seems fruitless for the enemy to ride straight at us. Two of them against us? And unable to pass through the gates unless we welcome them."

"Likely they aren't the enemy. But the gates aren't to be

raised until we know. Two men," she murmured as they rode close enough for her to be sure. "The one being led looks to be injured."

"No," Cian said after a moment. "Dead."

"How can you—" Niall cut himself off.

"You're certain?" Moira murmured.

"He's tied to the horse, and he's dead. So's the lead rider, but he's been changed."

"All right then." Moira let out a sigh. "Niall, tell the men to keep a sharp eye for others. They're to do nothing without a command. We'll see what this one wants. A deserter?" she said to Cian, then dismissed the idea before he answered. "No, a deserter would have gone as far east or north as possible, and kept hidden."

"Could be he thinks he has something to trade," Niall suggested. "Make us think the one he's bringing is still alive, so we'd let them in. Or he's got information he feels we'd value."

"No harm in listening," Moira began, then gripped Cian's hand. "The rider. It's Sean. It's Sean, the smithy's son. Oh God. Are you sure he's—"

"I know my own kind." And with eyes keener than Moira's he recognized the dead. "Lilith sent him—she can afford to lose one so newly changed. She sent him because you'd know him, and feel for him. Don't."

"He was little more than a boy."

"Now he's a demon. The other was spared that. Look at me, Moira." He took her shoulders, turned her to face him. "I'm sorry. It's Tynan."

"No. No. Tynan's at the base. We had word he reached it safely. Injured, but alive, and safe. It can't be Tynan."

She pushed away from Cian, leaning on the wall, straining her eyes. She could hear the murmurs now, then the shouts as the men began to recognize Sean. There was hope in the shouts, and welcome.

"It's no longer Sean." She lifted her voice, cut through the calls of the men. "They killed the one you knew and sent a demon with his face. The gates stay locked, and not a man here will pass what rides here through them. I command it."

She turned back. Every bone in her body went brittle as she saw Cian had been right. It was Tynan, or Tynan's mauled body, tied to the second horse.

She wanted to weep, wanted to burrow herself into Cian and scream and sob. She wanted to sink to the stones and cry out her grief and her rage.

She stood straight, no longer feeling the wind that blew at her cloak, at her hair. She notched the arrow, and she waited for the vampire to bring its vile gift.

"No one is to speak to it," she said coldly.

What had been Sean lifted its face, raised a hand to wave to those gathered on the wall.

"Open the gates!" it shouted. "Open the gates! It's Sean, the blacksmith's son. They may be after me still. I've Tynan here. He's badly hurt."

"You will not pass," Moira called out. "She killed you only to send you here to die again."

"Majesty." It managed an awkward bow as it pulled the horses to a halt. "You know me."

"Aye, I do. How did Tynan die?"

"He's hurt. He's lost blood. I escaped the demons and made my way to the farm, to the base. But I was weak and hurt myself, and Tynan, bless him, came out to help me. They set upon us. We barely escaped with our lives."

"You lie. Did you kill him? Did what she made you turn you so you'd kill a friend?"

"My lady." It broke off when she lifted the bow and aimed the arrow at its heart. "I didn't kill him." It held up its hands to show them empty of weapons. "It was the prince. The boy." It giggled, then pressed a hand to its mouth to muffle it in a gesture so like Sean's it ripped her heart. "The prince lured him outside and had the kill. I've only brought him back to you, as the true queen commanded. She sends a message."

"And what would it be?"

"If you surrender, and accept her as ruler of this world

and all others, if you place the sword of Geall in her hand, and set the crown on her head, you'll be spared. You may live out your lives here as you like, for Geall is a small world and of little interest to her."

"And if we don't?"

He took out a dagger, and leaning over, cut the ropes securing Tynan to the horse. A careless kick sent the body tumbling to the ground. "Then your fate is as his, as will be the fate of every man, every woman, every child who stands against her. You'll be tortured."

It ripped off its tunic, and the moonlight fell on the burns and gashes yet to heal on its torso. "Any who survive Samhain will be hunted down. We'll rape your women, we'll mutilate your children. When it's done, not a single human heart will beat on Geall. We are forever. You'll never stop the flood of us. Give your answer, and I'll take it to the queen."

"This is the answer of the true queen of Geall. When the sun rises after Samhain, you and all like you will be dust that blows out to sea on the wind. Nothing will be left of you in Geall."

She passed her bow back to Niall. "You have your answer."

"She'll come for you!" it shouted. "And for the traitor to his kind who stands beside you."

It wheeled the horse, kicked it to a gallop.

On the wall, Moira lifted her sword, and flinging it out, shot a stream of fire. The vampire screamed once as the flames struck, then the ball of fire that was left of it fell to the ground, and went to ash.

"He was of Geall," Moira murmured, "and deserved to end with its sword. Tynan—" Her throat simply locked.

"I'll bring him in." Cian touched her shoulder, and looked over her head into Niall's eyes. "He was a good man, and a friend to me."

Without waiting, Cian vaulted over the wall. He seemed almost to float to the ground.

Niall slapped the back of his hand on the arm of the

guard beside him when he saw the man made the sign against evil. "No man stands with me who insults Sir Cian."

Below, Cian picked Tynan up in his arms and, bearing his weight, looked up and met Moira's eyes.

"Open the gates," she ordered. "So Sir Cian can bring Tynan home again."

She tended the body herself, removing the torn and filthy clothes.

"Let me do this, Moira."

She shook her head, and began to wash Tynan's face. "This is for me. We were friends since childhood. I need to do this for him. I don't want Larkin to see him until he's clean."

Her hands trembled as she brushed the cloth gently over the tears and bites, but she never faltered.

"They were playmates, you see. Larkin and Tynan. Was it the truth, do you think, that the child did this to him?"

When Cian said nothing, she looked over.

"He's her child," Cian said at length. "He would be vicious. Let me wake Glenna, at least."

"She was fond of Tynan. Everyone was. No, there's no need for her to come now, so late. They tore my mother like this. Worse, even worse. And I turned away from that. I can't turn away from this."

"Do you want me to go?"

"You think because I see these wounds, these bites and tears, as if an animal had been at him, I could think you're the same as what did this? Do you think me so weak of mind and heart, Cian?"

"No. I think the woman I saw tonight, the woman I heard, has the strongest mind and heart I've ever known. I never ripped at a human that way."

He steadied himself as she turned those ravaged eyes on his again. "I need you to know that, at least. Of all the things I've done, and some were unimaginably cruel, I never did what was done to him."

"You killed more cleanly. More efficiently."

He felt the words slice into him. "Yes."

Moira nodded. "Lilith didn't train you, but abandoned you, so you have little of her in you. Not like this boy must. And, I think, some manner of your upbringing remained. Just as I heard Sean's tone, saw his mannerisms in that thing tonight, so some of yours stayed as they were. I know you're not human, Cian, just as I know you're not a monster. And I know there's some of both in you that has you constantly struggling to keep them balanced."

She washed Tynan's body as gently as she would have washed a child. When she was done she began to dress him in the clothes she'd had sent over from his quarters.

"Let me do that, Moira, for God's sake."

"I know you mean well. I know you're thinking of me. But I need to do this one thing for him. He was the first to kiss me." Her voice wavered a bit before she clamped down and finished. "When I was fourteen, and he two years older. It was very sweet, very gentle. Shy for both of us, as a first kiss in the springtime should be. I loved him. I think in a way like you loved King. She's taken that from us, Cian. Taken them from us, but not the love."

"I swear before any gods you wish, I'll end her for you."

"One of us will." She bent, brushed her lips over Tynan's cold cheek.

Then she stepped back from him.

Now she sank to the floor on a keening wail. When Cian knelt beside her, she curled into him and wept out her shattered heart.

Chapter 15

They buried Tynan on a brilliant morning with cloud shadows dancing over the hills and a lark singing joyfully in a rowan tree. The holy man blessed the ground before they lowered him into it, with a fife and drum sounding the dirge.

All who knew him, and many who didn't, were there so that mourners stretched across the sun-drenched graveyard and up the rise toward the castle. The three flags of Geall flew at half staff.

Moira stood beside Larkin, dry-eyed. Though she heard Tynan's mother weeping, she knew her time for tears had passed. The others of her circle stood behind her, and she could feel them, took some comfort from that.

Now two stones would stand for friends here, along with the markers for her parents. All of them victims of a war that had raged long before she'd known of it. And would end with her, one way or another.

At last, she moved away to give the last moments to the family and their privacy. When Larkin took her hand, she gripped it firmly. She looked at Cian, could just see his eyes under the shadow of his hood. Then she looked at the others.

"We have work to do. Larkin and I need to speak with Tynan's family again, then we'll meet in the parlor."

"We'll head in now." Blair stepped forward, laid her cheek against Larkin's. Moira couldn't hear the words Blair murmured to him, but Larkin released her hand and pulled Blair into a hard embrace.

"We'll be in shortly." Larkin eased back, then took Moira's hand again. She would have sworn she could feel his grief coming through his skin.

Before Moira could move back toward the family, Tynan's mother broke away from her husband and pushed her way to Cian. Her eyes were still spilling tears.

"It's your kind did this. Your kind killed my boy."

Hoyt made a move forward, but Cian shifted to block his path. "Yes."

"You should be in hell instead of my boy being in the ground."

"Yes," Cian repeated.

Moira stepped up to put an arm around her, but the woman shook it off. "You, all of you." She whirled, jabbing out an accusing finger. "You care more about this *thing* than my boy. Now he's dead. He's dead. And you have no right to stand here by his grave." She spat at Cian's feet.

As she wept into her hands, her husband and daughters carried her off.

"I'm sorry," Moira murmured. "I'll speak with her."

"Leave her be. She wasn't wrong." Saying nothing more, Cian walked away from the fresh grave, and the lines of stones that marked the dead.

Niall caught up with him as he reached the gates. "Sir Cian, a word with you."

"You can have as many words as you want once I'm out of this shagging sun."

He didn't know why he'd gone to the graveyard. He'd seen more than enough dead in his time, heard more than enough weeping for them. Tynan's mother wasn't the only one who looked at him with fear and hate, and here he was out in the daylight with the only things between him and the killing sun some rough cloth and a charm.

His blood cooled the moment he was inside, out of the light.

"Say what you need to say." Cian shoved back the detested hood of the cloak.

"So I will." A big man with his usually cheerful face tight and grim, Niall nodded sharply. His wide hand rested on the hilt of his sword as he looked hard into Cian's eyes. "Tynan was a friend, and one of the best men I've known."

"You're saying nothing I haven't heard before."

"Well, you haven't heard me say it, have you? I saw what had become of Sean, what had been a harmless and often foolish lad. I saw him kick Tynan's body from the horse as if it were no more than offal to be tossed in a ditch."

"To him it wasn't any more than that."

Again, Niall nodded, and his fingers tightened on the sword's hilt. "Aye, that's what was made of him. And of you. But I watched you lift Tynan's body off the ground. I watched you carry it in, as a man would carry a fallen friend. I saw none of what was Sean in you. Tynan's mother's grieving. He was her first-born, and she's mad with grief. And she was wrong in what she said to you by his grave. He'd not have wanted you insulted by his blood. So as his friend, I'm telling you that. And I'm telling you any man who fights with me fights with you. That's my word on it."

He lifted his hand from the hilt of his sword and held it out to Cian.

Humans never failed to surprise him. Irritate, annoy, amuse, occasionally educate. But most of all they continued to surprise him with the twists and turns of their minds and hearts.

He supposed that was one reason he'd been able to live among them so long and still be interested.

"I'll thank you for it. But before you take my hand, you need to know that what was in Sean is in me. There's a thin difference."

"Not thin by my measure. And I'm thinking you'll use what's in you to fight. I'll put my back to yours, Sir Cian. And my hand's still out."

Cian shook it. "I'm grateful," he said. But when he went up the stairs, he went alone.

Heartsick, Moira walked back to the castle. There was little time for grieving, she knew, little time for comfort. What Lilith had done to Sean, to Tynan, she'd done to cut at their hearts. And she'd aimed well.

So they would heal them now with action, with movement.

"Can the dragons be used? Are they trained enough to carry men?"

"They're smart, and accommodating," Larkin told her. "Easily ridden by any who have a good seat, and aren't afraid of the height. But so far, it's been like a game for them. I can't say how they'll do in battle."

"For now, it's more a matter of transportation. You'd know the best of them, you and Blair. We'll need—" She broke off as her aunt crossed the courtyard to her. "Deirdre." She kissed her aunt's cheek, held an extra moment. She knew Larkin's and Tynan's mothers were close. "How is she?"

"She's prostrate. Inconsolable." Deirdre's eyes, swollen from her own tears, locked on Larkin's face. "As any mother would be."

He embraced her. "Don't fret for me, or for Oran."

"Now you ask the impossible." Still she smiled a little. But the smile faded as she turned to Moira again. "I know this is a difficult time, and you've much on your mind, on your heart. But I would speak with you. Privately."

"Of course. I'll join you shortly," she said to the others, then laid her arm around Deirdre's shoulders. "We'll go to my sitting room. You'll have tea."

"You needn't trouble."

"It'll do us both good." She caught the eye of a servant as they passed into the hall, and asked that tea be brought up.

"And Sinann?" Moira continued as they climbed the stairs.

"Fatigued, and full of grief for Tynan, of worry for her husband, her brothers. I couldn't allow her to go to the grave today, and made her rest. I worry for her, and the babe she carries, her other children."

"She's strong, and has you to tend her."

"Will it be enough if Phelan falls as Tynan has? If Oran has already . . ."

"It must be. We have no choice in this. None of us."

"No choice, but for war." Deirdre entered the sitting room, took a chair. Her face, framed by her wimple, was older than it had been weeks before.

"If we don't fight they'll slaughter us, as they did Tynan. Or do what they did to poor Sean." Moira went to the hearth to add bricks to the fire. Despite the bright autumn sun, she was cold to the bone.

"And fighting them, how many will die? How many will be slaughtered?"

Moira straightened, and turned. Her aunt wasn't the only one who would question, who would look to their queen for the impossible answer.

"How can I say? What would you have me do? You who were confidant to my mother before she was queen, and all during her reign. What would you have had her do?"

"The gods have charged you. Who am I to say?"

"My blood."

Deirdre sighed, looked down at her hands lying empty in her lap. "I'm weary, to the bottom of my soul. My daughter fears for her husband, as I do for mine. And for my sons. My friend buried her child today. And I know there is no choice in this, Moira. This blight has come to us, and must be cut out."

A servant hurried in with the tea.

"Leave it please," Moira said. "I'll pour. Is food being sent to the parlor?"

The young girl curtseyed. "Aye, Your Majesty. The cook was seeing to it when I left with the tea."

"Thank you. That's all then."

Moira sat, poured out the tea. "There's biscuits as well. It's good to have small pleasures in hard times."

"It's pleasures in hard times I need to speak with you about."

Moira passed the cup. "Is there something I can do to ease your heart? Sinann's and the children's?"

"There is." Deirdre took a small sip of the tea before setting the cup aside. "Moira, your mother was my dearest friend in this world, and so I sit here in her stead, and I speak to you as I would my own daughter."

"I'd have it no other way."

"When you spoke of this war that's upon us, you spoke of no choice. But there are other choices you've made. A woman's choices."

Understanding, Moira sat back. "I have."

"As queen, one who's claimed herself a warrior, one who's proven herself as one, you have the right, even the duty, to use any and all weapons that come to your hand to protect your people."

"I do, and I will."

"This Cian who comes here from another time and place. You believe the gods sent him."

"I know it. He fought by your own son. He saved my life. Would you sit here and look at me, and damn him as Tynan's mother damned him?"

"No." Deirdre took a careful breath. "In this matter of war, he is a weapon. By using him you may save yourself, my sons, all of us."

"You're mistaken," Moira said evenly. "He's not to be used like a sword. What he's done, and what he will do to cut out this blight, he does of his own will."

"A demon's will."

Moira's eyes chilled. "As you like."

"And you've taken this demon to your bed."

"I've taken Cian to my bed."

"How can you do this thing? Moira, Moira." She reached out her hands. "He's not human, yet you gave yourself to him. What good can come of it?"

"Much has already, for me."

Deirdre sat back a moment, pressed her fingers to her eyes. "Do you think the gods sent him to you for this?"

"I can't say. Did you ask yourself that question when you took my uncle?"

"How can you compare?" Deirdre snapped. "Have you no shame, no pride?"

"No shame, and considerable pride. I love him, and he loves me."

"How can a demon love?"

"How can a demon risk his life, time and again, to save humanity?"

"It's not his bravery I question, but your judgment. Do you think I've forgotten what it is to be young, to be stirred, to be foolish? But you're queen, and you have responsibility to your crown, your people."

"I live and breathe that responsibility, every moment, every day."

"And at night you bed a vampire."

Unable to sit any longer, Moira rose, moved to the window. The sun still shone, she thought, bright and gold. It sparkled on the grass, on the river, on the gossamer wings of dragons who flew lazy loops around Castle Geall.

"I don't ask you to understand. I demand your respect."

"Do you speak to me as my niece, or as the queen?"

She turned back, framed by the window and the sunlight. "The gods have deemed me both. You come to me out of concern, and that I accept. But you also come with condemnation, and that I don't. I trust Cian with my life. It's my right, my choice, to trust him with my body."

"And what of your people? What of those who question how their queen could take one of these creatures of darkness as lover?"

"Are all men good, Aunt? Are they all kind and good and strong? Are we as we're made, or how we choose to make ourselves thereafter? I'll say this about my people, about those I'll give my life fighting to defend. They have more important things to worry about, to think about, to talk about than what their queen does in the privacy of her bedchamber."

Deirdre got to her feet. "And when this war is over, will you continue this? Will you put this thing you love on the throne at your side?"

The sun still shone, Moira thought again, even when the heart goes bleak. "When this is over, if we live, he'll go back to his time and his place. I'll never see him again. If we lose, I'll give my life. If we win, I'll forfeit my heart. Don't speak to me of choices, of responsibilities."

"You'll forget him. When this is done, you'll forget him and this momentary madness."

"Look at me," Moira said quietly. "You know I won't."

"No." Deirdre's eyes swam with tears. "You won't. I'd spare you from this."

"I wouldn't. Not a moment of it. I've been more alive with him than I ever was before, or will be again. So no, not a moment of it."

They were all gathered in the parlor around the table and food when Moira came in. Glenna reached over to remove a cover from the plate at the head of the table.

"It should still be warm," she told Moira. "Don't waste it."

"I won't. We need to eat, to stay strong." But she stared at the food on her plate as if it were bitter medicine.

"So." Blair gave her a bright smile. "How's your day been so far?"

The laugh, however quick and humorless, eased some of the knots in Moira's stomach. "Crappy. That would be the word, wouldn't it?"

"Right down to the ground."

"Well." She made herself eat. "She's struck at us, as is her habit, to incite fear and carve away at morale and confidence. Some will believe what she had Sean tell us. That if we surrender, she'll leave us in peace."

"Lies are often more attractive than the truth," Glenna commented. "Time's running out either way."

"Aye. We, we six, will have to make preparation to leave the castle, head toward the battleground."

"Agreed." Hoyt nodded. "Before we do, we'll need to be certain the bases we've set up are still in our hands. If Tynan was killed, they may have taken that stronghold. We've only the word of a demon it was the child who killed him, and him alone."

"It was the child." Cian drank tea that was nearly half whiskey. "The wounds on the body," he explained. "They weren't made by a full-grown vampire. Still, it doesn't answer if the strongholds are still secured."

"Hoyt and I can look," Glenna said.

"I'll want you to, but looking isn't enough." Moira continued to eat. "We need to gather reports from those who survived."

"If they did."

She looked at Larkin and felt what he felt. The constant thrum of fear for Oran.

"If they did," she repeated.

"If she'd wiped out the base," Cian put in, "the messenger she sent would have bragged about it, and likely she'd have sent more bodies."

"Aye, I can see that. But to keep what she accomplished from happening again, we'll want to add reinforcements."

"You want us to go by dragon." Larkin nodded. "That's why you asked if they were ready to be ridden."

"As many as can be used for this. Those who must go on foot or horseback from here will, from today on, be watched over by riders in the air. If you, Larkin, and Blair could go this morning, take a small number with you. On dragon-back, you can travel to all the bases, transport more weapons, more men, see to the reports and what you think must be done when you see for yourself where we stand. You could be back before nightfall, or failing that, stay at one of the bases until the morning."

"You're cutting too many of us out by sending two," Cian interrupted. "And I should be the one to go."

"Hey." Blair wagged a piece of soda bread. "How come you get to have all the fun?"

"Practicalities. First, all but Glenna and I have seen some of the ground of or near the battlefield firsthand. It's time I got the lay of it. Second, with that bloody cloak, I can start the journey during the day, but I can travel more quickly and more safely than any of you at night. And being a vampire myself, I'll recognize signs of them quicker than even our resident demon hunter."

"He makes a good argument for it," Larkin pointed out.

"I've been planning to go, nose around a bit in any case. So this will kill all the birds with one stone. And the last of it, I think we can all agree, the mood here would settle if I wasn't around."

"She was out of line," Blair muttered.

Cian shrugged, knowing she spoke of Tynan's mother. "All a matter of perspective—and where you draw that line. Time's getting short, and one of us should be on the battleground, particularly at night when Lilith might be scouting around herself."

"You don't mean to come back," Moira said slowly.

"There's no point in it." Their eyes met, held, and said a great deal more than words. "One of the men can come back with your reports and so on. And I'd fill in the rest of it when all of you arrive."

"You've already decided this." Moira watched his face carefully. "I see. We're a circle here, equal links. For such a decision, I think we should all have a say. Hoyt?"

"I don't like any of us going off without the others, truth be told. But it needs to be done, and Cian makes the most sense of it. We can watch as we watched when Larkin went to the caves back in Ireland. If need be we can intervene." He looked at his wife. "Glenna?"

"Yes. Agreed. Larkin?"

"The same. With one change in it. I think you're wrong, Cian, to say we'd be cutting it too thin to send two out. I think no one goes on their own. I can get you there in dragon form. And," he continued before there were objections, "I'm more experienced with the dragons than you, should there be any trouble with them, or the enemy. So I'm saying we go together, you and I. Blair?"

"Damn it. Dragon-boy's right. You may move faster alone, Cian, but you're going to need a dragon wrangler to get there, especially if you're leading men."

"Yes, it's smarter." Glenna considered. "All around smarter. It gets my vote."

"And mine as well," Hoyt said. "Moira?"

"Then that's what we'll do." She got to her feet knowing she was sending the two men she loved most away from her. "The rest of us will finish the weapons, secure the castle and follow in two days."

"Big push." Blair considered, nodded. "We can do it."

"Then we will. Larkin, I'll leave it to you to pick the dragons for this, and to you and Cian to pick the men." Moira laid it out in her mind, the overview, the details. "I'll want Niall left back, if you will, to go at the end of it with the rest of us. I'll go now, see to the supplies you'll need."

When she'd done all she could, and hoping she was calm, Moira went to Cian's bedchamber. She knocked, then opened the door without waiting for his response. With the curtains drawn there was barely enough light to see, so she flicked her hand, her power toward a candle. The way the flame spurted warned her she wasn't as calm as she'd hoped.

He continued to pack what he wanted to take in a duffle.

"You said nothing of these plans to me."

"No."

"Were you going to leave in the night, with no word?"

"I don't know." He stopped, looked at her. There were a great many things he couldn't give her, or ask of her, he reflected. At least honesty was a quality they could share.

"Yes, at least initially. Then you came to my door one night, and my plans changed. Or, they were postponed."

"Postponed." She nodded slowly. "And when Samhain's come and gone, will you leave without a word?"

"Words would be useless, wouldn't they?"

"Not to me." There was panic rising up in her at the knowledge they were moving toward the end. How could she not have known that was waiting in her to push its way out and choke her? "Words would be precious to me. You want to leave. I can see it. You want to go."

"I should have gone before. If I'd been quicker, I'd have been out the door and gone before you came to me. You'd be better off for it. This . . . with me. It's no good for you."

"How dare you? How *dare* you speak to me like a child who wants too many sweets? I'm sick to death of being lectured on what I should think, feel, have, do. If you want to go, you'll go, but don't insult me."

"My going has nothing to do with what's between us. It's just something that has to be done. You agreed, and so did the rest."

"If I hadn't, they hadn't, you'd have gone anyway."

He watched her as he strapped on his sword. Pain was already slicing thin wounds in both of them, as he'd known it would from the moment he'd touched her. "Yes, but it's less complicated this way."

"Are you done with me then?"

"And if I am?"

"You'll be fighting on two fronts, you right bastard."

He laughed, couldn't help himself. It wasn't only pain between them, he realized. He'd do well to remember that. "Then it's lucky for me I'm not done with you. Moira, last night you knew you had to be the one to end what had once been a boy you'd known, you'd been fond of. I knew it, so I stopped myself from doing it, from sparing you from that. I know I have to go, and go without you for now. You know that, too."

"It doesn't make it easier. We may never be alone again, never be able to be with each other as we were again. I want more time—there hasn't been enough time, and I need more."

She moved to him, held him hard and tight. "We didn't have our night. It didn't last till morning."

"But the hours mattered, every minute of them."

"I'm greedy. And already fretting that you'll go while I stay."

Not just today, he thought. Both of them knew she didn't speak only of today. "Do women of Geall follow the tradition of sending their men off with a favor?"

"What would you have from me?"

"A lock of your hair." The sentiment of it surprised him, and embarrassed a little. But when she drew back, he could see his request had pleased her.

"You'll keep it with you? That part of me?"

"I would, if you'll spare it."

She touched her hair, then held up a hand. "Wait, wait. I have something. I'll have to get it." She heard the trumpet call of dragons. "Oh, they're ready for you. I'll bring it to you, outside. Don't leave. Promise me you'll wait until I come to say goodbye."

"I'll be there." This time, he thought as she rushed out.

Outside, in the shelter of shade, Cian studied the dragons Larkin had chosen, and the men they'd decided on together.

Then he frowned down at the ball of hardened mud Glenna held out to him. "Thanks, but I had quite enough at breakfast."

"Very funny. It's a bomb."

"Red, it's a ball of mud."

"Yes, a ball of earth—charmed earth, holding a ball of fire inside. If you drop it from the air." She used her hands waving them down as she made a whistling noise—then a puff of breath to simulate an explosion. "In theory," she added.

"In theory."

"I've tested it, but not from a dragon perch. At some point you could try it out for me."

Frowning, he turned it over in his hands. "Just drop it?"

"Right. Somewhere safe."

"And it's not likely to explode in my hands and turn me into a fireball?"

"It needs velocity and force. But it wouldn't hurt to be sure you had good altitude when it's bombs away." She rose on her toes, kissed him on both cheeks. "Be safe. We'll see you in a couple of days."

Still frowning, he secured the ball into one of the pockets of the weapon harness Blair had fashioned for Larkin.

"We'll be watching." Hoyt laid a hand on Cian's shoulder. "Try to stay out of trouble until I'm with you again. And you as well," he said to Larkin.

"I've already told him I'll kick his ass if he gets himself killed." Blair gripped Larkin's hair, pulled his head down for a hard kiss. She turned to Cian.

"We're not doing a group hug."

She grinned. "I'm with you on that. Stay away from pointy wooden objects."

"That's the plan." He looked over her head as Moira ran toward the stables.

"I'd hoped to be quicker," she said breathlessly. "You're ready then. Larkin. Be safe." She hugged him.

"And you." He gave her a last squeeze. "Mount your dragons!" he called out, and with a last flashing grin for Blair, changed.

"I have what you asked me for." Moira held out a silver locket while Blair harnessed Larkin. "My father gave it to my mother when I was born, so she could keep a lock of my hair in it. I left that one, and put in another."

And had added what magic she could.

Rising on her toes, she put the chain over his head. To make a point, to him, to any who watched, she took his face in her hands, and kissed him long and warm and tender.

"I'll have another of those waiting for you," she told him. "So don't do anything foolish."

He put on the cloak, lifting the hood and securing it. He mounted Larkin, looked into Moira's eyes.

"In two days," he said.

He rose up into the sky on the golden dragon. Others soared behind him, trumpeting.

As she watched, as those glints of color grew smaller with distance, Moira was struck with a sudden knowledge, a certainty that the six of them would not come back from the valley to Castle Geall as a circle.

Behind her, Glenna gestured to Hoyt, sending him away. She hooked an arm around Blair's waist, around Moira's. "All right, ladies, let's get busy packing and stacking so we can get you back together with your men."

Chapter 16

He wished for rain. Or at the very least a thick layer of cooling clouds to smother the sun. The damn cloak was hot as the hell he was eventually bound for. He just wasn't used to feeling extremes in temperatures.

Being undead, Cian mused, tended to spoil a man.

Soaring on a dragon was a thrilling experience, no question. For the first thirty minutes or so. And another thirty could be spent admiring the green and pastoral countryside below.

But after an hour in a fucking wool sauna, it was just misery.

If he had Hoyt's patience and dignity, he supposed he would ride steely-eyed and straight-backed until doomsday. Even with the intolerable heat melting the flesh from his bones. But then he and his twin had had some basic differences even before he'd become a vampire.

He could meditate, he supposed, but it seemed unwise to risk a self-induced trance. He had the sun beating overhead just waiting to fry him like bacon, and a magic bomb strapped on Larkin that for all he knew could burst into flame just for the fun of it.

Why exactly had he thought he had to do this idiotic thing?

Ah yes. Duty, honor, love, pride—all those emotional weights that dragged a man down into the drowning pool, however hard he struggled to keep his head above the surface. Well, there was no going back now. Not on the flight, not on the feelings crowding inside him.

My God, he loved her. Moira the studious, Moira the queen. The shy and the valiant, the canny and the quiet. It was stupid, destructive, hopeless to love her. And it was more real than anything he'd known in a thousand years.

He could feel the locket she'd put around his neck—another weight. She'd called him a bastard one minute, then had given him one of what he was certain was her most valued treasures the next.

Then again, she'd once aimed an arrow at his heart, then apologized with a simple sincerity and flushed mortification. It was probably at that moment when he'd fallen for her. Or at least tripped.

He continued to study the land as his mind wandered. Good farmland, he mused, with rich, loamy soil and gentle rises. Streams and rivers thick with fish running through forests that teemed with game. The mountains in the distance rich with minerals and marbles. Deep bogs for cutting turf for fuel.

She'd brought orange seeds through the Dance. Who would think of such a thing?

She'd need to plant them in the south. Did she know that? Foolish thought, the woman knew everything, or had a way of finding out.

Orange seeds and Yeats. And, because he'd seen it on the writing table in her sitting room, a roller ball pen.

So she'd grow her orange saplings in the hothouse, then plant them in the south of Geall. If they pollinated—and how could they refuse her?—she'd have an orange grove one day.

He'd like to see it, he realized. He'd like to see her orange blossoms bloom from the seeds she'd taken from his kitchen in Ireland.

He'd like to see her lovely eyes light with humor and appreciation as she poured a glass of the orange juice she'd become addicted to.

If Lilith had her day, there'd be no grove, no blossoms, no life here at all.

Already he could see some of the death, some of the destruction. What had been tidy cottages and little cabins were rubble of scorched rock and wood. Cattle and sheep continued to graze in the fields, but there were carcasses rotting in the sun under a black cloud of flies.

Cattle killed by deserters, he decided. Scavenging where and when they could.

They'd have to be hunted down and destroyed, every last one. If even one survived, it would feed and it would breed. The people of Geall and their queen would have to be cautious and vigilant long after Samhain.

He began to put his mind to that particular problem until, at last, Larkin began to circle.

"Thank all your gods," Cian murmured on the descent.

It was a neat and pretty farm, as farms went. Soldiers were spread out, training, posted at points for guards. Women were among them, working alongside the men. And the smoke that rose from the chimney carried a scent that told him there was stew in a pot, likely simmering throughout the day.

On the ground, hands were shading eyes as faces looked up, or were being raised in waves and salutes of welcome.

They were surrounded the minute Larkin landed. Cian dismounted, began to unload the supplies. He'd leave it to Larkin and the other men to answer questions, and ask them. Now, he needed shadow and shade.

"We haven't had any trouble at all." Isleen spooned up stew Cian didn't want. But he thought it best to wait to dip into his supply of blood until he had privacy.

Larkin dove into his bowl the instant they were set down. “Thanks,” he said with his mouth full. “It’s fine stew.”

“You’re very welcome. I’m doing the cooking by and large, so I’m thinking our troop here is eating better than the others.” She dimpled into a smile. “We’ve been keeping up with our training, every day, and locking up tight before sunset. We haven’t seen hide nor hair of anyone since we arrived and sent the other troop on its way.”

“It’s good to know that.” Larkin picked up the tankard she’d set beside his bowl. “Could you do me a favor then, Isleen darling? Would you fetch Eogan—Ceara’s Eogan. We’ve some talking to do.”

“Sure I’ll do that right away. Oh, and you can bed down here, or upstairs if you’d rather.”

“We’ll be moving on to the next base after a bit, and leaving three of the men we brought behind here with you.”

“Oh. I noticed you brought red-haired Malvin along.” She said it casually, with just the hint of a laugh. “I wonder if he’d be one you’d leave behind with us.”

Larkin grinned and spooned up more stew. “That wouldn’t be a problem, not at all. Fetch Eogan now, won’t you, sweetheart?”

“You’ve had a bit of that, have you?” Cian murmured.

“Had— No.” Then his tawny eyes glinted with humor. “Well, a bit, but nothing substantial you could say.”

“How do you want to handle this business?”

“Eogan’s a sensible man, a solid one. He’d have heard of Tynan by now from those we brought with us. So, I’ll answer the questions he’ll have on that. I’d like it best if you’d go over the precautions and orders again with him. Then if he’s nothing more to report than we’ve just heard from Isleen, we’ll leave Malvin and two others here, and go on to the next. Aren’t you hungry then?”

“As a matter of fact, but I’ll wait.”

“Ah.” Larkin nodded his understanding. “You have what you need in that area?”

“I do. The horses and cows are safe.”

"I saw the carcasses along the way. Not like an army had fed, but a few scavengers. Deserters, would you say?"

"It's exactly what I'd say."

"An advantage now," Larkin murmured, "with her losing troops here and there. A problem for later."

"It will be, yes."

"We'll think of something." Larkin looked over as the door opened. "Eogan. We've much to talk about, and little time."

There was little more at the next stronghold, but at the third, Lilith had left her mark.

Two of the outbuildings had been burned to rubble, and in the fields the crops had been torched. The men talked of a night of fire and smoke, and the screams of the cattle as they were slaughtered.

With Larkin, Cian stood and studied the scorched earth.

"It's as you said, you and Blair. She would lay waste to the farms and the homes."

"Stone and wood."

Larkin shook his head. "Livestock and crops. Sweat and blood. Hearth and home."

"All of which can be bred and grown, shed and built again. Your men withstood the siege, with no casualties. They fought, and held the ground—and took some of Lilith's forces to hell. Your glass is miraculously half full, Larkin."

"You'd be right, I know it. And I hope if she tries to drink what's left in it, it burns her guts black. We'll move on then."

There were fresh graves at the next base, burned earth and wounded men.

The sick dread in Larkin's belly eased, finally, when he saw his younger brother, Oran, limp out of the farmhouse. He strode to Oran quickly, and in the way of men gave him a hard punch in the arm, then a bear hug.

"Our mother will be pleased you're among the living. How bad are your wounds?"

"Scratches. How is it at home?"

"Busy. I've seen Phelan at one of the other camps, and he's safe and well."

"It's good to hear. Good to hear. But I have hard news, Larkin."

"We know of it." He laid a hand on Oran's shoulder. His brother had been little more than a boy when he'd marched away from home, Larkin thought. Now he was a man, with all the weight that went with it. "How many besides Tynan?"

"Three more. And another I fear won't make the night. Two others taken, dead or alive, I can't say. It was a child, Larkin. A demon child who killed Tynan."

"We'll go inside, and talk of it."

They used the kitchen with Cian sitting back from the window. He understood why Larkin listened to the whole account, though they knew or could imagine most of it. Oran had to speak it all, see it all again.

"I'd had the watch before his, and was still sleeping when I heard the alarm. It was already too late for Tynan, Larkin, already too late. He'd gone out, alone, thinking there was a child hurt and lost and afraid. It lured him, you see, some distance from the house. And though there were men posted, bows ready, when it turned and ripped at him, it was too late."

He wet his throat with ale. "Men rushed out. I think back, I think, I was second in command, and should have ordered them to hold. It was too late to save him, but how could we not try? And because we did, more were lost."

"He would have done the same for you, for anyone."

"They took his body." Oran's young face was alive with grief, and his eyes very old. "We searched. The next morning we searched, for him and the two others, but found only blood. We fear they've been changed."

"Not Tynan." Cian spoke now, waited for Oran's weary gaze to meet his. "We can't say about the other two, but

Tynan wasn't changed. His body was brought back to Castle Geal. He was given a full burial early this morning."

"I'll thank the gods for that, at least. But who brought the body?"

As Larkin gave the account, Oran's face hardened again.

"Young Sean. We couldn't save him in the ambush along the road. They came out of the ground like hellhounds. We lost good men that day, and Sean was lost as well. Is he at peace now?" He looked to Cian. "Now that what took him over is gone, is he at peace?"

"I don't have the answer."

"Well, I'll believe he is, just as Tynan is, and the others we've buried. He can't be held accountable by men or gods for what was done to him."

They double posted guards for the night, and at Cian's instructions small bladders were filled with blessed water. These would be hooked to arrows. With this, even a miss of the heart would cause considerable damage, and possible death.

In addition, more traps had been set. Men who couldn't sleep whiled away the time carving stakes.

"Do you think she'll send out a raiding party tonight?" Larkin asked Cian.

They sat in what had been a small parlor, and was now in use for weapon storage.

"To one of the other points, she may. Here? Little point in it, unless she's bored—or wants to exercise some of her troops. She's done what she had in mind to do at this base." Since they were alone, Cian drank blood from a pottery cup.

"And if you were her?"

"I'd send out small parties to distract and harass. Chipping away at enemy troops and morale at every base. The trouble with that is your men tend to stand firm, while we know some of hers desert. But your individual losses echo with you, where hers mean less than nothing."

He drank again. "But then I'm not her. Being me, I'd find satisfaction in seeking out a raiding party, taking it by surprise before it reached its objective. And killing the hell out of it."

"Isn't that peculiar," Larkin said with a grin. "Not being her, and not being you, the exact same thought had planted itself in my mind."

"Well then. What are we waiting for?"

They left Oran in charge of the base. Though there was considerable argument, discussion, debate, Larkin and Cian set out alone. One dragon and one vampire, Cian had reasoned, could travel swiftly, and undetected.

If they found a party and opted to land for hand-to-hand, Larkin's weapon harness was well-loaded. Cian swung a quiver over his back, loaded extra stakes in his sword belt.

"It'll be interesting to see how the idea of aerial warfare flies—as it were."

"Ready then?" Larkin changed, stood gold and sinuous as Cian strapped on the harness.

They'd agreed to keep it short and simple. They would fly in widening circles, looking for any sign of a party or a camp. If they spotted one, they'd strike—quick and clean.

The flight up toward a moon approaching its third quarter was exhilarating. The freedom of the night swept over Cian. He flew without cloak or coat, reveling in the cool and the dark.

Beneath him, Larkin soared, his dragon's wings barely a whisper on the air, and so thin Cian could see the glimmer of stars through them when they swept the air.

Clouds drifted, thin wisps that slid like gauze over stars, sailed like ghost ships over the waxing moon.

Far below, the first fingers of fog began their crawl over the ground.

If nothing else, the pleasure of the flight balanced out the smothering discomfort of the day's journey. As if he sensed it, Larkin aimed higher, rising in lazy loops. For one indulgent moment, Cian closed his eyes and just enjoyed.

Then he felt it, a stroke along the skin. Cold, seeking fingers that seemed to slide into him and swirl through his blood. And a whisper inside his head, a quiet siren's song that called to what he was beneath the form of a man.

And when he looked down, the savage ground of the battlefield spread below.

Its utter silence was a scream of violence. It burned into him like molten steel, brilliant and dark, deep and primal. The grass was wild sharp blades, the rocks rough death. Then even they would give way to black pits of chasms and caves where nothing dared to crawl.

Guarded by the mountains the damned ground waited for blood.

He had only to lean forward—such a short distance—and sink his teeth in the neck of the dragon to find the blood of a man. Human and rich, that gush of life, and a taste no other living thing could match. A flavor he'd denied himself for centuries. And why? To live among them, to survive wearing the mask of one of them?

They were beneath him, so much less—fleas on a dog. They were nothing but flesh and blood, created for him to hunt. The hunger gnawed in him, and the desire, the feral thrill of it pumped through him like a heartbeat.

The memory of the kill, of that first hot spurt of life gushing into his mouth, riding down his throat, was glorious.

Shaking like an addict in the throes of withdrawal, he fought it. He would not end it this way. He would *not* go back to being a prisoner of his own blood.

He was stronger than that. Had made himself more than that.

His belly cramped with need and nausea as he leaned toward Larkin. "Put down here. Stay in this form. Be ready to fly again, to leave me if you need. You'll know."

It dragged at him, that cursed ground, as they lowered toward it. It murmured and sang and promised. It lied.

The heat was in him like a fever as he leaped down. He would not, he swore, he would not turn himself and kill a friend as he'd once tried to kill his brother.

"It's this place. It's evil."

"I told you not to change forms. Don't touch me!"

"I feel it inside me." Larkin's voice was calm and even. "It must burn in you."

Cian turned, his eyes red, his skin slicked with sweat from his inner war. "Are you stupid?"

"No." But Larkin hadn't, and didn't now draw a weapon. "You're fighting it, and you'll beat it back. Whatever it is this place calls to in you, there's more. There's what Moira loves."

"You don't know the hunger of it." Deep in his throat a groan waited. It hummed in Cian's ears, and with it, he could hear the beat of Larkin's pulse. "I can smell you, the human."

"Do you smell fear?"

Shudders ran through him, hard enough he thought his bones might crack to pieces. His head was screaming, screaming, and still he couldn't block out the sound, the vicious temptation of that beating heart.

"No. But there could be. I could bring it into you. Fear sweetens it. God, God, what sick hand forged this place?"

His legs wouldn't hold him, so he lowered to the ground and struggled to tighten his slippery grip on his will. As he did, he closed his fingers around the locket she'd put around his neck.

The sickness ebbed, just a little, as if a cool hand had stroked a fevered brow. "She brings me light, that's what she brings to me. And I take it, and feel like a man. But I'm not. This is a hard reminder that I'm not."

"I see a man when I look at you."

"Well, you're wrong. But I won't drink tonight, not from you. Not from a human. It won't swallow me tonight. And it won't take me like this again, now that I know."

The red was fading from his eyes as he looked up at Larkin. "You were a fool not to draw a weapon."

In answer, Larkin lifted the cross from its chain.

"It might have been enough," Cian considered. He scrubbed his sweaty palms dry on the knees of his jeans. "Fortunately for us both, we don't have to test it."

"I'll take you back."

Cian looked at the hand Larkin offered. Humans, he thought, trusting and optimistic. He took it, pulled himself to his feet. "No, we'll go on. I need to hunt something."

He'd won the battle, Cian thought as they rose into the air again. But he wouldn't deny he was relieved to be heading away from that ground.

And he was darkly thrilled when he spotted the movements below.

A dozen troops, he noted, on foot and moving with that fluid swiftness of his kind. For all the speed, there was a precision to it, an order in the ranks that told him they were trained and seasoned soldiers.

He felt the shift of the dragon's body when Larkin saw them, and once again Cian leaned down.

"Why don't we try out Glenna's newest weapon? When they cross the next field, fly directly over the center of the squad. They've got archers, so once the shit hits, you'll have to go into evasive maneuvers."

As Larkin flew into position, Cian reached into the harness pocket and took out the ball.

How is a dragon like a plane? he considered, and put his centuries of experience as a pilot to use gauging airspeed, distance, velocity.

"Bomb's away," he murmured, and let the ball drop.

It smashed into the ground, causing the baffled squad to stop, draw weapons. Cian was about to chalk Glenna's experiment up to a loss when there was a towering burst of flame. Those closest to it were simply obliterated, while a few others caught fire.

Watching the panic, hearing the screams, Cian notched an arrow. Ducks in a barrel, he mused, and picked off what was left.

Once again Larkin touched down, and changed. "Well." He kicked carelessly at a pile of ash. "That was quick."

"I feel better for having killed something, but it was detached, impersonal. Human style. Doesn't have the same kick as a true hunt. Same reason we don't use guns or modern weaponry," Cian added. "There's just no thrill in it."

"I'm sorry for that, but the results of it suit me well enough. And Glenna's fireball worked a treat, didn't it now?"

Larkin began to gather the weapons scattered over the ground. As he bent down, an arrow whizzed over his back, and planted itself in Cian's hip.

"Oh well, bugger it! I must have missed one."

"Take the harness." Larkin tossed it at Cian. "And get on."

He flashed to dragon, and since he considered the arrow might slow him down a little on foot, Cian vaulted up. He caught the next arrow in the air before it could strike. Then Larkin was rising and diving and swerving.

"There, I see them. Second party entirely. Likely a hunting party looking for stray humans or whatever comes to hand."

He used the bow again, taking out a few as they scattered and took cover.

"It's just no fun this way," he decided. Drawing his sword, he leaped off Larkin and dropped thirty feet to the ground.

If dragon's could curse, Larkin would have turned the air blue.

They came at Cian like the points of a triangle, two male, three female. He sliced the arrow coming at him in two with his sword, then spun the blade back to block the oncoming attack.

The dregs of what he'd felt on the battleground were in him, and he used them. That need for blood, if not to drink, then to shed it. He fought at first to wound, so he could smell it—the rich copper of it, and ride on it as he hacked and sliced.

The dragon's tail whipped down, slapped one of the females back as she lifted her bow again. Then its claws raked at the throat.

To amuse himself, Cian flipped back, shot a vicious kick into the face of an opponent. When it stumbled he took its head even as he yanked the arrow from its hip and plunged it into the heart of the one coming from his left.

He spun around, saw that Larkin had changed and was ramming a spent arrow in the heart of the last one.

"Is that it then?" Larkin said breathlessly. "Is that the last of them?"

"By my count."

"And you counted so well the last time." He rose, brushed himself off. "Bloody dust. Are you feeling more yourself now?"

"Top of the world, Ma." Cian rubbed absently at his wounded hip. Since it was pouring blood, he ripped off the sleeve of his shirt. "Give me a hand, will you? Quick field dressing."

"You want me to bandage your arse?"

"It not my ass, you git."

"Close enough." But Larkin walked over to see to it. "Drop your drawers then, sweetheart."

Cian spared him a single dark look, but obliged.

"And what do you think Lilith's mood will be when not a one of her raiding or hunting parties comes back?"

"She'll be pissed." Cian craned his head to watch Larkin's work. "Royally."

"Makes a body feel good, doesn't it? You'll have a fine hole in your bum for a bit."

"Hip."

"Looks like your ass to me. And I'm hungry enough to eat a donkey, hide and all. Time we went back, had ourselves a meal and a tankard. There, you'll do. It was a good night's work," he added when Cian pulled his pants up again.

"Turned out that way. It could have gone otherwise back there at the valley, Larkin."

Philosophically, Larkin pulled up some clumps of grass to wipe most of Cian's blood from his hands. "I don't think that's the truth of it. I don't think it could have gone any way but what it did. Now if your ass isn't too sore, you'll help me gather up all these nice weapons to add to our supply."

"Leave my ass out of it."

Together they began to gather swords, bows, arrows. "I'm sure that portion of you will be fine again shortly. If not, Moira'll kiss it well for you when they arrive."

Cian looked over as Larkin whistled a tune and loaded swords in the harness. "You're a funny guy, Larkin. A damn funny guy."

In Geall, Moira walked away from the crystal to stand at the window with her arms folded. "Am I mistaken in it, or were they not told to go check the bases, take no risks?"

"They disobeyed," Blair agreed. "But you've got to admit it was a good fight. And that fire ball was excellent."

"The delay's a little concern." Glenna continued to watch as they flew back toward base. "I'll work on that. I'm a little more worried about the effect the battlefield had on Cian."

"He fought it off," Hoyt replied. "Whatever tried to take hold of him, he fought it off."

"He did, to his credit," Glenna agreed. "But it was hard won, Hoyt. It's something we have to think about. Maybe we can work a charm or spell that will help him block it."

"No." Moira spoke without turning. "He'll do it himself. He'll need to. Isn't it his will that makes him what he is?"

"I suppose you're right." Glenna studied Moira's rigid back. "Just as I suppose the two of them had to go out tonight, and do what they did."

"That may be. Are they back safe yet?"

"Coming in for touchdown," Blair told her. "And all's quiet on the western front. Well, eastern front, but that doesn't have the same literary ring."

"Quiet for the moment." Moira turned back. "I think it's safe to say they'll be tucked up for the night now, and it's unlikely there'll be another raid on the base. We should all get some sleep."

"Good idea." Glenna gathered up the crystal.

They said good night, went their separate ways. But none of them went to bed. Hoyt and Glenna went to the tower to work. Blair headed to the empty ballroom to train.

Moira went to the library and pulled out every book she could find on the lore and legend and history of the Valley of Silence.

She read and studied until the first light of dawn.

When she slept, curled in the window seat as she'd often done as a child, she dreamed of a great war between gods and demons. A battle that had raged for a century, and more. A war that had spilled the blood of both until it ran like an ocean.

And the ocean became a valley, and the valley became Silence.

Chapter 17

"Sinann, you should be in bed still."

With her hand resting on her belly, Sinann shook her head at Moira. "I couldn't let my father leave without seeing him off. Or you." Sinann looked around the courtyard where horses and dragons and men were preparing for the journey. "It will seem so empty now, with so few of us left inside the walls." She managed a smile as she watched her father hoist her son high in the air.

"We'll come back, and the noise will be deafening."

"Bring them back to me, Moira." The strain began to leak through now, through her eyes, her voice. "My husband, my father, my brothers, bring them back to me."

She took Sinann's arms. "I'll do everything in my power."

Sinann pressed Moira's hand to her belly. "There's life. Feel it? Tell Phelan you felt his child move."

"I will."

"I'll tend your seedlings, and keep a candle lit until you all come home again. Moira, how will we know? How will we know if you . . ."

"You'll know," Moira promised. "If the gods don't send a sign of our victory, then we will. I promise. Now go kiss your father, and I'll kiss all your other men for you when I see them."

Moira moved to her aunt, touched a hand to Deirdre's arm. "I've spoken with the men I can leave with you. My orders are clear, simple and to be followed exactly. The gate stays locked, and no one leaves the castle—day or night—until word comes that the battle is done. I count on you as the head of my family who remains here, to see these orders are followed. You are my regent until my return. Or in the event of my death—"

"Oh, Moira."

"In the event of my death, you will serve until the next rightful ruler is chosen." She pulled off a ring that had been her mother's, and pushed it into Deirdre's hand. "This is a sign of your authority, in my name."

"I'll honor your wishes, your orders and that name. I swear it to you. Moira." She gripped her niece's hands. "I'm sorry we quarreled."

"So am I."

Though her eyes were wet, Deirdre managed a tremulous smile. "Though we both part here believing we had the right of it."

"We do. I don't love you less because of it."

"My child." Deirdre held her close. "My sweet girl. Every prayer I know goes with you. Come back to us. Tell my sons they have my heart and my pride."

"Sorry." Blair touched Moira's shoulder. "Everything's ready."

"I'll say goodbye to you." Deirdre stepped forward to kiss Blair's cheeks. "And trust you'll keep my eldest out of trouble."

"Do my best."

"You'll need to. He's a handful." She opened her mouth to speak again, then took a steadying breath. "I was going to say be safe, but that's not what warriors want to hear. So I'm saying fight well."

"You can count on it."

Without pomp or pageantry, they mounted horses and dragons. Groups of children were gathered, clucked over by the women who remained behind. The old leaned on walking sticks, or the arms of the younger.

There were tears glimmering. While they might look through the mist of them to loved ones leaving them behind, Moira knew they looked to her as well.

Bring them back to me. How many had that single desperate wish in their hearts and minds? Not all would have that wish granted, but she would—as she'd sworn to Sinann—do her best.

And she wouldn't leave them or lead them with tears.

Moira signalled to Niall who would lead the ground force. When he called for the gates to be raised, she lifted the sword of Geall high. And leading the last of the troops from Castle Geall, she shot an arc of fire into the pale morning sky.

The dragon riders arrived first to mobilize the troops. They would abandon the first base to begin the next leg of the march to the battlefield. Supplies and weapons were packed, and men were taken up on dragons, or onto horses when they arrived. Those who went on foot were flanked by riders—air and ground.

So they traveled across the land and the skies of Geall.

At the next stop they rested and watered their mounts.

"You'll have tea, my lady." Ceara joined Moira near a stream where dragons drank.

"What? Oh, thanks." Moira took the cup.

"I've never seen such a sight."

"No." Moira continued to watch the dragons, and wondered if any of them would see such a sight again. "You'll ride with your husband, Ceara."

"I will, my lady. We're near ready."

"Where is the cross you won, Ceara? The one you're wearing is copper."

"I . . ." Ceara lifted her hand to the copper cross. "I left it with my mother. Majesty, I wanted my children protected if . . ."

"Of course you did." She wrapped her fingers around Ceara's wrist and squeezed. "Of course." She turned as Blair strode toward them.

"Time to round them up. Mounts are rested and watered. Supplies and weapons are packed, except for what we're leaving behind with the squad that'll hold this base until tomorrow."

"The troops behind us should arrive well before sunset." Moira looked to the skies. "Do they have enough protection if there's a change in the weather. Natural or otherwise?"

"Lilith may have some snipers and scouts scattered this far west, but nothing the troops can't handle. We have to move on, Moira. Leap-frogging this way keeps soldiers from being exposed and vulnerable at night, but it takes time."

"And we've a schedule to keep," Moira agreed. "Give the order then, and we'll move on."

It was well past midday when the first of them arrived at their final destination. Below where she flew, men stopped and cheered. She saw Larkin come out of the house, lift his face. Then change into a dragon to fly up and join them.

And she saw the dark earth of fresh graves.

Larkin circled her with a quick, showy flourish, then paced himself to Blair's mount. Moira lost her breath when Blair stood on her dragon's back, then sprang off into the air. The cheers from below rose up like thunder as Blair landed on Larkin, and rode him down.

Like a festival, Moira thought, as other riders executed showy turns and dives. Perhaps they needed the show and the foolishness for these last few hours of daylight. Night would come soon enough.

She would have seen to her own mount as she had along the way, but Larkin plucked her off her feet, gave her a whirl and a kiss.

"That doesn't sweeten me up," she told him. "I've a bone to pick with you. You were to travel, gather reports and secure. Not go out looking for trouble."

"We do what we must when we must." He kissed her again. "And all's well, isn't it?"

"Is it?"

"It is. He is. Go inside. There are plenty here to see to the mounts. You've had a long journey. No trouble along the way, Blair says."

"No, none." She let him lead her inside.

There was a pot of stew simmering over the fire, and the scent of it, of men and mud filled the air. Maps were spread over a table where she imagined a family had once gathered. Hangings over the windows were homespun and cheerful, and the walls were clean and whitewashed.

Weapons stood at every door and window.

"You've a chamber upstairs if you want a bit of a rest."

"No, I'm fine. But in fact I could use a whiskey if there's any to be had."

"There is."

She could see by his face that Blair had come behind them.

"Mounts are being tended," Blair began. "Supplies and weapons unloaded. Hoyt's on it. What's the setup here?"

"We've troops bunking in the stables, the barn, the dovecote and the smokehouse as well as in here. There's a loft that's roomy enough, and we're using it as a kind of barracks."

He poured a whiskey as he spoke, cocked his head at Blair, but she shook hers.

"Sitting room here is serving as the main arsenal," he continued. "And we've weapons stockpiled in all the buildings. The men take shifts, day and night. Training continues daily. There were raids, as you know, but none since Cian and I arrived."

"Saw to that, didn't you?" Moira asked before she drank.

"We did, and gave Lilith a good boot in the arse. We lost

another man yesterday, one who was wounded in the raid that killed Tynan. He didn't die easy."

Moira looked down into her whiskey. "Are there more wounded?"

"Aye, but walking. There's a kind of parlor open to the kitchen, and we've been using that for tending those who need it."

"Glenna will have a look at that, and arrange it as she sees best. Well." She downed the rest of the whiskey. "We all know there's not enough room inside shelters for all the troops. Nearly a thousand here tonight, and half again that many who'll be here within the next two days."

"Then we'd better get busy making camp," Blair said.

There was some pride in it, Moira discovered, at seeing so many of her people—men and women, old and young—working together. Tents began to spread over the field while wood and turf was gathered for cook fires. Wagons of supplies were unloaded and stacked.

"You have your army," Glenna said from beside her.

"One day I hope crops will be planted here again instead of tents. There are so many. There never seemed so many before. Can you hold so many within a protective circle?"

Glenna's face tightened with sheer determination. "Lilith's pet dog managed to shield their entire base. I hope you're not suggesting Hoyt and I can't measure up."

"Wouldn't think of it."

"Damn big circle to cast," Glenna admitted. "And the sun's getting low, we'll have to get started. We could use you."

"I was hoping you could."

With them, Moira walked the field from end to end and, as Glenna had instructed, gathered blades of grass, small stones, bits of earth as she went. They met again in the center.

As word had passed that magic would be done, the troops fell silent. In the hush, Moira heard the first whispers of power.

They called on the guardians, east and west, north and

south. On Morrigan, their patron. She took up the chant with them as she'd been given it.

"In this place and in this hour, we call upon the ancient powers to hear our needs and grant our plea to shelter all in this company. Upon this grass, this earth, this stone, protection from harm bestow. Only life at its fullest may cross this ring, and none may enter with harm to bring. Within this circle that was cast no enemy nor his weapon may pass. Night or day, day or night shield earth and air within its light. Now our blood will seal this shield and circle it round this field."

As Hoyt and Glenna did, Moira cut her palm with an athame, then fisted it around the dirt, the grass, the stones she'd gathered.

It pumped and plunged through her, the heat—hers and theirs—and the wind they raised blew in widening circles, slapping at the tents, singing through the grass until it whipped around and around the edges of the field in a cyclone of light.

With Hoyt and Glenna, she threw down the blood-soaked earth, felt the shudder under her feet as three small flames bloomed and died. When they clasped hands, her body bowed back from the force of what joined them.

"Rise and circle," she shouted with them, "circle and close and bar this place from all our foes. Blood and fire here mix free, as we will, so mote it be."

Around the field red flames speared up. When the earth was scorched white in a perfect ring, the flames vanished in a thunderclap.

Moira's vision wavered, and the voices that spoke to her seemed to blur as well, as if the world were suddenly underwater.

When she came back to herself she was on her knees. Glenna was gripping her shoulders and saying her name.

"I'm all right. I'm all right. It was just . . . it was so much. Just need my breath back."

"Take your time. It was a powerful spell, only more so because we used blood."

Moira looked down at the slice on her hand. "Everything's a weapon," she stated. "As Blair says. Whatever it takes, as long as it works."

"I'd say it has," Hoyt said quietly.

Following his direction, Moira saw Cian standing outside the circle. Though the cloak protected him from the last rays of the sun, she could see his eyes, and the fury in them.

"Well then. We'll leave the men to finish setting up camp."

"Lean on me," Glenna told her. "You're white as a sheet."

"No, it won't do." Though her knees were still like pudding. "The men can't see me drooping now. I'm just a bit off in the stomach is all."

As she crossed the field, Cian turned on his heel and strode back to the house.

He was waiting inside, and something of his mood must have translated as he was alone.

"Are you trying to lay her out before Lilith gets the chance?" he demanded. "What are you thinking, dragging her into magicks like that, strong enough to brew up your own personal hurricane."

"We needed her," Hoyt said simply. "It isn't an easy matter to throw a net over an area so large that holds so many. And as it stopped you on the edge, the spell holds."

It hadn't just stopped him, but had shot jolts of electricity through him. He was surprised his hair wasn't standing on end. "She's not strong enough to—"

"Don't tell me what I'm not strong enough to do. I've done what was needed. And isn't that the same you'd say to me if I dared question your reckless journey to the valley? Both are done now, and we're able to stand here and argue about it, so I'd say both are well done. I'm told I have a chamber upstairs. Does anyone know where it might be?"

"First door, left," Cian snapped.

When she walked, haughtily, he thought, up the stairs, he cursed. Then followed her.

She sat in the chair by the fire that had yet to be lit, with her head between her knees.

"My head's light, and it doesn't need you bringing a scold down on it. I'll be myself again in a moment."

"You seem yourself to me." He poured water into a cup, held it down so she could see it. "Drink this. You're white as a corpse. I've made corpses with more color than you."

"A lovely thing to say."

"Truth is rarely pretty."

She sat back in the chair, studying him as she drank the water. "You're angry, and that's just fine and good, as I'm angry right with you. You knew I was here, but you didn't come down."

"No, I didn't come down."

"You're a great fool, is what you are. Thinking you'd ease back from me, that I'd let you. We've only days left before we end this thing, so you go ahead and take steps back from me. I'll just take them toward you until your back's in the corner. I've not only learned to fight, I've learned not to fight clean."

She gave a little shiver. "It's cold. I've nothing left after that spell to get the fire lit."

He moved toward the hearth, and before he bent down for the tinderbox, she took his hand. And she pressed it against her cheek.

It broke him, a snap like glass. He lifted her out of the chair, holding her off the floor while his mouth plundered hers. She simply wrapped herself around him, wantonly, arms and legs.

"Aye, that's better," she said breathlessly. "Much warmer now. The hours seemed endless since I watched you go. So little time, so little, for eternity."

"Look at me. Yes, there's that face." He held her close again so her head rested on his shoulder.

"Did you miss it, my face?"

"I did. You don't have to fight dirty when you've already carved yourself inside me."

"Easier to be angry with each other. It hurts less." She squeezed her eyes tight for a moment, then eased back when he set her on her feet. "I brought the vielle. I thought you might like to have it, to play it. We should have music, like we should have light and laughter, and all the things that remind us what we're ready to die for."

She walked to the window. "The sun's setting. Will you go back to the battlefield tonight?" She glanced around when he didn't speak. "We saw you go with Larkin two nights ago, and saw you go alone last night."

"Each time I go, I'm a little stronger. I won't be any good to you or myself if what's soaked into that ground turns me."

"You're right on that, and tonight I'll be going with you. You can waste time arguing, Cian," she said as he began to. "But I'll be going. Geall is mine, after all, and every inch of its ground, whatever is under it. I haven't been on the edges of that place since my childhood, except in my dreams of it. I need to see it, and at night, as it will be on Samhain. So I'll be going with you, or I'll be going alone."

"But I want to go! I want to. Please, please, please!"

Lilith wondered if her head could actually explode from the boy's incessant whining and wheedling. "Davey, I said no. It's too close to Samhain, and much too dangerous for you to leave the house."

"I'm a soldier." His little face went sharp and vicious. "Lucius said so. I have a sword."

He unsheathed the small blade she'd had made for him—to her current regret—after his field kill. "It's just a hunting party," she began.

"I want to hunt. I want to fight!" Davey slashed at the air with his sword. "I want to *kill*."

"Yes, yes, yes." Lilith waved him away. "And you will, to your heart's content. *After* Samhain. Not another word!"

She snapped the order out while a tinge of red smeared the whites of her eyes. "I've had enough from you for one day. You're too young and too small. And that's the end of it. Now go to your room and play with that damned cat you wanted so much."

His eyes gleamed red, and his lips peeled back in a snarl that stripped away even the mask of human innocence. "I'm not too small. I hate the cat. And I hate you." He stormed off, his little legs pumping in his tantrum. He swung his sword wildly as he went, slicing through the torso of a human servant who wasn't quick enough to leap aside.

"Damnation! Look at that mess." Lilith threw up her hands at the blood spatter on the walls. "That boy's driving me mad."

"Needs a good swat, if you ask me."

Face livid now, Lilith rounded on Lora. "Shut your mouth! Don't tell me what he needs. I'm his mother."

"*Bien sur.* Don't bite at me because he's being a brat." Sulking, Lora slumped into a chair. Her face was nearly healed now, but the scars that remained burned into her like poison. "Simple to see where he gets his bitchy attitude."

One of Lilith's hands curled, the red-tipped nails like talons. "Maybe you're the one who needs a good swat."

Knowing Lilith could do worse than a swat in her current mood, Lora shrugged. "I wasn't the one who hammered at you the last hour, was I? I backed you up with Davey, and now you're taking it out on me. Maybe we're all on edge, but you and I should stick together."

"You're right, you're right." Lilith dragged her hands through her hair. "He actually gave me a headache. Imagine."

"He's just, how do they say it? Acting out. He's so proud of himself for that kill in the field."

"I can't let him go out."

"No, no." Lora waved a hand. "You did absolutely right. We've lost a hunting party and a raiding party, and it's no place for Davey out there. I still say you should've given him a good slap for talking back to you."

"He may get one yet. Have someone clean that up." She gestured vaguely toward the body of the servant. "Then make sure the hunting party gets on its way. Maybe they'll be luckier tonight and track down the odd human. The troops are tired of sheep's blood.

"Oh, one more thing," she said as Lora started out. "I want a little something to eat—to calm myself down. Do we have any children left?"

"I'll check."

"Something small in any case. I don't have much of an appetite tonight. Have it sent up to my room. I need some quiet."

Alone, she paced the room as if it were a cage. Her nerves were stretched, she could admit that. So much on her mind, so many details, so many responsibilities with it all coming to the end of the circle at last.

The loss of troops was infuriating and worrisome. Deserters had been a problem, but she sent out scavengers nightly to hunt them down and destroy them. It simply wasn't possible two full squads had deserted.

More human traps? she wondered. They were costing her dearly—and would cost the humans a great deal more when she was done.

No one understood the pressure she was under, the weight of her responsibility. She had worlds to decimate. Her destiny was pressing down on her and she was surrounded by fools and incompetents.

Now her own sweet Davey, her own darling boy, was behaving like a snarling, spitting brat. He'd actually sassed her, something she took from no one. She wasn't certain if she should be proud or furious.

Still, she thought, he'd looked so cute and fierce waving that miniature sword. And hadn't he nearly cut that stupid servant in two, then stomped right out, almost swaggered, without a backward glance?

It was annoying, of course, but how could she not be a little proud?

She walked to the door, stepped out so she could feel the night slide over her, into her. He felt trapped in this house, poor Davey. So did she. But soon . . .

Of course, of course, what a terrible mother she was! She'd arrange a hunt right here, on the shielded grounds. Just the two of them. It would perk up her appetite, her spirits. And Davey would be thrilled.

Pleased with the idea, she went back in, and stepping over the bleeding body, went upstairs.

"Davey. Where's my bad little boy? I have a surprise for you."

She opened the door of his room. The smell came first. There was a considerable amount of blood, on the floor, on the walls, on the bed covers she'd had made for him of royal blue silk.

Pieces of the cat were strewn everywhere. It had been, she recalled, a very large cat.

She sighed, then felt a laugh bubbling up. What a temper her little darling had.

"Davey, you naughty boy. Come out from wherever you're hiding, or I might change my mind about the surprise." She rolled her eyes. Being a mother was such work. "I'm not angry, my sweetheart. I've just had so much on my mind, and I forgot you and I need to have some fun."

She searched the room as she spoke, then frowned when she didn't find him. There were little pricks of concern as she stepped again. Lora dragged a woman behind her by a neck shackle.

"We're out of children, but this one's small."

"No, no, not now. I can't find Davey."

"Not in his room." Lora peeked in. "Ah, creative. He's hiding somewhere because you're angry with him."

"I have something . . ." Lilith pressed a hand to her belly. "Something tight inside me. I want him found. Quickly."

They called out a search, scoured the manor house, the

outbuilding, the fields within the protected area. The tightness in Lilith's belly became strangling knots when they discovered his pony missing.

"He's run away. He's run off. Oh, why didn't I make certain he was in his room? I have to find him."

"Wait. Wait," Lora insisted and grabbed Lilith hard. "You can't risk going outside the safety area."

"He's mine. I have to find him."

"We will. We will. We'll send our best trackers. We'll use Midir. I'll go myself."

"No." Struggling for calm, Lilith closed her eyes. "I can't risk you. Lucius. Find Lucius, and have him come to me in Midir's lair. Hurry."

She cooled her blood and her mind. To rule took heat, she knew, but it also took ice. It was ice she needed to hold strong until the prince was safe again.

"I depend on you, Lucius."

"My lady, I'll find him. I give you my word, and my word that I would give my life to see him safely home."

"I know it." She laid her hand on his shoulder. "There's no one I trust more. Bring him back to me, and anything you ask of me is yours."

She whirled on Midir. "Find him! Find the prince in the glass."

"I am searching."

On the wall was a large oval of glass. It reflected the wizard in his dark robes, the room where he worked his dark magicks, and none of the three vampires who watched him.

Smoke slithered over the glass, swirled, and clawed its way to the edges. Through the haze of it, night began to bloom. And in the night came the shadow of a boy on a pony.

"Oh there, there he is." Crying out, Lilith gripped Lora's hand. "Look how well he rides, how straight in the saddle. Where is he? Where in this cursed land is the prince?"

"He's behind the hunting party," Lucian told her as he studied the vision in the glass. "And moving toward the battleground. I know that land, my lady."

"Hurry then, hurry. Willful brat," she muttered. "I'll take your advice this time, Lora. When he's back he'll have a good hiding. Keep him in that glass, Midir. Can you send me to him, the illusion of me?"

"You ask for many magicks at once, Majesty." Robes swirling, he moved to his cauldron and, letting his hands flow through the air over it, brought up a pale green smoke.

"I'll need more blood," he told her.

"Human, I suppose."

His eyes glittered. "It would be best, but I can make do with the blood of a lamb or young goat."

"This is the prince," she said coldly. "We don't make do. Lora, have the one I was going to have brought in. Midir can have it."

In the dark, Davey rode quickly. He felt strong and fierce and fine. He would show them, show them all that he was the greatest warrior ever made. The Prince of Blood, he thought with a glinting smile. He'd make everyone call him that. Even his mother.

She'd said he was small, but he *wasn't.*

He'd thought to trail behind the hunting party, then move in among them and order them to let him take the lead. None would dare question the Prince of Blood. And he would have the first kill.

But something was pulling him away from them, from the scent of his own kind. Something strong and tempting. He didn't need to stay with a hunting party, trail along after them like a baby. They were all less than he was.

He wanted to follow the music that was humming in his blood, and the smell of ancient death.

He rode slowly now, and with excitement bubbling inside him. There was something wonderful out in the dark. Something wonderful and his.

In the moonlight he saw the battlefield, and the beauty of it made him shake as he did when his mother let him put himself into her and ride as if she were a pony.

While it burned through him he saw figures on the high ground. Two humans, he thought, and a dragon.

He would have them all, slaughter them, drain them, and take their heads to drop at his mother's feet.

No one would ever call him small again.

Chapter 18

There was a hard place in the middle of Moira's chest, like a fist poised to strike. Breathing around it was an effort, but she stood as Cian did, at the edge of Silence.

"What do you feel?" she asked him.

"Pulled. You're not to touch me."

"Pulled how?"

"Chains on my feet, around my throat, pulled in opposite directions."

"Pain."

"Yes, but it's mixed with fascination. And thirst. I can smell the blood in the ground. It's thick and it's rich. I can hear your heartbeat, taste your scent."

Yet his eyes were Cian's eyes, she thought. They didn't burn red as they had the night he'd come here with Larkin. "They'll be stronger here than on other ground."

He looked at her then, realizing he should have known she would understand that. "They'll be stronger here. There'll be more of them than there are of you. Driven by what's bred in this place, by Lilith's power over them, death won't mean to them what it does to you. They'll come and they'll come without thought of their own survival."

"You think we'll lose. We'll die here, every one of us."

Truth, he thought, would shield her better than platitudes. "I think the chances of beating this diminish."

"You may be right. I'll tell you what I know of this place. What I've read, and what I think is the truth of it."

She looked out again, across the pitted land called *Ciunas*. "Long, long ago, before the worlds had separated, and were one instead of many, there were only gods and demons. Man had yet to come between to fight either, to tempt either. Both were strong and fierce and greedy, both wanted dominion. But still, the gods, however cruel, didn't hunt and kill their own kind, didn't hunt and kill demons for sport or food."

"So had the margin of good against evil?"

"There has to be a line, even if it's only that. There was war. Eons of it, all leading to this place. This was their last battle. The bloodiest, the most vicious, and most fruitless, I think. There was no victory. Only an ocean of blood that rose here, formed this harsh valley, and in time ebbed away, so that blood soaked into the earth, deep and deep."

"Why here? Why in Geall?"

"I think when the gods made Geall, deemed it would live centuries in peace, in prosperity, this valley was the price. The balance."

"Now payment's due?"

"It's always been coming to this, Cian. Now the gods charge the humans to fight the battle with this demon that began as human. Vampire against what is its source and its prey. It balances here, or it all falls. But Lilith doesn't understand what may happen if she wins this."

"We'll burn out. My kind." He nodded, having come to the same conclusion himself. "In chaos nothing thrives."

Moira said nothing for a moment. "You're calmer now, because you're thinking."

He let out a half laugh. "You're right. Still, it's the last place in this world or any I'd want to spread out for a picnic."

"We'll have a moonlight one, after Samhain. There's a place that's a favorite of mine and Larkin's. It's—"

Though he'd told her not to touch him, he gripped her wrist now. "Ssh. Something . . ."

Saying nothing, Moira reached into the quiver on her back for an arrow.

In the shadows, Davey grinned and drew his treasured sword. Now, he would fight the way a prince was supposed to fight. He'd slice and thrust and bite.

And drink, and drink, and drink.

He leaned low over the saddle, preparing to loose a war cry. And Lilith appeared before him.

"Davey! You turn that pony around this minute and come home."

The fierceness on his face turned into a childish pout. "I'm hunting!"

"You'll hunt when and where I tell you. I don't have time for this nonsense, this worry. I have a war to wage."

Now his face tightened into stubborn lines, and his eyes gleamed against the dark. "I'm going to fight. I'm going to kill the humans, then you won't treat me like a baby."

"I made you, and I can *un*make you. You'll do exactly what I . . . what humans?"

He gestured with his sword. As she turned, and she saw, true fear bloomed in Lilith's belly. Uselessly she grabbed for the bridle, but her hand passed through the pony's neck.

"Listen to me, Davey. Only one of them is human. The male is Cian. He's very powerful, very strong, very old. You have to run. Make this pony run as fast as it can. You're not meant to be here. We're not meant to be here now."

"I'm hungry." His eyes were turning, and his tongue flicked out over fang and lip. "I want to kill the old one. I want to drink the female. They're mine, they're mine. I'm the Prince of Blood!"

"Davey, no!"

But with a violent kick of his heels, he sent the pony racing forward.

It was all so quick, Moira thought. Flashing moments. The silver snick of Cian's sword leaving its scabbard, the shift of his body in front of hers like a shield. The rider flew out of the dark, and her arrow was notched and ready.

Then she saw it was a child, a little boy on a sturdy roan pony. Her heart stumbled; her body jerked. And her arrow went wide of the mark.

The child was screaming, howling, snarling. A wolf cub on the hunt.

Lilith flew behind the pony, an emerald and gold she-demon, streaking through the air, hands curled into claws, fangs gleaming.

Moira's second arrow spiked through her heart and soared into the air.

"She's not real!" Cian shouted. "But he is. Take the dragon and go."

Even as she reached for a third arrow, Cian shoved her aside, leaping over the charging pony.

A little boy, Moira thought. A little boy with eyes burning red and fangs spearing. It waved a shortened sword, as it dragged on the reins. Lilith's screams were like lances of ice through Moira's brain as the boy tumbled off the pony and fell hard on the rocky ground.

It bled, Moira saw, where the rocks struck and scraped. It cried, as a boy would when he had a fall.

Her breath caught in denial as Cian advanced with the illusion of Lilith clawing at him with intangible hands. Sick in heart and mind, Moira lowered her bow.

The second rider came out of the moon-struck dark like fury. Not a boy now, but a man armed for battle, his broadsword already cleaving the air.

Cian pivoted, and met the charge.

Swords clashed and crashed, the deadly music of them ringing over the valley. Cian leaped, dismounting the rider with a vicious kick to the throat.

With no clear shot, Moira tossed down her bow and

drew her sword. Before she could rush to fight with Cian, the boy gained his hands and knees. He lifted his head, stared at her with those gleaming eyes.

It growled.

"Don't." Moira backed up a step as Davey crouched to spring. "I don't want to hurt you."

"I'll rip out your throat." His lips peeled back as he circled her. "And drink and drink. You should run. I like it best when they try to run."

"I won't run. But you should."

"Davey, run! Run now!"

He whipped his head toward Lilith and snarled like a rabid dog. "I want to play! Hide-and-seek. Tag, you're it!"

"I won't play." Moira circled with him, trying to work him back with thrusts of the sword.

He'd lost his sword in the fall, but Moira told herself she would use hers if he sprang at her. He wasn't unarmed; no vampire ever was. And those fangs glinted, sharp and keen.

She spun, kicking out, aiming low to hit him in the belly and drive him back.

Lilith's form crouched over him, hissing. "I'll kill you for that. I'll peel the skin from your bones before I do. Lucius!"

Lucius hacked out at Cian. There was blood on them both, blood in their eyes. They leaped at each other, meeting violently in midair.

"Run, Davey!" Lucius shouted. "Run!"

Davey hesitated, and something came over his face. Moira thought, for an instant, she could see the child the demon had swallowed. The fear, the innocence, the confusion.

He ran as a child runs, limping on his scraped knees. And gaining speed, gaining that eerie grace as he rushed toward the slashing swords.

Dropping her own sword, Moira grabbed up her bow. A moment too late, as Davey leaped onto Cian's back, struck with fang and fist. If she shot now, the arrow could go through the boy, and into Cian.

A fingersnap. More flashes of time. The boy tumbled

through the air, propelled by a savage blow. He knuckled his hands over his burning eyes and cried for his mother.

Again, Lilith called out. "Lucius, the prince! Help the prince."

His loyalty, his years of service cost him. As Lucius turned his head a fraction toward Lilith, Cian took it with one singing strike of his sword.

Davey scrambled to his feet, wild panic on his face now.

"Take him," Cian called out as Davey began to run. "Take the shot."

Now those flashes of time slowed down. Wild screams, wild weeping, echoing through the dragging air. The figure of a child running on bleeding, tired legs. Lilith, her face alive with fear and horror, standing between the child and Moira, her arms spread in defense or plea.

Moira looked into Lilith's eyes as her own blurred. Then with a tear in her heart, she blinked them clear, and sent the arrow flying.

The shriek was horribly human as the arrow passed through Lilith. That shriek went on and on and on as the arrow continued, straight and true into the heart of what had once been a little boy who'd played in the warm surf with his father.

Then Moira was standing alone with Cian on the edge of a valley that hummed with the hunger for more blood.

Cian bent, picked up the swords. "We need to go, now. She'll have already sent others."

"She loved him." Moira's voice sounded strange and thin to her own ears. "She loved the child."

"Love isn't exclusive to humans. We need to go."

Her mind dull, she tried to focus on Cian. "You're hurt."

"And I don't relish leaving any more blood here. Get mounted."

She nodded, taking her own weapons before pulling herself onto the dragon. "She'd killed him," Moira murmured as Cian vaulted on behind her. "But she loved him."

She said nothing more as they flew away from the battlefield.

* * *

Glenna took over the moment they got back, herding them both into the parlor for first aid.

"I'm not hurt," Moira insisted, but sat heavily. "I wasn't touched."

"Just sit." Glenna got to work on Cian's buttons. "Off with your shirt, handsome, so I can see the damage."

"Some cuts, a few punctures." He bit back a wince as he shrugged out of the shirt. "He was good with a sword, quick on his feet."

"I'd say you were better and quicker." Blair handed him a cup of whiskey. "That's a nasty bite on the back of your shoulder, pal. What? This guy fought like a girl?"

"It was the boy," Moira said before Cian could answer. She shook her head at the whiskey Blair offered. "Lilith's boy, the one she called Davey. He came at us, riding a little pony, waving a sword no bigger than a toy."

"He wasn't a boy," Cian said flatly.

"I know what he was." Moira simply closed her eyes.

"A kiddie vamp did all this?" Blair demanded.

"No." With some annoyance, Cian scowled at her. "What do you take me for? The soldier—trained and seasoned—Lilith must have sent after the whelp did this, except for the shagging bite."

"How do I treat it?" Glenna asked him. "A vampire bite on a vampire?"

"Like any other wound. You can sure as hell hold the holy water. It'll heal quick enough, like the others."

"It was a foolish risk going out there," Hoyt said.

"It was necessary," Cian shot back. "For me. And our happy news is whatever holds that place doesn't stop me from dusting another vampire. Moira." Cian waited until she opened her eyes and met his. "It had to be done. There might have been others coming behind the one she called Lucius. If I'd gone after the young one, it would have taken time and left you alone. He was no less your enemy because of his size."

"I know what he was," she said again. "He was what killed Tynan, what tried to kill Larkin. What would have killed us both tonight if it had gone another way. Still, I saw his face—under what it was, I saw his face. It was young and sweet. I saw Lilith's face, and it was the face of a mother, terrified for her child. I put the arrow into it as it ran away, crying for its mother. I know, whatever comes now, nothing I ever do will be worse than that. And I know I can live with it."

She let out a shuddering breath. "I think I'll be having that whiskey now after all. I'll take it up with me if you don't mind. I'm tired."

Cian waited until Moira left the room. "Lilith will try for her. She may not be able to get physically into the house, but in dreams, or illusions."

Hoyt rose. "I'll see to it, make certain the protection we have is strong enough."

"She won't want me now," Larkin murmured. "Or any of us," he added with a quiet look for Cian. "She'll need to curl up with it for a while. And she will live with it, just as she said."

He sat now, across from Cian. "You said the one you fought was called Lucius?"

"That's right."

"That's the one I tangled with, along with the boy, in the caves. I'd say you've just taken out one of Lilith's top men. A kind of general. This would be a very hard night for Lilith, thanks to you and Moira."

"She'll come harder now because of it. We've destroyed or damaged those closest to her, and she'll come at us like bloody vengeance."

"Let her come," Blair said.

She would have come, then and there, so mad was her fury, her rage, her grief. It took six guards, and Midir's magic to hold her down while Lora dosed her with drugged blood.

"I'll kill you all! Every one of you for this. Take your hands off me before I cut them off and feed them to the wolves."

"Hold her!" Lora ordered and forced more blood down Lilith's throat. "You can't go to their base tonight. You can't go with the army and attack. Everything you've worked and planned for would be lost."

"Everything is lost. She put an arrow in him." She whipped her head, flashed fangs and sank them into one of the restraining hands. Her own screams mixed with the howls of the wounded.

"Release her, and I'll take more than your hand," Lora warned. "There's nothing to be done for him, my love, my darling."

"It's a dream. Just a dream." Bloody tears ran down Lilith's face. "He can't be gone."

"There now, there." Signalling the others back, Lora gathered Lilith into her arms. "Leave us. All of you. Get out!"

She sat on the floor, rocking Lilith, cooing to her while their tears mixed together.

"He was my precious," Lilith wept.

"I know. I know, and mine."

"I want that pony found. I want it slaughtered."

"It will be. There now."

"He only wanted to play." Seeking comfort, she nuzzled at Lora's shoulder. "In a few days, I could have given him everything. And now . . . I'll peel the skin from her bones, pour her blood into a silver tub. I'll bathe in it, Lora. I swear it."

"We'll bathe together, while we drink from that turncoat who took Lucius."

"Lucius, Lucius." Tears ran faster. "He gave his eternity trying to save our Davey. We'll build a statue of him, of both of them. We'll grind the bones of humans and build it from their dust."

"They'd be so pleased. Come with me now. You need to rest."

"I feel so weak, so tired." With Lora's help she gained her feet. "Have whatever humans we have left in stock executed and drained. No, no, tortured and drained. Slowly. I want to hear their screams in my sleep."

Moira didn't dream. She simply dropped into a void and floated there. She had Hoyt to thank for the hours of peace, she thought as she began to wake. Hours of peace where she hadn't seen a child's face blurred together with that of a monster.

Now there was work to be done. The months of preparation had whittled down to days that could be counted in hours. While the vampire queen mourned, the queen of Geall would do whatever needed to be done next.

She stirred, sat up. And saw Cian sitting in the chair near the simmering fire.

"It's still shy of dawn," he said. "You could use more sleep."

"I've had enough. How long have you watched over me?"

"I don't count the time." She'd slept like the dead, he thought now. He hadn't counted the time, but he had counted her heartbeats.

"Your wounds?"

"Healing."

"You'd have had fewer of them, but I was weak. I won't be again."

"I told you to go. Didn't you trust me to deal with two of them, especially when one was half my size? Less."

She leaned back. "Clever of you to try to turn this into a matter of my trust in your fighting skills instead of my lack of spine."

"If you'd had less spine and more sense, you'd have gone when I told you to."

"Bollocks. The time for running is well done, and I would never have left you. I love you. I should have taken him with the sword, quickly. Instead, I wavered, and tried to find a way to drive him off so I wouldn't be the one to end him. That moment of weakness could have cost us both. Believe me when I tell you it's burned out of me."

"And the misplaced guilt that goes with it?"

"May take a bit longer, but it won't get in the way. We have only two days left. Two days." She looked toward the window. "It's quiet. This time just before dawn is quiet. She killed a young boy, and came to love what she'd made of it."

"Yes. It doesn't make either of them less of a monster."

"Two days," she said again, almost in a whisper. Something inside her was already dying. "You'll go when this is done, if we win, if we don't, you'll go back through the Dance. I'll never see you again, or touch you, or wake to find you've watched over me in the dark."

"I'll go," was all he said.

"Will you come, hold me now, before the sun comes?"

He rose, went to her. Sitting beside her, he drew her against him so her head lay on his shoulder.

"Tell me you love me."

"As I've loved nothing else." He met her lips when she turned them to his.

"Touch me. Taste me." She shifted so she lay over him, trembling body, seeking lips. "Take from me."

What choice did he have? She was surrounding him, saturating his senses, stoking his needs till they burned. Offering as much as demanding as she pressed his lips to her breast.

"Take more. More and more."

Her mouth was hot and desperate as she pulled away clothes, her teeth nipping at his jaw in sharp, quick bites while her breath shuddered.

She was alive now, burning and alive, with everything inside her rising, aching. How could she step back from this? The love, the heat, the *life*.

If she was destined to die in battle, then she'd accept it. But how could she live—day after day, night after night—without her heart?

She straddled him, taking him in, hips whipping as she fought to feel more, to take more. To know more.

Her eyes gleamed, almost a madness, and stayed locked on his. Then she leaned to him, and her hair fell, curtaining them both, trapping him in its texture and fragrance.

"Love me."

"I do."

His fingers dug into her hips as she drove him toward the jagged edge of peak.

"Touch me, taste me, take me." On a cry, she lowered her throat to his lips, pressed that soft flesh with its pounding blood against him. "Change me."

It was beyond him to stop the flood, it gushed through him, hot, strong, turbulent—and through her, he knew, as her body bucked and quaked. And shuddering, she rubbed that throbbing pulse against his mouth.

"Make me what you are. Give me forever with you."

"Stop." As his body shook, he shoved her away with a force strong enough to nearly send her to the floor. "You'd use what I am against me?"

"Yes." Her chest burned with the tears that streamed through her voice. "Anything, anyone. Why should we find this only to lose it? Two days, only two days left. I want more."

"There's no more to have."

"There could be. Lilith loved what she'd made, I saw it. You love me now, and I love you. We wouldn't stop with the change."

"You know nothing of it."

"I do." She grabbed his hand as he rolled out of bed. "There's nothing I haven't read. How can we just turn away from each other, and go on? Why should I choose death on the field rather than by your hand? It's not true death if you change me."

He pulled his hand free, then seemed to sigh. With a gentleness she couldn't see in his eyes, he framed her face. "Not for all the worlds."

"If you loved me—"

"A poor female trick, that phrase. Not worthy of you. If

I loved you less, I might do exactly what you ask. I have before."

He moved to the window. Dawn was upon them, but there was no need to draw the drapes. Dawn had come with rain.

"I cared for a woman once, long ago. And she loved me, or loved what she believed I was. I changed her because I wanted to keep her." He turned back to where Moira knelt on the bed, silently weeping. "She was beautiful and amusing and bright. We'd make interesting companions, I thought. And we were, for almost a decade until she ran afoul of a well-aimed torch."

"It wouldn't be that way."

"She was twice the killer I was. She liked children best. She was beautiful and amusing and bright—and no less so for the change. Only once she was like me, she put those qualities to use luring toddlers."

"I could never—"

"You could," he said flatly. "And most certainly would. I won't turn the brightest light of my life into a monster. No, I'd never see you like me."

"I don't see a monster when I look at you."

"I would be, again, if I did this. It wouldn't just be you who changed, Moira. Would you damn me all over again?"

She pressed her hands to her eyes. "No. No. Stay then." She dropped her hands. "Stay with me, as we are. Or take me with you. Once Geall is safe, I can leave it in my uncle's hands, or—"

"And what? Live in the shadows with me? I can't give you children. I can't give you any kind of true life. How will you feel in ten years, in twenty, when you age and I don't? When you look in the mirror and see in your nature what you'll never see in mine? We've already stolen these weeks. They'll have to be enough for you."

"Can they be for you?"

"They're more than I ever had, or thought to. I can't be a man, Moira, not even for you. But I can feel hurt, and you're hurting me now."

"I'm sorry, I'm sorry. I feel as if everything in me is being squeezed. My heart, my lungs. I had no right to ask you, I know it. I knew it even when I did. Knew it was selfish and wrong. And weak," she added, "when I'd sworn not to be weak again. I know it can't be. I know it can't. What I don't know is if you can forgive me."

He came to her again, sat beside her. "The woman I changed didn't know what I was until that moment. If she had, she'd have run screaming. You know what I am. You asked because you're human. If I don't need to ask you to forgive me for being what I am, you don't need to ask me to forgive you for being what you are."

Chapter 19

For most of the day, Moira worked with Glenna forming, forging and charming the fireballs. Every hour or so two or three people would come into the tower and haul away what was done to store them in their stockpile outside.

"I never thought I'd say it," Moira began after the fourth straight hour, "but magic can be tedious."

"Hoyt would say what we're doing here is nearly as much science as magic." Glenna swiped at her damp face with her arm. "And yes, both can be boring as ever-living hell. Still, you're doing this with me cuts back on the time and increases the payload. Hoyt's bound to be closeted with Cian over maps and strategy all day."

"Which is probably just as tedious."

"Betcha more."

Once again Glenna walked the line of the hardened balls they'd made, hands stretched out, eyes focused as she chanted. From where she stood at the worktable Moira could see the constant use of power was taking its toll.

The shadows under Glenna's green eyes seemed to deepen every hour. And each time the flush the miserable heat brought to her cheeks faded, her skin looked more pale, more drawn.

"You should stop for a bit," Moira told her when Glenna completed the line. "Get some air, have a bite."

"I want to finish this batch, but I will take a minute first. It reeks of sulphur in here." She walked to the window, leaned out to draw in cool, fresh air. "Oh. This is a sight, Moira, come look. Dragons circling over tent city."

Moira wandered over to watch dragons, most of them mounted by riders training them to dive or turn on command. They were quick studies, she mused, and made a bold, bright show against a hazy sky.

"You're wishing you could take a picture of it, or sketch it at least."

"I'll spend the next ten years doing sketches and artwork of what I've seen these past months."

"I'll miss you so much when this is done and you're not here anymore."

Understanding, Glenna draped an arm over Moira's shoulders, then pressed a kiss to her hair. "You know if there's a way to come, we will. We'll visit you. We have the key, we have the portal, and if what we've done here doesn't earn the gods' blessing, nothing could."

"I know. As horrible as these past months have been in so many ways, they've given me so much. You and Hoyt and Blair. And . . ."

"Cian."

Moira kept her eyes on the dragons. "He won't come back to visit, with or without the blessing of the gods."

"I don't know."

"He won't, even if it were possible for him, he won't come back to me." Little deaths, Moira thought, every hour, every day. "I knew it all along. Wanting it different doesn't change what is, or can't be. It's one of the things Morrigan was telling me, about the time of knowing. Using my head and my heart together. Both my head and my heart know we can't be together. If we tried it would tear at us until neither of us could survive it. I tried to deny that, disgracing myself, hurting him."

"How?"

Before Moira could answer, Blair strode in. "What's up? A little girl time? What's the topic? Fashion, food or men? Oh-oh," she added when they turned and she saw their faces, "must be men, and me with no chocolate to pass around. Listen, I'll get out of your way, I just wanted to let you know the last incoming troops have been sighted. They'll be here within the hour."

"That's good news. No, stay a moment, would you?" Moira asked. "You should know what I was about to confess. Both of you have put your heart and blood into all of this. You've been the best friends to me I've ever had, or will have."

"You've got a serious voice on there, Moira. What did you do? Decide to turn to the dark side and hang out with Lilith?"

"It's not so far from that. I asked Cian to change me."

Blair nodded as she walked closer. "I don't see any bites on your neck."

"Why aren't you angry, or even surprised? Either one of you."

"I think," Glenna said slowly, "I might have done the same in your place. I know I'd have wanted to. If we walk away from this, Blair and I walk away with our men. You can't. Do you want us to judge you for trying to find some way to change that?"

"I don't know. It might be easier if you did. I used his feelings for me as weapons. I asked—all but begged him to make me like him when we were at our most intimate."

"Below the belt," Blair stated. "If I were going to do it, that's the method I'd have picked. He turned you down, which tells me there can't be any doubt what you are to him. Back to me again, I'd feel better knowing he was going to be just as miserable and alone as I was when he had to take a walk."

Moira let out a surprised and muffled laugh. "You don't mean that."

"I said it to lighten things up, but down in the gut? I don't know. I might. I'm sorry you're getting the shaft in this. Sincerely."

"Ah well, maybe I'll have a bit of luck and die in battle tomorrow night. That way I won't be miserable and alone after all."

"Positive thinking. That's the ticket." In lieu of chocolate, Blair gave her a hug. And met Glenna's eyes over Moira's shoulder.

It was important, Moira knew, for the last of the troops to be welcomed by their queen, and to show herself to as many as she could in the final hours before the last march. She walked among the tents as twilight came, as did the other members of the royal family. She spoke to all she could. She dressed as a warrior, with her cloak pinned with a simple claddaugh brooch and the sword of Geall at her side.

It was well after dark when she returned to the house, and to what she knew would be the final strategy meeting with her circle.

They were already gathered around the long table with only Larkin standing apart, scowling down at the fire. Something new, she thought with a little quiver in her belly. Something more.

She unpinned her cloak as she studied the faces of those she'd come to know so well.

"What plans are you making that has Larkin so worried?"

"Sit down," Glenna told her. "Hoyt and I have something. If it works," she continued as Moira walked to the table, "it would win this."

As Moira listened, the little quiver became a frozen knot. So many risks, she thought, so many contingencies, and so many ways to fail. For Cian most of all.

But when she looked into his eyes, she understood he'd already made his decision.

"It lays most on you," she said to him. "The timing . . . if it's off by a moment—"

"It lays on all of us. We all knew what we were taking on when we started this."

"No one of us should be risked more than the others," Larkin interrupted. "We may sacrifice one of us without need, without—"

"Do you think I bring this lightly?" Hoyt spoke quietly. "I lost my brother once, then found him again. Found more, I think, than either of us had before. Now doing this, doing what I was charged to do, I may lose him again."

"I'm not getting a sense of confidence in my abilities." There was a tankard on the table, and Cian lifted it to pour ale. "Apparently surviving over nine hundred years isn't considered a strong point on my résumé."

"I'd hire you," Blair said, and held out her cup. "Yeah, it's risky, a lot of steps, a lot of variables, but if it works, it'd be one hell of a thing. I'm figuring you'll make it through." She tapped her cup to Cian's. "So this has my vote."

"I'm not a strategist," Moira began. "And my magic is limited. You can do this?" she asked Hoyt.

"I believe it can be done." He reached for Glenna's hand.

"We got the idea, actually, from something you said back at Castle Geall," Glenna told her. "And we're using Geall's symbols. All of them. It would be strong magic, and—I think—though it takes blood to bind it, pure."

"I believe separately we have more true power than Midir." Hoyt scanned the faces around him. "Together, we'll crush him, and the rest."

Moira turned to Cian. "If you stayed back? A signal to you, to all of us once all the steps have been taken—"

"Lilith's blood on the battleground is essential. She has to be wounded, at least, by one of the six of us. And Lilith's mine," Cian said flatly. "If I get through or don't, she's mine. For King."

For King, Moira thought, and for himself as well. Once he'd been innocent, too. Once he'd been a victim and his life taken from him. She'd shed his blood, fed him hers. Now, what they'd shared might be vital to the survival of mankind.

She rose, carrying the weight of it, and walked to Larkin. "You've already decided." She looked back at the four who sat at the table. "Four of the six, so it would be done as you've planned however Larkin and I vote on this. But it's best if we're together. If the circle agrees, with no breaks, no doubts." She took Larkin's hand now. "It's best."

"All right. All right." Larkin nodded. "We're together then."

"If we could go over it oncemore." Moira came back to the table. "The details and the movements of it, then we'll pass this on to the squadron leaders."

It would be like a brutal and bloody dance, Moira thought. Sword, sacrifice and magic playing the tune. And the blood, of course. There must always be blood.

"The first preparations in the morning then." She'd risen to pour and pass short cups of whiskey for each. "Then we'll each do our part, and the gods willing, we'll end this. And end it, fittingly I think, with the symbols of Geall. Well, to us then and the hell with them."

When they'd drunk, she walked over to the vielle. "Would you play?" she asked Cian. "There should be music. We'll have music, and send it out to the night. I hope she hears it, and trembles."

"You don't play," Hoyt began.

"I didn't speak Cantonese once upon a time. Things change." Still Cian felt a little odd, sitting down with the vielle, testing the strings for tune.

"What is that thing?" Blair wondered. "Like a violin with gout?"

"Well, it would be a predecessor." He began to play, slowly, feeling his way back from war to music. The oddness faded away with the quiet, haunting notes.

"It's lovely," Glenna said. "A little heartbreaking." Because she couldn't resist, she went for paper and charcoal to sketch him as he played.

From outside, pipes and harps began to play, blending in with Cian's music.

Each note, Moira thought, like a tear.

"You've a hand with that," Larkin told Cian when the notes faded away. "And a heart for music, that's the truth. But would you be after playing something a bit livelier? You know, with a little jump to it?"

Larkin lifted his pipe and blew out quick, cheerful notes, so those echoes of melancholy were swept away in joy. More music poured in from outside, drums and fifes, as Cian matched melody and rhythm. With a quick hoot of approval, Larkin stomped his feet, his knees like loose hinges while Moira clapped the time.

"Come on then." Tossing his pipe to Blair, Larkin grabbed Moira's hands. "Let's show this lot how Geallians dance."

Laughing, Moira swung into step with him in what Cian saw was cousin to an Irish step-dance. Quick feet, still shoulders, all energy. He bent over the vielle, smiling a little at the persistence of the human heart as shadows and firelight played over his face.

"We won't let them get the better of us." Hoyt yanked Glenna to her feet.

"I can't do that."

"Sure you can. It's in the blood."

The floorboards rang with booted feet, and it flowed out into the night, the dance, the tune, the laughter. It was, Cian thought, so human of them, to take the joy, to not only use it, but to squeeze every drop of it.

There, his brother, the sorcerer who prized his dignity as much as his power, whirling around with his sexy red-headed witch who giggled like a girl as she tried to do the steps.

The kick-your-face-and-your-ass demon hunter mixing a little twenty-first-century hip-hop into the folk dance to make her shape-shifting cowboy grin.

And the queen of Geall, loyal, devoted and carrying the

weight of her world, flushed and glowing with the simple pleasure of music.

They might die tomorrow, every one, but by the gods, they danced tonight. Lilith, for all her eons, all her power and ambition would never understand them. And the magic of them, the light of them, might just carry the day.

For the first time, he believed—whether he survived or not—humankind would triumph. It couldn't be snuffed out, not even by itself. Though he'd seen, too often, it try.

There were too many others like these five, who would fight and sweat and bleed. And dance.

He continued to play when Hoyt paused long enough to drink some ale. "Send it to her," Cian murmured.

"Look at my Glenna, dancing as if she'd been born to it." Hoyt blinked, frowned. "What's that you said?"

Cian glanced up, no longer smiling though the music he played was as cheerful as a red balloon. "Send Lilith the music, send it out, just as Moira said. You can do that. Let's rub her fucking face in it."

"Then we will." Hoyt laid a hand on Cian's shoulder. "Damn right we will."

Power rippled, warming Cian's shoulder as he played, and played.

In the dark, Lilith stood watching her troops fight yet another training battle. As far as she could see—and her eyes were keen—vampires, half-vampires, human servants were spread in an army she'd spent hundreds of years building.

Tomorrow, she thought, they would swarm over the humans like a plague until the valley was a lake of blood.

And in it, she would drown that whore who called herself queen for what had been done to Davey.

When Lora joined her, they slid arms around each other's waists. "The scouts are back," Lora told her. "We outnumber the enemy by three to one. Midir is on his way, as you commanded."

"It's a good view from here. Davey would have enjoyed standing here, seeing this."

"By this time tomorrow, or soon after, he'll be avenged."

"Oh, yes. But it won't end there." She felt Midir as he climbed to the rooftop where she and Lora stood. "It begins soon," she said without turning to him. "If you fail me, I'll slit your throat myself."

"I will not fail."

"Tomorrow, when it begins, you'll be in place. I want you standing on the high ridge to the west, where all can see."

"Majesty—"

She turned now, her eyes cold and blue. "Did you think I'd let you stay here, locked and closeted within this shield? You'll do and be where I say, Midir. And you'll stand on that ridge so our troops, and theirs, can see your power. An incentive for them, and for you," she added. "Make your magic strong, or you'll pay the price of it during the battle, or after."

"I've served you for centuries, and still there is no trust."

"No trust between us, Midir. Only ambition. I prefer that you live, of course." She smiled now, thinly. "I have uses for you even after my victory. There are children inside Castle Geall, protected. I want them, all of them, when I've taken the night. From among them I'll choose the next prince. The others will make a fine feast. You'll stand on the ridge," she said as she turned back again. "And you'll cast your dark shadow. There's no cause for concern. After all, you've seen the outcome of this in your smoke. And so you've told me countless times."

"I would be more use to you here, with my—"

"Silence!" She snapped it out, tossed up a hand. "What's that sound? Do you hear it?"

"It sounds like . . ." Lora frowned out into the dark. "Music?"

"Their sorcerer sends it." Midir lifted face and hands

into the air. "I feel him reaching out, pale and petty power in the night."

"Make it stop! I won't be mocked on the eve of this. I won't have it. Music." She spat it out. "Human trash."

Midir lowered his arms, folded his hands. "I can do what you will, my queen, but they make a small and foolish attempt to anger you. See your own troops, training, wielding weapons, preparing for battle. And what does your enemy do with these final hours?" He dismissed them with a flick of his fingers that sizzled out fire. "They play like careless children. Wasting the short time they have left before the slaughter on music and dance. But if you will it—"

"Wait." She held up a hand again. "Let them have their music. Let them dance their way to death. Go back to your cauldron and smoke. And be prepared to take your place tomorrow, and hold it. Or I'll toast my victory with your blood."

"As you wish, Majesty."

"I wonder if he spoke the truth," Lora said when they were alone again. "Of if he hesitated to strike his power against theirs."

"It doesn't matter." Lilith couldn't let it matter, not this close to the fulfillment of all she coveted. "When everything is as I want it, when I crush these humans, drink their children, he'll have outlived his uses."

"*Certainement.* And his power could be turned against you once *he* has what he wants. What do you propose to do about him?"

"I'm going to make a meal of him."

"Share?"

"Only with you."

She continued to stand, watching the training. But the music, the damned music soured her mood.

It was late when Cian lay beside Moira. In these last hours, their circle was in three parts. He'd seen the fire flare and the candle flames flash, and knew Hoyt and Glenna were wrapped in each other.

As he'd been with Moira. As he imagined Larkin was with Blair.

"It was always meant to be this way," Moira said quietly. "The six of us making the circle, with each of us forming a stronger link with another. To gather together, to learn of and from one another. To know love. And this house is bright with love tonight. It's another kind of magic, and as powerful as any other. We have that, whatever comes."

She lifted her head to look down at him. "What I asked you to do was a betrayal."

"There's no need for that."

"No, I want to tell you what I know, as much as I know anything. It was a betrayal of you, of myself, of the others and all we've done. You were stronger, and now so am I. I love you with everything I am. That's a gift for both of us. Nothing can take it or change it."

She lifted the locket he wore. It held more than a lock of her hair, she thought. It held her love. "Don't leave this behind when you go. I want to know you have it, always."

"It goes where I go. My word on that. I love you with everything I am, and all I can't be."

She laid the locket back over his heart, then a hand over the stillness. Tears filled her, but she fought to hold them. "No regrets?"

"None."

"For either of us. Love me again," she murmured. "Love me again, one last time before dawn."

It was tender and slow, a savoring of every touch, every taste. Long, soft kisses were a kind of drug against any pain, silky caresses a balm over wounds that must be endured. She told herself her heart beat hard and strong enough for both of them now, this last time.

Her eyes stayed open and on his, drinking in his face so that at the peak of pleasure she saw him slide away with her.

"Tell me again," she murmured. "Once more."

"I love you. Eternally."

Then they lay together in the quiet. All the words had been said.

In the last hour before dawn they rose, the six, to prepare for the final march to battle.

They went on horse, on dragon, on foot, in wagons and carts. Above, clouds shifted over the sky, but didn't block out the sun. It beamed through them in shimmering fingers and sudden flashes to light the way to Silence.

The first arrived to lay traps in the shadows and in the caves while guards flew or rode over and around the valley with their eyes trained for any attack.

And there found traps laid for them. Under a man's feet, a pool of blood would spread, sucking him down. Ooze, black as pitch, bubbled up to burn through boots and into flesh.

"Midir's work," Hoyt spat as others ran to save who they could.

"Block it," Cian ordered. "We'll have a panic on our hands before we start."

"Half-vamps." Blair shouted the warning from dragon-back. "About fifty. First line, let's go." She dived down to lead the charge.

Arrows flew, and swords slashed. In the first hour, the Geallian forces were down fifteen men. But they held ground.

"They just wanted us to have a taste of it." With her face splattered with blood, Blair dismounted. "We gave them a bigger one."

"The dead and wounded have to be tended to." Steeling herself, Moira looked at the fallen, then away. "Hoyt's pushing back Midir's spell. How much is it costing him?"

"He'll have whatever he needs to have. I'm going up again, do a couple of circles. See if she's got any more surprises for us." Blair vaulted back on her dragon. "Hold the line."

"We weren't as prepared as we might have been for the traps, for a daylight attack." Sheathing his stained sword,

Larkin stepped to Moira. "But we did well. We'll do better yet."

He laid a hand on her arm, drawing her away so only she would hear. "Glenna says some are already here, under the ground. Hoyt can't work with her now, but she thinks between herself and Cian they can find at least some, and deal with it."

"Good. Even a handful will be a victory. I need to steady the archers."

The sun moved to midday, then beyond it. Twice she saw the ground open up where Glenna held a willow rod. Then the flash of fire as the thing burrowed in the earth caught the sun and flamed in it.

How many more, she wondered. A hundred? Five hundred?

"He's broken off." Hoyt swiped a hand over his sweaty face when he joined her. "Midir's traps are closed."

"You beat him back."

"I can't say. He may have gone to other work. But for now, he's blocked. This ground, it shakes the soul of a man. It pours up this evil it holds, all but chokes the breath. I'll help Cian and Glenna."

"No, you need to rest a few moments, save your energies. I'll help them."

Knowing he needed to gather himself, Hoyt nodded. But his eyes were grim as he scanned the valley, passed over where Glenna and Cian worked. "They won't be able to find them all. Not in this ground."

"No. But every one is one less."

Still when she reached Glenna, Moira could see the work was taking its toll. Glenna was pale, her skin clammy as Hoyt's had been. "It's time to rest," Moira told her. "Restore yourself. I'll work it awhile."

"It's beyond your power. It's on the edge of mine." Grateful, Glenna took the water bag Moira offered. "We've only unearthed a dozen. A couple more hours—"

"She needs to stop. You need to stop." Cian took Glenna's arm. "You're nearly tapped out, you know it. If you don't have anything left come sundown, what good will you be?"

"I know there are more. A lot more."

"Then we'll be ready when this ground spits them out. Go. Hoyt needs you. He's worn himself thin."

"Good strategy," Cian told Moira when Glenna walked away. "Using Hoyt."

"It is, but it's also true enough. We're draining them both. And you," she added. "I can hear in your voice how tired you are. So I'll say what you said to her. What good are you if you're worn out by sundown?"

"The bloody cloak smothers me. Then again, the alternative's not pleasant. I need to feed," he admitted.

"Then go, up to the high ground and see to it. We've done nearly all we can, all we set out to do by this time."

She saw Blair and Larkin with Hoyt and Glenna now. The six of them, together as the sun sank lower might push their strengths up again. They went across the broken ground, climbed over an island of pocked rock, and began up the hard slope.

Everything in her wanted to shudder when they reached the ridge. Even without Midir's spell, the ground seemed to pull at her feet.

Cian took out a water bag she knew held blood.

"Waiting on you," Blair began. "A lot of your troops have the jitters."

"If you're meaning they won't stand and fight—"

"Don't get all Geallian pride on me." Blair held up a hand for peace. "What they need is to hear from you, to get revved. They need their St. Crispin's Day speech."

"What's this?"

Blair arched her brows at Cian. "Guess you missed *Henry V* when you mowed through Cian's library."

"There were a lot of books, after all."

"It's about stirring them up," Glenna explained. "About getting them ready to fight, even die. Reminding them why they're here, inspiring them."

"I'm to do all of that?"

"No one else would have the same impact." Cian closed the water bag. "You're the queen, and while the rest of us might be generals, in a manner of speaking, you're the one they look to."

"I wouldn't know what to say."

"You'll think of something. While you are, Larkin and I will get your troops together. Add a little *Braveheart* to *Henry*," he said to Blair. "Get her on horseback."

"Excellent." Blair headed off to get Cian's horse.

"What did this Henry say?" Moira wondered.

"What they needed to hear." Glenna gave Moira's hand a squeeze. "So will you."

Chapter 20

"I don't have a thing in my head."

"It's not going to come from there. Or not only from there." Glenna handed Moira her circlet. "Head and heart, remember? Listen to both and whatever you say, it'll be the right thing."

"Then I wish you'd say it instead. Foolish to be afraid of speaking to them," Moira said with a weak smile. "And not as afraid to die with them."

"Put this on." Blair held out Moira's cloak. "Good visual, the cloak billowing in the wind. And speak up, kiddo. You have to project to the ones in the peanut gallery."

"I'll ask you what that means later." Moira took one huffing breath, then mounted the stallion. "Here we go then."

She walked the horse forward, then her heart gave a hard thud. There were her people, more than a thousand strong, standing with the valley at their backs. Even as the sun dipped lower in the sky, it glinted off sword and shield and lance. It washed over their faces, those who had come here, ready to give their lives.

And her head understood the words in her heart.

"People of Geall!"

They cheered as she trotted her horse in front of their lines. Even those already wounded called out her name.

"People of Geall, I am Moira, warrior queen. I am your sister; I am your servant. We have come to this time and this place by order of the gods, and so, to serve the gods. I know not all of your faces, all of your names, but you are mine, every man and woman here."

The wind caught at her cloak as she looked into those faces. "Tonight, when the sun sets, I ask you to fight, to stand this bitter ground that has already tasted our blood this day. I ask this of you, but you don't fight for me. You don't fight for the queen of Geall."

"We fight for Moira, the queen!" someone shouted. And again, her name rose up above the wind in cheers and chants.

"No, you don't fight for me! You don't fight for the gods. You don't fight for Geall, not this night. You don't fight for yourselves, or even your children. Not for your husbands, your wives. Your mothers and fathers."

They quieted as she continued to ride the lines, looking into those faces, meeting those eyes, "It's not for them you come here to this bitter valley, knowing your blood may spill on its ground. It's for all humankind you come here. For all humankind you stand here. You are the chosen. You are the blessed. All the worlds and every heart that beats in them is your heart now, your world now. We, the chosen, are one world, one heart, one purpose."

Her cloak snapped in the wind as the stallion pranced, and the dying sun glinted on the gold of her crown, the steel of her sword. "We will not fail this night. We cannot fail this night. For when one of us falls, there will be another to lift the sword, the lance, to fight with stake and fist the pestilence that threatens humanity and all it is. And if that next of us should fall, there will come another and another, and still more for we are the *world* here, and the enemy has never known the like of us."

Her eyes were like hell-smoke in a face illuminated with passion. Her voice soared over the air so the words rang out, strong and clear.

"Here, on this ground, we will drive them down even past hell." She continued to shout over the cheers that rippled and rose from the men and women like a wave. "We will not yield this night, we will not fail this night, but will stand and triumph this night. You are the heart they can never have. You are the breath and the light they will never know again. This night, they will sing of this Samhain, sing of The Battle of Silence, in every generation that comes after. They will sit by their fires and speak of the glory of what we do here. This night. The sun sets."

She drew her sword, pointed west where the sun had begun to bleed red. "Come the dark, we'll raise sword and heart and mind against them. And as the gods witness this, I swear it, we will raise the sun."

She sent fire rippling down the blade of her sword, and shooting into the sky.

"Not too shabby," Blair managed as the troops erupted with shouts and cheers. "Your girl's got a way with words."

"She's . . . brilliant." Cian kept his eyes on her. "How can they stand against that much light?"

"She spoke the truth," Hoyt stated. "They've never seen the likes of us."

The squadron leaders split the troops so they began to move into position. Moira rode back, dismounted.

"It's time," she said and held out her hands.

The six formed a circle to forge that final bond. Then released each other.

"See you on the flip side." Blair flashed a gleaming smile. "Go get 'em, cowboy." She leaped on her dragon, then shot skyward.

Larkin swung onto his own. "Last one to the pub when this is done buys the round." He flew up, and away from Blair.

"Blessed be. And let's kick ass." With Hoyt, Glenna started toward their posts, but she'd seen the look that had passed between the brothers. "What's going on with Cian? Don't lie this close to what might be bloody death."

"He asked for my word. If we're able to bring the spell into play, he asked for my word we not wait for him."

"But we can't—"

"It was the last he asked of me. Pray we won't have to make the choice."

Behind them, Moira stood with Cian. "Fight well," she said to him, "and live another thousand years."

"My fondest hope." He covered the lie by taking her hands a last time, pressing them to his lips. "Fight well, *mo croi*, and live."

Before she could speak again, he'd leaped onto his horse and galloped away.

From the air, Blair called out commands, directing her mount with her legs and scanning the ground for what would come with the dark. The sun fell, plunging the valley into night, and in that night, the ground erupted. They poured out of the ground, from earth, from rock, from crevice, in numbers too great to count.

"Show time," she whispered to herself, swinging south as arrows from Moira and her archers rained down. "Hold them, hold them." A quick glance to where Niall's foot soldiers' voices rose like chants told her Niall was waiting for the signal.

A little longer, a little more, she thought as vampires swarmed up the valley, as arrows pierced some, missed others.

She flashed the firesword and dove. As men charged, she yanked the rope on her harness, dropping the first bomb.

Fire and flaming shrapnel flew, and there were screams as vampires were engulfed. And still they spewed from the ground pushing their lines toward the Geallians.

Freed of his cloak, Cian sat his horse, his sword raised to hold the men at his back. Bombs exploded fire, scorching the enemy and the ground. But they came, slinking and slithering, clawing and leaping. On a cry of battle, Cian slashed his sword and led his troops into the firestorm.

With flashing hooves and hacking steel, he cleaved a hole in the advancing army's line. It closed again, surrounding him and his forces.

Screams came in a torrent.

On her sloping plateau, Moira gripped her battle-ax. Her heart knocked in her throat as she saw the vampires break through the line to the east. She led the charge even as Hoyt led his so that they took their warriors in a stream of steel and stake to flank the enemy's lines.

Over the screams, the crashes, the fire, came the trumpeting call of dragons. The next wave of Lilith's army was advancing.

"Arrows!" Moira shouted as her quiver emptied, and another, filled, was tossed at her feet.

She notched and loosed, notched and loosed until the air was so full of smoke the bow was useless.

She raised the fiery sword and rushed with her line into the thick of it.

Of all she'd feared, all she'd known, all she'd seen in the visions the gods had given her, what came through the smoke and stink was worse. Men and women already slaughtered, ash of vanquished enemy coating the bitter ground like fetid snow. Blood spurted like a fall of water, painting the yellowed grass red.

Shrieks, human and vampire, echoed in the dark under the pale, three-quarter moon.

She blocked a sword strike, and her body moved with the instinct of hard training to spin, to pivot, to block the next. When she leaped over a low slash, she felt the wind of the sword under her boots, and with a scream of her own slashed for the throat.

Through the haze she saw the dragon that held Blair spiraling to the ground with its side pierced with arrows. The ground was littered with stakes. Grabbing one in her free hand, she rushed forward, then flung it through the back and into the heart of one who charged at Blair.

"Thanks. Duck." Blair shoved Moira aside, and severed the sword arm of another. "Larkin."

"I don't know. They keep coming."

"Remember your own hype." Blair leaped up, striking with her feet, then rammed a stake through the one she'd kicked.

Then she was lost in the waves of smoke, and Moira was once again battling for her life.

As Blair hacked through the line, they closed in around her. She struck, sword, stake, fought to gain ground. And was suddenly soaked. As her attackers screamed from the flood of blessed water that rained down from above, Larkin flew out of the smoke, grabbing her lifted arm to haul her up behind him.

"Nice job," she told him. "Drop me off. There, big, flat rock."

"You drop me. It's my time to have a go down here. You're out of water, but there are two fireballs. She's pushing in hard from the south now."

"I'll give her some heat."

He leaped off, and she soared.

Through the melee, Hoyt searched with his eyes, with his power. He felt the brush of Midir's dark, but there was so much black, so much cold, he wasn't sure of its direction.

Then he saw Glenna, fighting her way back up a ridge. And standing on it like a black crow, was Midir. In horror, he watched a hand snake out of a fold of earth and rock and grab Glenna's leg. In his mind he heard her scream as she kicked, as she clawed to keep from being dragged into the crevice. Even knowing he was too far away, he rushed through swords. Continued to run even when the fire she shot from fingertips coated what dragged at her.

Sensing power, Midir hurled lightning, black as pitch, and had her flying back.

Mad with fear, Hoyt fought like a wild man, ignoring blows and gashes as he worked his way toward her. He could see the blood on her face as she answered Midir's lightning with white fire.

* * *

The stake missed Cian's heart by a hairsbreadth, and the pain buckled his knees. As he went down, he thrust his sword up, all but cleaving his attacker in two before he managed to roll. A lance dug into the stony ground beside him. He gripped it, heaved it up to strike at another heart. Then planting it, he vaulted up, kicking out to send another flying to the wooden stakes the Geallians had hammered into thc ground.

He saw Blair through the smoke that billowed from the fireballs and flaming arrows. With a pump of his legs, he leaped up, grabbing her dragon's harness to swing behind her an instant before she released another bomb.

"Didn't see you," she called out.

"Got that. Moira?"

"Don't know. Take over here. I'm going down."

She jumped down to the table of a rock. Cian saw her flip off, shooting stakes from both hands before the haze buried her. He swung his mount, aiming his sword, sending out fire. The ground continued to pull at him; its intoxicating scents of blood and fear driving hunger into him as keenly as a sharpened stake.

Then he saw Glenna, struggling her way up a sheer slope, and outnumbered three-to-one. Her battle-ax flamed, and each time she took an enemy, more crawled their way up toward her.

And when he saw the black figure on the high ridge, he understood why so many would go against a single woman.

The power of the circle battled back the hunger as he swept through the air toward his brother's wife.

He sent three tumbling down against rock, into traps of stakes and pools of holy water with a wild strike from the dragon's tale. His sword took two more even as Glenna's fiery ax turned enemies into flaming dust.

"Give you a lift?" He swooped down, circled her waist with his arm and hauled her up.

"Midir. The bastard."

Understanding, Cian soared up again. But when he struck out with the dragon's tail, it bounced off as if it hit rock.

"He's shielded. The coward." Breath short and choppy, Glenna searched the ground for Hoyt. And felt the lock on her lungs release when she saw him fighting his way up the slope.

"Set me down on the ridge, and go."

"The hell I will."

"This is what's needed, Cian. It's magic against magic for this. This is why I'm here. Find the others, get ready. Because by all the gods and goddesses, we're going to do this."

"Okay, Red. My money's on you."

He flew over the ridge, pausing while she slid down. And left her to face the black sorcerer.

"So, the red witch has come here to die."

"I didn't come for the ambiance."

She raised a hand, and charged with a swing of her ax. The widening of his eyes told her the move had surprised him. The flaming edge of the ax cut through the shield, but the blade missed its mark. She was propelled back, lifted into the air, slammed hard into the ground.

Though she threw out her own power, the scorching heat of his black lightning seared the palms of her hands. She held them out, held her power in them as she pushed painfully to her feet.

"You can't win this," he told her as dark shimmered around him. "I've seen the end, and your death."

"You've seen what whatever devil you sold yourself to wants you to see." She hurled fire, and though he deflected it with a snap of his wrist, she knew he felt her burn even as she'd felt his. "The end's what we make it."

With icy fury on his face, he brought a cutting wind that slashed at her skin like knives.

They were holding, Blair thought. She believed they were holding, but for every foot of ground the Geallians held, more vampires swarmed through the night and over it.

She'd lost track of her kills. A dozen at least with sword

and stake, at least that many with air attacks. And still it wasn't enough. Bodies littered the ugly ground, and even her strength was pushed to its limit.

They needed to pull the rabbit out of the hat, she thought, and screamed in vengeance as she slayed a vampire who'd stopped to feed on one of the fallen.

Whirling, slashing at others, she saw Glenna and Midir on the high ridge, and the firestorm of black against white as they battled.

She grabbed a lance from a dead hand, shot it out like a javelin. The spear tip went through two vampires fighting back to back, and the wood pole pierced hearts.

Something leaped down from above. Her senses caught just the edge of it, and her instincts had her pumping up into a high, wide flip. She slashed her sword as she touched ground, and clashed it against Lora's.

"There you are." Lora slid her blade down until it met Blair's to form a V. "I've been looking for you."

"Been around. You got something on your face there. Oh! Gee, is that a scar? Did I do that? My bad."

"I'll be eating your face shortly."

"You know that's wishful thinking, right? In addition to being disgusting. Enough small talk for you?"

"More than."

The swords sang as they slid apart. Then the music crescendoed as blade struck blade.

In moments, Blair understood she was facing the most formidable enemy of her career. Lora might look like a B movie dominatrix wrapped in snug black leather, but the French bitch could fight.

And take a punch, she thought when she finally got past Lora's guard long enough to slam a fist in the vampire's face. Blair felt the burn shoot a line across her knuckles as fangs sliced her flesh.

Blair flipped up to the jagged teeth of a rock, hacked down. And met air as Lora rose off the ground as if she had wings. Lora's sword whistled past Blair's face, and the tip of it sliced her cheek.

"Oh, will that leave a scar?" Lora landed on the rock with her. "My bad."

"It'll heal. Nothing about you is going to last much longer."

She answered first blood with a lightning parry of her own, gashing Lora's arm, then followed it through with a ripple of fire.

But Lora's sword struck the blade aside, going black against the red flame. The fire spurted and died.

"You think we weren't ready for that?" Lora bared her teeth as they hacked and thrust and swung. "Midir's magic is more than your magicians can ever hope for."

"Then why don't all of your troops have swords like yours? He couldn't pull it off." Blair flew up again, flipping over and striking Lora with her feet. The vampire used the momentum to soar up, driving down with the sword on her descent.

Raising hers to block, Blair didn't see the dagger that flew out of Lora's other hand. She stumbled from the shock, the pain, when it pierced her side.

"Look at all that blood. It's just pouring out of you. Yum." Lora laughed, a tinkling sound of delight, when Blair fell to her knees. And her eyes gleamed red as she raised the sword high for the killing blow.

With a mad, undulating howl, the gold wolf pounced from above. Claws and fangs raked as he leaped over the swinging sword, as he lunged and snapped. When he bunched to spring for the throat, Blair cursed.

"No! She's mine. You gave your word." Her breath whistled as she stayed on her knees, the dagger still lodged in her side. "Back off, wolf-boy. Back the hell off."

The wolf shimmered into a man as Larkin stepped back. "Get it done then," he snapped, his eyes grim. "And stop messing about."

"Pussy-whipped, is he?" Lora circled so that she could keep them both in her line of sight—the bleeding woman, the unarmed man. "But he's right, we really should stop messing about. I've a busy schedule."

She swung the sword down, and Blair thrust hers up to meet it, to block it, to hold it. The muscles in her arms screamed with the strain and her side wept blood and agony.

"I'm no pussy," she panted. "He's not whipped. And you're done."

She yanked the dagger from her side, stabbed it to its bloodied hilt into Lora's belly.

"That hurts, but it's steel."

"So's this." With all her remaining strength, Blair shoved Lora's sword aside, and plunged her own into the vampire's chest.

"Now you're just annoying me." Lora hefted her sword, point down. "Now who's done?"

"You," Blair replied as the blade still in Lora's chest erupted with flame.

Burning, screaming, Lora started to tumble from the rock. Blair yanked the sword free, swung it, hard and true, and cut off the flaming head.

"Fucking well done." Blair stumbled, swayed, would have fallen if Larkin hadn't sprung forward to catch her.

"How bad? How bad?" He pressed his hand to her bleeding side.

"Through and through, I think. No organs hit. Quick patch to stop the bleeding and I'm back in the game."

"We'll see about that. Get on."

When he shimmered into a dragon, Blair crawled onto his back. As they soared she saw Glenna on the ridge clashing with Midir. And she saw her friend fall.

"Oh God, she's hit. She's done. How fast can you get there?"

Inside the dragon Larkin thought: Not fast enough.

Glenna tasted blood in her mouth. There was more seeping out of a dozen shallow slices in her skin. She knew she'd hurt him, knew she'd chipped at his shield, his body, even his power.

But she could feel her own power ebbing out of her along with her blood.

She'd done all she could, and it hadn't been enough.

"Your fire's cooling. Barely an ember left to glow." Midir stepped closer now to where she lay on the scorched and bloody ground. "Still it might be enough to trouble myself to take, along with what's left of your life."

"It'll choke you." She gasped out the words. He'd bled, she thought. She'd made him bleed onto the ground. "I swear it will."

"I'll swallow it whole. It's so small, after all. Can you see below, can you? Where what I helped wrought runs over you like locusts. It's as I foretold. And as you fall, one by one, my power grows. Nothing will hold it now. Nothing will stop it."

"I will." Hoyt swung, bloody and battered, over the lip of the ridge.

"There's my guy," Glenna managed, gritting her teeth against the pain. "I softened him up for you."

"Now here is something more to chew on." Whirling, Midir shot black lighting.

It crashed, sizzled, spewed bloody flames when it struck against Hoyt's blinding white. The force blew them both back, searing the air between them. On the ground, Glenna rolled away from a streaking line of flame, then clawed to her hands and knees.

Whatever she had left, she gathered to send to Hoyt. Closing a trembling hand around the cross at her neck she focused her power into it, and to its twin Hoyt wore.

While she chanted, the sorcerers—black and white—battled on the smoke-hazed ridge, and in the filthy air above it.

The fire that sliced at Hoyt carried the burn of ice. It sought his blood—what was shed, what it aimed to shed, to draw away his power.

It clawed and slashed at him while the air flashed and boomed with magicks, sending smoke billowing high to drown the swimming moon. The ground beneath his feet cracked, splitting fissures under the enormity of pressure.

While his lungs labored and his heart pounded, he ignored those earthy demands on his body, ignored the pains from his wounds and the sweat that ran salt into them.

He was power now. Beyond that moment at the beginning of this journey when he'd wavered for an instant over the black. Now, on this ridge over blood and death, over the courage of man, the sacrifice and the fury, he was the white-hot flame of power.

The cross he wore flashed silver and brilliant as Glenna joined her magic to his. With one hand he reached for hers, gripping it firmly when she linked fingers with him and pulled herself to her feet. With the other he raised a sword, and the fire on it went pure white.

"It is we who take you," Hoyt began and slashed away a thunderbolt with his sword. "We who stand for the purity of magic, for the heart of mankind. It is we who defeat you, who destroy you, who send you forever into the flames."

"Be damned to you!" Midir shouted, and lifting both arms hurled twin thunderbolts. Fear rushed over his face when Glenna waved a hand over the air and turned them to ash.

"No. Be damned to you." Hoyt swung down the sword. The white fire leaped from the blade to strike Midir's heart like steel.

Where he dropped and died, the ground turned black.

High ground, Moira thought. She had to get back to higher ground, regroup the archers. She'd heard the shouts warning that their line had broken again to the north. Flaming arrows would drive that invading force back, give the troops in its path time to forge their lines again. She searched through the melee for a horse or dragon that would take her where she knew she was most needed.

And looking up saw Hoyt and Glenna bathed in brilliant white, facing Midir. A spurt of fresh hope had her racing forward. Even as the ground seemed to catch at her feet, she swung her sword at an advancing enemy. The gash she served it slowed it down, and as she poised to strike again, Riddock took it from behind.

With a fierce grin, he charged with a handful of men toward the broken line. He lived, she thought. Her uncle lived. As she raced to join him, the ground bucked under her feet, sent her sprawling.

As she pushed up she looked down into Isleen's dead and staring eyes.

"No. No. No."

Isleen's throat was torn open, the leather strap where Moira knew she'd worn a wooden cross was snapped and soaked with blood. Grief struck so strong, so deep, she gathered the body up against her.

Still warm, she thought as she rocked. Still warm. If she'd been faster, she might have saved Isleen.

"Isleen. Isleen."

"Isleen. Isleen." The words were a mocking mimic as Lilith flowed out of the smoke.

She'd dressed for battle in red and silver, a mitre like Moira's banding her head. Her sword was bloody to its jeweled hilt. Seeing her crashed waves of fear and fury through Moira that had her surging to her feet.

"Look at you." The grace and deftness with which Lilith spun the sword as she circled warned Moira this vampire queen knew the art of the blade. "Small and insignificant, covered with mud and tears. I'm amazed I wasted so much time planning your death when it's all so simple."

"You won't win here." Queen to queen, Moira thought, and blocked Lilith's first testing thrust. Life against death. "We're beating you back. We'll never stop."

"Oh please." Lilith waved the words away. "Your lines are crumbling like clay, and I've two hundred yet in reserve. But that's neither here nor there. This is you and me."

With barely a blink, Lilith shot out a hand, grabbing the soldier who charged her by the throat. And snapping his neck. She tossed him carelessly to the ground, while slicing down at Moira's swinging fire sword.

"Midir has his uses," Lilith said when the fire died.

"I want to take my time with you, you human bitch. You killed my Davey."

"No, you did. And with what you made of him destroyed, I hope what he was, the innocent he was, is cursing you."

Lilith's hand streaked out, flashing like the fangs of a snake. She raked her nails down Moira's cheek.

"A thousand cuts." She licked the blood from her fingers. "That's what I'll give you. A thousand cuts while my army feeds its belly full on yours."

"You won't touch her again." On his stallion's back, Cian rode slowly forward, as if time had stopped. "You'll never touch her again."

"Come to save your whore?" From her belt, Lilith drew a gold stake. "Gilded oak. I had this made for you, for when I end you as I made you. Tell me, doesn't all this blood stir you? Warm pools of it, bodies not yet cooled waiting to be drained. I know what's in you wants that taste. I put it in you, and I know it as I know myself."

"You never knew me. Go," he said to Moira.

"Yes, run along. I'll find you later."

She flew at Cian, then sprang up a sword's length away to spin over his head. As she sliced down, her sword met air while he threw his body up and back, with the heels of his boots barely missing her face.

They moved so fast, that eerie speed, that Moira saw little more than a blur, heard the clash of swords like silver thunder. This would be his battle, she knew, the one only he could fight. But she wouldn't leave him.

Leaping onto the horse, she drove Vlad up blood-slicked rock until she was positioned over their heads. There she shot fire from her sword to hold off Lilith's men who tried to reach their queen. She vowed that she and the sword of Geall would stand for her lover to the last.

Lilith was skilled, Cian knew. After all, she had centuries to learn the arts of war just as he had. Her strength and speed were as great as his. Perhaps greater. She blocked him, drove him back, slithered away from the force of his attack.

This ground was still hers, he knew. This pocket of black. She fed off it, as he didn't dare. She fed off the screams that echoed through the air and the blood that seemed to spew through it like rain.

He fought her, and the war inside him, the thing that struggled to claw free and revel in what it was. What she'd made him. Taking her advantage, she beat his sword aside, and in that flash of an instant he was open, plunged the stake at his heart.

It struck with a force that sent him staggering back. But as her cry of triumph echoed away, he continued to stand whole and unharmed.

"How?" was all she said as she stared at him.

He felt the imprint of Moira's locket against his heart, and the pain was sweet. "A magic you'll never know." He sliced out, scoring across the scar of the pentagram. The blood that welled from the wound was black and thick as tar.

Pain and fury brought the demon to her eyes, the killing red. Now her screams rang as she came at him with a new and wild strength. He slashed back, spilled more blood, drove as he was driven as the locket seemed to pulse like a heart on his chest.

Her sword ripped down his arm, sending his clattering against the rocks. "Now you! Then your whore!"

When she charged, he gripped the wrist of her sword arm in his bloody hand. She smiled at him. "This way then. It's more poetic."

She bared her fangs to strike at his throat. And he plunged the stake she had made for him into her heart.

"I'd say go to hell, but even hell won't have you."

Her eyes went wide, faded to blue. He felt the wrist he held dissolve in his hand, and still those eyes stared into his another moment.

Then there was nothing but the ash at his feet.

"I've ended you," he declared, "as you ended me so long ago. That's poetic."

The ground under his feet began to quake. So, he thought, it comes.

The black stallion leaped from the rocks, scattering ash. "You've done it." Moira vaulted from the saddle into his arms. "You've beaten her. You've won."

"This saved me." He dragged her locket out, showed her the deep dent in the silver from the force of the stake. "You saved me."

"Cian." As the rock behind her split like an egg, she jumped down, and her face went pale again. "Hurry. Go, hurry. It's begun. Her blood, her end, was the last of it. They've started the spell."

"It's you who beat her, you who won. Remember that." He pulled her into his arms, crushed his mouth to hers. Then he was flying onto the horse, and was gone.

Everything around her was chaos. Screams and shouts through the haze, the moans of wounded, the rush of the enemy in mad retreat.

A gold dragon speared through it, Blair on its back. With the ground rippling in waves under her, Moira lifted her arms so Larkin could cradle her in his claws. She flew over the quivering land toward the high ridge.

On it, Hoyt gripped Moira's hand. "It must be now."

"Cian. We can't be sure—"

"I gave my word to him. It must be now." He raised their joined hands, and together they lifted their faces, their voices to the black sky.

"In this place once damned we hold the power, and we wield it in this final hour. On this ground blood was shed in blackest night, theirs for dark and ours for light. Black magic and demon here are felled by our hand, and now we claim this bloody land. Now call forth all we have done. Now through dark we raise the sun. Its light will strike our enemy. As we will, so mote it be."

The ground trembled, and the wind blew like a fury.

"We call the sun!" Hoyt shouted. "We call the light!"

"We call the dawn!" Glenna's voice rose with his, and the power grew as Moira clasped her free hand. "Burn off the night."

"Rise in the east," Moira chanted, staring through the

smoke that swirled up around them while Larkin and Blair completed the circle. "Spread to the west."

"It's coming," Blair cried. "Look. Look east."

Over the shadow of mountains the sky lightened, and the light spread and speared and grew until it was bright as noon.

Below, fleeing vampires burned to nothing.

On the rocky, broken ground, flowers began to bloom.

"Do you see that?" Larkin's hand tightened on Moira's, and his voice was thick, reverent. "The grass, it's greening."

She saw it, and the sweet charm of the white and yellow flowers that spread over its carpet. She saw the bodies of the fallen on the meadow of a lush and sun-lit valley.

But nowhere did she see Cian.

Chapter 21

Though the battle was won, there was still work. Moira labored with Glenna in what Glenna called triage for the wounded. Blair and Larkin had taken a party out to hunt down any vampires that might have found shelter from the sun while Hoyt helped transport those whose wounds were less severe back to one of the bases.

After rinsing blood from her hands again, Moira stretched her back. And spotting Ceara wandering as if in a daze, rushed to her.

"Here, here, you're hurt." Moira pressed a hand to the wound on Ceara's shoulder. "Come, let me dress this."

"My husband." Her gaze roamed from pallet to pallet even as she leaned heavily against Moira. "Eogan. I can't find my husband. He's—"

"Here. He's here. I'll take you. He's been asking for you."

"Wounded?" Ceara swayed. "He's—"

"Not mortally, I promise you. And seeing you, he'll heal all the quicker. There, over there, you see? He's—"

Moira got no further as Ceara cried out and in a stumbling run rushed to fall to her knees beside where her husband lay.

"It's good to see, good for the heart to see."

She turned, smiled at her uncle. Riddock, his arm and leg bandaged, sat on a supply crate.

"I wish all lovers would be reunited as they are. But . . . we lost so many. More than three hundred dead, and the count still coming."

"And how many live, Moira?" He could see the wounds she bore on her body, and in her eyes the wounds she bore on her heart. "Honor the dead, but rejoice in the living."

"I will. I will." Still she scanned the wounded, those who tended them, and feared for only one. "Are you strong enough to travel home?"

"I'll go with the last. I'll bring our dead home, Moira. Leave that for me."

She nodded, and after embracing him went back to her duties. She was helping a soldier sip water when Ceara found her again.

"His leg, Eogan's leg . . . Glenna said he won't lose it, but—"

"Then he won't. She wouldn't lie to you, or to him."

On a steadying breath, Ceara nodded. "I can help. I want to help." Ceara touched her bandaged shoulder. "Glenna looked after me, and said I'm well enough. I've seen Dervil. She came through very well. Cuts and bruises for the most of it."

"I know."

"I saw your cousin Oran, and he said Sinann's Phelan's already on his way back to Castle Geall. But I haven't found Isleen as yet. Have you seen her?"

Moira lowered the soldier's head, then rose. "She did not come through."

"No, my lady, she must have. You just haven't seen her." Again, Ceara searched the pallets that stretched over the wide field. "There are so many."

"I did see her. She fell in the battle."

"No. Oh no." Ceara covered her face with her hands. "I'll tell Dervil." Tears flowed down her cheeks when she lowered her hands. "She's trying to find Isleen now. I'll tell her, and we'll . . . I can't fathom it, my lady. I can't fathom it."

"Moira!" Glenna called from across the field. "I need you here."

"I'll tell Dervil," Ceara repeated and hurried away.

Moira worked until the sun began to dim again, then exhausted and sick with worry, flew on Larkin to the farm where she would spend one last night.

He would be here, she told herself. Here is where he would be. Safe out of the sunlight, and helping organize the supplies, the wounded, the transportation. Of course, he would be here.

"Near dark," Larkin said when he stood beside her. "And there'll be nothing in Geall that will hunt in it tonight but that which nature has made."

"You found none at all, no enemy survivors."

"Ash, only ash. Even in caves and deep shade there was ash. As if the sun we brought burned through it all, and there was none of them could survive it no matter where they hid."

Her already pale face went gray, and he gripped her arm.

"It's different for him, you know it. He'd have had the cloak. He'd have gotten it in time. You can't believe any magic we'd bring would harm one of our own."

"No, of course. Of course, you're right. I'm just tired, that's all."

"You'll put something in your belly, then lay your head down." He led her into the house.

Hoyt stood with Blair and Glenna. Something on their faces turned Moira's knees to water.

"He's dead."

"No." Hoyt hurried forward to take her hands. "No, he survived it."

Tears she'd held for hours spilled out of her eyes and flooded her cheeks. "You swear it? He's not dead. You've seen him, spoken to him?"

"I swear it."

"Sit, Moira, you're exhausted."

But she shook her head at Glenna's words and kept her eyes on Hoyt's face. "Upstairs? Is he upstairs?" A shudder passed through her as she understood what she read in Hoyt's eyes. "No," she said slowly. "He's not upstairs. Or in the house, or in Geall at all. He's gone. He's gone back."

"He felt . . . Damnation, I'm sorry for this, Moira. He was determined to go, straight away. I gave him my key, and he was going by dragon-back to the Dance. He said . . ."

Hoyt took a sealed paper from a table. "He asked if I'd give you this."

She stared at it, and finally nodded. "Thank you."

They said nothing as she took the paper and went upstairs alone.

She closed herself in the room she'd shared with him, lit the candles. Then sitting, simply held the letter to her heart until she had the strength to break the seal.

And read.

Moira,

This is best. The sensible part of you understands that. Staying longer would only prolong pain, and there's been enough of it for a dozen lifetimes. Leaving you is an act of love. I hope you understand that, too.

I have so many pictures of you in my head. Of you sitting on the floor in my library surrounded by books, poring through them. Of you laughing with King or Larkin as you so rarely laughed with me in those first weeks. Courageous in battle or lost in thought. You never knew how often I watched you, and wanted you.

I'll see you in the morning mists, drawing a shining sword from a stone, and flying a dragon with arrows singing from your bow.

I'll see you in candlelight, holding out your arms

to me, taking me into a light I've never known before or will know again.

You've saved your world and mine, and however many others there might be. I think you were right that we were meant to find each other, to be together to forge the strength, the power needed to save those worlds.

Now it's time to step away.

I'm asking you to be happy, to rebuild your world, your life, and to embrace both. To do less would be a dishonor to what we had. To what you gave me.

With you, somehow with you, I was a man again.

That man loved you beyond measure. What I am that is not a man loved you, despite everything. In all the centuries I've loved you. If you loved me, you'll do what I ask.

Live for me, Moira. Even a world apart, I'll know that you do and be content.

Cian

She would weep. A human heart needed to shed such a deep well of tears. Lying on the bed where they'd loved each other for the last time, she pressed the letter to her heart, and let it empty.

New York City
Eight weeks later

He spent a great deal of time in the dark, and a great deal of time with whiskey. When a man had eternity, Cian figured he could take a decade or two to brood. Maybe a century since he'd given up the love of his endless bloody life.

He'd come around, of course. Of course he would. He'd get back to business. Travel for a while. Drink a bit longer first. A year or two of a sodding drunk never hurt the undead.

He knew she was well, helping her people recover, planning the monument she would build in the valley come the next spring. They'd buried their dead, and she herself had read every name—nearly five hundred of them—at the memorial.

He knew because the others were back now as well, and had insisted on giving him details he hadn't asked for.

At least Blair and Larkin were in Chicago now and wouldn't be hammering at him to talk or get together with them. You'd think humans, after spending such an intense amount of time with him, would know he wasn't feeling sociable.

He was going to wallow, goddamn it. The lot of them would be long dead, by his estimation, before he was finished wallowing.

He poured more whiskey. He told himself at least he had enough standards left not to drink it straight from the bottle.

And here were Hoyt and Glenna nagging at him to spend Christmas with them. Christmas, for bleeding Judas's sake. What did he care for Christmas? He wished they would go the hell back to Ireland and the house he'd given them and leave him be.

Did they have Christmas in Geall? he wondered, running his fingers over the dented silver locket he wore night and day. He'd never asked about that particular custom—but why should he have. It would likely be Yule there, with burning logs and music. Whatever, it was nothing to him now.

But she should celebrate, Moira should. Light a thousand candles and set Castle Geall glowing. Hang the holly bushes and strike up the bloody band.

When the hell was this pain going to ebb? How many oceans of whiskey would it take to dull it?

He heard the hum of the elevator and scowled over at it. He'd told the shagging doorman no one was to be let up, hadn't he? He ought to snap the idiot's neck like a used chopstick.

But no matter, he mused, he'd locked the mechanism from inside as second line of defense.

They could come up, but they couldn't get in.

He could barely drum up a curse when the doors slid open, and he saw Glenna step into the dark.

"Oh for pity's sake." Her voice was impatient, and an instant later, the lights flashed on.

They seared his eyes so that this time his curses were loud and heartfelt.

"Look at you." She set aside the large and elegantly wrapped box she'd carried in. "Sitting in the dark like a—"

"Vampire. Go away."

"It reeks of whiskey in here." As if she owned the place, she walked into his kitchen and began making coffee. While it was brewing she came out to find him exactly as he'd been.

"Merry Christmas to you, too." She angled her head. "You need a shave, a haircut—and one day when you're not sulking I'm going to ask how you accomplish that sort of thing. A shave," she repeated, "a haircut, and since whiskey's not the only reek in here, a bath."

His eyes remained hooded, and his lips curved without a whiff of humor. "Going to give me one, Red?"

"If that's what it takes. Why don't you clean yourself up, Cian, come back to the apartment with me? We have plenty of leftover Christmas dinner. It's Christmas Day," she said to his blank look. "Nearly nine o'clock Christmas night, actually, and I've left my husband home alone because he's as stubborn as you and won't come back here without an invitation."

"That's something anyway. I don't want leftovers. Or that coffee you're making in there." He lifted his glass. "I've got what I want."

"Fine. Stay drunk and smelly and miserable. But maybe you'll want this, too."

She marched over to the box, hefted it, then brought it over to drop it in his lap. "Open it."

He studied it without interest "But I didn't get anything for you."

She crouched at his feet now. "We'll consider your opening it my gift. Please. It's important to me."

"Will you go away if I open it?"

"Soon."

To placate her, he lifted the lid with its silver paper and elaborate bow, brushed aside the top layer of sparkling tissue.

And Moira looked out at him.

"Ah, damn you, damn you, Glenna." Neither whiskey nor will could hold against the image of her. Emotion shook in his voice as he lifted the framed portrait. "It's beautiful. She's beautiful."

Glenna had painted her in that moment Moira had drawn the sword free from the stone. The dreaminess and power of it, with green shadows, silver mists, and the new queen standing with the shining sword pointed toward the heavens.

"I thought, hoped, that having it would remind you what you helped give her. She wouldn't have stood there without you. There'd be no Geall without you. I wouldn't be here without you. None of us would have survived this without each one of us." She laid a hand on his. "We're still a circle, Cian. We always will be."

"I did the right thing for her, leaving. I did the right thing."

"Yes." She squeezed his hand now. "You did the right thing, an enormous and pure act of love. But knowing you did the right thing for all the right reasons doesn't stop the pain."

"Nothing does. Nothing."

"I'd say time will, but I don't know if it's true." Sympathy swam in her voice, in her eyes. "I will say you have friends and family who love you, and will be there for you. You have people who love you, Cian, who hurt for you."

"I don't know how to take what you want to give me, not yet. But this." He traced his finger around the frame. "Thank you for this."

"You're welcome. There are photographs, too. Ones I took in Ireland. I thought you might like to have them."

He started to lift the next layers of tissue, then stopped. "I need a moment."

"Sure. I'll go finish the coffee."

Alone, he uncovered the large manila envelope, and opened it.

There were dozens of them. One of Moira and his books, and with Larkin outside. One of King reigning over the stove in the kitchen, of Blair, eyes intense, sweat sheening her skin as she held a sword in warrior position.

There was one of himself and Hoyt he hadn't known she'd taken.

As he studied each one his feelings swirled and mixed, pleasure and sorrow.

When he looked up at last he saw Glenna leaning against the doorjamb with a mug of coffee in her hand. "I owe you more than a gift."

"No, you don't. Cian, we're going back to Geall for New Year's. All of us."

"I can't."

"No," she said after a moment, and the understanding in her eyes nearly broke him. "I know you can't. But if there's any message—"

"There can't be. There's too much to say, Glenna, and nothing to say. You're sure you can go back?"

"Yes, we have Moira's key, and an assurance of Morrigan herself. You didn't wait around long enough for the thanks of the gods."

She walked over, set the coffee on the table beside him. "If you change your mind, we're not leaving until midday, New Year's Eve. If you don't, after that Hoyt and I will be in Ireland. We hope you'll come see us. Blair and Larkin are taking my apartment here."

"Vampires of New York, beware."

"Damn right." She leaned over, kissed him. "Happy Christmas."

He didn't drink the coffee, but he didn't drink any more whiskey either. Surely that was a step somewhere. Instead he sat and studied Moira's portrait, and the hours passed that way toward midnight.

A swirl of light brought him out of the chair. Since it

was the closest weapon, he grabbed the whiskey bottle by the neck. As he wasn't nearly drunk enough for hallucinations, he decided the goddess standing in his apartment was real.

"Well, this is a red-letter day. I wonder if such as you has ever paid a call on such as me before."

"You are of the six," Morrigan said.

"I was."

"Are. Yet you hold yourself apart from them again. Tell me, vampire, why did you fight? Not for me or mine."

"No, not for the gods. Why?" He shrugged, and now did drink from the bottle in a kind of defiance, of disrespect. "It was something to do."

"It's foolish for such as you to pretend with such as me. You believed it was right, that it was worth fighting for, even ending your own existence for. I've known your kind since they first crawled through the blood. None would have done what you did."

"You sent my brother here to see I fell into line."

The god lifted her brow at his tone, then inclined her head. "I sent your brother to find you. Your will was your own. You have love for this woman." She gestured toward Moira's portrait. "For this human."

"You think we can't love?" Cian's voice shook with rage, with grief. "You think we aren't capable of love?"

"I know that you are, and while that love may run deep in your kind, its selfishness runs as strong. But not yours." Robes flowing, she walked to the portrait. "She asked you to make her one of you, but you refused. You could have kept her had you done as she asked."

"Like a goddamn pet? Kept her? Damned her is what it would have done, killed her, crushed out that light in her."

"Given her eternity."

"Of dark, of a craving for the blood of what she'd been. Condemned her to a life that is no life. She didn't know what she asked me."

"She knew. Such a strong heart and mind she has, and courage, yet she asked and she knew, and would have given you her life. You've done well, haven't you? You have culture and wealth, skills. Fine homes."

"That's right. Made something of my dead self. Why shouldn't I?"

"And enjoy it—when you're not sitting in the dark brooding over what can't be. What you can't have. You enjoy your eternity, your youth, your strength and knowledge."

He sneered now, damning the gods. "Would you rather I beat my breast over my fate? Endlessly mourn my own death? Is that what the gods demand?"

"We demand nothing. We asked, and you gave. Gave more than we believed you would. If it were otherwise, I wouldn't be here."

"Fine. Now you can go away again."

"Nor," she continued in the same easy tone, "would I give you this choice. Continue to live, grow wealthier yet. Century upon century, with no age, no sickness, and the blessings of the gods."

"Got that already, without your blessing."

Her eyes sparkled a little, but he couldn't tell—didn't care—if it was amusement or temper. "But now it's given to you, the only of your kind who has it. You and I know more of death than any human can. And fear it more. There need be no end to you. Or you can have an end."

"What? Staked by the gods?" He snorted out a laugh, took another long pull from the bottle. "Burned in godfire? A purification of my condemned soul?"

"You can be what you were, and have a life that comes to an end as all do. You can be alive, and so age and sicken and one day know the death as a man knows it."

The bottle slipped out of his fingers, thudded on the floor. "What?"

"This is your choice," Morrigan said, holding out both hands, palms up. "Eternity, with our blessing to enjoy it. Or a handful of human years. What will you, vampire?"

* * *

In Geall, a quiet snow had fallen, a thin blanket over the ground. The morning sunlight glinted off it, and sparkled on the ice that coated the trees.

Moira passed her cousin's infant back to Sinann. "She's prettier every day, and I could spend hours just looking at her. But our company's coming after midday. I haven't finished preparing."

"You brought them home to me." Sinann nuzzled her daughter. "All I love. I wish you could have all you love, Moira."

"I had a lifetime in a few weeks." She gave the baby a last kiss, then glanced around in surprise as Ceara rushed in.

"Majesty. There's someone . . . downstairs, there's someone who wishes to see you."

"Who?"

"I . . . I was only told there's a visitor who's traveled far to speak with you."

Moira's eyebrows shot up when Ceara dashed away again. "Well, whoever it is has her fluttered up. I'll see you again later."

She went out, brushing at her trousers. They'd been cleaning for days in preparation of the new year and her most anticipated guests. To see them again, she thought, to speak with them. To watch Larkin grin over his new niece.

Would they bring any word, any at all, of Cian?

She pressed her lips together, reminded herself not to let her inner grieving show. It was a time of celebration, of holiday. She would not put a pall over Geall after all they'd fought to preserve.

Something trembled along her skin as she started down the stairs. Shivered up her spine and to the base of her neck where her lover had liked to press his lips.

Then it trembled in her heart, and she began to run. That trembling heart began to race. And then to soar.

What she believed never could be was, and he was there, standing there, looking up at her.

"Cian." The joy that had been shut away burst out of her, like music. "You came back." She would have launched herself into his arms, but he was staring at her so intently, so strangely she wasn't sure she'd be welcomed. "You came back."

"I wondered what I'd see on your face. I wondered. Can we speak in private?"

"Of course. Aye, we'll . . ." Flustered, she looked around. "It seems we are. Everyone's gone." What could she do with her hands to stop them from touching him? "How did you come? How—"

"It's New Year's Eve," he said, watching her. "The end of the old, the start of the new. I wanted to see you, on the edge of that change."

"I wanted to see you, no matter when or where. The others come in a few hours. You'll stay. Please say you'll stay for the feasting."

"It depends."

Her throat burned as if she'd swallowed flame. "Cian. I know what you said in your letter was true, but it was hard, so hard, not to see you again. To have our last moment together standing in blood. I wanted . . ." Tears flooded her eyes, and she nearly lost the war to will them back. "I wanted just a moment more. Now I have it."

"Would you take more than a moment, if I could give it?"

"I don't understand." Then she smiled and choked back a sob when he drew the locket she'd given him from under his shirt. "You still wear it."

"Yes, I still wear it. It's one of my most treasured possessions. I left nothing of me behind for you. Now I'm asking, would you take more than that moment, Moira? Would you take this?" He lifted her hand, pressed it to his heart.

"Oh, I was afraid you didn't want to touch me." Her breath shuddered out with relief. "Cian, you know, you must know, that I . . ."

The hand beneath his trembled, and her eyes went wide. "Your heart. Your heart beats."

"Once I told you if it could beat, it would beat for you. It does."

"It beats under my hand," she whispered. "How?"

"A gift from the gods in the last moments of Yule. They gave me back what was taken from me." Now he drew out the silver cross that hung around his neck with her locket. "It's a man who stands before you, Moira."

"Human," she whispered. "You live."

"It's a man who loves you." He pulled her toward the doors, flung them open so the sun poured over them. And because it was still so miraculous, he lifted his face, closed his eyes and let the stream of it bathe his face.

She couldn't stop the tears now, or the sobs that came with them. "You're alive. You came back to me and you're alive."

"It's a man who stands before you," he said again. "It's a man who loves you. It's a man who asks if you'll share the life he's been given, if you'll live it with him. If you'll take me as I am, and make a life with me. Geall will be my world, as you're my world. It will be my heart, as you're my heart. If you'll have me."

"I've been yours from the first moment, and I'll be yours until the last. You came back to me." She laid a hand on his heart, and the other on her own. "And my heart beats again."

She threw her arms around him, and those who'd gathered in the courtyard, and on the stairs cheered as the queen of Geall kissed her beloved in the winter sunlight.

"So they lived," the old man said, "and they loved. So the circle grew stronger, and formed circles out from it as ripples spread in a pool. The valley that had once been silent sang with music of summer breezes through green grass, the lowing of cattle. Of pipes and harps and the laughter of children."

The old man stroked the hair of a little one who'd climbed into his lap. "Geall flourished under the rule of Moira, the warrior queen and her knight. For them, even in the dark of night, a light shone.

"And that brings the tale of the sorcerer, the witch, the

warrior, the scholar, the shifter of shapes and the vampire to its own circle."

He patted the rump of the child on his lap. "Off with you now, all of you, while there's still sunlight to enjoy."

There were shouts and whoops, and he smiled as he heard the arguments already starting for who would be the sorcerer, who would be the queen.

Because his senses were still keen in some areas, Cian lifted his hand to the back of the chair, and covered Moira's.

"You tell it well."

"Easy to tell what you've lived."

"Easy to *enhance* what was," she corrected, coming around the chair. "But you stayed very close to the truth."

"Wasn't the truth strange and magical enough?"

Her hair was pure white, and her face as she smiled at him, lined with the years. And more beautiful than any he'd known.

"Walk with me before twilight comes." She helped him to stand, hooked her arm through his. "And are you ready for the invasion?" she asked, tipping her head toward his shoulder.

"When it comes, at least you'll be finished fussing over it."

"I'm so anxious to see them all. Our first circle, and the circles they've made. Once a year for the whole of them is so long to wait, even with the little visits between. And listening to little pieces of the tale brings it all back so clear, doesn't it?"

"It does. No regrets?"

"I've never had a one when it comes to you. What a fine life we've had, Cian. I know we're in the winter of it, but I don't feel the cold."

"Well, I do, when you put your feet on my arse in the night."

She laughed, turned to kiss him with all the warmth, all the love of sixty years of marriage.

"There's our eternity, Moira," he said, gesturing toward

their grandchildren, and great-grandchildren. "There's our forever."

Hands linked, they walked in the softening sunlight. Though their steps were slow and measured from age, they continued through the courtyards and the gardens, and out through the gates while the sound of children playing rang behind them.

High above on the castle peaks, the three symbols of Geall, the claddaugh, the dragon and the sun, flew—gold against the white.

Glossary of Irish Words, Characters and Places

a chroi (ah-REE), Gaelic term of endearment meaning "my heart," "my heart's beloved," "my darling"

a ghrá (ah-GHRA), Gaelic term of endearment meaning "my love," "dear"

a stór (ah-STOR), Gaelic term of endearment meaning "my darling"

Aideen (Ae-DEEN), Moira's young cousin

Alice McKenna, descendant of Cian and Hoyt Mac Cionaoith

An Clar (Ahn-CLAR), modern-day County Clare

Ballycloon (ba-LU-klun)

Blair Nola Bridgitt Murphy, one of the circle of six, the "warrior"; a demon hunter, a descendant of Nola Mac Cionaoith (Cian and Hoyt's younger sister)

Bridget's Well, cemetery in County Clare, named after St. Bridget

Burren, the, a karst limestone region in County Clare, which features caves and underground streams

cara (karu), Gaelic for "friend, relative"

Ceara, one of the village women

Cian (KEY-an) ***Mac Cionaoith/McKenna,*** Hoyt's twin brother, a vampire, Lord of Oiche, one of the circle of six, "the one who is lost"

Cirio, Lilith's human lover

ciunas (CYOON-as), Gaelic for "silence"; the battle takes place in the Valley of Ciunas—the Valley of Silence

claddaugh, the Celtic symbol of love, friendship, loyalty

Cliffs of Mohr (also Moher), the name given to the ruin of forts in the south of Ireland, on a cliff near Hag's Head, "Moher O'Ruan"

Conn, Larkin's childhood puppy

Dance of the Gods, the Dance, the place in which the circle of six passes through from the real world to the fantasy world of Geall

Davey, Lilith, the Vampire Queen's, "son," a child vampire

Deirdre (DAIR-dhra) ***Riddock,*** Larkin's mother

Dervil (DAR-vel), one of the village women

Eire (AIR-reh), Gaelic for Ireland

Eogan (O-en), Ceara's husband

Eoin (OAN), Hoyt's brother-in-law

Eternity, the name of Cian's nightclub, located in New York City

Faerie Falls, imaginary place in Geall

fàilte à Geall (FALL-che ah GY-al), Gaelic for "Welcome to Geall"

Fearghus (FARE-gus), Hoyt's brother-in-law

Gaillimh (GALL-yuv), modern-day Galway, the capital of the west of Ireland

Geall (GY-al), in Gaelic means "promise"; the city from which Moira and Larkin come; the city which Moira will someday rule

Glenna Ward, one of the circle of six, the "witch"; lives in modern-day New York City

Hoyt Mac Cionaoith/McKenna (mac KHEE-nee), one of the circle of six, the "sorcerer"

Isleen (Is-LEEN), a servant at Castle Geall

Jarl (Yarl), Lilith's sire, the vampire who turned her into a vampire

Jeremy Hilton, Blair Murphy's ex-fiance

King, the name of Cian's best friend, whom Cian befriended when King was a child; the manager of Eternity

Larkin Riddock, one of the circle of six, the "shifter of shapes," a cousin of Moira, Queen of Geall

Lilith, the Vampire Queen, aka Queen of the Demons; leader of the war against humankind; Cian's sire, the vampire who turned Cian from human to vampire

Lora, a vampire; Lilith's lover

Lucius, Lora's male vampire lover

Malvin, villager, soldier in Geallian army

Manhattan, city in New York; where both Cian McKenna and Glenna Ward live

mathair (maahir), Gaelic word for mother

Michael Thomas McKenna, descendant of Cian and Hoyt Mac Cionaoith

Mick Murphy, Blair Murphy's younger brother

Midir (mee-DEER), vampire wizard to Lilith, Queen of the Vampires

miurnin (also sp. miurneach [mornukh]), Gaelic for "sweetheart," term of endearment

Moira (MWA-ra), one of the circle of six, the "scholar"; a princess, future queen of Geall

Morrigan (Mo-ree-ghan), Goddess of the Battle

Niall (Nile), a warrior in the Geallian army

Nola Mac Cionaoith, Hoyt and Cian's youngest sister

ogham (ä-gem) (also spelled ogam), fifth/sixth century Irish alphabet

oiche (EE-heh), Gaelic for "night"

Oran (O-ren), Riddock's youngest son, Larkin's younger brother

Phelan (FA-len), Larkin's brother-in-law

Prince Riddock, Larkin's father, acting king of Geall, Moira's maternal uncle

Region of Chiarrai (kee-U-ree), modern-day Kerry, situated in the extreme southwest of Ireland, sometimes referred to as "the Kingdom"

Samhain (SAM-en), summer's end (Celtic festival); the battle takes place on the Feast of Samhain, the feast celebrating the end of summer

Sean Murphy (Shawn), Blair Murphy's father, a vampire hunter

Shop Street, cultural center of Galway

Sinann (shih-NAWN), Larkin's sister

sláinte (slawn-che), Gaelic term for "cheers!"

slán agat (shlahn u-gut), Gaclic for "good-bye," which is said to the person staying

slán leat (shlahn ly-aht), Gaelic for "good-bye," which is said to the person leaving

Tuatha de Danaan (TOO-aha dai DON-nan), Welsh gods

Tynan (Ti-nin), guard at Castle Geall

Vlad, Cian's stallion

Turn the page for a look at

Angels Fall

by

Nora Roberts

Chapter 1

Reece Gilmore smoked through the tough knuckles of Angel's Fist in an overheating Chevy Cavalier. She had two hundred forty-three dollars and change in her pocket, which might be enough to cure the Chevy, fuel it and herself. If luck was on her side, and the car wasn't seriously ill, she'd have enough to pay for a room for the night.

Then, even by the most optimistic calculations, she'd be broke.

She took the plumes of steam puffing out of the hood as a sign it was time to stop traveling for a while and find a job.

No worries, no problem, she told herself. The little Wyoming town huddled around the cold blue waters of a lake was as good as anywhere else. Maybe better. It had the openness she needed—all that sky with the snow-dipped peaks of the Tetons rising into it, sober and somehow aloof gods.

She'd been meandering her way toward them, through the Ansel Adams' photograph of peaks and plains for hours. She hadn't had a clue where she'd end up when she'd started out that day before dawn, but she'd bypassed Cody, zipped through Dubois, and though she'd toyed with veering into Jackson, she'd dipped south instead.

So something must have been pulling her to this spot.

Over the past eight months, she'd developed a strong belief in following signs, and impulses. Dangerous Curves, Slippery When Wet. It was nice that someone took the time and effort to post those kinds of warnings. Other signs might be a peculiar slant of sunlight aimed down a back road, or a weather vane pointing south.

If she liked the look of the light or the weather vane, she'd follow, until she found what seemed like the right place at the right time. She might settle in for a few weeks—or as she had in South Dakota, a few months. Pick up some work, scout the area, then move on when those signs, those impulses, pointed in a new direction.

There was a freedom in the system she'd developed, and often—more often now—a lessening of the constant hum of anxiety in the back of her mind. These past months of living with herself, essentially *by* herself, had done more to smooth her out than the full year of therapy.

To be fair, she supposed the therapy had given her the base to face herself every single day. Every night. And all the hours in between.

And here was another fresh start, another blank slate in the bunched fingers of Angel's Fist.

If nothing else, she'd take a few days to enjoy the lake and the mountains, and pick up enough money to get back on the road again. A place like this—the signpost had said the population was 623—probably ran to tourism, exploiting the scenery and the proximity to the national park.

There'd be at least one hotel, likely a couple of B and Bs, maybe a dude ranch within a few miles. It might be fun to work at a dude ranch. All of those places would need someone to fetch and carry and clean, especially now that the spring thaw was dulling the sharpest edge of winter.

But since her car was now sending out thicker, more desperate smoke signals, the first priority was a mechanic.

She eased her way along the road that ribboned around the long, wide lake. Patches of snow made dull white pools in the shade. The trees were still there, wintering brown, but there were a few boats on the water. She could see a couple of guys in windbreakers and caps in a white canoe, rowing right through the reflection of the mountains. It was so clear she glanced up, almost expecting to see the canoe mirrored on the rough hills.

Across from the lake was what she decided was the business district. Gift shop, a little gallery. Bank, post office, she noted. Sheriff 's office.

She angled away from the lake to pull the laboring car up to what looked like a big barn of a general store. There were a couple of men in flannel shirts sitting out front in stout chairs that gave them a good view of the lake.

They nodded to her as she cut the engine and stepped out, then the one on the right tapped the brim of his blue cap that bore the name of the store—Mac's Mercantile and Grocery—across the crown.

"Looks like you got some trouble there, young lady."

"Sure does. Do you know anyone who can give me a hand with it?"

He laid his hands on his thighs and pushed out of the chair. He was burly in build, ruddy in face, with lines fanning out from the corners of friendly brown eyes. When he spoke, his voice was a slow, meandering drawl.

"Why don't we just pop the hood and take a look-see?"

"Appreciate it." When she released the latch, he tossed the hood up and stepped back from the clouds of smoke. For reasons she couldn't name, the plumes and the fuss caused Reece more embarrassment than anxiety. "It started up on me about ten miles east, I guess. I wasn't paying enough attention. Got caught up in the scenery."

"Easy to do. You heading into the park?"

"I was. More or less." Not sure, never sure, she thought and tried to concentrate on the moment rather than the before or after. "I think the car had other ideas."

His companion came over to join them, and both men

looked under the hood the way Reece knew men did. With sober eyes and knowing frowns. She looked with them, though she accepted that she was as much of a cliché. The female to whom what lurked under the hood of a car was a foreign as the terrain of Pluto.

"Got yourself a split radiator hose," he told her. "Gonna need to replace that."

Didn't sound so bad, not too bad. Not too expensive. "Anywhere in town I can make that happen?"

"Lynt's Garage'll fix you up. Why don't I give him a call for you?"

"Lifesaver." She offered a smile and her hand, a gesture that had come to be much easier for her with strangers. "I'm Reece, Reece Gilmore."

"Mac Drubber. This here's Carl Sampson."

"Back East, aren't you?" Carl asked. He looked a fit fifty-something to Reece, and with some Native American blood mixed in once upon a time.

"Yeah. Way back. Boston area. I really appreciate the help."

"Nothing but a phone call," Mac said. "You can come on in out of the breeze if you want, or take a walk around. Might take Lynt a few to get here."

"I wouldn't mind a walk, if that's okay. Maybe you could tell me a good place to stay in town. Nothing fancy."

"Got the Lakeview Hotel just down aways. The Teton House, other side of the lake's some homier. More a B and B. Some cabins along the lake, and others outside of town rent by the week or the month."

She didn't think in months any longer. A day was enough of a challenge. And homier sounded too intimate. "Maybe I'll walk down and take a look at the hotel."

"It's a long walk. Could give you a ride on down."

"I've been driving all day. I could use the stretch. But thanks, Mr. Drubber."

"No problem." He stood another moment as she wandered down the wooden sidewalk. "Pretty thing," he commented.

"No meat on her." Carl shook his head. "Women today starve off all the curves."

She hadn't starved them off, and was, in fact, making a concerted effort to gain back the weight that had fallen off in the past couple of years. She'd gone from health club fit to scrawny and had worked her way back to what she thought of as gawky. Too many angles and points, too many bones. Every time she undressed, her body was like that of a stranger's to her.

She wouldn't have agreed with Mac's *pretty thing.* Not anymore. Once she'd thought of herself that way, as a pretty woman—stylish, sexy when she wanted to be. But her face seemed too hard now, the cheekbones too prominent, the hollows too deep. The restless nights were fewer, but when they came they left her dark eyes heavily shadowed and cast a pallor, pasty and gray, over her skin.

She wanted to recognize herself again.

She let herself stroll, her worn-out Keds nearly soundless on the sidewalk. She'd learned not to hurry—had taught herself not to push, not to rush, but to take things as they came. And in a very real way to embrace every single moment.

The cool breeze blew across her face, wound through the long brown hair she'd tied back in a tail. She liked the feel of it, the smell of it, clean and fresh, and the hard light that poured over the Tetons and sparked on the water.

She could see some of the cabins Mac had spoken of, through the bare branches of the willows and the cottonwoods. They squatted behind the trees, log and glass, wide porches and—she assumed—stunning views.

It might be nice to sit on one of those porches and study the lake or the mountains, to watch whatever visited the marsh where cattails speared up out of the bog. To have that room around, and the quiet.

One day maybe, she thought. But not today.

She spotted green spears of daffodils in a half whiskey barrel next to the entrance of a restaurant. They might have trembled a bit in the chilly breeze, but they made her think: spring. Everything was new in spring. Maybe this spring, she'd be new, too.

She stopped to admire the tender spouts. It was comforting to see spring making its way back after the long winter. There would be other signs of it soon. Her guidebook had boasted of miles of wildflowers on the sage flats, and more along the area's lakes and ponds.

She was ready for flowering, Reece thought. Ready for blooming.

Then she shifted her eyes up to the wide front window of the restaurant. More diner than restaurant, she corrected. Counter service, two- and four-tops, booths, all in faded red and white. Pies and cakes on display, and the kitchen open to the counter. A couple of waitresses bustled around with trays and coffee pots.

Lunch crowd, she realized. She'd forgotten lunch. As soon as she'd taken a look at the hotel, she'd . . .

Then she saw it in the window: the sign, hand-lettered.

COOK WANTED
INQUIRE WITHIN

Signs, she thought again, though she'd taken a step back before she caught herself. She stood where she was, taking a careful study of the set-up from outside the glass. Open kitchen, she reminded herself, that was key. Diner food—she could handle that in her sleep. Or would have been able to, once.

Maybe it was time to find out, time to take another step forward. If she couldn't handle it, she'd know, and wouldn't be any worse off than she was now.

The hotel was probably hiring, in anticipation of the summer season. Or Mr. Drubber might need another clerk at his store.

But the sign was right there, and her car had aimed

toward this town, and her steps had brought her to this spot, where daffodil shoots pushed out of the dirt into the first hesitant breaths of spring.

She backtracked to the door, took a long, long breath in, then opened it.

Fried onions, grilling meat—on the gamey side—strong coffee, a jukebox on country, and a buzz of table chatter.

Clean red floors, she noted, scrubbed white counter. The few empty tables had their lunch setups. There were photographs on the walls—good ones to her eye. Black and whites of the lake, of white water, of the mountains in every season.

She was still getting her bearings, gathering her courage, when one of the waitresses swung by her. "Afternoon. You're looking for lunch you've got your choice of a table or the counter."

"Actually, I'm looking for the manager. Or owner. Ah, about the sign in the window. The position of cook."

The waitress stopped, still balancing a tray. "You're a cook?"

There'd been a time Reece would have sniffed at the term—good-naturedly, but she'd have sniffed nonetheless. "Yes."

"That's handy, 'cause Joanie fired one a couple of days ago." The waitress curled her free hand, brought it up to her lips in the mime for drinking.

"Oh."

"Gave him the job in February when he came through town looking for work. Said he'd found Jesus and was spreading his word across the land."

She cocked her head and her hip, and gave Reece a sunny smile out of a pretty face. "He preached the Word, all right, like a disciple on crack, so you wanted to stuff a rag in his mouth. Then I guess he found the bottle, and that was that. So. Why don't you go right on and sit up at the counter. I'll see if Joanie can get out of the kitchen for a minute. How about some coffee?"

"Tea, if you don't mind."

"Coming up."

Didn't have to take the job, Reece reminded herself as she slid onto a chrome and leather stool and rubbed her damp palms dry on the thighs of her jeans. Even if it was offered, she didn't have to take it. She could stick with cleaning hotel rooms, or head out and find that dude ranch.

The juke switched numbers, and Shania Twain announced joyfully she felt like a woman.

The waitress tapped a short sturdy woman at the grill on the shoulder, leaned in. After a moment, the woman shot a glance over her shoulder, met Reece's eyes, then nodded. The waitress came back to the counter with a white cup of hot water, with a Lipton tea bag on the saucer.

"Joanie'll be right along. You want to order some lunch? Meatloaf 's house special today. Comes with mashed potatoes and green beans and a biscuit."

"No thanks, no, tea's fine." She'd never be able to hold anything more down, not with the nerves bouncing around in her belly. The panic wanted to come with it, that smothering wet weight in the chest.

She should just go, Reece thought. Go right now, and walk back to her car. Get the hose fixed and head out. Signs be damned.

Joanie had a fluff of blond hair on her head, a white butcher's apron splattered with grease stains tied around her middle, and high-topped red Converse sneakers on her feet. She walked out from the kitchen wiping her hands on a dishcloth.

And she measured Reece out of steely eyes that were more gray than blue.

"You cook?" A smoker's rasp made the brisk question oddly sensual.

"Yes."

"For a living, or just to put something in your mouth?"

"It's what I did back in Boston—for a living." Fighting nerves, Reece ripped open the cover on the tea bag.

Joanie had a soft mouth, almost a Cupid's bow, in contrast with those hard eyes. And an old, faded scar, Reece noted, that ran along her jawline from her left ear nearly to her chin.

"Boston." In an absent move, Joanie tucked the dishrag in the belt of her apron. "Long ways."

"Yes."

"I don't know as I want some East Coast cook can't keep her mouth shut for five minutes."

Reece's opened in surprise, then closed again on the barest curve of a smile. "I'm an awful chatterbox when I'm nervous."

"What're you doing around here?"

"Traveling. My car broke down. I need a job."

"Got references?"

Her heart tightened, a sweaty fist of silent pain. "I can get them."

Joanie sniffed, frowned back toward the kitchen. "Go on back, put on an apron. Next order up's a steak sandwich, med-well, onion roll, fried onions and mushrooms, fries and slaw. Dick don't drop dead after eating what you cook, you probably got the job."

"All right." Reece pushed off the stool and, keeping her breath slow and even, went through the swinging door at the far end of the counter.

She didn't notice, but Joanie did, that she'd torn the tea bag cover into tiny pieces.

It was a simple setup, she decided, and efficient enough. Large grill, restaurant-style stove, refrigerator, freezer. Holding bins, sinks, work counters, double fryer, heat suppression system. As she tied on an apron, Joanie set out the ingredients she'd need.

"Thanks." Reece scrubbed her hands, then got to work.

Don't think, she told herself. Just let it come. She set the steak sizzling on the grill while she chopped onions and mushrooms. She put the pre-cut potatoes in the fry basket, set the timer.

Her hands didn't shake, and though her chest stayed

tight, she didn't allow herself to dart glances over her shoulder to make sure a wall hadn't appeared to close her in.

She listened to the music, from the juke, from the grill, from the fryer.

Joanie tugged the next order from the clip on the round, and slapped it down. "Bowl of three-bean soup—that kettle there—goes with crackers."

Reece simply nodded, tossed the mushrooms and onions on the grill, then filled the second order while they fried.

"Order up!" Joanie called out, and yanked another ticket. "Reuben, club san, two side salads."

Reece moved from order to order, and just let it happen. The atmosphere, the orders might be different, but the rhythm was the same. Keep working, keep moving.

She plated the original order, turned to hand it to Joanie for inspection.

"Put it in line," she was told. "Start the next ticket. We don't call the doctor in the next thirty minutes, you're hired. We'll talk money and hours later."

"I need to—"

"Get that next ticket," Joanie finished. "I'm going to go have a smoke."

She worked another ninety minutes before it slowed enough for Reece to step back from the heat and guzzle down a bottle of water. When she turned, Joanie was sitting at the counter, drinking coffee.

"Nobody died," she said.

"Whew. Is it always that busy?"

"Saturday lunch crowd. We do okay. You get eight dollars an hour to start. You still look good in two weeks, I bump in another buck an hour. That's you and me and a part-timer on the grill, seven days a week. You get two days, or the best part of two off during that week. I do the schedule a week in advance. We open at six-thirty, so that means first shift is here at six. You can order breakfast all day, lunch menu from eleven to closing, dinner five to ten. You want forty hours a week, I can work you that. I don't pay any overtime, so you get stuck behind the grill and go over, we'll take it off your next week's hours. Any problem with that?"

"No."

"You drink on the job, you're fired on the spot."

"Understood."

"You get all the coffee, water, or tea you want. You hit the soft drinks, you pay for them. Same with the food. Around here, there ain't no free lunch. Not that it looks like you'll be packing it away while my back's turned. You're skinny as a stick."

"I guess I am."

"Last shift cook cleans the grill, the stove, does the lockdown."

"I can't do that," Reece interrupted. "I can't close for you. I can open, I can work any shift you want me to work. I'll work doubles when you need it, split shifts. I can flex time when you need me over forty. But I can't close for you. I'm sorry."

Joanie raised her eyebrows, sipped down the last of her coffee. "Afraid of the dark, little girl?"

"Yes, I am. If closing's part of the job description, I'll have to find another job."

"We'll work that out. We've got forms to fill out for the government. It can wait. Your car's fixed, sitting up at Mac's." Joanie smiled. "Word travels, and I've got my ear to the ground. You're looking for a place, there's a room over the diner I can rent you. Not much, but it's got a good view and it's clean."

"Thanks, but I think I'm going to try the hotel for now. We'll both give it a couple of weeks, see how it goes."

"Itchy feet."

"Itchy something."

"Your choice." With a shrug, Joanie got up, headed to the swinging door with her coffee cup. "You go on, get your car, get settled. Be back at four."

A little dazed, Reece walked out. She was back in a kitchen, and it had been all right. She'd been okay. Now that she'd gotten through it, she felt a little light-headed, but that was normal, wasn't it? A normal reaction to snagging a job, straight off the mark, doing what she was trained to do again. Doing what she hadn't been able to do for nearly two years.

She took her time walking back to her car, letting it all sink in.

When she walked into the mercantile, Mac was ringing up a sale at a short counter opposite the door. The place was what she'd expected. A little bit of everything: coolers for produce and meat, shelves of dry goods, a section for hardware, for housewares, fishing gear, ammo.

Need a gallon of milk and a box of bullets? This was the spot.

When Mac finished the transaction, she approached the counter.

"Car should run for you now," Mac told her.

"So I hear, and thanks. How do I pay?"

"Lynt left a bill here for you. You can run on by the garage if you're going to charge it. Paying cash, you can just leave it here. I'll be seeing him later."

"Cash is good." She took the bill, noted with relief it was less than she'd estimated. She could hear someone chatting in the rear of the store, and the beep of another cash register. "I got a job."

He cocked his head as she pulled out her wallet. "That so? Quick work."

"At the diner. I don't even know the name of it," she realized.

"That'd be Angel Food. Locals just call it Joanie's."

"Joanie's then. I hope you come in sometime. I'm a good cook."

"I bet you are. Here's your change."

"Thanks. Thanks for everything. I guess I'll go get myself a room, then go back to work."

"If you're still looking at the hotel, you tell Brenda on the desk you want the monthly rate. You tell her you're working at Joanie's."

"I will. I'll tell her." She wanted to take out an ad announcing it in the local paper. "Thanks, Mr. Drubber."

The hotel was five stories of pale yellow stucco that boasted views of the lake. It harbored a minute sundry shop, a tiny stand selling coffee and muffins, and an intimate linen-tablecloth dining room.

There was, she was told, high-speed Internet connection for a small daily fee, room service from seven A.M. to eleven P.M. and a self-service laundry in the basement.

Reece negotiated a weekly rate on a single—a week was long enough—on the third floor. Anything below the third was too accessible for her peace of mind, and anything above the third made her feel trapped.

With her wallet now effectively empty, she carted her duffle and laptop up three flights rather than use the elevator.

The view lived up to its billing, and she immediately opened the windows, then just stood looking at the sparkle of the water, the glide of the boats, and the rise of the mountains that cupped this little section of valley.

This was her place today, she thought. She'd find out if it was her place tomorrow. Turning back to the room, she noted the door that adjoined the neighboring guest room. She checked the locks, then pushed, shoved, dragged the single dresser in front of it.

That was better.

She wouldn't unpack, not exactly, but take the essentials and set them out. The travel candle, some toiletries, the cell phone charger. Since the bathroom was hardly bigger than the closet, she left the door open while she took a quick shower. While the water ran, she did the multiplication tables out loud to keep herself steady. She changed into fresh clothes, moving quickly.

New job, she reminded herself, and took the time and effort to dry her hair, to put on a little makeup. Not so pale today, she decided, not so hollow-eyed.

After checking her watch, she set up her laptop, opened her daily journal, and wrote a quick entry.

Angel's Fist, Wyoming
April 15

I cooked today. I took a job as a cook in a little diner-style restaurant in this pretty valley town with its big, blue lake. I'm popping champagne in my mind, and there are streamers and balloons.

I feel like I've climbed a mountain, like I've been scaling the tough peaks that ring this place. I'm not at the top yet, I'm still on a ledge. But it's sturdy and wide, and I can rest here a little while before I start to climb again.

I'm working for a woman named Joanie. She's short, sturdy, and oddly pretty. She's tough, too, and that's good. I don't want to be coddled. I think I'd smother to death that way, just run out of air the way I feel when I wake up from one of the dreams. I can breathe here, and I can be here until it's time to move again.

I've got less than ten dollars left, but whose fault is that? It's okay. I've got a room for a week with a view of the lake and the Tetons, a job, and a new radiator hose.

I missed lunch, and that's a step back there. That's okay, too. I was too busy cooking to eat, and I'll make up for it.

It's a good day, April fifteenth. I'm going to work.

She shut down, then tucked her phone, keys, driver's license, and three dollars of what she had left in her pockets. Grabbing a jacket, she headed for the door.

Before she opened it, Reece checked the peep, scanned the empty hall. She checked her locks twice, cursed herself, and checked a third time before she went back to her kit to tear a piece of Scotch tape off her roll. She pressed it over the door, well below eye level, before she walked to the door for the stairs.

She jogged down, counting as she went. After a quick debate, she left her car parked. Walking would save her gas money, even though it would be dark when she finished her shift.

Couple of blocks, that was all. Still, she fingered her key chain, and the panic button on it.

Maybe she should go back and get the car, just in case. Stupid, she told herself. She was nearly there. Think about now, not about later. When nerves began to bubble, she pictured herself at the grill. Good strong kitchen light, music from the jukebox, voices from the tables. Familiar sounds, smells, motion.

Maybe her palm was clammy when she reached for the door of Joanie's, but she opened it. And she went inside.

The same waitress she'd spoken to during the lunch shift spotted her, wiggled her fingers in a come-over motion. Reece stopped by the booth where the woman was refilling the condiment caddie.

"Joanie's back in the storeroom. She said I should give you a quick orientation when you came in. We got a lull, then the early-birds will start coming in soon. I'm Lindagail."

"Reece."

"First warning: Joanie doesn't tolerate idle hands. She catches you loitering, she'll jump straight down your back and bite your ass." She grinned when she said it in a way that made her bright blue eyes twinkle, deepened dimples in her cheeks. She had doll-baby blond hair to go with it, worn in smooth French braids.

She had on jeans, a red shirt with white piping. Silver and turquoise earrings dangled from her ears. She looked, Reece thought, like a western milkmaid.

"I like to work."

"You will, believe me. This being Saturday night, we'll be busy. You'll have two other waitstaff working—Bebe and Juanita. Matt'll bus, and Pete's the dishwasher. You and Joanie'll be manning the kitchen, and she'll have a hawk eye on you. You need a break, you tell her, and you take it. There's a place in the back for your coat, your purse. No purse?"

"No, I didn't bring it."

"God, I can't step a foot outside the house without mine. Come on then, I'll show you around. She's got the forms you need to fill out in the back. I guess you've done this kind of work before, the way you jumped in with both feet today."

"Yeah, I have."

"Restrooms. We clean the bathrooms on rotation. You've got a couple of weeks before you have that pleasure."

"Can't wait."

Linda-gail grinned. "You got family around here?"

"No. I'm from back east." Didn't want to talk about that, didn't want to think about that. "Who handles the fountain drinks?"

"Wait staff. We get crunched, you can fill drink orders. We serve wine and beer, too. But mostly people want to drink, they do it over at Clancy's. That's about it. Anything else you want to know, just give me a holler. I've got to finish the setups or Joanie'll squawk. Welcome aboard."

"Thanks."

Reece moved into the kitchen, took an apron.

A good, wide, solid ledge, she told herself. A good place to stand until it was time to move again.

A